PART ONE

EDGE GLIDING

'. . . the Goddess starts her endgame in Britain, where nobody's looking . . .'

Fraser Clark, August, 1994

FAIRYLAND

PAUL McAULEY

The right of Paul McAuley to be identified as the author
of this work has been asserted by him in accordance with
the Copyright, Designs and Patents Act 1988.

First published in Great Britain in 1995 by
Victor Gollancz Ltd

This edition published in Great Britain in 2009 by
Gollancz
An imprint of the Orion Publishing Group
Orion House, 5 Upper St Martin's Lane, London WC2H 9EA
An Hachette UK Company

10 9 8 7 6 5 4 3 2 1

A CIP catalogue record for this book
is available from the British Library

ISBN 978 0575 08658 6

Typeset at The Spartan Press Ltd,
Lymington, Hants

Printed in the UK by CPI Mackays,
Chatham, Kent

The Orion Publishing Group's policy is to use papers that
are natural, renewable and recyclable products and made
from wood grown in sustainable forests. The logging and
manufacturing processes are expected to conform to the
environmental regulations of the country of origin.

www.orionbooks.co.uk

1
King's Cross

The room is full of ghosts.

Transparent as jellyfish, dressed in full Edwardian rig, they drift singly or in pairs around and around the newly restored Ladies' Smoking Room of the Grand Midland Hotel at St Pancras, adroitly avoiding passengers waiting to board the 1600 hours Trans-Europe Express. Alex Sharkey is the only person in the room who pays the ghosts any attention; to pass the time, he has been trying to derive the algorithm which controls their seemingly random promenade. He arrived twenty minutes early, and now, according to the watch he bought on his way here, it is twelve minutes past three, and his client is late.

Alex is edgy and uncomfortable, sweating into his brand-new drawstring shirt of unbleached Afghan cotton. The raw cotton is flecked with nubbles of chaff that scratch his skin. The jacket of his suit is tight across his shoulders; although the salesman assured him that its green tweed check complemented his red hair, Alex thinks it makes him look a little like Oscar Wilde, who wouldn't be out of place in the lovingly restored heritage décor of the Ladies' Smoking Room, with its salmon pink and cream walls, marble pillars and plush red upholstered easy chairs, its potted palms and flitting population of Edwardian ghosts.

Alex is wedged into a low, overstuffed armchair, chain-smoking and feeling the buzz from his second cup of espresso. One thing he's learned today is they make wonderful espresso here, oily and bitter and served scalding hot in decently thick thimble-sized cups, with a twist of lemon in the bowl of the dainty silver spoon, and a bitter mint chocolate and a glass of flash-filtered water served on the side.

Caffeine is such a simple, elegant, *necessary* drug – Alex remembers one of Gary Larson's Far Side cartoons, goofy lions sprawled around a tree and off in the distance a rhino pouring a

3

cup of coffee for its mate, who's saying, 'Whoa, that's plenty.' The title was *African Dawn*, and Alex smiles now, remembering the way he laughed out loud the first time he saw it. Which was when? One Christmas back before the end of the twentieth century, he must have been five or six. It would have been in the damp, ant-infested, twelfth floor council flat on the Isle of Dogs, looking out over the Thames. Lexis always got him a book for Christmas, somehow or other. To improve him.

And now here he is, surrounded by hologram ghosts and waiting for his man, trying to blend in with the suits and the rich tourists waiting for the express train out of this shitty country. Most of them are chattering in French, the *lingua franca* of the élite of the increasingly isolationist European Union. The women are defiantly tanned, in flimsy blouses and very short shorts, or mini-skirts with artfully tattered hems. A few, this is the very latest in BodiCon fashion, are enveloped in chadors made of layers of translucent chiffon woven with graphic film that flashes odd images and shifting patterns, revealing and concealing breasts, the curve of a hip, smooth tanned skin hollowed over a collar bone. The men wear chunky suits in earth colours, a lot of gold on their wrists, and discreet makeup. Earrings flash when they speak or glance at themselves in the tall gilt mirrors behind the bar. Unnervingly, the mirrors do not reflect the ghosts. At the bar's mahogany counter, half a dozen Ukrainians in shiny black suits make a lot of noise, toasting each other with rounds of malt whisky.

One woman has a pet doll. It sits quietly beside its mistress, dressed in a pink and purple uniform edged with gold braid. A chain leash is clipped to the studded dog collar around its neck. Its prognathous blue-skinned face is impassive. Only its eyes move. Dark, liquid, sad-looking eyes, as if it knows that something's wrong deep down in every cell of its body, knows the burden of sin that's been laid on it.

Alex feels sorry for it – it's displaced from Nature, dazed by the violence done to its genome. It's a crufty creature, he thinks, the epitome of his belief that there's no point gengineering anything more advanced than yeast: the more complex the organism, the more unpredictable the side-effects.

Alex lights another cigarette and checks the time again. He has an edgy sliding feeling that things have gone wrong. He has always hated waiting around, having to be on time. For this one occasion, when he had to be punctual, he bought a watch, and all it does is make him more nervous. It is a piece of recyclable Polish street shit that cost less than a single espresso, graphic film on a hexagon of varnished fibreboard, a bright orange cloth strap. It runs on the faint myoelectric field generated by Alex's wrist muscles – it's a time-binding parasite. There's a black eagle impressed on the watch-face, and the eagle raises its wings and breathes fire when Alex tilts his wrist to look at it. The hands are black slivers generated by the same chip that runs the eagle. The graphic film is already wrinkling: the eagle has a broken wing; the hour hand is kinked. It is eighteen minutes past three.

Alex once had a genuine antique stainless steel oyster Rolex; it came with a certificate proving it was manufactured in Switzerland, in 1967. It was given to him by the Wizard – the Wizard was always giving him stuff like that, in the days when Alex was the brightest and best of the Wizard's apprentices. But Alex lost the Rolex when he was banged up with the Wizard and the rest of his crew. Either the cops or one of Lexis's asshole toy boys swiped it. Alex lost a lot, then, which is one reason why he's in a hole with Billy Rock, and making risky, desperate deals with junior grade Indonesian diplomats.

Twenty-eight minutes past. Shit. Alex signals to the waiter and orders another espresso, speaking slowly and carefully because the tall, silver-haired man is an Albanian refugee who has only a glancing relationship with the English language.

It's twenty to four, and the boarding announcement for the Trans-Europe Express has been made, and the passengers are beginning to leave, when the waiter brings Alex his espresso. Alex pays with a credit card which doesn't have his name on it, knocks back the coffee and walks over to the woman with the leashed doll. He stands there, looking at her. It's silly and he knows it won't really make him feel better, but he has to do it.

When she finally looks up, a tanned woman of about forty with that tightness around her jaw that indicates a facelift, Alex says, 'I only just figured out that the animal at the end of the lead is the one getting smashed on Campari,' and walks out of there, straight through two ghostly women in small-waisted day dresses who break apart around him in spangles of diffracted laser light.

Gilbert Scott's great curving stair takes Alex down to the busy lobby. He shakes out his black, wide-brimmed hat (yeah, Oscar Wilde) and claps it on to his head, trying to look nonchalant despite the ball of acid cramping his stomach. A doorman in plum uniform and top hat opens a polished plate glass door and Alex walks out into bronze sunlight and the roar of traffic shuddering along Euston Road.

To the north, black rainclouds are boiling up, bunching and streaming as if on fast forward. There's a charge in the air; everyone is walking quickly, despite the heavy heat. Every other person carries an umbrella. It's monsoon weather.

Alex takes the pedestrian underpass to King's Cross Station. There's a row of phone kiosks at the edge of the pavement, tended by a crone in a kind of wraparound cape made of black plastic refuse bags. Alex tips her and, cramped in a booth that stinks equally of piss and industrial deodorant, its walls scaled with the calling cards of the face workers of the sex industry, dials his contact number. The Wizard taught him never to ring clients from a mobile phone – the locations of switched-on mobile phones are constantly updated on lookup tables, microwave junctions are tapped, with AIs patiently listening in for keywords, and anyone within fifteen kilometres can eavesdrop using an over-the-counter scanner.

The screen of the phone is cracked, and someone has spilled a bottle of black nail varnish over its lower quadrant. There's a blood-tinged hypo barrel on the floor. Alex kicks it around while the phone rings out, then leaves with a curious sense of exhilaration, a floating rush like being in free fall. He is well and truly fucked. Sooner or later this will catch up with him, but right now it's as if he has escaped something.

Just as he starts towards the Underground, the rain comes down.

It comes down with a black fury, rebounding a metre in the air. Alex dodges into the station entrance, half-drenched. The brim of his hat sheds water down his back. The rain is so intense you could drown in it. The temperature drops ten degrees in an instant. The weather has been doing weird things lately. It's in a hurry. It wants to get some deep change over with.

Black taxis suddenly all have orange occupied signs. Trucks plough up bow waves in the flooded road, swamping the pastel bubbles of microcars. Alex sees blue flickers far up Pentonville Road, and tenses. No, it could be just an accident.

Wind gusts turn umbrellas and parasols inside out, snatch hats from heads. There is a refugee encampment on the traffic island at the road junction of King's Cross. Lashed by crisscrossing ropes to railings and the posts of traffic signs, the tarpaulin and plastic sheeting of the benders and bivouacs belly and crack in the wind. A sheet of black plastic suddenly winnows out in the pouring rain, goes sailing off above the traffic like a bat, then drops on to the windscreen of a truck. The truck slews to a halt in the flooded road, belching vast clouds of black smoke that smells like boiling year-old cooking oil and blocking both eastbound lanes. Horns, angry flickers of brake lights: red stabs in dark teeming air.

Distant blue lights revolve in the rain. Sirens start up, are cut short in frustration. Alex sees someone run into the stalled traffic, a small guy pursued by two big beefy men in suits who grab his arms, pull him back. One of the men waves a bit of laminated plastic at a taxi which blows its horn.

Oh Jesus, there goes his contact. Alex is suddenly certain that it's Perse. Perse has found out and fucked him over.

Two police cruisers are caught in the jam of vehicles behind the jackknifed truck. The doors of one of the cruisers slam open and policemen in yellow slickers scramble out.

Suddenly, Alex is intensely aware of the security cameras everywhere. He pulls his wet hat lower and walks into the crowded station concourse. A vagrant in a filthy full-length overcoat belted with string grins at him. The vagrant's forehead is cratered with a purple and yellow crusted wound. He sees he's got Alex's attention and says, 'This bloke gave me some bleach this morning and I triaged myself. Poured it right on to my forehead and didn't even get a drop in my eye. What do you think of that?'

Alex pulls the case from the inside pocket of his jacket – the striations of its black plastic cover seem to flex as it scans his prints – and thrusts it at the man. He says, 'Fifteen minutes ago I was going to be rich. Never trust a copper.'

The vagrant stares at what looks like a matt black CD jewel box and says, 'Do you think I want to dance?'

But he takes it anyway, and that's that. Contact with unrecognized fingerprints activates the suicide sequence, and in seconds the case will cook its contents.

Alex is already hurrying away. The sound of rain on the high glass roof echoes above him like God's impatient fingers, drumming, drumming. He pushes through a line of passengers waiting to board one of the new radiation-proofed trains to Scotland, and takes the stairs down to the Underground station. He doesn't even bother to try and make a deal with one of the sellers of secondhand travelcards, but feeds a machine with a five pound coin, grabs his ticket and runs down escalators and along tiled corridors. Ozone-laden wind sandpapers his throat as he runs, a fat young man in a suit of vivid green check one size too small for him, his face as pink as a skinned seal's, clutching a broad black hat to his head, in a hurry to get somewhere else.

2
Home Run

Straphanging on the rattly old Metropolitan Line, Alex Sharkey just breathes for a while. Sweat soaks his shirt: he can feel its nubbly material stick and unstick to his back as the train smashes through the dark. The carriage is crowded, and Alex is squashed by one of the doors. A safety notice above his head has been detourned to read *Obstruct the doors cause delay and be dangerous*. Alex can almost believe it's a message directed at him.

Alex changes on to the East London Line at Whitechapel for the short jog over to Shadwell, where he climbs the stairs and waits a long while on the wet, windy platform for one of the little Docklands trains. After the Radical Monarchist League blew up the

Jubilee extension, travel between the centre of London and the East End has once again become terrifically inconvenient.

A middle-aged man in a suit, probably a journalist, hunches over a Bookman at the front of the carriage; weary East End women sit with their shopping between their feet; a black kid, the hood of his poncho pulled up and the top half of his face masked by an iridescent visor, talks into a mobile phone. Every now and then the kid leans his arm across the back of his seat and turns towards Alex, who wonders if maybe the kid thinks he looks like a copper.

He starts to laugh, a little constricted giggle that makes him shake all over. Because, Jesus, he really is in deep shit now. He doesn't even know if it's safe to go home, but where else can he go? Leroy won't thank him if he drags his trouble into the shebeen, and there's no way he's going to put his mother through it again. When the police moved against the Wizard, an armed team punched out the door of Lexis's flat with a pneumatic jackhammer.

Alex gets off at Westferry. It's stopped raining. Raw sunlight heats the air. Steam boils up from the road. There's a smell like fresh baked bread. Everywhere, light is shattered by water films. Mosquitoes whine, and even though he's had shots against yellow fever and malaria and blackwater fever, Alex pulls down the veil of his big black hat.

He remembers the years just after the birds died, the plagues of grasshoppers, aphids, flying ants and flies, the food shortages and the long lines outside supermarkets. The little world Lexis drew around them both, back then – he should go and see her, once this is over, once it's safe. She's getting on, and her current boyfriend is younger than Alex, for Christ's sake. If he's safe, he'll go and see her. He offers this up like a prayer. Home, safe and free. Playing tag in the stairwells of the tower blocks, Alex was always anxious about being left out, being left behind – he was overweight even then, although he could run as fast as most of the other kids, could wrestle most of them into submission, too. His weight gave him a presence – he still likes to think that. He remembers the one girl who could outrun everyone. Tall, knock-kneed Najma, her thick black braid sticking out as she flew across the ground. Gone now, gone away. Her family caught in one of the repatriation sweeps and sent to India although they'd all of them been born here. If she's

9

still alive, what must life be like for her now? Alex should count his blessings.

He thinks all this as he takes underpasses beneath busy roads and skirts a threadbare acre of grass between tattered deck access housing projects where kids play football amongst burnt-out cars, so many cars abandoned here it looks like a parking lot. The pyramid-capped monolith of Canary Wharf disappears and re-appears behind the tower blocks. The sun beats down, baking the crown of Alex's skull inside his black hat.

He has a bad moment in the unmade alley that runs past a scrap yard under the cantilevered Docklands line, but the two figures at the far end of the alley are just a crack dealer and one of his runners. Alex vaguely knows the dealer, a muscled Nigerian who always wears wraparound shades. There's a baseball bat tucked under his arm, for sorting out argumentative customers. The dealer nods languidly and asks Alex how it's going, is he still making that strange shit?

'You want to sell some for me?'

'Oh man, there's no percentage in that stuff. My customers know exactly what they want. You should be getting into that, man. You cook me some DOA, I can move it for you no problem. You worked for the Wizard, man. Any stuff you cook up will sell, I guarantee it. The punters appreciate a good pedigree.'

They've had this conversation before, but Alex isn't crazy or desperate enough for this sort of deal. Not yet, at least. He starts to sidle past the dealer, saying, 'It's just that I'm not into industrial chemistry.'

'Well, you think about it,' the dealer says genially. 'This here is a steady trade, and I hear the law is about to catch up with the weird shit you make. But I can't talk now, man, people be quitting work, hurrying over to get their fix. Later, eh?'

Past the elevated railway line is the back end of the dilapidated row of workshop units where Alex lives, half a dozen in a row, overlooked by the gutted wreck of a toytown yellow brick office block dating from the eighties, its blue and red plastic fittings faded and broken, every window smashed. Weeds push up through the tarmac of the access road; buddleia bushes have established them-selves on the flat roofs. The sharp smell of solvents from the chip-assembly shop at the far end. Frank, the old geezer who sells second-hand office furniture, is sitting in the sun on a black leather swivel chair, and nods to Alex as he goes past. Alex thinks he's exchanged about ten words with Frank, and they've been neighbours for the last three months. On the other side, there's the busy chorus of Malik Ali's industrial sewing machines: three of the units are used by Bangladeshis in the rag trade.

Alex has another bad moment when he ducks through the little access door set in the double doors that front his own unit – someone could be waiting for him in the dark – but then he clicks on the fluorescent lights, and of course no one's there. He gets a quick shot of reassurance from a couple of tabs of Cool-Z, which he washes down with that day's carton of Pisant, this orange cinnamon drink he discovered in a vending arcade on the Tottenham Court Road. Pisant lasted about a week in the frenzied sharkpool of niche marketing, probably because of the name, but Alex tracked down the supplier before it disappeared, and the last of the world's supply of Pisant is stacked in one of his three industrial fridges.

For the rest, there's an extruded stainless steel kitchen, empty except for a big cappuccino machine and the microwave Alex uses to heat up reconstituted Malaysian army rations – he has about a thousand unlabelled packs crated in the back of the workshop – and the food he orders from the Hong Kong Gardens takeaway. There's a bed in the back, too, behind a Chinese screen of lacquered paper, and a little toilet and shower cubicle rigged up in what was once an office. The rest of the space is taken up with lab benches littered with glassware, a containment hood, ultracentrifuge, freeze-drier and benchtop PCR, a second-hand bioreactor, a metal-framed desk with the computer Alex uses for sequence modelling and for running his artificial life ecosystem, and, in the middle of the bare concrete floor, the machine for which he sold his soul: Black Betty, a sleek state-of-the-art Nuclear Chicago argon laser nucleotide sequencer and assembler.

The smell of the place, a potent cocktail of solvents edged with hydrochloric acid fumes, reassures Alex's backbrain. He's been here three months now, and he still likes it. Black Betty is purring and clicking, the mini-Cray which controls her scrolling through the assembly program a line at a time. She's making another batch of the stuff he trashed at King's Cross, but he doesn't have the heart to switch her off. Of course, he should never have bought her and put himself in hock to Billy Rock's family, which was the only place he could get the money. But what can he say? It was love at first sight.

Alex checks his mail, but there are no messages. His online daemon tells him it's logged a couple of interesting discussion threads, and asks if he wants a new database of chemical suppliers, but Alex tells it he's busy. The daemon – a dapper red devil with a forked tail and a pitchfork – knuckles its horned forehead and does a slow fade.

Right now Alex's contact could be spilling his guts in some police station interview room, although since he has diplomatic immunity he should be smart enough to say nothing even if it does incriminate him. Alex thinks about this, and knows he should get out even if the guy doesn't talk. But it isn't as if he's done anything illegal, and besides, he can't leave his stuff.

The Cool-Z is working now, an icy sheath of calm closing around him. Alex does what he should have done at King's Cross, if he hadn't panicked at the sight of the squad cars. He calls up Detective Sergeant Howard Perse.

Perse answers on the first ring, as if he's been waiting for the call. He is sitting close to the camera of his phone, distorting Alex's view of his heavy, pockmarked face.

'You look fucked,' Perse says.

'You should know.'

'I heard that something went down at King's Cross,' Perse says. He seems to be smiling, but it's hard to tell. 'Was that your drop, Sharkey?'

'You know it was, you fucker,' Alex says, angry despite the Cool-Z.

'Now, now.' Perse is amused. 'I could tell you it doesn't matter, Sharkey, that there are always other clients. Is that what you want to hear? What were you selling anyway? HyperGhost? You're a naughty boy, Sharkey. The slants watch enough TV as it is.'

'It isn't illegal.'

'But you know it will be. The Bill comes up for its final reading in two weeks. Is that why you were in a hurry to offload it?'

'Yeah, and when it does you'll always be there to do me down, keep me small, under control. Maybe I won't cooperate any more, Perse.'

Perse says nothing.

Alex adds, 'I'll have to talk to Billy Rock. I'm not going to be able to pay my insurance this month.'

Perse says, 'It's always a good idea to keep on the right side of Billy Rock.'

And Alex makes a connection he should have made right at the beginning. Perse's foot. He's being fucked over because of Perse's fucked up foot!

'This is more than keeping me down, isn't it? You've got some kind of bullshit scheme to get me close to Billy Rock. You've been told to keep away from Billy, you've been told not to hassle him. So you want to use me.'

Perse doesn't bother to deny this accusation. Everyone knows that he wants to nail Billy Rock after the little bastard broke his foot, even though it was an accident. He says, 'How deep are you in with Billy?'

Alex swivels back and forth. The air suspension of the chair sighs under his weight. He says, 'I had to take the protection along with the loan. It wasn't optional.'

Perse says, with his infuriating smile right up against his phone's lens, 'You ever think that Billy Rock might have something to do with your run of bad luck?'

'He can call up a couple of squad cars? Because that's what happened at King's Cross.'

'Sharkey, he can call out a fucking Chief Inspector if he wants to, because his family has at least two on retainer. You know the way it works, so stop dicking around.'

Alex knows the way it works. It's like an eternal triangle. Triad Families like Billy Rock's run both the Yardies and the bent coppers. The Yardies do the necessary streetwork, and the police keep the Yardies under control. Anything that might perturb the relationship is rubbed out or incorporated.

Alex says, with a bad taste in his mouth, 'What would I do if he did fuck up my deal?'

'Why don't you talk to him about your problem, let him make his move? He might reveal something.'

'Yeah.' Alex is thinking that if it was Billy Rock, someone still had to tell him about the deal in the first place.

'Son, if Billy Rock lends anyone money to expand, the next thing is that he'll want a piece of the action. That's the way it is.'

'Why should I want to expand?'

'What's that stuff you drink called? You have a fridge full of it.'

'Pisant?'

'Yeah, whatever. You're going to run out of it one day, you ever think of that?'

And then Perse cuts the connection. Alex still doesn't know who fucked him over, but he does know that Perse is right about one thing. He should call Billy Rock.

3
Billy Rock

An expert system, masquerading on the phone as a sleekly groomed receptionist with pneumatic breasts scarcely concealed beneath a wispy blouse, takes Alex's message and promises to pass it to Mr Rock. While he's waiting for Billy Rock to call back, Alex spends a lot of time tracking the latest changes in his a-life ecosystem, and more time on the Web Bulletin Board that a-life freaks use, talking with a Professor of Biology in the University of Hawaii about edge gliders. It seems that someone with the ethertag Alfred Russel Wallace has a new twist on the parasite problem that's pushing the edge gliders towards extinction.

Still no reply from Billy Rock, who at this time of night is probably higher than the Moon. Fuck him, Alex thinks. It is late enough to go and see his friend Ray Aziz, who runs a Total Environment Club called Ground Zero, and Alex needs to make a deal to at least try and cover the beating he's just taken at King's Cross.

Alex arrives just in time for the second ground burst of the night, a vast glare and an earth-shaking boom contracting into a hologram mushroom stalk that seems to rise beyond the huge video screens and roof girders of the club, dancers thrashing away like damned souls in the middle of all this light to a pulsing technoraga beat. The club isn't called Ground Zero for nothing.

Alex talks with Ray in the mixing booth high above the dance floor, where three tech jockeys keep the music and lights and effects jumping. Ray is a mellow fifty-year-old E-head, his serotonin level so low he can't get angry at anything, but he has been doing the club scene a long time, and runs a tight ship where it counts. He is also a good customer of Alex's from way back, from before the bust that netted the Wizard and his apprentices. Alex was one of the first gene hackers to crack the code for Serenity, and his very own psychoactive RNA virus, variously called Ghost or Fade or Firelight, is popular in the TECs because it enhances the flicker effect of TVs and holo systems, makes them appear to be saturated with coded meanings, revealing ghosts in the electronic glimmer. Clubbers like as much information density as possible, along with the sense that they've been transported to another dimension, and Ghost helps them along. If Alex could have patented Ghost, he would have made a fortune, but of course being a gene hacker cuts both ways. And thanks to Perse or Billy Rock, his chance at going international with a new version of Ghost, before psychoactive viruses are made illegal in the UK, has just gone down the toilet.

The deal with Ray takes a while to complete. There are sensibilities to satisfy, forms as elaborate as Japanese tea ceremonies to be observed. It is too late to even think about sleep by the time Alex gets back to his workshop and finds a message from Billy Rock's expert system telling him that a limo will pick him up at ten in the morning. Apparently Billy Rock was expecting Alex to make contact. He wants to meet.

Fuelled with amphetamines and paranoia, Alex calls up Alice, his regular amongst Ma Nakome's string of part-time whores, sleepy, plump Alice who expertly relieves him of his tensions and stays over to have breakfast. He likes Alice – their relationship is entirely commercial, but there's also a nice mutual pretence at an intimate familiarity.

While he waits for the limo to arrive, Alex catches a cycle of the BBC Breakfast News and switches back and forth between three of the greater metropolitan area cable news channels, but there is no mention of any Indonesian diplomat arrested at King's Cross. Not that he expects any news. Instead of carrying the batch of Hyper-Ghost to Paris, by now the guy will be on a stratocruiser on his way back to Jakarta, a luckless pawn in the campaign to harass Alex Sharkey.

Alex is too restless to sit still. He wishes now that he hadn't called up Billy Rock, but it's too late to unring that bell. He goes out into the hot, bright sunshine and chats to old Frank, who is already sitting in his customary place outside his office furniture store, until the limo arrives.

Billy Rock's runner is this sixteen-year-old black kid with a razorcut, a white Joseph T-shirt and baggy blue jeans with transparent cutouts in the thighs, box-fresh Nikes and a bad attitude. Alex has met the kid a couple of times before: he calls himself Doggy Dog, after some dead rap singer. He's a small wiry fucker, sitting right back in the deep blue oxhide upholstery as if he owns the limo; his Nikes don't even reach the nice blue carpet. There are LEDs in the soles of the sneakers, little red blips chasing each other round and round. The kid sees Alex staring at them and grins – he's got a diamond chip set in one of his front teeth.

The limo glides off. Alex pulls out a cigarette and lights it without asking permission.

'You'll get cancer,' the kid says, giving Alex a contemptuous hooded gaze, seeing this balding fat guy in blue denim bib overalls over a rumpled purple sweater with both elbows out, and scuffed, no-fashion, orange construction boots.

Alex blows out a riffle of smoke and returns the kid's look. 'Maybe I'll give you cancer first.'

'No way, bwoy. I've had my shots.'

'Billy Rock has a health plan for his runners?'

'Runner, shit. I got out of that two months ago. You be sorry you don't show me more respect.'

The limo swings out on to the East India Road. Alex settles back in the plush upholstery and smokes his cigarette and watches the cluster of Docklands skyscrapers catch the light of the sun. The limo's smoked glass shades everything blue. Alex didn't sleep last night. He is running on coffee and amphetamines, and feeling a weird nervous high. He is almost tempted to ask Doggy Dog how Billy Rock gives it him – in the mouth or in the arse, and is that why he's called Doggy Dog? – but the reason the kid is sitting slumped in the seat is he has a pistol tucked in the waistband of his jeans.

The limo speeds through the Rotherhithe Tunnel, turns past the Norwegian Church, and comes out in a little road cramped between high warehouses somewhere by Canada Dock. It drives around two sides of a big muddy pit where little yellow electric bulldozers are working and pulls up in the shadow of a gutted warehouse.

The kid, Doggy Dog, waits for the driver to get out and open the door. Alex has to slide over to follow Doggy Dog out into the soggy heat. The driver, a big impassive man in a cutaway T-shirt to show off the carbon whisker spurs implanted in his muscular forearms, gets back into the limo and drives off, and Doggy Dog leads Alex into the warehouse. Alex has the bad feeling that he's somehow being led to the slaughter, and maybe Doggy Dog senses this, because he catches hold of Alex's arm just above the elbow, as if to restrain him.

There's a big bare high space inside the warehouse. At the far end, in the concentrated glare of arc lights on scaffold towers, is a circular arena fenced with wooden boards, with tiered benches rising above it. Billy Rock is sitting ringside, his boots cocked on the wooden palisade.

Billy Rock – he's about twenty-five, small and wiry, not much bigger than Doggy Dog. He wears a raw linen suit, with a panama hat pulled low over his face and a cane cradled between his knees. White gloves, ostrich skin boots with cuban heels. His jacket is slung like a cape around his shoulders, and he sort of hunches into it as he stares down into the arena. His smooth-skinned petulant face is masked by shades. Alex suspects that Billy's high cheekbones are the result of plastic surgery, but of course no one would ever ask.

Alex leans at the palisade and looks down, and the thing in the pit snarls, bounds forward, and slams on to its back as a chain brings it up short.

Alex jerks away and Doggy Dog laughs, a kind of snorting giggle.

The floor of the arena is covered in sawdust. In the centre, an iron stake anchors a chain. The thing at the end of the chain has gouged deep tracks in the sawdust, down to the grey sand beneath. It springs to its feet now, very fast, very limber. It is a blue-skinned doll, heavily modified by selective somatic mutation or surgery. Probably both, Alex thinks. It's naked – and female, although its dugs are little more than enlarged nipples. The wide powerful jaws are like something found on an old tree bole blasted by lightning and infected with fungus and rot, layers of knotted cankerous growth. The doll has a crest of muscle on the top of its skull to work these big jaws, a nose so flattened that the nostrils are slits, little black eyes close set under a craggy brow.

Billy Rock is watching Alex. His almond-shaped eyes are just visible behind the shades. He says, 'You like her? Want to go a couple of rounds maybe?'

Bow legs splayed, the doll stamps and pulls at the chain, which is welded to an iron ring around its left ankle. The nails of its toes and fingers are thick and yellow and raggedly sharp. There is a ruff of carbon whisker quills around its neck, and a kind of mane of quills twitches and clatters down its back as the creature rakes the air, hissing. Thick saliva drips from pointed teeth.

Alex sees that blood sprays have darkened the wood of the palisade fence around the arena. He fumbles out a cigarette and says, 'She's what, your runner's girlfriend?'

Doggy Dog scowls. 'Don't you be dissin' me, fat boy.'

Billy Rock laughs. 'Anyone tried to fuck her, she'd have their guts out in a minute. She'd claw out your liver and your lungs and eat them right in front of your eyes while you were still wondering what happened. She doesn't know when to stop. That's what makes her good. She's been in three bouts and won every one in less than two minutes. Three more, then I retire her and use her as breeding stock.'

This shocks Alex more than the sight of the thing. He coughs out smoke and says, 'She's fertile?'

'Not yet,' Billy Rock says, 'but there's a way to do it. Maybe if I tie her up you could help out, uh? You sit down, now. You look pale.'

He gives Alex a nasty smile. The thing about Billy Rock is this: he's both dumb and mean. He's the youngest of five brothers. Three were killed in the vendetta that gave his family control of this part of South London after they moved in from Hong Kong. The fourth survived being shot in the head and losing most of his forebrain, but he spends all the time in a room in the basement of the family house, hunting for imaginary enemies and howling like a dog. Which, because his father died of Creutzfeldt-Jakob's, means that Billy Rock is the *de facto* head of the family.

Billy's uncles handle most of the day-to-day business, and he is left with little to do except indulge in his drug of choice. Crack, mostly, which is how he got his street name; that, and his fondness for speed metal. The last time Alex had to talk with Billy Rock, maybe the worst half hour of his life, Billy Rock was lying flat out in the back of his limo, smoking pipes of crack and scratching patterns on his skinny bare chest with a penknife while, the soundsystem blasted out the crank rock of the Bad Brains so loud the big car was rocked back and forth on its cushioned suspension.

But Billy Rock seems clean now, almost animated. He spends about fifteen minutes talking about fighting dolls, which is his family's latest scheme, it turns out, or one half of it. Billy Rock has been running fighting dolls for a year, taking a percentage of the bets laid, but now he's building a big arena where punters can hunt down unmodified dolls and kill them for real. He tells Alex that he wants to call it Mortal Kombat, after some old computer game he played when he was a kid, although it will be mortal only for the dolls. They will be armed with laser tag guns, while the punters will have the real thing.

'Mortal Kombat would be a keen name, but my fucking uncles are calling it after some old film.'

'The Killing Fields,' Doggy Dog offers.

'Whatever. Some pussy name. Although maybe we could stage gladiator stuff, too. Set fighting dolls against guys with swords and nets, shit like that. Make it more sporting. What do you think?'

Alex lights another cigarette. He thinks that someone has been feeding Billy a line. There's no way he could have come up with this on his own. The kid, Doggy Dog, is watching Billy the way a teacher watches an educationally challenged pupil trying to recite the ten times table. Alex thinks that he will have to be careful around Doggy Dog.

Down in the arena, a handler is swiping at the doll with a long bamboo pole. The handler wears a heavily padded suit, chain mail gloves, and a kind of crash helmet with a cage of bars in front of his face. After a minute of this goading, the doll suddenly wrenches the pole from the man's grasp and chews down on its end: bamboo three centimetres thick shatters with a noise like a gunshot. The doll tosses the pole away, spits splinters, and glares at the handler with dumb, triumphant malevolence.

Alex says, 'I think the dolls would win.'

Billy Rock likes this answer. 'Sure they would,' he says seriously. 'The point is, how many could someone kill before they got him? Something like that would bring in some sincere attention, don't you think?'

'If you could find people dumb enough to go against those things.'

'That's hardly a problem,' Billy Rock says.

Doggy Dog says, 'Listen, boss, tell him the deal, OK? There's somet'ing you need to see out on the site.'

'Hey,' Billy Rock says, turning around and fixing Doggy Dog with his shades. 'Who's in charge here, huh?'

'It's the concrete they be pouring—'

'Fuck the concrete. You see these boots?'

Alex and Doggy Dog look at Billy Rock's boots, cocked up on the palisade.

'They cost a thousand pounds,' Billy Rock tells Alex, 'and this little turd expects me to go walking through the fucking mud to look in a fucking hole full of wet concrete. These are genuine ostrich skin boots. They just can't make them any more. You think I put them on because I want to go walking through all that shit? I wanted to do that, Dog, I would have dressed like you.'

Doggy Dog says petulantly, 'Oh man, you're being ripped off, like I said you would when you went for the cheapest bid. How you t'ink they g'win make a profit on what you pay if they don't cut corners? Which is just what they be doing, cheating on you and generally showing you disrespect. You got to do something.'

Billy Rock tells the kid, 'You just tell them to get it right or they'll be part of the foundations.' He says to Alex, 'Details – that's what I pay people for. See, they all said I couldn't run a business, but this is the cutting edge of entertainment, believe me. We'll have families out here wanting to buy popcorn and T-shirts and gimme hats and shit like that. Maybe I should start a franchise. What do you think? Want to get in on the ground floor?'

'I wish I could,' Alex says, feeling a little better now. Billy Rock will want him to do something to help this along. He can live with that. He says, 'You really think that you can get dolls to breed?'

Doggy Dog says, 'It be against the law.'

'That's right,' Billy Rock says, 'but that doesn't mean it can't be done. This is a separate thing, you understand, from the Killing Fields thing. My own private thing my uncles don't need to know about.'

Doggy Dog explains, 'This will be for sporting types who want to breed their own stock, like racing horses. Breeding is like an art, understand, and people pay a lot more for art than technology. Dolls those fucking Koreans sell be male, and all of them guaranteed sterile. But they have all the equipment, it just isn't developed. It needs starting up.'

Alex has been wondering where they got a female doll, but it isn't the kind of question you can ask in circumstances like this. He says, 'And you want me to work out a way of doing this? That would be worth a lot of money.'

'You want to talk about money,' Billy Rock says lazily, 'we can start talking about what you owe. I hear you fucked up a deal yesterday, maybe can't make this month's payment. Man in your position should be glad of a business opportunity.'

So Billy Rock did have something to do with screwing the deal. And Alex is certain that Perse somehow found a way to let Billy Rock know about it. Maybe Doggy Dog is doing a deal with Perse behind Billy Rock's back.

Alex asks, 'You'll square what I owe with the family, if I do this for you?'

He is thinking of Billy Rock's uncles, sober, dignified men who look like barristers or bankers, immaculate in silk pinstripe suits from Jermyn Street. They don't approve of Billy Rock screwing around on the street like this. It is bad for the family's reputation. But if this goes wrong, Billy Rock won't be the one hurt.

Billy Rock waves this away. It is another detail. He says, 'You come along to the party I'm giving. We're floating this Killing Fields thing on the stock market in a few days.'

Alex drops his cigarette butt and grinds it under the heel of his construction boot. He says carefully, 'I'd be pleased to come along. Of course I would.'

Doggy Dog says, 'You have a hormone synthesis problem to solve. See, we can get female dolls, but they be as sterile as the males. Your job is to make the stuff to bring them on heat. Understand, we'd send it to a real biotech company, but they'd pass it straight on to the Korean fuckers who make the dolls.'

Alex says, 'There's got to be more to it than giving them the right hormones.'

Doggy Dog says, 'Don't you be worrying about that. You just make the hormone.'

'For one thing,' Alex says, 'the things you've had done to change that thing down there into a fighting doll are all somatic. They won't be inherited.'

Doggy Dog says, looking amused, 'There be ways to make the changes down at the blastula level, before separation of the somatic tissue and . . . how you call it?'

'Generative tissue.' Alex wonders how the little gangster knows this stuff.

'Yeah, whatever. So that way the changes get passed on.'

'It's illegal to make genetic changes to generative tissue,' Alex says. 'Even in this country. I mean, *really* illegal.'

Doggy Dog cracks up at this. He laughs so hard he can hardly stand, finally calms down enough to be able to say, 'Man, that be the *least* of your worries.'

'You don't have to worry about a thing,' Billy Rock says, 'as long as you do right by me.'

4
Dealing

The next day, Alex meets Howard Perse in a pub off the White-chapel Road. Perse is working on a double murder, two Uzbeki-stanis found that morning in a corner of Bethnal Green Cemetery, tied back to back and both shot through the head.

Perse says, with weary irony, 'We're looking for the people who did it so we can recruit them. The victims were a couple of pieces of shit dealing in heroin from the old country. But that's too crude for the likes of you to bother with, isn't it, Sharkey?'

'That's Mister Sharkey to you,' Alex says. He's tired and irrit-able, sweating into his green tweed suit and perched uncomfortably on a stool at a little round table with a cracked marble top and a heavy cast iron frame. The table is crowded with empty beer glasses. A drowsy wasp buzzes from one glass to another and back again. Overhead, a ceiling fan stirs the layers of cigarette smoke but does nothing to cut the heat. The sun, striking through the greasy window, glows incandescently on nicotine-stained red flock wall-paper and haloes the heads of the people around the bar, as if they are saints crowding for a glimpse of the Messiah.

Alex has been up early, has already been to pay the visit to his mother that he promised himself he'd make if he wasn't arrested after the deal was fucked. Lexis has a new boyfriend, a scrawny kid barely out of his teens. All the time Alex is there, the boyfriend sits in the other room drinking canned lager and watching football on interactive TV, switching restlessly from viewpoint to viewpoint, the volume turned up so loud it rattles the paper-thin walls of the flat. Ten in the morning, for Christ's sake.

When Alex had money, when he was working for the Wizard, he bought his mother the satellite TV system, a new suite of lounge furniture and the air conditioning unit that hums above the sliding glass door on to the narrow balcony. He offered to buy her a house in the suburbs, but she has lived all her life in the East End and says she would never move. All of life is here. Out in the suburbs they're dead and don't know it.

Lexis Sharkey. His mother. A peroxide blonde who always, it

23

seems to Alex, wears full makeup, powder and lipstick and mascara, this morning in a cheap nylon kimono that, carelessly tied, exposes her loose, freckled breasts in their black lace cradle. She keeps herself in shape, this feisty forty-eight-year-old broad. She knows right away Alex is in trouble – they have never been able to hide anything from each other.

Alex grew up in a tower block flat much like this one, with black mould on the walls and Pharaoh ants in the kitchen, and a view from the wind-battered picture window across the Thames' glittering loops to the *terra incognita* of South London. The tower block was demolished to make way for an access road to the London City Airport, but the cheap shabby furniture of his childhood has persisted, along with dozens of undusted pottery figures, plastic souvenirs and artificial flowers in plastic baskets imitating woven straw, the empty budgerigar cage with its mirror and bell, a ceramic dray horse with a broken hind leg mended with superglue – Alex knocked it off the wooden shelf above the electric fire when he was four or five – and a leather pouffe with a rip down one side dating from the day Alex cut it open convinced there was money inside. He vividly remembers finding only yellow and green foam rubber chunks. They'd never had any money, but they'd always managed. Lexis is a fighter.

Lexis says that if there is anything he needs, he only has to ask, and Alex tells her that it's all right, he has a deal going, and she smiles and lights another cigarette – he brought her a big carton of Benson and Hedges, like a gold brick, and a bottle of Lamb's Navy Rum.

'You only have to ask,' she says again, exhaling a cloud of smoke. 'And if you get in trouble, you come and tell me. The boys down the club can sort it out for you. That's what friends are for.'

The club is Leroy's shebeen, currently located in the basement of an abandoned office block, where a crowd of middle-aged Jamaicans spend the nights playing pool and dominoes and listening to old reggae tunes. Bob Marley and the Wailers. Burning Spear. Max Romeo. Lexis is a dealer herself in a small way, mostly homegrown weed now, but she sold E and whizz in the raves and clubs in the good old days of the nineties, when she'd been a single mother trying to stretch diminishing welfare payments. Alex has sworn never to supply his mother with even a single infective unit of the psychoactive viruses he splices, not that she has ever asked him.

'Your problem,' Lexis tells her son, 'is that you don't have any friends. You think you don't need people, but you do. What kind of trouble are you in?'

Alex does have friends, but they are safely distributed through the hyperconnective geography of the Web. He likes to gossip and boast as much as any gene hacker, he just doesn't want to meet up with the people he talks to. The thought of actual live face-to-face conferences on gene hacking makes Alex's skin crawl.

Alex tells Lexis that everything will be fine, that business is just a little slow. What else can he say?

But his mother just looks at him and says, 'Alex, you haven't been sleeping. Don't think I can't see it. And that's a fucking awful suit. It makes you look like Oscar Wilde. What possessed you to buy it? If you ask me, you haven't been the same since you went in the nick.'

Alex can't deny it. He woke in the early hours, and found himself standing by the computer console, drenched in sweat and convinced that he'd been talking to someone. Somehow he could hear an echo of a voice. He'd switched on all the lights and looked around, wondering if a rat had got in. He even checked the security cameras, but they showed nothing but moonlight-drenched tarmac.

And now, in the hot, crowded pub, Detective Sergeant Howard Perse crushes a cigarette in the overflowing tin ashtray and lights another and says, 'Whatever you're going to ask me, you'd better do it, Sharkey. There's pressure to get a result with this case.'

'Someone cares about a couple of dealers?'

'A couple of dealers who were taking payment for their stuff in hardened electronics. The sort of electronics used in smart weapons, the sort that can survive being shot out of a cannon, and then guide the shell down to target. Mind you, this is strictly off the record.'

'Everything you tell me is off the record.'

Perse takes a long drag on his new cigarette, followed by a swallow of his Guinness. He is a stocky man in his mid-forties, with a comfortable swag of beer belly straining his striped shirt, and a face pockmarked and cratered by old acne. With black hair combed back from a widow's peak, and a truculent saturnine glare, he looks like a low rent Count Dracula. When he lifts his Guinness, his jacket tugs sideways to show his pistol holster under his armpit. He is looking over Alex's shoulder, and Alex turns on the stool to see what has caught Perse's attention.

The pub is crowded with old men in straw hats and bright leisure clothes. The local dealer is in one corner. Every five minutes or so, someone comes up and puts money on the bar in front of the dealer, and he hands a packet over and his customer turns and shoves through the crowd out into the sunlight. There's a gang of crusties in the back, all dreadlocks, beads and ethnic clutter. Dogs on string leads wind themselves around their masters' legs. The crusties are smoking blow and taking long theatrical snorts from a little bottle of clear liquid they pass amongst themselves. But Perse isn't watching the passing trade – he could start arresting people up and down the Whitechapel Road and not be finished by Christmas. He's watching the television hung in the angle above the bar, which shows a helicopter shot of billowing columns of black smoke rising from a cluster of mirrorglass skyscrapers into an achingly blue sky.

'Where's that,' Perse says. 'Houston?'

'Atlanta, I think. The army pulled out of Houston two weeks ago.'

'Thank Christ for our system,' Perse says. 'Always had a fatal weakness, the Yanks. Never had a strong central government.'

Alex thinks this is a pile of shit. There's as much unrest here as anywhere in the States: it's just that the American population is better organized and more heavily armed. The Christer coalition used nerve gas and helicopter gun ships in Houston.

He says, although he knows Perse will not rise to it, 'Strong on law and order, that's how you like it?'

Perse smiles sourly. 'I got another sweet case today. Matter of fact, I was pulled off it to come down here. Some bloke filling up at a petrol station early this morning got the shit beaten out of him. Three guys in a van jumped him, stabbed him, cracked his skull with a two by four, then drove his car over him, back and forth, back and forth, three or four times. Broke his legs. Then one of them took off in the bloke's Mercedes, and the other two followed in their van. They lost control of the van on the Chiswick Flyover, and they're down at the nick right now. Still don't know what happened to the Merc.'

'So what has that got to do with you?'

'The poor bastard they beat up was carrying half a key of DOA. But that wasn't why they beat him up. Know why they did it? He was black, and these shitheads saw his white girlfriend coming out of the petrol station toilet. What a sweet world, eh? So I'm a busy boy, Sharkey. Tell me about your meeting with Billy.'

'You fucked up my deal, didn't you? I don't care if it was Billy Rock's pet Chief Inspector who actually sent in the squad cars – someone had to tell Billy in the first place. You did it so I'd stay in the hole with him. Admit it, Perse, you're going after him again.'

'Even if you pay off the loan, Sharkey, you never will pay off the debt. You know that. And then there's the protection. Why are you pissing and moaning at me?'

'Everyone knows you have it in for Billy Rock.'

Perse fixes Alex with his patented heavy-duty Look, and Alex knows he's pressed the right button. He is caught in the middle of the war of Flatfoot Perse's fucked-up foot.

Perse says, 'You keep your mouth shut, you little shit. You can't even begin to know the favours I've done you. Stop complaining and tell me what Billy Rock wants from you.'

So Alex tells Perse about Billy Rock's plan to breed dolls, and the job he's been given. It isn't as if he has any choice, and besides, he doesn't think that he's doing anything wrong, grassing like this. Cops are part of the information economy like everyone else – there's even a bulletin board called CopWatch which posts information on police operations and techniques. According to the anarcho-liberationists who set it up, the police check it out more frequently than anyone else.

Perse thinks it over, then says, 'Billy Rock has to have someone else working for him. Some kind of rogue biotech company, perhaps. You know Billy Rock never had an idea of his own in his life.'

'Of course he has someone else. He more or less told me.'

Or at least, the kid, Doggy Dog, did. Alex hasn't told Perse about his suspicions concerning Doggy Dog.

Perse says, 'I'll see what I can find out. It might be a way in. You can talk to this guy, one hacker to another.'

'Why should I help you?'

'You're paying Billy, what? Five K per month?'

'Something like that,' Alex says, sweating because Perse is almost bang on the nail. He adds, 'With what I've told you, you can have Billy Rock on a plate. Isn't that enough? The Hyundai Magic Doll Corporation won't be too happy if someone starts hacking their patented genome. You have violation of copyright right there, and definitely a slew of broken biotech regulations.'

'The point is being able to prove it,' Perse says, lighting up another cigarette. He smokes Craven As, not being a man who likes to compromise. The first two fingers of Perse's right hand are stained nicotine yellow to the knuckles. He sneers when Alex takes out one of his Benson and Hedges, and says, 'What Billy's asked you to do would earn him nothing more than a fine and a slap on the wrist, if that. But if you get close to whoever put Billy up to this, then we have a lead on a conspiracy to defraud. I'm just a street copper, thank Christ, but I'm sure the commercial enforcement boys would be glad of the case.'

'And I'll be a material witness. Fuck off, Perse.' Alex knows what happens to witnesses against the Triads.

'You won't have to testify,' Perse says coolly.

Alex lights his cigarette. 'I'm sure. And I'd still be in debt to Billy's family, or someone else will have the paper, so what good does this do me?'

'I've always looked after you, Sharkey. No one will finger you for this.'

Alex says, 'I don't have to stay around to get whacked by Billy's family. I can move on, operate anywhere. I just need a little seed money.'

Alex has already thought it through. The hormone specs are straightforward. He isn't worried that he can't do it; he is worried that once Billy Rock's people test everything out, Billy will decide that Alex Sharkey is disposable.

Perse says, 'You're a London boy, like me. Where else are you going to go?'

'Somewhere cool,' Alex says. 'Finland, maybe.'

'They've got malaria in Finland, these days.'

'Sweden, then. Iceland. What does it matter?'

'They've got leprosy in Sweden. A holdout from the Middle Ages. The one place it never went away. And then there's the radioactivity. Don't you worry, Sharkey,' Perse says, stubbing out his cigarette, 'I'll look after you. It's time I got back to work. It's starting to stink in here.'

Alex walks with Perse to the crime site. The sun is brutal, and when Alex puts on his big black hat Perse laughs and says it makes him look like a nun in drag. Perse limps slightly, favouring his right foot. That's the one that was run over after Perse stopped Billy Rock's limo with the intention of shaking it down, a month after he'd been relocated to the Drug Squad. Billy Rock just laughed and ordered his driver to move on. The driver was a nervous get-away merchant who pulled away so fast he left smoking rubber on the tarmac. So fast that Perse couldn't get his foot out of the way. The limo's rear wheel went over it and broke twelve bones. Then gangrene set in and Perse lost two toes. More importantly, Perse lost so much face that he spent all of his time trying to nail Billy Rock, until one of Billy's tame Chief Inspectors put a stop to it by sticking Perse with a case-load of unsolved drug-related murders. And now, two years later, it's started all over again, with Alex piggy-in-the-middle.

Cars are parked on either side of the road, with goods piled on their bonnets: TVs, portable phones, bootleg CDs and sticks, clothing, cased computers, all kind of electronics. There are operators who can open a carton, slit the plasticwrap, slip out the goods and replace it with a slab of concrete weighing exactly the same, and reseal the wrap and carton so sweetly you'll never know until after you've bought it. At the corner, a white van is parked with its door cracked a handswidth at the bottom. People are queuing to buy, bending to pass money through the slot and receive their packet or tube, shuffling off to find a quiet spot to get their hit. A skinny guy lurches up clutching a leather coat, saying they can have it for ten pounds, five pounds, he needs the fare home, that's all . . . There's blood still wet on the coat's orange fake fur collar.

Perse says to Alex, 'One of your customers?'

'Maybe one of the Wizard's ex-customers.'

'You're not really a hard bastard, Sharkey. Not like you pretend to be. You should get out of the game.'

'I'm not doing anything against the law.'

'Not now, perhaps, but in a few weeks psychoactive viruses will be illegal. And once upon a time you were benchtesting new narcotic substances for a well-known pot-boiler who even now is serving a long stretch for possession with intent. You were lucky you were caught with nothing on you, and even luckier that no one fingered you.'

'I was held in jail for six months and released without trial.'

'But that doesn't make you innocent, Sharkey. You know that.'

'I know you think no one's innocent.'

'How is the Wizard these days?'

'Making methamphetamine out of household chemicals. He'll be richer coming out than he was when he went in. He once told me that he used to say to the people he sold stuff, "This is going to kill you. It's going to destroy your life and ruin your world." They bought it anyway. They still buy DOA, even though it'll kill them if it isn't properly cut, because it's such a fantastic high. With a name like Dead On Arrival the punters think it has to be. But I don't deal in stuff like that.'

Alex really doesn't like hard drugs. The thing about something like heroin is that it only works on people with clinical or sub-clinical depression. Any normal person feels nothing but nausea and lassitude after their first taste and doesn't understand why anyone would want to try it twice, but one little girl told Alex that the first time she smoked junk she felt this click in her head, like a door opening into a world of sunshine. The psychotropic viruses Alex hacks are more subtle, enhancing highly specific states of consciousness, and totally non-addictive. The problem is that the government doesn't see it his way.

Perse says, 'All the same, word is that someone's interested in you. I've heard that the spooks might be on your case. They pulled your jacket, although don't worry, it's clean.'

Alex laughs. It seems the only sane response. 'What kind of spooks? Five?'

'Something along those lines.' Perse isn't smiling.

They've reached the crime scene. A couple of uniformed officers chat beside an ambulance waiting with its doors wide open. Just inside the cemetery gate, yellow tape is stretched to make a rough square amongst blackened headstones. Stevie Cryer, Perse's boyish partner, is watching a forensic tech work on two bodies lying on plastic sheeting.

Perse says, 'We've got the Colombians trying to muscle in again. I don't know why anyone should be interested in a small-time artist like you, Sharkey, unless you're servicing some MP someone wants fitted up. What haven't you told me?'

Alex says, 'If my jacket is clean, what could they know?'

'They have these tricks. Want to hear one? They call you up, put a subliminal signal on the screen. You come around with a blinder of a headache, and you can't remember spilling your guts.'

Alex thinks about how he woke up this morning. He says, 'If you want me to help you with Billy Rock, then find out more about this spook stuff.'

'That's the spirit, Sharkey. And if you hear about someone trying to shift a half a key of DOA, let me know, I'm still after the shithead who took off in the Mercedes.'

Perse lifts the yellow tape and ducks under it and leaves Alex standing next to Stevie Cryer. Cryer is a lanky, amiable fellow, tough but straightforward. Alex likes him a lot more than he likes Perse. Today, Cryer is dressed for the heat, in baggy blue shorts and a long-sleeved grey T-shirt, a floppy straw hat perched jauntily on his thinning blond hair. He says, 'I hear you're making some new kind of gear, Alex. Is that why you can afford those snappy threads?'

Alex says, 'I have a problem with your partner.'

Cryer fixes Alex with his washed-out blue eyes. He always looks wearily amused, as if he's seen everything the world has to offer and isn't impressed. He says, 'You'll just have to work it out with him.'

'It's about Billy Rock. Perse is starting it up again.'

'That's his call.'

'Has he talked to you about it?'

Cryer says, 'Well, that's between him and me.'

'I'd hate to see you get involved.'

'Where is this heading, Alex? You have something to tell me?'

'I'd like to think I can call you if I need to. If things get out of hand.'

'We're always there, Alex. Excuse me now. I've got to deal with a couple of dead people.'

5
Deep Hacking Mode

Alex spends the rest of the day making a list of what he will need to realize Billy Rock's order. The way to go, he decides, after running a matching search that compares the putative doll hormones with a library of equivalents, is to buy commercially available bacteria which have been gengineered to produce the cocktail of hormones used in Hormone Replacement Therapy – the secret of the Prime Minister's post-menopausal vigour – and use site-specific mutagenesis to alter the plasmids which have been inserted into them.

It is an old technique, one that harnesses the boundless mutability of bacterial metabolism. The serfs of the biosphere, bacteria are easy to manipulate because they have a simple genetic structure. Unlike plants and animals, which package their genetic information into as many as a hundred separate chromosomes, each an immensely long complexly folded string of DNA, bacteria have a single loop of DNA which can be augmented by smaller satellite loops, plasmids. Bacteria exchange plasmids promiscuously. Naturally occurring plasmids add capabilities like antibiotic resistance; artificial plasmids can be inserted to transform bacteria into self-replicating factories that will synthesize a single product on command. Site-specific mutagenesis will selectively alter the DNA of the plasmids of the gengineered bacteria Alex plans to purchase, so that they will manufacture doll-specific hormones instead of human hormones.

The site-specific mutagenesis and plasmid reinsertion will take a day. After screening, Alex will grow up a batch of suitably transformed bacteria in his little bioreactor, and after three or four days he'll have enough purified hormones for testing.

It's late in the night when Alex has finished, but compared to his own work this is a trivial project. The essence of gene hacking is nothing more than altering the sequence of nucleotide bases along a DNA helix. Once you've identified which genes you want to modify, the rest is no more than simple wet chemistry using tech-nology as old and tried as manufacturing enzymes for biological washing powders. Designing psychoactive drugs and viruses is of an entirely different order of complexity.

Alex read George Gamow's classic, *Mr Tompkins Explores the Atom*, when he was a kid. The book was lent to him by a teacher who glimpsed a spark in the surly quiet fat boy who hardly ever talked to anyone, who seemed to live inside his head most of the time. The book clicked with something in Alex. It helped him define what he wanted to be; one of the mind tools he uses to engage in the zen-like deep hacking mode needed to work out his complex syntheses is to imagine himself as a nucleus at the heart of an atom, fat and happy and strong, binding his swarm of electrons and watching the reactions around him.

Organic synthesis is still a black art resembling alchemy, in that all operations have to be conducted in an exact and precise way that approaches ritualization, often for complicated reasons that are difficult to fully figure out. Many psychoactive molecules are big and complex, and often their effect depends on the way in which the chains and rings of carbon, oxygen and hydrogen are doped with single atoms of phosphate or sulphur. Working out how to get those atoms in exactly the right place, and knowing just where the right places are, intuitively understanding the subtle interactions that twist and bend molecular conformations in new and interesting ways, is what Alex is good at, better than any of the so-called expert systems used by big drug companies. And that's only half the story, because after something is synthesized, the impurities have to be removed. Any intelligent school kid can make LSD from readily available chemicals – the trick is to purify it of the secondary products which can cause anything from recurrent flashbacks to pseudo-Parkinson's.

The interface between psychoactive molecules and the intricate metabolic and ionic processes which sustain consciousness is fractal, sensitively dependent upon a myriad initial conditions. Before the Millennium, it could be crudely disrupted by drugs like Prozac, which interfered with the subtle checks and balances of serotonin metabolism. Most psychoactive drugs are no better. But now there are psychoactive RNA viruses which stimulate single points on consciousness's fractal surface.

The psychoactive viruses, like those which cause HIV or herpes, have a very high specificity. Compared to the saturation bombing of drugs, they operate with the cool precision of snipers. HIV viruses infect only T-lymphocytes; herpes viruses are active only in epithelial cells around the mouth or genitals; psychoactive viruses infect as few as a dozen specialized neurones. Like all RNA viruses, they inject a string of RNA and an enzyme, reverse transcriptase, into their target cells. Normally, RNA is the messenger between DNA, which encodes genetic information, and the cellular machinery which translates that information into proteins. RNA is a single-stranded mirror-image of the nucleotide code of the active strand of double-stranded DNA. Reverse transcriptase drives the machinery backwards, making DNA from viral RNA: DNA which can insert itself inside the host cell's genome, remaining inert until something activates it and it subverts the host cell's machinery to manufacture new viruses.

The DNA made by psychoactive viruses, though, cannot make new viruses, and it is not inserted into the host genome. Instead, it manufactures enzymes which in turn synthesize chemicals that are normally present only when the host neurone is activated, enhancing the particular fractional state of consciousness controlled by the infected neurones. Because the viruses can't replicate, and because the unbound DNA they make is ephemeral, users need to buy a hit every time they want to turn themselves on. If you can hack a psychoactive virus that targets an interesting component of consciousness's *Gestalt*, you can make a lot of money very quickly.

So far, Alex has only been successful with two strains of virus. One, Serenity, was actually hacked by someone else; Alex simply cracked its code and pirated it. The other, Ghost, was quickly broken by other gene hackers, and Alex has put its full details on shareware bulletin boards, with a request for a token contribution from anyone who uses the information. Perhaps one per cent users pay. It's pin money, but useful pin money, because Alex has more than used up his capital making a more potent variant, Hyper-Ghost. And now all psychoactive viruses are about to be made illegal. Which is why he's doing this dumb piece of gene hacking for Billy Rock, instead of getting on with his real business.

Alex saves his notes on hormone synthesis and has his daemon order a minicab. The driver is a Bengali Alex knows slightly. His minicab is done out in red plush and gold braiding. Little trinkets hang from bead-chains on the dashboard. There's a hologram of Shiva the Destroyer right next to the driver's laminated photo ID, and the slogan *God gives me speed* is lettered across the top of the windscreen. The Wizard would give God a run for his money, Alex thinks, when he reads this pious boast.

Postcards of religious images are pasted on the cloudy plastic screen that divides passenger from driver. The driver has pushed open the sliding window in the screen so that he can talk to Alex. It's as hot as an oven in the minicab, and a joss stick wedged into the air vent on the driver's side sends up a thick sweet smoke, the smell of Alex's childhood. Lexis was into that post-hippy New Age shit when she was a single mother no older than Alex is now. He could be, Alex thinks, in a little bubble of Fairyland.

Old London Town is growing strange and exotic in the grip of what they are now calling the Great Climatic Overturn. Lights drift past the minicab like stars seen from some hyperlight spaceship. Streetlights, the scattered lights of the tower blocks behind screens of hardy sycamores and ginkgoes, the lights of the pyramid-capped tower of Canary Wharf rising into the sodium orange sky. A helicopter slowly crosses the sky from west to east, the needle of its laser spotlight intermittently stabbing amongst the flat roofs of deck access housing.

The driver tells Alex about the latest drive-by shooting out on the Whitechapel Road. 'A whole bunch of skinheads, screaming past in an old Cosworth Sierra, out where the youth fucked up on crack hang out. You know that café?'

'The Gunga Din?' Alex knows it's where Billy Rock's family supplies half the Bengali crackheads. He adds, 'I always like to think the owner has a sense of humour, although I've never been in.'

'No good man goes in,' the minicab driver says. 'The youth and their gangs are gone bad and crazy. We disown them, we disown the lot of them.'

'Well, I don't know if I'm a good man, but I still wouldn't go in there. Nights like this, don't you think you could just drive forever?'

Alex feels alert, buzzing with a tab of whizz, good old-fashioned methamphetamine sulphate, the kind mother used to make. The Wizard in his cell, churning it out to turn on his fellow inmates, brighten their grey routines. Alex remembers the Wizard's searching gaze, arctic blue behind the slab-like lenses of his glasses, his intellect vast and cool and unsympathetic.

Alex sometimes feels guilty that the Wizard is banged up and he is free – but the Wizard always said that he was free wherever he was, free inside his own head. He'd had to explain his syntheses to the police techs after he was arrested – he'd even given them the right kind of masks when they'd arrived. Part of the game, taking a pride in showing the blundering coppers what he'd been getting away with for so long.

The minicab driver says, 'I don't have the ration to drive as much as I'd like to, Mr Sharkey. You'll notice how carefully and sweetly I drive. It is to conserve fuel. You wonder where those white trash motherfuckers get their petrol, eh? Criminals, all of them, and criminals aren't supposed to get petrol. But they have more than me, an honest man doing his job. They have enough to drive around all day looking for targets.'

'I know,' Alex says.

'Five shots. *Bang bang!* Just like that!' The driver takes his hands off the wheel and claps twice. His eyes meet Alex's in the rearview mirror. 'They think this one youth, he'll die. Shot in the head. Two others wounded, but they will live, and perhaps learn their lesson. Stay away from there for now, Mr Sharkey. It's not a good place for a white guy.'

'I'm a man of circumscribed habits,' Alex says.

The driver drops him across the street from Ma Nakome's.

'I'm going to hang out for fares up by Aldgate,' he says, after Alex has paid him. 'You come over and find me, OK?'

'Sure,' Alex says, although he knows he'll call for a cab right here in Ma Nakome's, which even close to midnight is busy, people sitting at the plastic tables scattered on the pavement outside and the little bar crowded, Hi Life Dub blaring out across the heads of the customers in the hot dark air.

Alex is a regular, and Ma Nakome herself comes out of the kitchen to greet him. She seats him at a table at the edge of the raised area in back, a prime spot where he can see and be seen. Ma Nakome is a fat woman, heavier and rounder than Alex, swathed in red and gold cotton, with a gold-flecked smile in a shiny black face. Like half her customers, she's Somali, part of a community that has established itself in East London over the past twenty years. There are even newer immigrant communities now: Nigerians, Tongans, Albanians, refugees from drowned Polynesia. At the beginning of the last century it was Poles and White Russians and Lithuanian Jews. The East End has always been the point of entry for each wave of war-driven immigration into London.

The Somalis have done well. Most of them were professionals – lawyers, teachers, scientists, the cream of their country's intellectual élite. Even when their men sank into khat-induced torpor to escape the bleak reality of Brick Lane, the women worked and organized. They've formed a tight-knit but inclusive community, embracing British culture while retaining or modifying the best of their own.

Alex eats a huge plate of lamb and green bean stew served on baked plantain leaves, with okra and sweet potatoes on the side, and drinks a litre of freezing cold Sappora beer. The speed is wearing off, leaving him dry-mouthed.

He's working his way through a bowl of chilled, cumin-flavoured goat's milk yoghurt when someone drops a hand on his shoulder. He turns and Billy Rock's boy runner, Doggy Dog, is standing there. The big driver is right behind him, bare arms folded across a black leather vest, showing off the quills laid along his muscled forearms.

'You fucker,' Doggy Dog says, 'why don't you be working, eh? You work for us, man, you work, 'stead of sitting here wallowing in your food like a pig.'

Doggy Dog dips his fingers in Alex's yoghurt, scoops up a dripping gobbet and sticks it in his mouth. He has a ring of raw unworked gold on his thumb; it is laid along his cheek as he sucks on his fingers.

'Tastes like fucking pig food, too,' Doggy Dog says loudly.

The other diners look at him, and then look away.

Alex says, 'You have a message from Billy?'

'Billy, Billy, they named that man good, he be billied out all the time on crack, wiggling around like a worm on his genuine cow leather upholstery to that Satanist music of his.'

'Are you billied up, to be talking like this?'

Alex speaks from a calm quiet space that is not yet fear. He doesn't believe that even Doggy Dog will do anything here.

The boy says, with regal disdain, 'Man, I don't be needing no shit.'

Alex sees that this is the truth. Doggy Dog is lifted up by his own craziness. He wears a long T-shirt with hoops of green, red and gold over the same baggy blue jeans he wore yesterday. A little leather cap is pitched on his shaggy hair. Alex can see the outline of an automatic pistol under Doggy Dog's T-shirt. It is tucked into the waistband of his jeans.

The boy leans forward until his face is a few centimetres from Alex's. Alex keeps quite still.

'I know I frighten you,' Doggy Dog says. 'That's OK. You see I'm a powerful man. Billy Rock is used up. He lets his contractors fuck him over, you believe it?'

'It isn't Billy Rock you have to worry about,' Alex says, looking right into Doggy Dog's bloodshot eyes. 'It's his family.'

'I don't be knowing anything about families. Bunch of old men in suits, in that big old house in Hampstead? Shit, bwoy, they don't know anything 'bout the street, nor do you, right?'

'Right.'

Doggy Dog says, 'The deal you have with Billy Rock? He wants dolls to fuck each other, make baby dolls. You ever t'ink about fucking dolls yourself? Men fucking dolls?' The boy spears three fingers into Alex's chest, pushes himself upright. 'You t'ink about that,' he says, and walks off.

The imperturbable driver nods to Alex and follows.

Ma Nakome comes over to apologize. She tells Alex that she'll never let that little scorpion in her house again. She sends for more yoghurt and coffee, and sits at Alex's table.

'He was here for the insurance,' she says.

'I don't think he's working for Billy Rock any more,' Alex says.

'That boy is wrong in the head, if he thinks he can take money away from Mr Rock.'

Alex agrees. The thing about Yardies is not that they're fools, but that they are crazy. They have no hierarchy but that sustained by alpha male domination games, no territory except where they have women stashed away, no real plans. Most of their violence is impulsive, and most of it is directed at each other. Their idea of a plan is to ramraid a drugdealer's crib, pile out shooting, grab the stuff and any money, and get away. No such thing as an old Yardie, except for a few very violent, very rich and very cunning men. Doggy Dog is setting out on a rising curve, and he'll kill his way up until he's killed by someone luckier or smarter or hungrier.

Alex tells Ma Nakome about his latest project, although not what it's for. He never tells her that. He respects her too much. She was a research technician at Queen Mary Hospital until the health service was taken over by the big insurance companies and the research budget was cut to nothing. She appreciates his shoptalk. She has used the same techniques, she tells him, and he offers her a job that she laughingly declines – she has too many children, he must find a woman of his own to look after him, it is what all men do.

Alex agrees, thinking of his mother, the times they had up in the windy air above the Thames. A nation of two, with the city at their feet. Sitting in the dark, watching the lights, Lexis slowly getting smashed on rum and coke. Fairyland, she'd tell her son. There's anything you want out there, anything at all. Alex must get rid of that little parasitic shit of a toy boy, see if Lexis will find a steady man, a good man. She deserves that, at least.

Ma Nakome says that he's troubled. Maybe he'd like her to send one of her girls around? 'She'll be round today, tomorrow. When you like, Alex.'

'Tomorrow,' Alex says, feeling obscurely bullied. Sex will never be a big thing in his life, he knows, so he tries not to think about it too much.

'Alice,' Ma Nakome says firmly. 'That's who you like. I know she was with you just the other night.'

'Sure,' Alex says distractedly.

It's true that he likes his routines, but right now he feels momentum gathering like a wind at his back, the feeling he had before he was arrested, as if he was accelerating through the nighttime city, no traffic lights to stop him, everything getting out of his way as he sped by, faster and faster and faster, invincible in his speed. But then they caught him and sent him down without even charging him. The world is implacable – you can't escape it.

Still, he does like Alice. She's a little older than the rest of Ma Nakome's girls, most of whom are barely in their teens. Alice waits tables at the restaurant some nights, works only a few chosen customers. He can tell her stuff, after, and she lies there listening, or pretending to listen, and it's comforting.

'Sometimes I wish I was a Catholic,' Alex says.

Ma Nakome laughs and punches him in the arm and starts to get up, like a summery mountain rising. 'You are a crazy man,' she says.

Alex pays the bill and rides a gypsy cab driven by a young Armenian who has to be given instructions to find the way back to Alex's crib. The Armenian tries to sell Alex a lid of DOA, and can't understand why Alex laughs in his face.

6
Alfred Russel Wallace's Dream

Alex fights up from sleep. He's standing by the computer, his bare feet cold on gritty concrete. He's naked except for a T-shirt. Sweat streams down his flabby, hairless chest and heavy flanks. It's three thirty-three a.m. An omen. He has the feeling that someone has been talking to him, and just then the phone rings, loud in the still black air.

Alex accepts the call cautiously, using the lightest possible pressure to punch the code. There's nothing at first, a dance of static snow on the phone's little screen, a roar like the sea from the speaker, like the sound of his own blood rushing through the arteries of his inner ear. Then the static snow starts to whirl and billow, as if driven by some electronic wind, blowing away to show the face of a young girl in grainy black and white that slowly bleeds into colour.

'I know you,' she says. 'You're Captain Marvel.'

She is perhaps twelve, her round, serious face framed by straight black hair. She has some kind of middle European accent.

'Miracle Man,' Alex says. It's the ethername he uses on the a-life bulletin board.

The little girl says, 'I'm Alfred Russel Wallace. We've talked before, on the board. And I've lurked around while you were talking to others. That's how I know you. That's why I decided I could use you.'

Alex can't help laughing. Alfred Russel Wallace, named for the naturalist whose theories on natural selection finally persuaded Darwin to publish, is the ethername of a notorious and brilliant a-life hacker, almost certainly some maverick academic, who burst on to the scene a year ago. No way can this little girl be who she claims she is.

'Sometimes I think I dreamed you all up,' the girl says. Her smile is hardly there. Her dark eyes are serious and serene, fixed on infinity. 'In a fever dream.'

Alex remembers that the idea of natural selection by survival of the fittest came to Wallace while he was tossing and turning in his hammock, burning with swamp fever in the Borneo jungle. Darwin suffered from recurrent fevers, too. Evolution was a fever dream burning away the fossilized hierarchies of the Victorian Age.

'You're having problems with your edge gliders,' the little girl says.

'Well, everyone is having trouble with their edge gliders.'

Alex was discussing this on the a-life bulletin board only that night, after he got in from Ma Nakome's. Edge gliders inhabit the margins of the tableland maps in which the traditional a-life ecologies run. They skim a thin living at the brink of oblivion, but recently their marginal habitat has been invaded by a clade of parasites which hook on to them and gradually drain their energy. The parasites have evolved from piggyback organisms which infiltrate the mass configurations of clusterfucks, voracious, amorphous colonies which feed on their own dead as much as the informational energy all a-life organisms need to perform the algorithms necessary to survive and reproduce. At the risk of being absorbed by their hosts, piggybacks grab stray bits of informational energy at the shifting margins of the clusterfucks' huge agglomerations. The two kinds of a-life organism have achieved a stable relationship, necessary if the clusterfucks are not to grow so large that they would fuse and take over the entire a-life ecosystem, like algae choking out a fishtank. But the fragile edge gliders have no resistance to these parasite, and so far no one has worked out how to prevent the edge gliders being decimated by piggybacks without also destroying the clusterfucks and unravelling the complex web of interrelationships that stabilizes the a-life ecosystems.

The little girl tells Alex, 'I can help you. I can download something that will take care of it.'

'Why are you talking to me?'

'Think of it as a test,' she says. Her image is breaking apart in a snow of white pixels. 'Do you want it? I haven't long on this line.'

Alex opens a buffer, and it fills with the little girl's program.

She says again, 'Think of it as a test. You work out how to use it, I'll know.'

Then she's gone.

7
Hyperconnectivity

Detective Sergeant Howard Perse hands Alex a folded piece of paper and says, 'It was so easy, I'm beginning to think this is some kind of set-up.'

'What do I do, read this and eat it?'

Perse takes a long drag on his cigarette and says, 'Do what you like with it, but be careful.'

'You really are worried. Is that why you dragged me here?'

They are standing under the trees at the riverside edge of the car park in the shadow of the Tower of London, both smoking cigarettes they hold cupped inside their palms, a habit Alex learnt in prison. They might be a couple of old lags, discussing some scam in one of those old Ealing films that have recently become popular all over again, in a wave of nostalgic yearning for the thumbsucking comfort of a safe stable past that never really was. Across the car park, tourists queue patiently as they wait to be allowed to pass through the metal detector at the security fence. A family stands stiffly around a sweating Beefeater while the father videos them. It is ten in the morning, but already swelteringly hot under a milky white sky. The river is at low tide, flowing as sluggishly as brown jelly between stinking mud banks. On the far side, HMS *Belfast* shimmers in a haze.

Perse looks at the ancient wall that looms above the car park. He is wearing mirrored shades that flash in the sunlight. He says, 'Have you ever been inside?'

'The Tower? Christ, no. Why should I?'

'Exactly.'

'It isn't as if the Crown Jewels are in there any more. Do you think that story about the ravens was true?'

Perse shrugs. 'They didn't leave. They died. The point is that you wouldn't even go in if the King was brought back and put on exhibition. No one living in London would. So it's a safe place to meet.'

'You've done this before.'

Perse doesn't deny it.

A gaggle of tourists go past, trooping up from the river boat that docked at Tower Pier a few minutes before. They are Americans, all well past retirement age – Alex suppresses the impulse to ask them how the war back home is going. At least half the men wear a hybrid costume of tartan tam-o'-shanters, T-shirts and Bermuda shorts that will do nothing to protect them from UV burn; the women, more sensibly, wear floppy straw hats or carry parasols, like aging Southern belles. A woman who must weigh all of two hundred kilos, so heavy that even Alex thinks she's really fat, is encased in a carbon fibre exo-frame. As the frame walks the fat woman up the road, the whine of its motors rises above the chatter of her companions.

Alex draws a last mouthful of tarry smoke from his cigarette and squashes it out on the green-painted iron railing. He says, 'Where did you get the address from?'

'Billy Rock's case file. We do keep a case file on Billy Rock, in spite of what you might think.'

'And they let you access it?'

'Don't push your luck, Sharkey. Now listen. This address is the only update there's been on the file in the last year, just this one little thing slipped in amongst the old records. I had to look around for it, but I think I was supposed to find it.'

'This is scary stuff, Perse. Your paranoia is catching.'

Perse takes off his shades and pinches the bridge of his nose between thumb and forefinger. He's tired, Alex sees. His eyes look bad, like bruised pits.

Perse says, 'You should be scared. Billy Rock's family is bidding to become legitimate. And if they do become legitimate, they'll want to tidy up loose ends.'

Alex takes off his big black hat and mops his face and neck with his handkerchief. 'They're working you hard. Maybe you're seeing things that aren't there.'

He thinks of what Doggy Dog told him, in Ma Nakome's. He won't tell Perse, though – he just might need an edge.

Perse says, 'I interviewed about twenty Uzbekistanis last night. Most didn't speak English. Or pretended not to. I had to wait three hours to get a translator, and he could hardly speak English either. Every one of the bastards claimed they knew who killed those two, and every one of them came up with a different set of names. And we found the Mercedes that was stolen after the stabbing, but it was burnt out, the driver's long gone, and his mates aren't talking. And there's no chance of calling any extra bodies in to help because of the explosion at Heathrow.'

'What explosion?'

'A medium-sized bomb on the roof of Terminal Four last night. No warning, it was pure luck no one was killed. So far we have the Monarchists and the Animal Liberation Brigade claiming it, and because of all the other crazy fuckers who'll crawl out of the woodwork to claim the publicity there's nothing about it on the news, not yet, and when it comes out it will be explained away as a transformer explosion. Whoever did it got through about ten layers of security. So I'm fucking tired, and I don't need any shit from you, Sharkey. Not when I'm trying to help you. So listen. I'm damn sure someone is running this deal as some kind of entrapment scam. Maybe it's Billy Rock's family. They can't just whack Billy. They have to do him in a way that means they don't lose face. Entrapment would be the perfect thing.'

With thumb and forefinger, Perse pushes up the skin at the corners of his eyes, to make them into slits. 'Very cunning, Johnny Chinaman.'

'I don't like being used as a way to get Billy, Perse. Why not let his uncles get rid of him, if that's what they want?'

'Because I want him,' Perse says. 'I want his ears in my little collecting bag.'

'Fuck off, Perse. I won't do it.'

'Oh, but you will, Sharkey. What other choice do you have? If Billy doesn't fuck you over, then I will. I'll bust your premises every day, eight a.m. on the dot, until you run to Billy and beg to be put out of your misery. All I'm asking for is a little cooperation, and that's not much to ask after two years of watching your fat arse and listening to your pathetic line in hacker boasts.'

Alex unfolds the piece of paper. There's a single line, a street name and a number.

He says, 'Did you check this out?'

'What do you think I am, a private eye?' Perse puts on his shades. 'Be careful, Sharkey. This is the big time.'

The address is in Bridle Lane, one of the narrow little streets behind the shops and theatres around Piccadilly Circus. Alex, sweating, with the feeling of forces massing over his head, pays off the cab – money is sifting through his fingers – and then spends ten minutes hunting for the house number.

It is a tall narrow building squashed like a last slice of pie between the backs of offices and shop service entrances. Four storeys, windows blanked with white security shutters. There's a railing at the roof line, and Alex glimpses greenery, some kind of garden up there. The door is a scarred slab of iron-bound oak behind a locked security gate. There's no name-plate or video camera, just an old-fashioned brass bell-push.

A few homeless people have set up benders along the edge of the street, little more than slabs of packing foam leaning against this or that wall. None of them know anything about the house, non-information that costs Alex all but one of his cigarettes.

There's a closed-up loading bay a little way down, and for a while Alex sits there under a roaring air conditioner outlet. He fans himself with his hat, feeling sweat gather in the folds of fat at the back of his neck. Traffic ghosts by at either end of the little street. In a second floor office across the road, no more than ten steps away, a man is working at a drafting table. Its green light, striking up under his chin, makes him look as if he's underwater. By and by, an old woman in widow's weeds lets herself out of the entrance door of a little block of flats. She gives Alex a sour, suspicious look before shuffling off, back bent under a dowager's hump.

Alex badly needs a cigarette, but if he smokes his last one he'll have to go off and buy another pack and then he might miss something. One thing he does figure out, there in the loading bay entrance, is that between Billy Rock's cracked ideas, Perse's thirst for revenge, and whoever is running the covert entrapment, if that's what it is, he's a dead man unless he can figure out which way to jump, and when.

Alex is certain that the little girl who called him last night is part of this tangle. That package she downloaded, he'd be crazy to even peek in it. She probably isn't even a little girl, but some expert system, or someone using a morphing program to alter what they look like on screen. Alex himself uses a weak morphing program that makes him look a little thinner, a little less obviously balding. You can get packages that make you look like Elvis or Elle or Fred Flintstone, anyone or anything you like.

A limo makes the turn into the narrow street. It sweeps past Alex in a blowing wave of wastepaper and fast food containers – so close he sees his face flow over its mirrored windows and black lacquer finish – and pulls up outside the tall narrow house. A big man gets out – it is Billy Rock's driver – and opens the passenger door. Alex isn't surprised to see Doggy Dog, dressed down in a Bob Marley T-shirt and red shorts, and a big knitted hat like a floppy bowl.

Alex presses back against the metal door under the noisy air conditioner. Someone else gets out of the limo. It is the little girl who called him up last night.

The little girl and Doggy Dog exchange a few words, and both of them laugh. While she unlocks first the security gate and then the door of the house, the big driver leans on the hood of the limo, his muscular arms folded. The girl blows a kiss to Doggy Dog and then she's inside, and the kid and the driver climb back inside the limo and are gone, like a smooth silent dream.

Alex heaves himself out of his inadequate hiding place, and walks over to the grilled door. He thumbs the brass bell-push and hears, deep within the house, a slow sonorous chime.

8
Typhon Coming In

A bell is ringing somewhere, electric and insistent. Alex is standing in front of a big oil painting in a heavy gilt frame, so close that his nose is almost touching its lumpy varnished surface. Someone takes his arm and tells him politely but firmly he'll have to step back.

'You'll have to move away, sir,' the guard says again, his grip tightening. His other hand is near the taser on his hip.

Alex mumbles an apology and takes a backwards step over a brass rail on to the worn maroon carpet. The other people in the skylit gallery turn away, already bored by the minor incident, this dazed-looking fat guy in bib-overalls and orange construction boots staring at, what is it?

It is one of Turner's stormy seascapes with the sun sinking through gorgeous unfocused reds and golds, and a wallowing ship lost in the middle of it all.

Slaver Throwing Overboard the Dead and Dying – Typhon Coming In.

Alex gives the guard his best shit-eating smile and says, 'It's just that it's such a wonderful painting.'

The guard is a tall tough man in his fifties, very upright in his button-down light blue shirt and grey trousers. His taser is the kind that can leave permanent burn scars.

He says, 'It was done right in the middle of his best period of oil-painting. But stay on this side of the rail, sir, or I'll have to throw you out.'

'I'll be good,' Alex promises.

What he wants to ask is how he got here, but that would be looking for trouble.

As Alex makes his way out of the crowded gallery rooms, he fingers through his pockets, finds the ticket stub. It's stamped 14:32. Shit, he's lost more than three hours.

It's blazing hot outside. The air is soggy with unshed moisture, the sky as blank as a sheet of paper. Traffic snarls at a sullen stop-and-go pace either side of Trafalgar Square and the shattered stump of Nelson's Column, which still shows the black searing of the explosion that brought it down five years ago. Twenty or so students are holding a protest under the serene gaze of one of Edwin Landseer's bronze lions. They are masked with caricatures of the Prime Minister, or with red or black cloth hoods in which eye-holes have been roughly torn. Police watch from a distance. One constable is openly videoing the gathering. The police out-number the protestors two to one. Alex is too far away to hear the students' unamplified chants, or read the slogans on their T-shirts. Then one of the students holds up a placard showing a doll's blue, apish face overprinted with broken manacles, and Alex must smile at the irony.

The fighting doll, its imbecilic fury. The pets affected by the rich. The black figures drowning in the corner of Turner's painting, an arm or a leg lifted from weltering waves where nightmare fish fight to feed on flesh. Shit, he doesn't even like Turner.

His stomach growling with acid, Alex finds a pizza stand and eats six slices loaded with onions, anchovies and pepperoni. One thing he didn't do in those lost hours was have lunch, although somewhere or other he smoked his one remaining cigarette. He buys a new pack, wanders past the barriers which secure the West End in the evening, wanders in the heat and humidity and stink all the way up Charing Cross Road and then back again, past second-hand bookshops where bargain books burst in white hosannas from wooden racks, past the shuttered theatre at Cambridge Circus, the rows of boarded-up or burned-out shops where the homeless and dispossessed squat amongst blankets and shopping trolleys piled with bundles of clothing wrapped in torn black plastic.

Someone is going through the pockets of a dead child lying facedown in the gutter. Blood is pooled under the child's head – some streetkid shot by vigilantes, or by another streetkid. The man treats the body with a strange tenderness as he rolls it on its side to check its pockets. Three tramps have made a kind of encampment in the shuttered doorway of a wrecked shop. They squat in its meagre shade, watching passers-by. One gives Alex the finger when he glances at them. Another rackingly coughs into a scrap of paper: viral TB.

There's a shebeen in another wrecked shop, with a radio blasting out the latest Beijing pop song. Alex buys a couple of tabs of Cool-Z from the skinny nervous kid who's dealing from a corner table. The tabs are individually wrapped in scraps of greasy cling-film. Alex swallows them both, dry, and walks on, waiting for the kick. He needs something to get his head straight.

He remembers seeing Doggy Dog and the little girl, and remembers standing up when they had gone, dizzy in the soggy heat. He remembers the dizziness, and with that a glimpse of a room all in white, with toys marching back and forth and a woman standing in the middle. Someone had said something then. A name.

He says the name out loud now, relishing the syllables in his mouth: 'Nanny Greystoke.'

No one takes any notice, not when within twenty metres there are three hawkers shouting their wares, an old woman is shaking her fist at the shuddering traffic, and a man is pissing up against a lamppost and muttering, his head trembling so hard that his matted hair whips back and forth across his vacuous gaze. His brain is probably a sponge riddled by the last stages of Creutzfeldt-Jakob's.

A gorgeous woman, expensively dressed in a gauzy body-wrap, walks through all this with regal disdain, trailed by a blue-skinned doll on a leash and an armed bodyguard. The doll is dressed in red silk pantaloons and gold Arabian Nights slippers with curled toes. There are rings through its flat black nipples. It looks back and forth as it trots along after its owner. Its brown eyes are sad and human.

He isn't crazy, Alex thinks. He's certain of that, because he remembers craziness from the inside, the exhilarating speed and the invulnerable certain momentum of craziness. Maybe he's confused, but he isn't crazy. Something happened to him, and he can't remember what it was. He went away, and then he came back.

Perhaps someone has infected him with a rogue strain of what people are starting to call fembots, little robots spun out of buckyballs and buckytubes doped with rare earths. True nanotechnology that can't be called nanotech by its manufacturers because some American company which makes clunky mechanical critters ten times bigger has patented the term. There are fembots that can trigger false memories. Maybe the half-remembered glimpse of toys marching around and around the woman in the white room is a false memory, generated from packages of RNA inserted in certain of his cortical neurones. Or maybe it's part of a flashback from a drug Alex contaminated himself with when he was working with the Wizard – but Alex dismisses this thought because he knows he's too good a potboiler to fuck himself up that way. The Wizard taught him well. Just a speck of some of the stuff he's helped cook up would have killed him ten or twenty times over before it was cut. He remembers the care the Wizard took to cut the batches individually, doping them with different impurities so they couldn't be traced back to a single lab.

What he should do, Alex thinks, is get himself PET-scanned at a clinic to check his nervous system for the clusters of rare earth atoms which indicate the presence of fembots, and then get a shot of universal phage to knock them out. Except that right now he can't afford it.

He plunges into the crowded tube station at Leicester Square, finds a dealer in the throng and after a brief hassle buys a second-hand travelcard for twenty per cent face value. The homeless are everywhere down here: workers whose skills have become irrelevant; people who have never had a job, some nearing retirement age now; middle-class dropouts destroyed by bad luck or bad health. Many exhibit the black and yellow tags of contaminated refugees from the Sellafield plume, although a large proportion of these, despite realistic weeping sores on faces and arms, are professional beggars masquerading as radiation victims.

Alex fights his way down the stalled escalators. He's drenched in sweat before he's reached the bottom of the first flight. Leicester Square was one of the first stations to be invaded by the homeless, and there are people living in permanent hutches in the corridors, and more on the platforms.

The noise is incredible, the stench worse. Alex takes a deep breath to kill his sense of smell. Passengers must pick their way amongst the tube dwellers, who seem oblivious to the chaos around them, as if the world is a TV and they are watching it in the privacy of their own homes. Braided wires and cables rise up from their pitches, running into access hatches to illegal junctions with electricity, telephone and cable TV lines. Some of the more enterprising sell long-distance calls at fractional rates, or sticks of badly recorded movies, or bootleg games and datasets you'd be crazy to download into your computer. Over at Temple, both platforms of the Circle Line are lined with the cages of black market currency changers.

Here, many of the tube dwellers have erected makeshift screens around their two square metres of platform, although these screens hardly hide lives lived right there in public: a woman breast-feeding a baby; an old woman spooning mush into her toothless mouth; a family sitting on plastic chairs around a flickering TV, as if around a campfire; a tiny little girl being washed in a plastic bowl, her skin so pale you can almost see the organs that pulse in her swollen stomach. Tiny black mice scatter from a litter bin as an old man wrapped in fraying rags starts sifting through it; beneath the platform, more mice scamper between the greasy rails.

The train is a long time coming. Alex stares at the bright poster ads pasted on the wall across the tracks and ignores the children who now and then thrust their grimy paws in front of his face. Start giving and you'll never stop. Since the collapse of the welfare state and the flight from the north, perhaps half the population of London consists of homeless refugees, living in tube stations, on the street, in abandoned tower blocks and deck access housing no one can be bothered to tear down.

Lexis fighting to keep her and Alex together, two castaways afloat on a hostile sea. Alex feels a pathetic wave of gratefulness: the Cool-Z is kicking in.

The train roars into the station, pushing a wave of hot fetid air ahead of it. Every carriage is crammed. Alex has to straphang, and as more people crowd on he loses even that support. His feet leave the floor as he is buoyed up by the crush of people. A woman starts to scream somewhere in the carriage. Maybe someone is raping or robbing her, but what can you do?

At the next station, the train stops but the doors don't open. The people start to murmur, grumbling in the low-key British way at the system, at the all-powerful faceless conspiracy that controls every aspect of their lives. Alex hears someone saying that there's been an explosion in Aldgate; someone else adds that the BBC at Portland Place was hit with a car bomb that crashed through the doors.

Alex thinks of what Perse told him about a bomb at Heathrow, and then, a handspan from his face, a terrified man is trying to prise open the doors by pulling at the rubber flanges. There's a flat sound and the man's face is slammed against the glass as stuff bursts from the back of his head. The Cool-Z makes it look like a bad special effect to Alex, too sudden to be convincing.

A policeman, his face hidden by a black reflective visor, bangs on the door with the stock of his pistol. The people inside, Alex included, flinch away. The train starts with a jerk and makes its long rising roar as it plunges into the tunnel.

Half the people around Alex affect the Londoner's cool weariness of having seen it all before; others are talking, indignant, scared, excited by the rumours floating around. Someone declares, in a plummy authoritarian voice, that summary execution is too good for terrorists, the police should castrate them and hand them over to the people.

Alex thinks of the streetkid, dead in the gutter. The blood and matter spattered on the door's glass looks black in the carriage's yellow light. It's already happening.

Alex makes the change at King's Cross to the Metropolitan Line.

The train is every bit as crowded and slow as the one on Piccadilly, and stops not once, not twice, but three times between stations. Alex changes on to the East London Line and then at last gets a seat on the little Docklands railway train. Two days ago he rode this very same train home in the rain, heartsick and angry. The anger's still there, but mixed with fear now, and trapped beneath the icy veneer of Cool-Z.

The setting sun burnishes Canary Wharf as Alex walks through underpasses and open spaces to his workshop. Billy Rock's limo is parked on the weedy tarmac. Alex isn't surprised. Nothing can touch him at the moment. Loud music shakes the limo's mirrored windows. Looking through the windscreen, Alex glimpses Billy Rock thrashing about on the back seat, kicking his legs in the air like an upturned bug.

Alex's neighbour, Malik Ali, is working with the double doors of his workshop unit wide open. A fan droning on the floor pushes the heat around inside. Malik tells Alex that someone saw two men go into Alex's place, although one was a kid really, one of those rude boy gangster types.

'What did the other one look like?'

'Big. Muscles.'

Malik is sewing the halves of a jacket together. He doesn't stop because he's on piecework. Alex can feel the vibration of the industrial sewing machine through the thick soles of his construction boots. Its noise drowns out the muffled thudding of the limo's sound system.

Malik says, 'You know them?'

'Yeah, I know them.'

'Alex, man, you stay for a cup of tea. Maybe they go away. They've been in there half an hour now. Arrived just after the woman.'

'Woman?'

Then Alex remembers Ma Nakome's promise to send Alice around. Oh shit.

Malik says with a little smile, 'You've not been paying your insurance?'

Alex thinks that Malik would shit his pants if he knew that Billy

53

Rock was inside the limo. He says, 'Something like that. Let me deal with it, but if I'm not out in an hour, call the police.'

Alex gives Perse's cellphone number to Malik. It's not likely Perse would do anything if it came down to it, but it's all he has.

The little access door is unlocked. When Alex steps into the workshop, Doggy Dog raises his pistol. He's sitting in the chair by the computer. He makes a clicking sound, jerks the pistol as if in recoil, and says, 'Now you're a dead man.' The pistol is a Glock 17, the tried and tested weapon of choice for Yardies.

'You better not have touched anything in here,' Alex says, 'or *you're* dead.'

'Hey, listen to the fat man,' Doggy Dog says.

The driver is leaning against the stainless steel kitchen counter, arms folded. He shrugs, unimpressed.

'I mean it,' Alex says. He feels amazingly calm. 'There's some dangerous shit in here. Where's Alice?'

'The ho? Oh, she back there, someplace,' Doggy Dog says casually. He swivels back and forth in the chair. He is wearing the same Bob Marley T-shirt and bright red shorts that Alex saw him in this morning, but the hat is gone. 'Don't you be worrying, bwoy. I wouldn't be touching your girlfriend, or anything else your scabby white man's dick's been near.'

'I'm going back there to take a look at her. OK?' Alex makes his appeal to the driver, who shrugs again.

Behind the Chinese screen, Alice is sitting up on the bed with her back against the rails of the brass bedstead. There is silver duct tape over her mouth, more tape wrapped in a fat knot around her wrists and the bedstead. Alex carefully peels the tape from her mouth and she spits sideways and says, 'The fuckers jumped me, made me unlock the door.'

Alex has forgotten that he gave her a copy of the card that works the lock. 'I'm sorry,' he says. They seem to have used a whole roll of tape on her hands; he'll have to find something to cut it with. He adds, 'I've got to talk with them.'

'That kid felt up my tits, but that's about all they did. The big bloke told me to be quiet and I wouldn't be hurt. He took my pager. Get it back, won't you? Don't let him walk off with it.'

Alice grins, showing the gap between her front teeth. She's

about two years younger than Alex, and quite fearless. She moves her legs around on the bedspread and says, 'Come on back here, maybe you can get off on a little bondage.'

'Does this really excite you? Jesus, Alice, those guys are serious.' Yet Alex feels his penis flex inside his jockey shorts. There *is* something exciting about this.

Alice says, 'They're losers. Besides, Ma Nakome knows where I am. If I don't call in soon, someone will be round. What do you say? I don't mind, with you, and it won't cost more than twice what we work out on, OK?'

'How long until your friend gets here?'

'Maybe ten, fifteen minutes. Keep them talking, Alex. That's what you're good at.'

Doggy Dog is rooting in one of the three fridges, the middle one where Alex keeps his supply of Pisant. 'You don't got no Coke,' Doggy Dog says accusingly. He has shoved the automatic pistol into the waistband of his red shorts.

'I'll get some for next time.'

'There'll need to be no next time, if you do right by us,' the driver says.

'Which means you stay away from that bitch,' Doggy Dog says. He shuts the fridge door. 'How you know she lives there?'

'She phoned me,' Alex says.

'Bull*shit*,' the driver says.

'Switch on the radio, Delbert,' Doggy Dog says to the driver, and says over the noise of Capital Radio, 'See, Delbert, I told you she would try to pull something like this. She isn't like normal people, that's what you got to understand. She's, like, curious about everything. So if she phone this fat fuck, it's only because she want to know who she be working with. That's all it is.'

Delbert says slowly and thoughtfully, 'I don't know, Dog. This is getting out of control.'

Alex says, 'Who is she?'

'One thing you don't need to know,' Doggy Dog says, 'is who she is, or what she does. All you have to do is make the stuff Billy Rock asked you to make. OK?'

'And give it to you. Wow. Either you guys are really dumb, or you have the biggest pairs of balls outside of a bull elephant. Billy could get tired of listening to his music. Or bored. He could walk right in here, and then what would you say?'

'He's a happy camper,' the driver, Delbert, says. 'He's just done himself a load, and he won't be getting up for at least an hour. I've been working for Mr Rock for three years now, and I do believe I know him better than you.'

Doggy Dog takes out his pistol again. He aims it at Black Betty, at each of the three fridges, one after the other. Alex and Delbert watch him. On the radio, a pop song finishes and there's a bright, bouncing ad about Sanyo's home virtuality entertainment system.

Doggy Dog says, 'You be smart, right? I know guys like you. You all think you be better than anyone like me. Delbert, you show him how smart he is.'

The driver pushes away from the counter, says, 'Nothing personal,' and punches Alex in the mouth.

Alex sees it coming, but hardly has time to start to turn his head when the driver's fist slams into him. Light bursts in his eyes. Then he's sitting on the floor, tasting blood in his mouth where his front teeth have cut into his lower lip.

Doggy Dog is standing over him. Alex looks up at the maw of the pistol. It is a little round black hole in a rectangular profile. Doggy Dog's finger is on the trigger.

Alex says, 'Point that thing somewhere else.'

'Now maybe you'll begin to forget all that white man disrespect you be showing me. Down on the floor you be no better than anyone else. You listening?'

'Just nod,' Delbert says genially.

Alex nods. He can sweep Doggy Dog's legs out from under him, but unless he can grab the pistol Delbert will be on him in a moment. Alex is probably stronger than Doggy Dog, but he's pretty certain the big driver is skinpopping one of the commercial synapse enhancers. Most bodyguards do.

'All you got to do is make the stuff,' Doggy Dog tells Alex. 'You don't tell Billy you done it, and if he asks, you tell him there's a difficulty. You make something up, won't take much to confuse Billy Rock. Tell him one more day.'

Delbert says, 'You listening, Alex? I'm sorry I had to hit you, but you overstepped the mark. I would have hit you in the gut, but that's risky with a man big as you.'

'Can I get up now?'

Alex is wondering just when Alice's backup will get here, and if he'll be armed. Well, *of course* he'll be armed.

'You stay on the floor,' Doggy Dog says. 'I like you down there, your big belly going up and down like you be a woman 'bout to give birth.'

Alex says, 'You two are crazy. If Billy doesn't kill you, his uncles will.'

'Yeah, and how will Billy know unless you tell him? You do that and you be dead. You t'ink me and Delbert here are the only ones on this t'ing? We get hurt, so do you. You and your mother, right. I know where she lives, bwoy. You t'ink about that.' Doggy Dog tucks his pistol in the waistband of his shorts. 'We be watching you. Be good.'

Then they're gone. Alex waits a long minute, looking up at the dusty stays under the concrete slab roof and letting his fear tremble out of him, before he can get up and cut Alice free.

She looks at him and says, 'I guess you're not ready for it just yet.'

'You better call off your backup,' Alex tells her, and while she uses his phone he sticks his head around the door of Malik Ali's workshop and tells him everything is OK.

Alice makes a pot of tea, and she and Alex sit drinking it side by side on the bed, just as if they've had sex, Alex holds a plastic baggie of crushed ice against his tender bottom lip, taking it away each time he sips the sweet milky tea. Alice wants to know what kind of trouble Alex is in, and he tells her some of the story, but not about the way Billy Rock's runner and driver are planning to double-cross him, and especially not about their partner. Alex is certain he knows who that is. Those two are too dumb to think of a scam like this all on their own.

Alice rubs at the strings of adhesive the tape has left on her wrists. She says, 'You could sell the film rights on a story like that.'

'It isn't so exciting when you're in the middle of it.'

Alice sort of looks at him from under her eyelashes. 'So you're still not up, huh? Come on, big guy. Didn't it even excite you a little?'

'I just had a gun put on me, for Christ's sake.'

Alice is suddenly angry. 'Oh yeah? Well listen, I've had to *do* it with a gun to my head. More than once. What happened here is nothing. That kid is nothing. You've never lived on the street, you don't *know*. Billy Rock wouldn't really hurt you. He needs you enough to give you protection.'

'This wasn't about protection,' Alex says.

'It wasn't anything,' Alice says. Her anger is gone, as suddenly as it arrived. She adds, 'Don't listen to what I say, baby. Maybe I'm a little shook up.'

'That's OK,' Alex says, but it isn't, not really. Their cosy pretence at happy families has been punctured. He pays her and she promises him she won't tell Ma Nakome, and then she's gone.

9
Artificial Life

Alex finds that he can't sit down. He prowls around the big workshop, suddenly finds himself kicking the breezeblock wall with his steel-capped construction boots, blazing with an anger that's spent as quickly as it arose. He has work to do. Work is the universal solvent of care.

He checks the sequencing of the point-mutated genes, then sets up the PCR block incubator. By tomorrow, the polymerase chain reactions, driven by temperature-sensitive DNA-replicating enzymes cycling over and over, will have made millions of copies of the DNA strings which code for the suite of enzymes capable of assembling the hormones. He will have enough copies to guarantee successful insertion into a plasmid, which in turn will be inserted into cells of *Bacillus subtilis*. Once an active gene is inserted, the bacteria will be transformed into chemical factories that produce the desired product. The particular plasmid Alex plans to use will subvert the bacteria's protein-making machinery if the culture is fed tryptophan. Instead of making the hundreds of different proteins needed to produce new bacteria, the bacteria will make only the enzymes which make the oddly differentiated doll sex hormones. Two days at the outside, and it'll be done.

Alex opens a pack of Malaysian army rations – banana curry, fuck – and nukes it in the microwave. While he's spooning down rice and sour-sweet banana-flavoured pap, he thinks about the package the little girl downloaded into his system buffer. Crack it open, she said, and he'll know to get in touch with her again.

It's a risk, but he opens a carton of Pisant and sets to. After all, he can hardly walk up and bang on the door of the house, not after what happened last time.

In fact, cracking the data package is insultingly easy. After he's decompressed the package, he runs a debugger on its dense lines of codes, which are definitely the algorithmic genes of some kind of a-life critter. Buried in them is a single non-operational line. He extracts it and converts the bin-hex code into ASCII. It's an address in the Web.

'Alfred Russel Wallace, I presume,' Alex mutters.

He could have encrypted the address in half a dozen more subtle ways. Either the little girl's naïve, or she wants him to think she is. He isn't certain which is the less worse alternative.

Still, she is his only clear line into the tangled heart of this trouble, he's certain of that. And if she's what she claims to be, this a-life creature she's given him really will solve the edge glider parasite problem.

With some misgiving, Alex loads copies of the new creature into his a-life ecosystem. Just a few of them in one area, because if this does turn out to be some kind of system gobbler, then maybe he can cauterize the copies before they spread too far. Then he puts on the VR goggles, sits back, and watches.

The a-life system has various levels of monitoring. Alex toggles it for the global view, with different organisms appearing as variously shaped icons whose colour indicates how much energy they possess. He seems to be hovering above a green, rumpled table-top world that is teeming with vibrantly coloured flecks. The green world's edges are sharply defined against the black void in which it floats. The flecks pulse and flicker, as, with each tick of the ecosystem's clock, the a-life organisms examine and react to the bitstream density and the configurations of other organisms in their vicinity.

There are over two hundred species, close to the stable limits for this type of a-life ecosystem. More advanced a-life freaks are into PondLife systems now, teaspoonfuls of simulated water teeming with simulated protozoans, bacteria, algae and viruses in which Real Life processes are modelled on a molecular scale. Alex's computer doesn't have the RAM to run something that complicated at anything more than geological speed, and besides, he enjoys the illusion of being a microcosmic God floating benignly over his flatland world.

Most of Alex's a-life ecosystem has stabilized as a kind of open prairie of small, densely growing plantoids, organisms that feed on the bitstream density of the system just as plants feed on sunlight, air and water. Here and there are islands of scrubby tangles of things like thong ferns, and just off-centre is a patch of triple-tiered jungle, where a kaleidoscopic variety of huge plantoids intensely recycle a bitstream density too low to sustain the prairie.

On the global view this jungle is a fuzzy bump in the table-top flatness of the ecosystem. Animal-like bugoids are reduced to twenty-bit icons. Some move slowly, in herds – herbivores which directly feed on the plantoids. Predators which feed on the information space coding; other bugoids pursue solitary trajectories. Here and there are pulsing masses of clusterfucks, shaded from bright red at the edges through green and indigo to dull dead black in the centre.

The new bugoids, yellow hook-legged snowflakes, don't reproduce, or not at once. Nor do they feed, or not at once. Instead they move away from the spot on the map Alex assigned them, moving in different directions towards the nearest edge of the a-life ecosystem.

Alex downloads four. One runs straight into a clusterfuck colony and is absorbed. The others reach the edge, which in this system is a real boundary, and move out along it. Several times the new bugoids interact with fuzzy wimps, which bumble along the edge picking up detritus left by more active feeders, but they don't touch the wimps, even though some are richly red with energy. Twice, the new bugoids avoid the stretched lozenges of healthy edge gliders – and then an edge glider captures one and it is gone, and the edge glider changes colour from green to orange.

Two left. Alex is beginning to wonder just what these things do when one crosses the path of an edge glider which has a piggyback riding it – and the new bugoid eats the edge glider and its parasite, turns red, and splits in two.

After Alex has watched for half an hour, turning back and forth in his swivel chair to survey the whole world, he's pretty sure that he knows how the new bugoids operate. They can only eat edge gliders which have been weakened by infection with piggyback parasites. Otherwise, they can be eaten by anything else, and because the new bugoids are strongly tropic for the edge of the virtual map, where edge gliders are the dominant predators, they are most likely to fall prey to healthy edge gliders. Already, the population of new bugoids is increasing at the expense of parasitized edge gliders, and Alex is pretty sure that a balance will be reached, with numbers of edge gliders, piggybacks and the new bugoids oscillating around a strange attractor in a complex but dynamically stable interaction.

Alex strips off his goggles and sends a message to the Web address that was hidden in the a-life codes. He's hardly finished typing when the phone rings. He answers, and the little girl says, 'It's about time.'

10
Leroy

Leroy's shebeen is almost empty. Business only picks up once the pubs have shut, and it's not yet ten. On the far side of the dimly lit basement room, a few old men hover at the billiard table, their faces dipping in and out of the glow of the light hung above the table's brilliant green rectangle. Two other customers are playing dominoes at one of the square formica-topped tables; the clicks of their pieces are louder than the mumble of the TV over the bar.

Leroy Edwards is behind the counter, and when he sees Alex

coming down the stairs he shakes a bottle of tomato juice, flips off its cap and pours the juice into a shot glass without being asked.

'Your mother be along later,' Leroy says.

Alex says, 'I wanted to talk to you.'

The tang of the tomato juice, spiced with Worcester sauce, cuts through the taste of blood from his split lip. His jaw tenderly aches.

Leroy says, with a teasing twinkle and an exaggerated islands accent, 'What you want, white bwoy? Come down here to buy some blow? I always got Dutch Dragon, but for you I could maybe fetch up some righteous 'igh Mountain Jah-maican 'erb. You look like you be steppin' out tonight. Is that a new shirt?'

'Yeah, well I've kind of got a date later on.'

'But first you come and see your old uncle Leroy. What's the problem? I see someone popped you on the mouth. About time.'

Leroy is in his early sixties, almost as fat as Alex, but still strong and alert, still something of a local hero. He has rolled up the sleeves of his white shirt high on his biceps. There are blurry blue jail tattoos on his forearms, done with biro ink and a sewing needle. His grey hair is cut short, nappy on his skull, and his nose is so flattened that his nostrils are scarcely more than creases. Someone did that with a cricket bat, and Leroy, bleeding and roaring like a stuck pig, took the bat away from the guy and broke both his arms. Alex knows that story and a hundred others; Leroy and Lexis were friends before Alex was born, which, if it wasn't for his red hair and cave-dweller's pallor, would make Alex wonder.

Lexis first worked for Leroy when he owned a pub on the Brixton Road. The Commercial Arms, a utilitarian brick palace built in the fifties, with a knocked-through bar, bare wood floors and white tile walls. Leroy ran a soundsystem before he became a publican, and still has a box of 12 inch vinyl 45 rpm singles of his one hit, a toast with a Lover's Rock style lilting backbeat that made Number 26 in the charts in 1983. Leroy used the royalties from that to buy the Commercial Arms.

The pub was a big punk and ska venue in the seventies and early eighties – the Clash and the Specials played some of their early gigs there – but it lost its music licence just before Leroy became the landlord. In the mid-eighties, it was at the centre of a riot when National Front boneheads tried to hold a march through Brixton.

There was another riot in the late nineties, after a protest against armed policing was broken up, five thousand police against ten thousand marchers. That was the time when British National Party supporters had the habit of driving through Brixton in stolen cars and taking random shots at passers-by. The pub was shot up twice, and someone tried to burn it down during the Millennium celebrations, one of more than ten thousand arson attacks in London that night, an end-of-century fever which came close to recreating the Great Fire.

Leroy held on to the pub through thick and thin for twenty years. His father came over in the fifties, when Jamaicans were actively recruited to remedy post-war labour shortages, and he worked on the Underground until it was privatized two years short of his retirement. Leroy's father knew all about hard work and persistence, but his pension was privatized along with the rest, and quickly dwindled into a derisory lump sum. Then his wife died, and like many Jamaicans at that time, sickened by a tide of overt racism, Leroy's father took the ticket back.

Leroy stayed. He knows something about persistence, too. When things started to go downhill he found it harder and harder to pay insurance money demanded by the Triad New Families, after they moved into South London when the People's Republic of China took back Hong Kong. In the end the Triads did what the Millennium firebug failed to do, and had the pub torched one crowded Saturday night. Five people died then, and Leroy went to prison for a while.

For as long as Alex has known him, Leroy has sworn that one day he'd retire to the islands. But here he is, sixty-two next birthday and only out of London twice in his life: once when he was moved to Leeds jail after the Scrubs was burned down; once when he went to Jamaica for his father's funeral.

Now Lexis works for Leroy in the shebeen, an unlicensed drinking den which has had three addresses in the last five years. With each move, Leroy has taken with him the heavy slate-topped billiard table, the two one-armed bandits and the old-fashioned purple neon CD jukebox. His clientele are mostly middle-class second and third generation Brixton Jamaicans who run small businesses – minicab franchises, clothing or electronics shops, garages, off-licences. There's even a doctor, and a solicitor or two. They treat the shebeen as a private club, help keep Leroy straight with the police. Alex has known most of them most of his life.

Leroy pours Alex another tomato juice and says, 'Tell me about the smack on the mouth there, white boy. Who did it? Don't tell me you ran into the fridge door, because I can see the mark his ring made. You give him reason?'

'They were trying to frighten me. Give me some of those crisps, the prawn-flavoured ones? You're the only person I know who still sells them.'

'Your busted mouth to do with some busted deal? Alex, Alex, I thought you were making easy money fucking up the heads of the rich clubbers. I thought you had the sense to stay out of trouble. You'll break your poor mother's heart.'

'Actually, it's Lexis I came to see you about.'

Reluctantly, Alex tells Leroy about Doggy Dog's threat.

Leroy reacts angrily. 'You surely fucked up this time, bringing this shit on your own mother's doorstep.'

'I didn't go looking for it,' Alex says, knowing it sounds weak. 'I thought maybe she could stay with you for a few days. It will be over by then, I swear.'

'You said you would keep on the right side of the law. I distinctly remember it because the day you said it was the day you came out of prison.'

Alex stuffs a handful of crisps into his mouth and says around them, 'It isn't illegal. I can tell you that. You know that nothing I've been doing has been strictly illegal.'

'I remember when blow used to be illegal,' Leroy says.

'Yeah, but the stuff I make isn't a drug. It just stimulates cells in your brain as if they've been hit by a drug. Besides, when was the last time you paid tax?'

'Don't get smart, little white boy. I'm not too old to tan your fat arse.'

Alex dredges the last fragments of crisps from the bottom of the packet, licks grease from his fingers, wipes his fingers on his shirt. 'Smart is what I am. That's what I've been all my life. It got me where I am.'

'With a bruise swelling up your lower lip, and someone threatening your mother? Days like these I'm glad I'm dumb.'

'That's the last thing I'd call you, Leroy.'

'Blow, now, it's a natural high. It's an 'erb, something God Himself made for us to use. The stuff you make, Alex, it's devil work. It's the way the world got fucked up.'

'Come off it, Leroy. The world was fucked up before I was born. Psychoactive viruses just make cells do what they do normally, only in a more coordinated way. What's more natural than that? Here you are, selling alcohol, and you know why? Because micro-organisms in your gut produce alcohol as a byproduct of their metabolic activities, and as a consequence we've evolved the ability to metabolize the stuff. Our brains are built to process psychoactive drugs because they need naturally produced psychoactive chemicals to function properly. There's a theory that intelligence and language evolved because when our apeman ancestors were grubbing up food on the African plains they'd get stoned from eating mushrooms growing in herbivore shit. They got smart because that was the only way they could relate to the hallucinations the mushrooms gave them. My viruses don't do anything unnatural. They just enhance what's already there.'

'I don't know about any of that,' Leroy says stubbornly. 'All I know is that you're a smart boy with a smart mouth, and you're not making the world better. No one is in this country. Maybe it's time I—'

'—retired to the islands. Maybe one day, Leroy, I'll make a difference.'

'In your dreams,' Leroy says. 'You're dumb for a clever boy, Alex. Always were. You think you can take what you want and never owe. You're a clever white boy, and you think you know the street because you hang out with a few gangsters. You think you can play at God, but this is the real world, it'll always smack you in the chops if you don't look out for yourself. The world doesn't work on dreams.'

'Not yet. Will you look after Lexis, make sure she's OK?'

'She can stay at my place. Long as she leaves her boyfriend behind.'

'Yeah, I saw him.'

'Something in him reminded me of you, white boy.'

'Hey,' Alex says, hurt.

Leroy levels a finger, fixes his gaze on Alex's face. He has his stern and unforgiving prophet-in-the-wilderness look. He says, 'I'll watch out for her, but I can't watch out for you. You get hurt and it'll break your mother's heart. You don't know how hard it was for her when you were doing time.'

Alex finishes his tomato juice. 'I have to get somewhere. Listen, don't worry. And don't worry Lexis, OK? I told you I'm doing nothing illegal. Trust me, Leroy.'

'I did that once,' the old man calls after him.

Leroy is still angry, but Alex knows he'll cool down. Leroy just hasn't changed with the world, Alex thinks, which is why he's so angry all the time. Which is why he hides away down in the basement, where every night is the same, and time might have looped back to the old days of the Brixton Road, the old century not yet worn out and Leroy a respectable landlord, not a jailbird down for double manslaughter.

What Leroy did after the Commercial Arms was fire-bombed, the thing that turned him into a local hero, was track down the two Yardies who were paid to do it, knock them unconscious, lock them in their silver Mercedes SL500 and set it on fire. Leroy has a righteous, biblical sense of justice.

11
Dr Luther

Now all Alex has to do is follow instructions. The little girl, a.k.a. Alfred Russel Wallace, gave him no choice in the matter. It is almost eleven, and there's a queue at the security barrier at the exit of Charing Cross tube station, where a couple of bored guards in Kevlar vests over short-sleeved shirts check IDs. A third stands behind the wire mesh with a neat little automatic rifle slung under his arm.

Alex, in his squarejohn costume of loose cotton trousers and a shirt with big prints of birds on it, gives the security guards one of his false IDs (tonight he's Evan Hunter) and looks as bored as they do while they check it and then wave him through. Saturday, and the secured section of the Strand is busy, brilliant with flickering neon. People swirl in and out of the electronics emporia. The smell of fried food is heavy in the hot, humid air. Clouds of mosquitoes whirl and topple around luminous signs. Most of the shops sport the violet glow of insect-o-cutors above their doors; the continual, almost subliminal sizzle of flash-frying bugs undercuts the noise of the crowd and the pulsing beat of soundsystems that spills from shop doorways.

Alex skirts the back of St Martin-in-the-Fields and plunges across Charing Cross Road into Leicester Square. Fairy lights are strung from the sycamore trees in the little park. People queue to pass through metal detectors into cinemas and clubs. Big video screens play snatches of the latest movies between blocks of advertisements. Groups of salarymen shout and whoop as they reel past prostitutes of all five sexes. A heavy bald man in a pinstripe suit is on his knees in the gutter, being noisily sick.

Private security guards go by, patrolling two by two, with fat stickyfoam pistols holstered at their hips. It is even hotter here, under cascades of gold and white and pink neon, the heat ripe with the stink of garbage spilling from black plastic bags. A group of screeching secretaries half-heartedly pursue a gorgeous trans-vestite clubber, who's six foot six in stiletto heels. He turns, lifts his dress and waggles his dick at them before diving through a cinema queue after his friends. A helicopter thumps overhead, and its spotlight sweeps across the crowded square like the finger of an unforgiving God. Leroy, patient and judgemental behind his bar. Despite what he says, he's not in the world, not like Alex.

At the corner of Gerrard Street, beneath the red lattice gateway at the entrance to Chinatown, a crowd has gathered around two bare-chested men who are fighting it out with knives. One is already badly cut; blood mixed with sweat streams down his belly. He feints sluggishly, and his opponent, stepping back from the jabbing blade, seems equally weary: it is as if both are half-asleep in the fuggy heat.

A pair of security guards are watching from the back of the crowd, and Alex ducks his head when one glances at him incuriously. He's suddenly acutely aware of the cameras and microphones mounted on the walls of buildings, atop the poles of traffic signs. It's said that the Triads tap into the security network, use an AI to pull specific faces from the crowds. And here he is, heading into the symbolic heart of their territory at the bidding of a little girl he doesn't even know.

She told him to meet her in the Dean Street branch of Pizza Express, an upmarket place favoured by media types. Although it's half empty, Alex is stuck with a small table near the kitchen. A party of suits, their jackets hung on the backs of their chairs, their ties askew, are making a lot of noise at the long table by the big picture window. Alex orders a bottle of white wine and works his way through two portions of blueberry cheesecake. He's just looking around for the waiter when, suddenly, she's there, slipping into the chair opposite him.

She looks older than she did on the phone. She is wearing knee-length green shorts, and a white T-shirt that leaves her thin arms bare. Her eyes, under heavy eyebrows that make a single line across her brow, are so dark that they look black. Mediterranean genes in there, Alex thinks. She has woven her thick black hair into a French braid. She seems quite at ease, ordering a pizza for both of them and a Pepsi for herself, then sitting back and giving Alex a level, appraising look.

Alex asks what to call her. Alfred Russel Wallace doesn't seem appropriate. She tells him that Milena will do, and when he asks her if that's her real name, she smiles and says, 'It's as good as anything.'

Alex, figuring he has nothing to lose, tells her about the threats that Doggy Dog made, and she tells him not to worry about it.

'The boy is charming in a rough sort of way, but he isn't important. There are thousands like him. In my opinion, Mr Billy Rock should be better advised in his choice of personnel.'

Alex's curiosity wins out over his caution. He wants to know. He wants to understand. 'The kid and Delbert, you're running them, aren't you?'

'Am I?'

Milena looks over her shoulder at a burst of laughter from the party of suits, looks back at Alex with a teasing smile. A naughty little girl out past her bedtime, flirting with a strange man.

Alex sticks to his point. 'Delbert and Doggy Dog are too dumb to have thought of using dolls that way, and you're . . . not.' He realizes that he doesn't know anything about her. He says, 'That house – you live with your parents?'

'Oh no,' Milena says calmly. 'I don't have parents. I have a company.'

'I see,' Alex says, although he doesn't.

The pizza arrives and Alex eats most of it while the little girl, Milena, nibbles delicately at a single slice and sips her Pepsi. Alex smokes a cigarette, drinks the last glass of the chalky Chardonnay.

At last, Milena blots her lips with her napkin and says, 'You're cross with me.'

'I want to know what's going on. That's why I'm here.' Alex stubs out his cigarette. 'I can cause trouble if I want to.'

'I expect you can, but you're too smart to try. That's why I chose you.'

'You chose me? Why do you even need me?'

'Because I'm not allowed to work in the area you work in. I need a gene hacker. My own specialty is nanoware. Did you ever get zapped?'

'You mean by those things? Fembots?'

'That's what they call them now. For the same reason that people call vacuum cleaners hoovers. You should be interested in fembots, Alex. They do what your viruses do, only it's purer, very intense and very precise. I made the first strain. It gives you a vision of the Madonna – the Mother of God, not the pop star. I let it loose, and the hackers took over. There are fifty-eight strains I know of, now, all developed inside a year. Some reveal Elvis Presley or Princess Di, others God Herself in clouds of glory, or LGM.'

'LGM?'

Alex is thinking of the white room – she zapped him for sure. His brain crawls under his skull.

Milena is eager to explain. 'Little Green Men. You know, like flying saucers. Right brain visions. There's one strain, the Streiber, that gives you a complete abduction experience, even with fuzzy false memories of rape. It's amazing what you can pack down inside a bunch of metal-doped superconducting buckyballs.'

'*Klaata barada nikto*,' Alex says, and isn't surprised to see that she doesn't get it. She's probably the intense serious type who listens to Bach's *Well Tempered Clavier* if she listens to anything at all, and hasn't watched a single movie in her life. He says, 'But it isn't as if they do anything permanent, is it?'

'Not yet. I made a Universal Phage that gets rid of any fembots, not only those in your blood but also any bound to your neurones or their synaptic junctions. The company loved that when I threw it to them. I have to give them something occasionally, so I can do my real work. You're following this?'

'I do know something about the fembots. But it seems like . . . cheating. And crude.'

The little girl laughs. 'You're so old-fashioned. Oh, I'm not making fun of you! It's really quite delightful.'

Alex says doggedly, 'But you need me.'

'One day I'll be able to design fembots that can do everything. I'll make assemblers that will set up factories within liver cells and manufacture the hormones for sexual maturity, and the effector fembots needed to increase neuronal connectivity. But at the moment the changes fembots make must be chemically supplemented.'

'You could simply use gene therapy to insert the DNA to make the hormones.'

The little girl, Milena, is suddenly serious. She says, 'Gene therapy will be part of the package, but it's slow, and the makeover has to be as catastrophic as a phase change to take permanently. It isn't easy, Alex. The people who make the dolls have worked hard to make sure that their design can't be subverted. But they made a fundamental error: they used point deletions to neuter the dolls. The breeding stock from which they harvest gametes are simply the base models. What's been taken out of the neutered dolls can be put back. Then there's the question of sex change. Did you know that most dolls sold are fundamentally male? I was lucky to get hold of any females, but in fact that's a minor consideration.'

Alex leans across the table. 'This isn't about making dolls into sex toys, is it?'

'Of course it is, but that's the *easy* part. I want to show you something. It's neat. You'll have to pay the bill. I'm too young for a credit card, and I don't like carrying cash around at this time of night.'

Milena leads Alex through the neon brawl of nighttime Soho to a comic book shop. The bored, middle-aged skinhead at the cash register waves them through a curtain of dangling plastic strips, and Alex follows Milena up a flight of uncarpeted stairs lit by a bare fluorescent tube.

'There are places like this all through Soho,' Milena says. 'But there are few places like Dr Luther's. He specializes.'

There is a long corridor floored with cracked linoleum, which creaks under Alex's feet. He suddenly feels his clumsy weight; he's like a doomed bull following this little girl, bemused and be-fuddled, to the slaughter. They pass doors with panes of frosted glass that bear, in faded gilt lettering, the names of vanished import/export companies, personal finance advisors, and dubious aromatherapy and 'mind relaxation' parlours.

There's a light behind one of the doors at the end of the corridor. Milena raps lightly on the door's glass pane, and it is opened by a tall, slightly stooped man who ushers them inside. The room is bare except for a few plastic stacking chairs and a metal-framed desk with an ancient keyboard computer on it. A half-open door leads into an inner room tiled from floor to ceiling, white tiles that gleam under a wash of lights. Alex thinks he knows what's behind that door. He wants to see it, and yet he doesn't.

'Dr Dieter Luther,' Milena says. 'He makes what you might call living sex toys.'

'You may call them that, but I would not,' Dr Luther says.

He is in his late forties, and has a cadaverous yet handsome face, like that of an aging alcoholic actor. He wears a green doctor's gown fastened down the back, and disposable latex gloves. The gloves squeak and rustle as he clasps his hands under his chin and gives Alex a cold, appraising stare.

'Dr Luther supplies several houses of ill-repute,' Milena says. 'His work is held in wide regard.'

She is matter-of-fact about this, a very demure little girl calmly explaining commerce in the worst kind of sex.

Dr Luther allows himself a small smile. 'There are a number of cognoscenti who depend on my services. Some of them, fortunately, high-placed. I am, you understand, not an independent operator, but who is, these days?'

Milena says, 'You will be one day, Dieter, I know it.'

Dr Luther lights a cigarette, draws on it with a flourish, then holds it up by his neck, its filter pinched delicately between thumb and forefinger. He says, 'I do have plans, it is true. Amsterdam is very liberal, very understanding. Here, more and more, there are these so-called morality laws. Well, young man, you know how it is. You are a kind of artist also, I understand.'

'I suppose so,' Alex admits.

'Dr Luther is employed by Billy Rock's family,' Milena says.

Alex looks at Dr Luther, who returns his gaze with a faint, amused smile. 'What are you trying to tell me?'

'I'm not trying to *tell* you anything,' Milena says. 'I'm letting you learn. You take from it what you will.'

'Milena is testing you,' Dr Luther says. 'It's how she gets her fun. Such a bright little girl, and so easily bored.'

His smile has grown by a millimetre. It is not a nice smile. It seems to imply that Dr Luther can look into Alex's soul, and is not impressed by what he sees there.

Milena says, 'That's not true!'

Dr Luther says to Alex, 'Ah, but she *is* a bright young thing, don't you think? Quite unique. She gave me much help with modifications to the control chip.'

'You were doing fine without me.'

'Milena, sweetheart, while some customers are quite content with, let us say, *quiescent* partners, there are many more who prefer a reaction to their actions.

'Milena,' Dr Luther tells Alex, 'showed me how to reprogram the chip. Now, if you'll forgive me, I am rather busy . . . There is such a high turnover, you understand.'

'You change dolls into sex toys,' Alex says. He wants to get this over with. Sweat prickles across his scalp.

'In here,' Milena says, and takes Alex by the hand. Her skin is cold and dry. She leads him into the white-tiled room, where something lies on a steel table under a rack of brilliant lights.

It is like a bald, blue-skinned child. It is a doll. It looks like it is wearing a green bandage above a red loincloth, but then Alex registers the sweet smell and sees blood dripping from a corner of the table into a white plastic bucket. The green bandage on its chest is a cloth on which stainless steel surgical instruments are laid out.

'Nothing interesting,' Dr Luther says. 'Just a standard vaginal reconstruction, the kind that would fulfil a transvestite's deepest wish. Dolls have a cloaca, you understand, like the birds you wear so colourfully, Mr Sharkey. From the point of view of most customers it is not a satisfactory entrance. Do look, please, if it interests you.'

'You expected me to throw up or faint,' Alex says to Milena. 'I'm sorry to disappoint you.'

'My,' Dr Luther says, 'such anger, and so sudden. My hat is off to you, Milena. Perhaps he'd like to stay, while I carve this thing a new asshole.'

Then Alex is stumbling along the corridor, and Milena is calling after him. He almost falls down the stairs, and the customers browsing the racks of comics give him startled looks as he rushes past. Outside, at the gutter, he gives up macerated cheesecake and pizza in a smooth rush. He spits and wipes his mouth on the back of his hand. The night's heat is like a tight bandage on his forehead.

Behind him, Milena says, 'I won't apologize for Dr Luther. He's necessary.'

Alex turns.

Milena faces him with cool defiance, with a poise beyond her years. She says, 'If you want to know why I need him, you'd better come with me. Or you can go home and wait for Billy Rock or Doggy Dog to close your end of the deal.'

She walks away, and after a moment Alex follows her. She says, without looking around, 'Dr Luther customizes dolls by giving them vaginas, or by constructing other, more novel orifices. Some of his customers have very strange tastes.'

Alex says, 'Dr Luther is as strange as anyone I'd care to meet.'

'He's very intelligent, and he's also a borderline psychopath. I think that the surgery is the only thing that keeps him on the level. But he has a regular supply of dolls, and he allows me to experiment on their control chips, in return, of course, for knowledge. He allowed me to visit with you because I told him you'd supply the right cocktail of hormones to give them secondary sexual characteristics, fat under the skin, real breasts, that kind of thing. He has plans to open his own brothel. At the moment, he is simply a supplier.'

'Doggy Dog doesn't know about this, does he?'

'He really is very stupid. Delbert, although he works hard at it, is no brighter. They have no conception at all of the extent of the business interests of Billy Rock's family.'

'What happens to the dolls? The ones Dr Luther modifies.'

At last, Milena turns to face Alex. They are standing at the western end of Gerrard Street, by the gate into Chinatown. The knife fighters and the crowd have gone, leaving only a patch of blood-soaked sawdust.

Milena says, 'The dolls are used up. The clients that Dr Luther caters for really do have very special interests. You're shocked. Do you need to know anything else?'

'Why are you doing this?'

Milena strikes an attitude. Flickering light from the nearby gaming arcade turns her white skin blue. 'To set them free. You want Utopia? I can take you there. The elements of the new age are all around us, and I'm drawing them together. Some must suffer so others are free, but it's not as if the dolls are human. Nor will they be, because I'll make them more than that. Are you with me or not?'

Alex knows then that they are bound together, by blood and by the thirst for knowledge. He knows why she chose him, and knows that he is lost. Of course, she could have done something to him to make him feel this way, in the lost hours after he rang her doorbell, but the thought is only a flicker, gone. It doesn't matter.

'Yes,' he says. 'Yes.'

'Good,' Milena says. She yawns, as quick and oblivious as a cat. 'I have to go home now.'

'I'll walk you there.'

'It isn't necessary. In fact, I'd rather you didn't. I'm being watched.'

'By Doggy Dog?'

'By my company. They don't trust me. They think I'm working

on enhancing doll control systems. The control chips that make dolls do what they are needed to do, that simulate intelligence. Dear Alex, if only they knew!'

'Who are you, Milena?'

'I'm something new, like the dolls. My company made me, you might say, although it doesn't yet know quite what it has. I'm smarter than they know, and I plan to live forever. How far along are you with the synthesis?'

'Another day and I can give you all you'll need. The bacteria are growing. The next stage is to harvest and purify their product.'

'That's good,' Milena says, 'because we might not have much longer than that. Don't follow me,' she adds, and walks away, disappearing amongst people strolling past the brightly lit plate glass windows of the restaurants of Chinatown.

12
Abuse of Power Comes as No Surprise

Ray Aziz tells Alex, 'You look like shit, man. I'm saying that in the most friendly way, of course.'

'I've been up all night.'

It is noon, the next day. Alex has just made his delivery of HyperGhost. He suspects that he'll soon need all the cash he can lay his hands on.

'Let me get you something,' Ray says. 'On the house. Really.'

'Water will be fine. Really.'

Ray laughs. 'Well, we have ten different kinds. The kids get thirsty.'

'Whatever. But nothing flavoured.'

Ray walks around the freeform steel counter of the bar. Ground Zero looks dusty and bleak in the daylight that leaks through half-open shutters. Sound and lighting rigs hang like giant black insect chrysalises over a row of crashed cars inhabited by tumbled, blood-spattered test dummies, heat-stained concrete walls with the shadows of vaporized people, slicks of puddled glass that dot the floor.

Ray hands Alex a blue bottle shaped like a miniature dumbbell. Alex plucks out the slice of lime which Ray has wedged in the bottle's neck before taking a long swallow.

He really has been up all night. Harvesting the modified oestradiols and thyropic hormone excreted by his genetically modified bacteria. Running tests. The chromatography system is purifying the hormones now, and by the end of the day he should have more than fifty grams of product. He should feel relaxed, but instead he feels an intense foreboding, a kind of unfocused dread intensified by the post-apocalyptic décor of Ground Zero.

When Ray asks if he's OK, Alex says, 'I've never seen the club like this, in the daylight.'

Ray nods. 'It really is spooky when you don't have VR enhancement . . . Kind of dead without the firestorms and the groundbursts, huh? Let's go outside, man, sit in the shade a while.'

'I should get going. There's just one thing—'

'Come on, sitting down for a moment won't hurt. You know I'm supplying my best VJ for Billy Rock's thing tonight?'

'Really?'

'For this new thing of his, the Killing Fields.'

'I thought you were straight, Ray.'

'I'm a paper millionaire, but I work in this funny area, at the cutting edge of culture.'

'I heard you say that on Capital Radio a few months ago.'

Ray shrugs. 'What I didn't say then is that occasionally I have to put up with assholes like Billy Rock. I shouldn't complain. I mean, I was invited to the party.'

They sit in the shade of the concrete platform that used to be a loading dock, back when the long, steel-framed building was a warehouse supermarket. Ray squats on his haunches, a fifty-year-old pixie in tight black cycling shorts and a baggy T-shirt printed with a Holzerism, *Abuse of Power Comes as No Surprise*. His grey hair is done in a braid that hangs halfway down his back.

Alex asks, 'Are you going?'

'Don't count on it.' Ray pauses, then adds, 'I hear you're in trouble with Billy Rock.'

Alex takes a sip of water. 'I'm sort of helping him out. Something to do with this Killing Fields thing, actually.'

Ray looks off into the distance. All around the old warehouse, on what used to be the parking lot, are rows and rows of old cars waiting their turn to be crushed and recycled. Across a sleeve of water, a STOL fanjet is manoeuvring away from the terminal of London Airport, wavering in and out of focus in the waves of heat that ripple across the expanse of concrete.

Eventually, Ray says, 'Word is that Billy Rock is moving up. There are some heavy dudes coming in to catch a demonstration of that thing he's building across the river.'

'The Killing Fields arena.'

'You know, Kubrick made that Vietnam movie of his around here. Put in artificial palm trees, made it look like Vietnam.' Ray laughs. 'He should have waited thirty years, man, for the world to catch up with where he was at. I hear Billy Rock has Michelle Rocha working for him.'

'Oh yeah?' Alex doesn't want to appear not to know who Michelle Rocha is.

'You catch the ambient sets she did for *Mao and Me*? Prima numero uno weirdness. Billy Rock's getting slick. Moving up, like I said. Power finds its own level.'

Alex thinks about the phone message that was waiting for him when he got back from the strange, unsettling meeting with the little girl, Milena. Howard Perse saying that he had to call back no matter what the time. And when Alex did, Perse was drunk, and raving about some huge conspiracy.

Alex tells Ray, 'I don't think it's really Billy Rock. It's really his family, but they can't show their hand because Billy Rock's the number one son. He can't be allowed to lose face, so it has to look as if he's in charge.'

Perse had said something like that. Connections were being made, further up. A scenario in which dolls were actually killed in for-real combat games was ideal counter-propaganda to the arguments of that weird alliance of militant Christians, Muslims and animal rights activists who were, for their different reasons, trying to get doll labour banned.

'I'm being leaned on,' Perse had said. He looked worse than Alex felt. Although it was past midnight, he was still in the Drug Squad's operations room. He stubbed out a cigarette in a plastic cup at the blurry edge of the phone's field of vision, lit another with his Zippo. 'There's heavy stuff going down, and you're seen as expendable.'

'You got me into this with this fucking vendetta of yours. And now you're just going to drop it?'

'Look,' Perse said, with the grave intensity of the very drunk, 'all I know is that this Killing Fields thing of Billy's is coming out into the open. That party he told you about, turns out it's been planned for weeks. Half of London's glitterati will be there. Even a Cabinet minister. You think I can walk in and arrest the little shit with weight like that backing him up?'

'You're fucked, Perse.'

Perse pulled back from the camera, grim and dishevelled. 'We'll see, Sharkey. I still have one or two options, but you'll have to watch your fat arse from now on.'

Alex started to say, 'That's just so much bullshit—' but he was already talking to a blank screen. Leaving Alex with only one way out, which is why he worked all night to finish the synthesis.

Remembering that conversation, Alex tells Ray, 'This is something big. Billy Rock is about to go legit.'

'Someone should kill that nasty little fucker,' Ray says, with a vehemence that surprises Alex. Usually Ray is a gentle soul, an old E-head whose synapses are fried open on a permanent mellow buzz of peace, love and understanding.

The STOL jet makes a hollow roar as it accelerates through heat ripples. Suddenly it is airborne, making a wide turn to the south, to Europe. Ray and Alex watch it go, dwindling towards the white stacks of the Thameside nuclear power plant.

Ray stands and slaps his spandexed thighs. 'London,' he said. 'Fucking kills you, huh? I better get on, man. Thanks again for the stuff.'

Alex finally gets out his question. 'Hey, Ray? I know you have a couple of vans here. Do you think I could borrow one?'

13
Who By Fire

Alex drives the Transit van he has borrowed from Ray Aziz, a rusty clunker almost as old as he is, back to his workshop, and is not surprised to find Delbert and Doggy Dog waiting for him. They lean against the white limo and watch as he parks the van and clambers out.

'Nice wheels,' Delbert says. He has a toothpick stuck at a jaunty angle in one corner of his mouth, is wearing black leather jeans and a black leather waistcoat. Carbon whisker quills rattle together when he folds his arms. 'Thinking of going somewhere?'

'I had a delivery to make.'

'Bull*shit*,' Doggy Dog says, pushing away from the limo. Under the broad bill of his cap, his smooth young face is twisted with sudden anger. 'You keep just one t'ing on your mind, and that's making the stuff for us. Where the fuck is it? You said today.'

Alex tells him, 'It'll be ready.'

'Hey, Delbert? I t'ink we toss his crib, make sure this pasty motherfucker don't be holding out on us.'

'I'm busy. If you came here to threaten me, consider me threatened.'

'Billy Rock sends you a message. He wants you at his party tonight.'

Doggy Dog drops a gilt-edged envelope at Alex's feet, but Alex doesn't give him the satisfaction of bending to pick it up.

Doggy Dog says, 'You better be there, with the stuff. The timing of this t'ing of ours has extreme cruciality.'

'Or what?' Alex asks, innocently.

'Be there,' Doggy Dog says and climbs into the limo, giving Alex a hard look under the bill of his cap before shutting the door.

Delbert backs the limo out of the yard at high speed; horns blare as it screeches in a U-turn into the traffic. Old Frank, sitting outside his unit on a broken swivel chair, slowly claps. Alex salutes him, picks up the envelope and goes inside.

He leaves a message on the a-life bulletin board, sticks a couple of packs of army rations in the microwave, and begins the arduous job of testing the finished batches of doll-specific hormones. By the time he's satisfied and has, after some thought, packaged a mix of dosages in lipodroplet form, it is early evening, and Milena still has not called.

While he's waiting for the phone to ring, Alex accesses the a-life ecosystem to check on the new bugoids. Things have changed. The edge gliders are no longer restricted to the margins of the habitat, but are ranging across the entire tabletop virtual space. When an edge glider encounters a whirling dervish, Alex understands what's happening. The edge glider carries one of the selective predators that Milena designed. The two organisms have entered into a symbiosis: the predator fastens on the whirling dervish and swiftly drains its energy to a level that enables the edge glider to absorb the rest of it.

There are, Alex sees from his God-like viewpoint, edge gliders everywhere. They outnumber everything else. They are taking over. The edge is eating the centre.

This seems like a message in itself, if only he could fathom it. He is combing through the a-life bulletin board messages, hoping that he might spot some clever twist Milena has used to disguise her reply, when the phone rings.

It is Leroy, calling from a kiosk.

'You had better get your ass over here,' Leroy says. 'Some fuckers just torched your mother's flat.'

The first thing Alex sees, when he drives up in the rattling Transit van, is an ambulance waiting by the entrance to the block of flats. Its back doors are flung open, and the two attendants are chatting to a policeman in shirtsleeves. None of them look at Alex as he runs past and hurries up the stairs. The stairwell seems as hot as an oven. He can smell smoke and wet ashes.

Neighbours stand around on the walkway behind stretched scene-of-crime tapes, gossiping and trying to peek through the blackened doorframe of Lexis's flat. Alex hears an old woman say that someone was killed in there, and he feels everything fall away.

He lifts the red and yellow tape and ducks under it. Inside the flat, firemen in helmets and yellow slickers are raking over the wet, charred rooms. The intense smell of burnt wood and plastic assaults Alex's eyes and nose. A fireman shouts at him, but just then Leroy comes out of the lounge, a cardboard box in his arms. He looks older, diminished, in the ordinary daylight.

'It's OK,' Leroy says to Alex. 'It's OK. Your mother, she's fine.'

It was Lexis's boyfriend who was killed. Neither the police nor the firemen seem much interested in Alex once they learn that he doesn't live there and hardly knows the dead man.

Leroy steers Alex down the stairs. The cardboard box he is carrying reeks of smoke; the same smell clings to Alex's clothes.

'This here's stuff your mother wanted saved,' Leroy explains. 'People will strip that place clean soon as the police clear off.'

'I'll make it up to her,' Alex says. He sniffs hard, and something the size of an oyster slides down the back of his throat. 'I swear I will. I know exactly who did this.'

'So do I,' Leroy says grimly. 'Your mother was staying with me, but I had people keep an eye on her place. That no-good boyfriend of hers wouldn't move out, and she let him stay. I suppose maybe I was hoping the little fucker would do something dumb, bring a girl back or whatever. Instead, a couple of fellows smashed the window by the door, splashed in petrol and dropped a match. My friend saw it all, jumped in his car and followed them. Had his phone with him and called me up. We caught up with them when they stopped off at a corner shop.'

'Delbert and Doggy Dog.'

'You know them. Now I wonder why that doesn't surprise me.'

'Tell me what happened, Leroy. Give me the hard time later.'

'The skinny young fellow saw us coming and ran off, but the other tried to get back in the car and we boxed him in. He won't tell us his name. He just says we're in a world of trouble. When I get back I'm going to pull out the spikes he has on his arms, see if that loosens up his tongue.'

Alex says, his heart sinking, 'You're holding on to him?'

'*Of course* I'm holding on to him,' Leroy says. He puts down the box to unlock the door of his car. 'Man tried to kill your mother, white boy. What you want us to do?'

Alex sees the ceramic carthorse on top of the pile of scorched, smoke-stained souvenirs. Its mended hind leg has cracked off again; its harness is charred. He says, 'You got to let me talk with this guy you're holding.'

Leroy straightens up and fixes Alex with his fierce patriarchal look.

'I don't have to do anything. I'm thinking of your mother, white boy, even if you aren't. Right now she's sort of numb. You should know you don't shit on your own doorstep. Sometimes I don't think you could possibly be . . . Fuck, you aren't even listening to me.'

'Look, I have that van over there. I'll follow you, Leroy,' Alex says, knowing how weak it sounds. 'It's *important*. Trust me.'

'But I don't trust you,' Leroy says, and the soft way he says it nearly breaks Alex's heart.

'Leroy, this one favour. I know the man you're holding. I can make him talk.'

'This is the last time I help you, Alex. I swear.'

'It *is* the last time,' Alex says. Milena. If she doesn't call, then he really is fucked. Yet despite this he feels a singing in his heart. He's free and running, and he can't stop now until he's dead or off the map.

14
Delbert

Leroy has Delbert stashed away in the storeroom of his shebeen. The bodyguard is tied to a plastic chair with electrical cable. He sits proud and straight under a flickering fluorescent circlet, like a captive king amongst the crates of beer bottles and boxes of crisps and salted peanuts, the lager barrels and black carbon dioxide cylinders.

Alex goes straight to Delbert, smacks him across the mouth with an open hand and says, 'Nothing personal. I just needed to do that.'

Alex has just spent a painful half hour with Lexis. She didn't want to blame her son for the firebombing, but Alex saw how much it cost her not to.

'I'll always be here for you, Alex. You know that.'

'You always were. Do you remember when you showed me the lights of the city, and said it was Fairyland? I really believed you.'

'You were just a little boy, Alex, and I was probably high on something or other. You shouldn't take your old mum seriously.'

'But I always do,' Alex said, and although Lexis didn't understand she smiled, and made him promise he wouldn't go to jail again.

'You've got that look,' she said. 'Like you had just before the last time.'

'I do? Don't worry. I have the police on my side this time.'

Lexis listened as Alex told her how he would make it up to her, and just smiled and took another sip of rum and coke and told him to be careful.

'Never trust a copper. You're an East End boy, Alex. You should know that.'

The worst thing was that she didn't yet know that her boyfriend was dead. Leroy told Alex that he would break the news once Lexis was over the shock of the firebombing.

Now, with the force of the blow still stinging Alex's palm, Delbert returns his gaze. Both of Delbert's eyes are puffed, and there's blood crusted around his nostrils.

'I thought better of you,' the bodyguard says coolly.

'Why did you firebomb the flat?'

'Go ask Doggy Dog. I had nothing to do with it.'

'You were *seen*, Delbert.'

'Oh man, you been hanging out with the police too long, you know that? I already told the old man he's in serious shit, I shouldn't need to tell you, Alex. You want to talk about the law, let's talk about kidnapping.'

Leroy says, 'You leave him with me for two minutes, Alex. I'll get him to talk.'

'Hey, Alex? Tell the old man to take a flying fuck at the moon.'

Alex looks at Delbert. This childishly defiant big man with cable biting into the hypertrophied muscles of his arms, looking at Alex as if daring him to make the next move in the game. But Alex isn't playing Delbert's game.

Very much aware of Leroy watching from the doorway, Alex says, 'You know what I do for a living, don't you, Delbert? I make psychoactive viruses. Mostly for recreational use, of course, but I've things that can fuck you up permanently. I can give you stuff that'll turn your brain into cottage cheese. One shot, and you'll be out in the streets shouting at the traffic for the rest of your life. I can put you right there this minute, Delbert, unless you tell me exactly what you did.'

'We thought the flat was empty, man. Shit, we waited until the old woman left. Waited half the fucking afternoon. It wasn't our fault someone else was in there.'

Alex walks around the chair, trying to calm himself. He has a tab of Cool-Z in his pocket, but Leroy is watching. He says, 'What is it, Delbert? What do you want from me that I haven't promised?'

'Oh man, we were just making sure, you know. Making sure that you wouldn't sell us out to Billy Rock. We warned you, man, but you didn't seem to be taking any notice. We wanted to catch your attention.'

Leroy says, 'What's this all about, Alex? You mind telling me?'

So Alex has to explain about being in the hole with Billy Rock, about promising to make a batch of stuff for him, about how Doggy Dog and Delbert want to rip off their own boss. He expects Leroy to start in with how he told Alex that all this would lead to grief, but Leroy just shakes his head. Which in a way is worse, because for once Alex would feel better for hearing that he's done wrong.

Delbert says, trying to be reasonable, 'It was just business, you understand, so why are you keeping me tied up like this? Man, I really could sue you for kidnapping if I wanted. In fact that's the *least* I could do. You ought to realize you're in over your head.'

Alex says, 'You just tell me what you know about that little girl.'

Delbert thinks about it, looking off into the corner of the room and mumbling to himself. Then he smiles and says, 'Shit, why not? You haven't got the balls to kill me, have you? And sooner or later this'll catch up with you. I swear it. So go ahead. What you want to know?'

'You can start by telling me her phone number.'

'Hey,' Alex says, when Milena answers the phone, and Milena says, 'Very good, Alex. What do you want?'

Alex says, 'Delbert and Doggy Dog are out of the game. If you want the stuff you'll have to show me that it works. And we'll have to do it tonight.'

'That would be very nice, Alex, but I don't have a subject. It was never in the plan to do anything straight away.'

'It is now.' Alex tells her where to meet him, and switches off the phone before she can reply. Let her wonder what's going on for a change.

On the other side of the bar counter, Leroy says, 'Go kiss your mother goodbye, Alex. I'm not sure we're going to see you again.'

15
The Killing Fields

Alex flashes the Transit's headlights when Milena comes out of the entrance of the Aldgate Underground station. She crosses the road and clambers on to the van's bench seat. She is wearing a pink denim jacket over a demure long-sleeved blue dress with a floppy white bow at her neck, the kind of dress Japanese schoolgirls wear, the kind of dress that implies virginity and guileless innocence. A shoulder bag of seamless, silvery material is tucked under one of her skinny arms.

Alex says straight away, 'You were going to have those two fools take the hormone away from me.'

'It isn't that I don't trust you personally,' Milena says. 'The fact is that I don't trust anyone. What do you want, Alex? It's costing me a lot to meet you like this. My company expects me to go to a forward planning meeting tonight.'

'You're scared. I can understand that, because I'm scared too.'

Alex pulls out into the traffic. It is that time of the evening when half the cars are driving with headlights on, half off. Clouds draw black bars across the red sunset.

Milena looks at the voodoo dolls taped to the cracked vinyl dashboard, the loops of beads and crosses that swing from the rearview mirror, the garish laminated 3-D postcard of Jesus, crucified and crowned with thorns.

She says, 'This isn't your style, Alex. What's possessing you?'

There's an edge to her voice – good, let her stay scared.

Alex says, 'We're going to a party.'

'To Billy Rock's party? Is that why you're dressed like that?'

Alex is wearing his green check suit over a white cotton turtle-neck. The party is supposed to be black tie, but this is the best he can do at short notice. He steers the van around a man in rags who stands in the road shouting at the traffic. Fitfully illuminated by oncoming headlights, the man jabs at the air with a dog's head impaled on a stick. On the building site behind the man, figures crouch around a fire. They're probably spit-roasting the rest of that dog.

Alex remembers how he threatened Delbert, and laughs. Milena looks at him, looks away.

He says, 'Do you have the control chip?'

Milena pats the silvery bag in her lap. 'Everything I need is in here. Do you have the hormones?'

Alex doesn't answer straight away. He makes the turn into Commercial Street. Shops are mostly boarded up or shuttered. An armed guard is standing at the lighted door of an electronics supermarket. A hologram cross slowly revolves above the Seventh Day Adventist church that was once a cinema. Alex waits until he has stopped the van in a queue at traffic lights before turning to Milena and telling her that Delbert and Doggy Dog firebombed his mother's flat.

Milena is staring through the windscreen at the itinerant fruit seller who lifts a string bag of oranges, shrugs, moves on to the car behind them. At last she says, 'They weren't supposed to do anything like that.'

Alex says, 'Well, the world isn't a logical place, is it? It isn't like an a-life ecosystem. It's for real. You've been playing around with crazy people, and if Doggy Dog thinks you're screwing him over, he'll hurt you.'

Milena says, 'You mean he'll kill me. Oh Alex, you really don't know very much about me, do you?'

Alex tells her the name of the company that employs her. 'They own that house, too.'

'You could say they own me,' Milena says lightly, 'but you'd be wrong, even though that's what *they* believe.'

Alex says, 'Delbert told me they did something to you.'

'All my life,' Milena says. 'You can't begin to understand how it is, Alex. I'm the only success of the programme – the rest went mad.'

The light changes. Alex puts the van in gear and moves off. He says, 'They made you brighter.'

'Perhaps they did. Or perhaps I would be this way anyway – there's no single gene for intelligence, although that didn't stop the company trying to create its own R&D force of baby supergeniuses. I don't have parents, just gamete donors. I know who *they* are, I found that out for myself, when I was four. I also found out that I don't care who they are.

'My sisters and I were treated with neuron growth substance while we were in our host mothers. Increased neuronal connectivity – that's what they gave me, although it was effected by very crude chemical interference. What I've brought along will do the job much more efficiently. Anyway, we were brought up in seclusion, given a hyperconnected education that started before we could crawl, and tested continually. Test after test after test. Most of my sisters suffered spectacular psychoses. They built their own worlds inside their own heads, and retreated into them. The rest turned out to be no more intelligent than average.

'I'm the only one left, Alex, and sometimes I think that I'm mad, too. Mad, but functional. What they don't know is that I'm smarter than the company psychologists suspect. I long ago worked out how to manipulate their tests. I control those around me. Nanny Greystoke especially.'

'I don't think you're mad,' Alex says, but he then remembers his fugue.

The White Room. The woman in the White Room, standing empty-eyed amongst the toys. Perhaps it wasn't a fugue after all. Perhaps it was real.

He tells Milena, hoping he doesn't sound afraid, 'We wouldn't have come this far if you were crazy. But you shouldn't have tried to exploit me the way you did.'

'You're smarter than I thought, Alex. I'm glad I chose you to be my Merlin.'

'I'll take that as a compliment.'

Milena is silent for a while. Alex turns off Commercial Street, threads through back streets until he's pretty sure he isn't being followed. When they come out on to Cable Street, heading towards the Rotherhithe Tunnel, Milena asks what he plans to do. And when he tells her, she laughs and says she may or may not be crazy, but he certainly is.

Alex parks the van at the end of one of the narrow streets by the river, in the shadow of an abandoned block of flats built in the Legoland style of the boom-and-bust 1980s. As they walk towards the Surrey Docks and Billy Rock's party, Alex and Milena see thin lines of white laser light crossing and recrossing, making a kind of tent in the twilight air. It begins to speckle with rain, fat, greasy drops that pock and patter on Alex's scalp. Milena puts her pink jacket over her head and carefully tucks her silvery bag under her arm.

The gate to the building site is lit by spotlights that make the yellow brick façade of the *faux* warehouse block of flats across the road shine like butter. Chauffeured BMWs, Mercedes and Jaguars are unloading passengers. Armed, uniformed flunkies check tickets. As Alex and Milena join the queue, Howard Perse walks up to them.

Perse's face is white and unshaven, his eyes sunken and ringed with shadow. He says, 'What the fuck are you doing here, Sharkey?'

Alex feels a curious calm. 'Hello, Mr Perse. This is my cousin, Milena. I'm taking her to the party.'

Milena gives the policeman a bright sappy grin, but Perse barely glances at her. 'You're in with him. Aren't you, Sharkey? Is that why you're here?'

People in the queue glance around.

Alex says, 'Should you be here, Mr Perse?'

Perse crowds close, reeking of whisky. 'A spot of surveillance, that's all. We're gathering useful information. You watch your fat arse, Sharkey.'

'He's out of control,' Milena says thoughtfully, as Perse reels away, pushing through a knot of men in dinner jackets.

A security guard runs Alex's invitation through a scanner to read its embedded chip, and then ushers Alex and Milena through a metal detector. A covered walkway runs past the excavated pit to the warehouse, where there's a bower of real tropical foliage in which a welcoming line of dolls, dressed in black pyjamas and coolie hats, bow as the guests move past.

Inside the warehouse, Ray Aziz's sound and light system pulses and thunders. Threads of laser light sweep above the heads of the crowd. Men in black tie and dinner jackets; women in cocktail dresses – randomly slashed crushed velvet is popular, but a fair number wear diaphanous head-to-heel chadors over body stockings or graphic film or nothing at all. Alex recognizes the TV star who plays the matriarch in a long-running soap, a bouffant-hair-styled VJ he remembers from when he watched MTV as a kid. A Cabinet minister with a girl on either arm is being interviewed by a TV crew. The lead singer and the keyboard player of the trash asthetique band *du jour*, Liquid Television, are sharing a bottle of Jack Daniel's over by the bar. Hard-eyed Chinese men in hired dinner jackets, the foot soldiers of Billy Rock's family, move amongst the glitterati. Alex doesn't doubt that at least half the women are working girls.

Dolls, dressed as waiters and bearing silver salvers piled with delicacies, trot through the crowd in tireless criss-cross trajectories. Alex picks up a disc of moist black bread speckled with white caviar, peppery nuggets of squid in a glaze of aspic, a purée of seaweed coiled and peppered on a Bath Oliver. Milena watches him consume these delicacies with a mixture of amusement and disdain. The dolls are coming from somewhere behind the arena at the far side of the warehouse space, and Alex makes his way towards it.

Big liquid crystal screens slant down from the high roof, showing people in baggy orange coveralls and black flak jackets running through light and shadow and falling rain, ducking and weaving amongst wrecked cars and torn-up sections of wall. They are chasing dolls in black pyjamas. A doll caught by crossfire spasms as bullets smack home; the cameras zoom in as a head shot spatters blood and brains.

Hardly anyone in the party is watching the screens.

Alex holds on to Milena's hand as he steers her through the crowd towards the arena. He is halfway there when he sees Doggy Dog. For a moment their eyes lock. Then a waiter moves between them, and Doggy Dog is gone. Chills snarl Alex's spine. He bulls his way through the crowd, with Milena holding tight to his hand and telling him to slow down.

Billy Rock is sitting in the upper row of the seats that rise above the arena, flanked by two of his sober-suited uncles. Billy Rock is dressed entirely in black, from a snap-brimmed Homburg to cobra-hide cowboy boots. Mirrorshades mask half his face. Below him, an eager crowd fills the tiers of benches, their heads limned by the glare of spotlights aimed into the arena.

Milena surprises Alex by running ahead of him up the steps and bowing to Billy Rock, to his uncles. Billy Rock is as high as a kite, and grins and claps his hands, pointing past Alex at the arena.

At opposite sides of the sawdust-strewn ground, two handlers in heavily padded overalls, thick gloves and helmets with grilled faceshields are each holding back a fighting doll. A quick flicker runs through the crowd as money changes hands. A bell rings, barely audible above the stuttering pulse of the soundsystem, and at once the handlers let go of their charges.

The fighting dolls meet with a rush in the centre of the arena. They roll over and over, clawing at each other with hands and feet. The crowd is on its feet, screaming with one voice. Suddenly, one doll is on top, and rips out the other's throat with a quick jerk of its massive jaws. It is spattered by a sudden spurt of rich red blood before loops of braided wire drop over its gnarled head and it is dragged away by both handlers.

Billy Rock claps loudly, then gestures up at the screens. 'You try it, Alex. Go outside and kill yourself a doll. Isn't difficult, and very safe. This is some party, huh? You never forget it.'

'I certainly won't.'

Billy Rock says, 'Who's your girlfriend?'

'She's my niece,' Alex says.

He is acutely aware of the level, unfathomable stares of Billy

Rock's uncles. They both bear a remarkable similarity to ancient toads, with black hair greased back from age-spotted foreheads.

Billy Rock laughs. 'If you say so, Alex, Let her try it too. It's for all the family.' He leers at Milena. 'You come along with me, little girl, and have some fun.'

The right-hand uncle catches Billy Rock's arm and murmurs something, but Billy Rock shakes off the old man's restraining hand and says loudly, 'I show my friend here a good time. It is not a problem. Come on, Alex. You come along with me, you and your little niece.'

Behind a tall screen of bamboo and black lacquered paper at the back of the arena is a long, brightly lit space with racks of overalls and helmets and guns down one side. The dead fighting doll is wheeled past on a steel gurney. Three of its live fellows, excited by the smell of its blood, dash at the thick steel bars of their individual cages. Beyond, unmodified dolls in black pyjamas squat apathetically in a holding pen. The odour of animal musk and sawdust reminds Alex of the time he went to a tattered circus which set up its tent in Southwark Park: the aged, dignified elephant which ponderously followed its routine, quite unaware of applause; the half-hearted clowns; the perfunctory trapeze show whose participants doubled not only as tumblers but also as a knife-throwing act. That had been before the turn of the century, strange to think, before the park was taken over by an organized tribe of the homeless.

Milena wanders over to the cages as a fighting doll is dragged out by a handler in padded overalls. The black pyjamaed dolls in the holding pen turn to look at her. All have exactly the same prognathous jaw, the same close-set brown eyes peering under a craggy brow.

The handler, his mask pushed up, collars the doll with a wire loop around its neck and opens the cage door by tapping out a code on the lock's keypad. A second handler, standing by with a pistol at the ready, politely tells Milena to keep away. She smiles brightly at the man and says, 'But they're so cute!'

Alex watches this with an anxious ache in his gut. He is no longer angry. Anger has carried him this far, and then left him stranded, with Perse waiting at the gate and Doggy Dog out there in the crowd.

Billy Rock is allowing an attendant to fasten a set of orange overalls over his clothes. He has taken off his black Homburg and his mirror-shades. He takes a deep sniff from a small bottle half-full of a clear liquid, smiles starrily, and tells Alex to hurry up, he'll miss the fun. His pupils are shrunken to pinpricks.

'I just came to say hello, Billy. Really.'

'You'll have fun,' Billy Rock says, wiping his nose with the back of his hand. 'You never have fun, hiding away in that dingy dreary weary lockup.'

Then, quick as a weasel, he darts forward and claps a hand over Alex's mouth, shoves the bottle under his nostrils.

Alex tries to shake him off and takes a breath and it's as if a light has exploded in his head. For a moment he can't see. He blinks tears and snorts out what seems like half a litre of snot. He's suddenly foolishly happy, happier than he's ever been in his life.

Billy Rock makes an imperious gesture, and an attendant sits Alex down, zips him into a set of coveralls, buckles on a black flak-jacket. Alex feels he should protest, but he'd rather concentrate on the dizzy feeling of well-being that's trembling all the way-out to his fingertips.

Billy Rock has a gun now. He giggles, and aims it at Alex, at the fighting dolls inside their cages, at the people who, already in coveralls and flakjackets, are waiting to enter the game area.

Billy laughs and Alex laughs too.

'It's for fun!' Billy Rock yells, and raises both arms above his head like a winning boxer. An attendant, seizing the moment, fits a flakjacket over Billy's head.

Alex's attendant fastens a holstered pistol around his waist and explains mechanically, 'Your weapon will only discharge inside the game area, sir, and only if it is pointed at a target with a skin temperature of forty-two degrees centigrade. That is the skin temperature of the dolls. It will not fire at anyone wearing a protective vest. Squeeze the trigger slowly and regularly when you fire; the rate is controlled at one round per five seconds. The dolls are armed with low energy laser pistols. If you are tagged three times your gun will cease operation. It is most sporting that way, sir. Here is your helmet. The visor is armoured for your full protection, but allow me to reassure you that the bullets are gel, and there is no chance at all of fragmentation or ricochet injuries. Do enjoy your game, sir, and good hunting.'

Alex laughs, because it makes no sense at all. The attendant slaps Alex on the back and turns to the next customer, a man with a bodybuilder's physique who's stripped to black jockey underpants.

Suddenly Milena is in front of Alex. She glances at Billy Rock and shouts, 'They don't have coveralls my size.'

Things keep coming at Alex from different angles. He just sits there happily, staring at her. His heart is pumping at the same rate as the sound system's music and the jerky flicker of the fans of red and green laser beams overhead.

Milena catches his arm and leans close to whisper, 'I fixed the locks of the cages, so sober up and get ready,' and skips away before he can reply.

Billy Rock, waving his gun and whooping, is jogging towards the people waiting their turn to enter the game area. Alex takes a step and falls on his hands and knees and starts laughing. Some remote part of him observes that he's truly fucked in every sense of the word. There's a sudden crash. Alex rolls over to see what it is.

A fighting doll has slammed open the door of its cage.

The creature steps out and looks around. It shakes its massive head, opens its heavy, malformed jaws in a careless yawn. Ropes of saliva glisten between the spiky racks of its teeth. Attendants and customers shrink back against the racks of coveralls and flakjackets but the fighting doll doesn't even glance at them; it simply turns and runs straight into the main part of the warehouse. A woman starts to laugh. Maybe she's on the same stuff that Billy Rock used on Alex.

Now two more fighting dolls are shouldering out of their cages. A handler lumbers towards them, awkward in his padded suit. The fighting dolls look at him as he raises his pistol and snaps off three quick shots. One of the dolls is knocked backwards; the other runs straight at Billy Rock, who grins and woozily aims his pistol.

He snaps the trigger, snaps it again, but of course nothing happens.

The fighting doll knocks him down and takes most of his face off in a single bite, bounces up and runs straight at the people waiting to get into the game area. Screams, panic. The handler takes aim and fires twice. The fighting doll tumbles forward and kicks out with both bandy legs and is still. Billy Rock lies face down. Blood is soaking into the sawdust beneath him.

'Come *on*,' Milena says.

She grabs Alex's hand. Behind her is a doll from the holding pen. It is exactly her own height. She leads them both out through a firedoor into the open air.

It is still raining. Alex tips his face and lets it get wet, breathes in wet warm air, breathes it in and breathes it in. His heart is galloping but he feels calmer. People are running towards the gate. Tines of laser light claw the teeming sky above them. Security guards, pistols drawn, battle through the crowd towards the warehouse. In the distance is the thready whoop of sirens.

Milena says, 'Now you've got what you want, what are you going to do with it?'

The doll stands behind her, its eyes dull under its ridged brow.

Alex starts to unbuckle his heavy flakjacket. 'I'll tell you later. Will it follow us?'

'Of course. Its control chip understands basic commands.'

Alex drops the flakjacket and, still in the loose orange coveralls, goes to the doll, sinks on one knee and pulls off its black pyjamas. It doesn't try to resist – it is like handling a sleepy child. Its blue skin is hot against his fingers: forty-two degrees centigrade. Its breath, like that of a diabetic, is edged with acetone. It has a flat chest and a smooth crotch, and the blurred, androgynous build of a small child.

'Tag,' Milena says to it, and the doll obediently pads along on long-toed flat feet as Alex and Milena push through the crowd to the gate.

Outside, expensive cars crowd the street in a tangle of headlights and angry horns. A fighting doll suddenly jumps on to the roof of a limo, stamping and flinging its arms around. Flecks of foam fly from its muzzle. A shot stars the limo's windscreen and its horn starts to blare. The doll is gone. Someone flings open the door of the limo and the dead driver falls from his seat on to the tarmac.

Alex and Milena and the doll walk straight past this into the rainy night.

'What we need,' Alex says, 'are bicycles,' but Milena doesn't get it.

He feels a faint trembling under his skin, the reaction to the endorphin blast evoked by Billy Rock's drug. In the rainy half-darkness, stroked by the headlights of cars fleeing the party, he starts to feel afraid. He is in the twilight zone, alone with two aliens.

Alex half expects the van to have gone, but it is still there, at the end of the little street. Dimmed by rain, the lights of Wapping glitter across the river. He's actually beginning to think that they might have made it when the van's headlights come on.

Howard Perse opens the door and gets out, taking his time. He's close to being drop-down drunk. 'You're fucked,' he tells Alex.

'Go home, Mr Perse.'

'Interfering with a police operation. That'll do for starters.'

'Billy Rock is dead.'

Perse blinks at him owlishly, then starts to laugh. He takes a swig from a flat, quarter-litre bottle of whisky and says, 'I still want you, Sharkey. I want to know what you're up to.'

'I did what you asked. That's all.'

'Well, that's what I want to find out.'

'You can't do this to me, Mr Perse. We're finished.'

'Damn right,' another voice says, and Doggy Dog comes around the back of the van. He grins at Alex and shows him his pistol and says, 'Time for you to deliver, motherfucker.'

Perse suddenly doesn't seem drunk. He straightens his back and looks Doggy Dog in the eye and says, 'Put the weapon down, son.'

'I know you,' Doggy Dog says.

'Exactly. So put away the weapon before you get into trouble.'

Doggy Dog laughs and Perse takes a step forward. There's a loud flat crack that echoes off the abandoned block of flats. Perse is howling, hopping on his right foot while clutching his left in both hands. Blood drips between his fingers.

'Flatfoot Perse,' Doggy Dog says. 'You be one sorry mother-fucker.'

Sudden as a striking snake, Doggy Dog reverses the pistol and slams it against Perse's head. The policeman falls against the side of the van, too dazed to stop Doggy Dog hitting him again.

'Hey,' Alex says. 'Enough. Enough, OK?'

Doggy Dog turns, flicking his pistol back and forth between Alex and Milena, finally settling on Milena. 'She's the dangerous one,' he says to Alex.

'She does magic,' Alex says. His whole body is suddenly trembling. Perhaps she can magic away Doggy Dog's pistol.

But Milena more or less ignores Doggy Dog. She walks past him, jumps up on to the little wall at the edge of the river and looks down into the black water. Rain softly fells around her. The naked doll pads up behind her and she turns and pats the top of its bald head.

'You did the deed,' Doggy Dog says. He sounds as scared as Alex feels. 'You did it right under Billy Rock's nose, though I don't know why you bothered. I could get you one of those t'ings anytime, night or day.'

'That's the point,' Milena says. She has a flashlight in her hand.

Doggy Dog laughs and says, 'You try and shoot me down with a ray gun, little girl?' and then there's a stuttering flash of red light and Alex is on his belly on wet tarmac, rain splashing into a puddle right by his face.

At first Alex thinks Milena has shot Doggy Dog, but then he sees that the kid is crawling around in the middle of the road. He is looking for his pistol, but Milena has it. She grins at Alex and says, 'Magic.'

Doggy Dog stands up and extends his arm. He has a knife in his hand. He says, 'Give that back and I don't hurt you.'

'Run away,' Milena says, 'and I won't hurt *you*.'

It's the wrong thing to say. Doggy Dog springs at Milena, his knife slashing wildly, and there's a stutter of red light and Alex is flat on his belly again. He's bitten his tongue, and spits out a mouthful of blood as he gets up.

Doggy Dog is in a half-crouch, staring at Milena. 'Fucker!' he yells, but his voice cracks with fear.

Milena holds up the knife so that its blade glitters in the glare of the van's headlights, then carelessly tosses it away. 'Silly little boy,' she says.

Making a noise half-way between a scream and a yell, Doggy Dog charges at Milena. She raises the pistol. There is a cold, intent expression on her face.

The flat report of the first shot is loud in the narrow street. Doggy Dog bangs into the side of the van. Milena fires three more times, the shots spaced exactly five seconds apart, and Doggy Dog falls forward on to his face.

Alex stays on his knees in the rain, his hands clasped around the swag of his belly. He is shivering. She made the kid angry, he thinks, so she could kill him.

Milena tells the doll to climb up into the van. 'You too,' she says to Alex. 'I don't know how to drive.'

'What are you going to do if I don't? Shoot me?'

'You can walk away,' Milena says. 'I'll survive. I know it, now. I can survive anything. You can walk away, Alex. You can walk away if you want to. You can let it go.'

He can't. They are bound together by blood and guilt. Besides, he has to know. He has to see. 'Come on,' he says. 'Let's get out of here.'

16
Born to Run

They leave Perse lying half-unconscious next to Doggy Dog's body, with Doggy Dog's pistol in his hand, but Alex knows it won't be as easy as that. As he turns the van on to Brunel Road he tells Milena, 'You better hope no one out here saw you ex the kid.'

Milena is looking at the orange streetlights flipping past. She clutches the silvery bag in her lap. The doll crouches under the dashboard, by her feet. She says, 'If that policeman has any sense, he'll claim the kill. But it won't matter soon. You do have a place to hide out, I hope.'

Alex doesn't have a place, not exactly, but he has thought about this contingency. He drives west for a while, his heart-rate spiking every time a police cruiser goes past, then crosses the river at Tower Bridge, skirts the Square Mile, where even at this hour curtains of lights rise up towards pinnacles topped by winking red warning beacons, and turns along the Embankment. The Houses of Parliament shine in a cocoon of white light above their reflection in the Thames's black water. The span of Westminster Bridge, aimed at the South Bank Plaza and Waterloo, is outlined in fairy lights.

They cut past Victoria and Hyde Park, swing around the spotlit wedding cake decoration of Marble Arch. Alex has to stop for petrol, and, in the blue light under the service station's canopy, at the armoured cashier's window, buys a dozen chocolate bars, cans of Coke, sandwiches in clear plastic wedges. Fear has made him hungry.

He's stripping off his orange coveralls when Milena comes out of the toilet, white faced, her eyes watery. She's been sick to her stomach, she says. In a way, Alex is relieved at this sign of weakness. She is only human, after all. She gets back in the van without speaking. The doll sits where she told it to sit, quiet and uncomplaining.

Alex eats as he drives through the cluttered streets of Paddington, turning out at last into the mazy encampments beneath the flyovers of the Westway. The Transit van slowly bumps along a muddy track as Alex searches for an empty space in this, the largest congregation of the dispossessed in London.

There have been people living here since the middle of the last century, an official camp of gypsies that was slowly surrounded by ring after ring of the homeless and refugees from the Sellafield plume. There are still a few caravans, but mostly the accommodation is improvised: vans and cars up on blocks; tepees and benders; shacks made of shingled flattened oil drums or built around and beneath the support pillars of the flyovers; subdivided freight containers; big concrete pipes sealed by crude wooden partitions. A wheelless double-decker bus has a vegetable garden on its roof.

Green bioluminescent lamps glow here and there, singly or in clusters. The air stings with smoke from a big bonfire where a hundred or more people are dancing to the surfing rhythms of a group of freestyle drummers.

After Alex has found a space and parked, a burly black guy with dreadlocks down to the small of his back comes up and asks, with a gap-toothed easy smile and a broad Birmingham accent, if he wants to be connected, mains or telecommunications, the same flat fee for both. Alex declines, but gives the guy a five pound coin and asks him to keep a look-out. It's almost the last of his cash; and Milena has no money at all. She has, it turns out, never bought anything in her life.

The man spins the coin and pockets it before leaning in at the side window. He says, 'Round 'ere we look out for each other. You and the little girl in trouble? She your daughter?'

'Sister,' Milena says. She suddenly seems close to tears. 'Our p-parents went crazy on drugs. Please don't tell them we're here!'

'No one don't trouble anyone,' the man tells Alex, 'unless they look like trouble. Seen?'

'Of course,' Alex says.

'There's a standpipe,' the man says, pointing along the track. 'Man who run it give a fair price. Storm drain beyond it for your sanitary needs. Don't go dumping your shit out your window and driving off. Samaritans come by about two o'clock you want something to eat, if you don't mind the prayers. You missed the do-gooders from the 'burbs, but Samaritan food is better.'

Alex offers a chocolate bar, but the man shakes his head. 'That shit isn't natural. You want natural food, come asking after me. I'm Mister Benny. I cook up natural food, food from the earth. People know me all over, even come from outside to eat at my place. If you had turned left instead of right you would have gone right past it. You stop by for breakfast, now.'

And then he's gone, moving off through the shadows between a bender wrapped in black polythene and a wheelless Sierra with a candle flickering behind its windscreen.

'King of the hill,' Milena remarks, matter-of-factly. She cranks down the window on her side, sticks her head out to look around. 'Some hill,' she adds. She seems to have recovered her poise. 'So, Alex, tell me about your plan.'

Alex is suddenly afraid. He says, 'I want to see how it's done.'

Milena laughs, and reaches down to pat the doll which crouches in the shadows by her feet. 'I've never done it before. But now's the time, I think.'

So they do the doll right there in the back of the van, by the green light of a biolume stick Alex cracks in half and wedges in one of the roof braces. Milena puts on spectacles with pop-eyed turret lenses that zoom in and out and a little fibreoptic light attached to the bridge. She has the doll sit on the plywood decking and tells Alex to close his eyes, or he'll be affected by the pulse.

Alex says, 'You did something to my head, back at your house. You did something to Doggy Dog, too.'

'It isn't my house. The company owns it. They own everything.'

'Not everything. They're not the world.'

'Close your eyes, Alex. This was your idea.'

Alex does as he's told, is allowed to open them maybe thirty seconds later. The doll is lying on its back, its eyes wide but unfocused.

Milena says, 'Of course I did something to you. And to Delbert and Doggy Dog. If Delbert gives you any trouble, just pop him with a two hundred c.p.s. strobe and he'll do anything you ask. I put the same strain of fembots in all of you. It infects the visual cortex and responds to light cues, just as the doll's control chip does. I developed it so I could work around my supervisor.'

'Nanny Greystoke.'

The white room – the woman – her blank stare.

Milena says, 'Let's say Nanny Greystoke has an unusually rich fantasy life.'

She explains she used an aerosol spray on Alex when he came through the door, buckyball fembots suspended in a fluorocarbon carrier. They entered the blood vessels at the back of his throat, crossed the blood-brain barrier while he was taking tea with her. As well as modifying his visual cortex, they tagged and removed almost all of the last couple of hours of his memory – he'll never remember what she said to him, Milena says, or the taste of the tea.

'What kind was it?'

'Earl Grey. Does it matter?'

'I suppose not.'

Milena promises Alex that she didn't plant any subconscious commands in him, but Alex isn't so sure. She has this urge to manipulate, to control. Her love of explanations is part of that – how it must have taxed her to keep secrets from her company! She is something new, all right. She should be walking around with a biohazard symbol tattooed on her forehead.

Converting the doll takes three hours. Milena's silvery shoulder bag contains nothing but tools for the job. She erects a kind of scaffolding around the doll's head, anchored at a dozen points by screw calipers. She drops curarine in the doll's right eye to immobilize it and inserts something like a teaspoon between eyeball and bony orbit. The scaffolding has thumb-operated waldoes for microsurgery work. Milena hunkers down and, with the turret lenses of her spectacles popping in and out for the fine work, uses the waldoes to disconnect and dismantle the doll's control chip.

Alex asks why she just can't reprogram it, and she tells him that it is a PROM, a Programmable Read-Only Memory chip that can be loaded with information just once. After the chip has been blown with code, the information it contains can only be read. The information – the software – becomes the hardware which dictates the control protocols for the doll's routines. If a doll is redeployed, its chip has to be replaced.

Milena tells Alex this as, using fine tweezers, she loads a chip into the microsurgery scaffolding and slides it into place in the doll's eyesocket. Alex breaks another biolume stick as Milena connects the new chip. His back and thighs ache from squatting, but Milena is intent on her work and has hardly moved for the last two hours. Once the chip is connected, she breaks open an ampoule of milky liquid, a soup of nanoware assemblers, and administers a single drop to each of the doll's eyes. Then she injects a massive dose of the cocktail of artificial hormones Alex manufactured, and that's that.

Alex stretches out as best as he can on the bench seat in the front of the van, his jacket rolled up inside the orange coveralls for a pillow. Milena curls up next to the doll. It's hot and close, and a mosquito has got in. Its divebomber whine dopplers past Alex's ear a dozen times before it finally lands on his wrist. He lets it slide its needle-fine proboscis into his skin before he mashes it. Its brown blood – his blood – stains his thumb. The drummers have long ago given up, but traffic still rumbles and sighs on the cantilevered overpass. A dog barks monotonously, as if barking is the one idea it has left.

Alex falls into an uneasy, exhausted sleep. Once, he half-wakes, dimly aware of the dull orange night sky beyond the windscreen, cut in two by the overpass, from which hang constellations of little green biolume lamps.

Fairyland.

In the back of the van, the doll is squatting with a Watchman in its lap, intent on the screen's lozenge of moving colour. The earpiece is plugged into its ear, and its lips move as it mumbles in imitation of unheard speech.

Milena sits zazen, watching the doll watching TV. She turns and grins at Alex in the half-darkness inside the van, and then there's a stutter of red light.

17
The White Room

When Alex wakes, he's sticky with old sweat and his eyes are gummed. He can smell himself in his day-old clothes. Above the overpass, the sky is white with early morning heat. The back door of the Transit van hangs open. Milena is gone, and so is the doll.

What has woken him is the chirping of his portable phone. Alex sits up and pulls the thing out of its holster. Perse's voice says in his ear, 'You've been a busy boy, Sharkey.'

Alex says, 'I can't do anything for you, Perse.'

'That's not what I hear. If you think that Billy Rock's death puts you in the clear, you're very wrong. A runner, kid by the name of Doggy Dog, was found shot dead, and tyre prints match those of a van we traced to Ray Aziz. Mr Aziz has a cast-iron alibi, and he says that he lent the van to you.'

Alex is sweating all over. He says, 'He would have killed you, Perse. What do you want?'

'I want the whole story, Sharkey. You fucked up. You didn't deliver. I still want a material witness, and it comes down to you.'

Alex cuts the connection, remembering too late about portable phones, about how easily they can be traced. He pulls on his jacket and goes to look for Milena, hoping that she has taken the doll for a drink of water. He walks all the way down the track to the standpipe where an old woman, wrapped from head to foot in greasy rags, is filling a blue plastic bucket.

There's no sign of Milena. Alex walks back, walks past the van and keeps on walking. He doesn't feel any panic, just a mellow hazy calm, as if he's dropped a tab of Cool-Z.

There's a shack by the broken-down wire fence at the edge of the encampment. Its walls and roof are scaled with flattened oil cans. Benches and plastic chairs are scattered around an ashy barbecue pit; goats placidly munch on cabbage leaves in a chicken wire pen. An Alsatian chained to a stake near the goat pen starts to bark as Alex approaches.

A man comes out of the shack, scratching at his dreadlocked hair and blinking sleepily. It is Mister Benny. He doesn't seem surprised to see Alex, and tells him, 'Your little sister was here an hour gone.'

'Was she with anyone?'

'No, man. She bought a little breakfast from me, then she go off out. Said she had to work the commuters. Cute little thing. Begged me to give her ape some fruit, and I found it a hand of bananas. You pay me, she said. Where did you run away from, the circus?'

The Underground station at Ladbroke Grove is just opening when Alex arrives, sweating in his green tweed suit and completely out of breath. He uses his last two five pound coins to buy a ticket – he doesn't dare use any of the credit cards he carries – and rides all the way into the centre of London.

A black electric car, sleek as a raindrop, is parked on the double yellow lines outside the tall, narrow house in Bridle Lane. The door stands open. Alex walks in, climbs a half-remembered flight of stairs towards me sound of a man's voice.

The room at the top of the stairs must take up the whole of the first floor. It is painted white. White paper blinds are pulled down over the windows. The floor is blond ash, gleamingly polished and littered with toys. Every surface shines as if irradiated with an inner light.

There are two people in the room. A man in a black suit steps amongst the toys, describing each one into a portable phone. A thin, middle-aged woman in a plain white dress stands in a corner, watching the man with empty eyes.

Alex knows that he has seen the woman before, although he doesn't remember it. He says her name, and the man in black turns on his heel to Alex, snaps the phone shut and says, 'Where is she?'

'She isn't here?'

'Nanny Greystoke thinks she is, but something has happened to Nanny Greystoke. Where is she?'

'I don't—'

Alex is suddenly backed up against the wall. The man holds his throat in one gloved hand. The gloves are black, and seamed with myoelectric pseudo-musculature. His grip is incredibly strong. His breath is flavoured with cloves. His eyes are grey. The pupil of his left eye is flecked with brown in the upper quadrant.

Alex can't stop noticing these little things. His every nerve is laid bare by fear.

The man says, his voice loud and flat, 'Where is she?'

Alex makes a fist, and the man looks him straight in the eye and says, 'You're a big man, but you're out of condition, and this is my job. So don't even think about it, Mr Sharkey.'

Alex laughs. It's a line from an old film. He's supposed to lash out at the man, who'll then hurt him. But he doesn't have to follow any script now. He's free. Milena let him go, just as she freed the doll. He relaxes in the man's grip and looks past him at Nanny Greystoke, who stands staring at something beyond the far wall.

'Two hundred cycles per second,' Alex says. 'It happened to me, too.'

The man lets Alex go and steps back. Toys move away from his expensive black brogues.

There are dozens of toys, all amniotronic. A monkey in a gold vest and red fez clashes cymbals as it totters up and down. A turtle cautiously bumps along the skirting board. A couple of racing cars chase each other in and out of the other toys, flashing their headlights.

A teddy bear is saying over and over in a gruff, plaintive voice, 'Come back. Please come back. Come back to us.' When the man picks it up, the teddy bear windmills its stubby arms in alarm, and says indignantly, 'You can't play with me. It's not *allowed*.'

'We'll interrogate them,' the man says, setting the teddy bear down, 'but I don't think they'll tell us very much. There might be something on their chips. They all store a week's worth of visual and auditory data. Where is she, Mr Sharkey?'

'I don't know.' It hurts to speak.

The man flexes his gloved hands. 'I have to be careful with these. I could poke a brand new hole in your face with my forefinger. Be a good boy. Tell me where she is.'

By one of the shuttered windows, a canary in a gilded cage bursts into brief song. The rushing burble of trills stirs something in Alex that brings the prickle of incipient tears to his eyes. He remembers the budgerigar Lexis kept in the flat. It lasted a full two weeks after the pigeons and sparrows and starlings started falling out of the sky. Alex found its corpse early one morning. He still remembers the crisp dry lightness of its body, its delicate coral-coloured clawed feet, each claw with a tiny transparent nail. The canary, caught in a blade of light that pries between the shutters, turns its head back and forth as it sings and sings and sings.

'It's a toy,' the man says. 'It isn't real.'

Alex says, 'The toys will tell you that I was here. They'll tell you that Milena did something to me, the same kind of thing that she did to Nanny Greystoke. But I don't know *what* it was. You can tell me: what did she do?'

'I'm just a foot soldier, Mr Sharkey. Someone else will inter-rogate the toys. I'm picking up here before the trail goes cold. Where is she?'

'She fucked up my head,' Alex says.

He is shivering, and angry, and close to tears. It's this room, this white, white room. It stirs up vague memories, but he can't remember what she did. He can't remember.

The man, implacable in his anonymous black suit and black gloves, stands in the middle of all the whiteness, watching with professional patience. Alex walks around in tight circles, and realizes that the racing cars are following him. He kicks out and they split up, zooming away to different corners of the room.

Alex says, 'I have to know.'

The man shrugs.

'You knew what she was doing. What she was doing to me.'

'We know everything up to the point when she let the fighting dolls loose. You two got away in the confusion, and one of our agents was later found dead.'

Alex says, 'Doggy Dog was working for you?'

'He wasn't what you'd call reliable, but we were taking what we could at that point.'

'Who else? Billy Rock? Dr Luther?'

'Dr Luther works for Billy Rock's family. Billy Rock, before a fighting doll bit off his face, was an unstable gangster with a heavy drug addiction.' The man's gaze is unwavering. 'What happened to her, Mr Sharkey? You went with her when she ran away. The company allowed that. It wasn't my idea. I wanted her brought in, but I'm just the guy who clears up the shit on the streets. I was overruled. Make my job easy. Tell me what happened.'

Alex tells him. Why not? He hasn't got anything to lose at this point. It doesn't take long. As he talks, men come and go, moving stuff from rooms above. One comes in and starts to pack up the toys; he has a hard time catching the racing cars. Another leads Nanny Greystoke away.

Alex says, 'That's not her real name is it? Greystoke, I mean.'

'One of Milena's little jokes,' the man says. He is flexing his hands inside the black gloves. Or perhaps the gloves are flexing and moving his hands of their own accord, because the man lifts his hands and looks at them as the fingers bend and straighten. He adds, 'She was very fond of stupid little jokes like that.'

'What was she?'

'I can't tell you that.'

'She told me something of what you people did to her. She thought she was better than us. She thought that she was a superior being who was raised up by animals, like Tarzan and the apes, or like Mowgli and his wolves. But she was just a little girl, very bright and, I think, very unstable, and your people let her loose to play in the world.'

This at least seems very clear to Alex. Perhaps Milena whispered it all to him after she zapped him. Here in the white room, or in the van.

He says, 'I think she wanted company, so she's trying to make something out of the dolls. The way she was made, the way she was changed.'

106

'We don't know what she wants,' the man says.

Someone comes into the room, another smooth-shaven burly type in an expensive black suit. He carries a video camera. The first man tells him, 'One minute,' and says to Alex, 'You go home, Mr Sharkey. If we need you we'll be in touch.'

'Just like that.'

'We already know most of your story. The rest may not matter. You're an interesting man, Mr Sharkey, but at present we have other concerns. You run along now, and don't cause us any more trouble.'

So there's nothing there for Alex, except the knowledge that Milena got away. She is more ruthless and resourceful than even her owners suspect. Alex has seen her operate, and has learnt all about ruthiessness from the Wizard. He is pretty sure he knows where she has gone, too, when he finds that Dr Luther has quit his premises.

'Left owing me two months' rent,' the aging skinhead owner of the comic book shop says. His hairy belly pushes out of the bottom of his T-shirt and makes a fold over the top of his jeans. 'Was he a friend of yours?'

'I only met him once,' Alex says, and refuses an offer to buy Dr Luther's stainless steel table.

Alex has to walk all the way to Leroy's shebeen. He stops half a dozen times to use his phone, and on the last try gets Perse's partner, Stevie Cryer.

Alex says, 'I want to clear this up. Tell Perse that.'

'You'd better come in and talk about it.'

'He wants to lay the murder on me.'

'Which murder would that be, Alex?'

'I didn't kill Doggy Dog. I mean I was there but I didn't kill him.'

'Well, we can talk about it.'

Alex tells Cryer where to find him. 'Give me a few minutes, and I'll give you Doggy Dog's partner. He'll tell you what they were up to.'

'I can't make any promises,' Cryer says.

By the time Alex gets to Leroy's shebeen, there's an unmarked police car waiting outside. Alex goes past without looking to see who's in it.

Persuading Leroy to let him talk with Lexis is harder than persuading him to fix up Delbert. It isn't an easy conversation, especially as Lexis forgives him so easily. She'll be all right, she says, and Alex makes all sorts of promises he's not sure he can keep.

At last, Alex says, 'Remember the time you showed me the lights? I've realized that it isn't a place. It's an idea.'

'You were always making things up, Alex,' his mother says, and gives him money and tells him to send a postcard.

Alex zaps the bodyguard with an old strobe left over from Leroy's sound system days and tells him to forget what happened here, tells him to walk up to the street.

Alex follows after a minute. Three policemen are sitting on Delbert while a fourth cuffs the bodyguard's hands behind his back. Cryer gets out of the unmarked police car, and Alex walks over to him.

18
No Big Deal

Alex waits a long time in a shabby interrogation room in the bowels of New Scotland Yard. The usual green paint, the usual big mirror everyone knows is one-way, the usual scuffed carpet tiles. Cheap plastic chairs, a beat-up wooden desk with a cassette recorder and an overflowing ashtray. Even the tea is just as Alex remembers, milky and lukewarm, with a dusty aftertaste.

He smokes two packets of cigarettes, waiting there. He feels clammy in clothes he hasn't changed for more than a day. The sharp creases in his green check suit are wilting. He is deeply aware that with every minute Milena is moving further and further away. After a while, Perse gimps past the open door on crutches, his left foot wrapped in white bandages. He doesn't look at Alex.

Alex waits some more, and at last Stevie Cryer comes in. He takes one of Alex's cigarettes and says, 'You've a day to get out of the country.'

'I need to sell my stuff.'

Cryer fixes Alex with his weary blue eyes. 'Your stuff may have been bought with profits from drug dealing. We're going to impound it at noon tomorrow. There's your deadline.'

'This isn't much of a deal,' Alex says.

'Are you complaining?'

'I suppose not.'

'That's smart of you.'

'Perhaps I'm smarter than you think.'

Cryer exhales a riffle of blue smoke. He looks tired, his clean boyish complexion sallow in the harsh fluorescent light. He says, 'Being smart – it's no big deal. For one thing, there's always going to be someone smarter than you. For another, it gives you a dangerous contempt for other people. You think you can use them. Well, now you've been used. Welcome to the world, Alex.' He stubs out his cigarette. 'Come on, I'll sign you out.'

On the way to the front desk, they pass a room where half a dozen policemen, Perse amongst them, are watching a big TV. They are laughing at this scared-looking fat man in orange coveralls puffing along in the dark, in the rain, after a little girl and a naked, blue-skinned doll. The camera pans to show a boxy white blur. The Transit van. Alex realizes that security cameras must have caught the whole thing.

Alex looks at Cryer, who smiles and taps the side of his head. 'I'm curious,' Cryer says. 'Where are you going?'

Alex smiles right back. Perhaps the impulse to move on, his sudden restlessness, his urge to follow Milena, is an infection Alex could cure with a shot of universal phage. But he knows he won't. He has a place to get to, if he can find it, if it exists. Perhaps it is no more than an idea, but these days ideas are as real as the common cold. It is an idea whose time has come. It is pushing its way into the world.

He says, 'I'm going to look for Fairyland.'

PART TWO

LOVE BOMBING

1
Europa

Europe in the early years of the Third Millennium is not an easy place to find a preternaturally intelligent little girl who has deliberately gone to ground. Alex Sharkey makes a long journey of it, across France and Germany and through the little kingdoms and republics of Eastern Europe. He searches for twelve years. Although the products of Milena's imagination are all around him, in all that time he only once comes close to finding her.

Dolls are no longer the novelty toys of the rich. They are used as cheap, versatile computer-controlled labour in industries where working conditions are traditionally hazardous – chemical refineries, deep coal mines, intensive horticulture, nuclear fission power stations. Gradually, they replace human workers in the emergent nanotechnology industries: driven by plug-in chips and fembot-grown neural nets, dolls can work for twenty hours a day accurately electron-etching primary fembot templates no bigger than bacteria. Killing Fields franchises are built in Rotterdam, Hamburg, Budapest and Moscow. Every day, more than a thousand dolls are hunted down and killed for sport in arenas across the European Union. There are women-only arenas, arenas for senior citizens, arenas where the clinically disturbed therapeutically discharge the murderous fantasies of their superegos.

It is an age of excess.

In the Europe of the First World, most people enjoy a universal unearned wage and unlimited leisure in booming economies driven by new technologies that are making techniques of mass production, hardly changed since the days of Henry Ford, finally obsolete. They live at the edge of the old conurbations in ribbon arcologies, vast conglomerations of apartment complexes, leisure parks and shopping centres that are part built, part grown. More than fifty per cent of the population of First World Europe is over eighty, the baby boomer generation of the last century come into a post-Millennial paradise. Nanotechnology and gene therapy promises that at least half of them will live into their second century.

But there's also the Europe of the Fourth World, the Europe of the dispossessed, the people of the fringe. Half the population of the old Communist Bloc countries have been displaced by civil wars, and their numbers are swollen by refugees from the economic and ecological disasters in Africa, migrants who flock through Italy into the heart of Europe like swallows. They are uncountable, although tag and recapture methods used by UN relief teams estimate that refugees are roughly equal in number to the official population of Europe. Sometimes, especially in summer, it seems that all of Europe is on the move, a giantess tossing restlessly but never quite waking, displacing and distorting the maps which cover her.

After five years of travelling, Alex settles for a while in the café and beer hall culture of the demi-monde of Prague, where two generations of American exiles have established an easygoing Bohemia. There arc fairies here – there are fairies everywhere, now, if you know how to recognize their enigmatic traces – but they are fey, wild and elusive, and still heavily outnumbered by their human creators and collaborators.

Alex falls in with an aging punk who calls herself Darlajane B., her stage name from the 1980s, when she was lead singer in an East German thrash metal group, the Thalidomide Babies. After four years of playing the semi-legal clubs of East Berlin, half the band was thrown in prison by the Stasi, the East German secret police. A year later, they were let out in time to celebrate the fall of the Berlin Wall. Darlajane B. has a fuzzy recording of herself dancing by searchlight on top of the wall in T-shirt and lycra cycle shorts, soaked by the play of firehoses.

For a year, Darlajane B. made a good deal of money selling pieces of the wall to gullible American and Japanese dealers ('So much we sold, a wall they could have built from Stockholm to Beijing.'), along with Stasi torture equipment, Soviet military uniforms and badges and even weapons. She gave that up after someone with a high velocity rifle took a shot at her as she was crossing a St Petersburg bridge, minutes after leaving a hotel room where a couple of Ukrainians had offered her two kilos of weapons grade plutonium.

With finely tuned empathy for the *Zeitgeist* of the end of the twentieth century, Darlajane B. migrated to Prague shortly after Czechoslovakia split into two. She set up the city's first coin-operated launderette and lost the profits from that in a venture in exporting beer, started over as bartender in a folk-rock café, and is now part-owner of an ambient club, Zone Zone, deep in the maze of alleys and passageways of the Starê Mesto.

She also grows chips that can make over dolls into fairies.

For two years, Alex lives in two rooms above Zone Zone's arena. Of necessity, he sleeps by day, but he doesn't mind that. He's having fun, and beginning to hope that Milena's glamour has eased its pull. He grows psychoactive viruses for the clubbers and brews batches of doll-specific thyrotropic hormone for the liberationists, but he doesn't quickly discover who Darlajane B.'s associates are, nor where she's learned her skills or obtained the fembot templates.

'Such things,' Darlajane B. declares when he asks her, 'you don't need to know.'

But Alex persists in asking. Eventually, Darlajane B. lets him know that she has contacts with a cell of a radical Muslim group which is held to be responsible for sabotaging doll-associated enterprises all over Eastern Europe, including the firebombing of a hatchery in Budapest that killed the plant supervisor and four technicians as well as thousands of newborn and unborn dolls. This association makes Alex more than uneasy. There are dozens of liberationist groups, from political pressure groups to underground organizations with names like Daughters of Morlock or Blue Star Liner, when they have names at all. But the Muslims aren't interested in freeing dolls and making them over into fairies; instead, they want to destroy every trace of these blue-skinned devils.

Darlajane B. doesn't share Alex's concern. She says she will talk to anyone. Information should be free: it is not information that destroys, but people who use it. She does spend just about half her waking life on the Web, it's true. She's almost evangelical about it.

At last, Alex gets to meet with two of the Muslim group. One is a Moroccan student with a ferocious knowledge of molecular biology, the other a tall loose-limbed drummer in his fifties. Alex gets very high with them on harsh strong mountain hashish from Tunisia, smoked in a hookah over peppermint oil, and he learns that as a teenager the drummer once played with the Rolling Stones, and that the student's grandfather was working in the Hotel Minzah in Tangiers when Brian Jones stayed there.

'Connections everywhere,' Darlajane B. says. 'It's a very wiggly world.'

They all laugh – they are so stoned that everything seems funny. When the student says that one day they will cleanse all palaces of sin, including Zone Zone, they all laugh at that, too.

'By then I will be so old I will want it destroyed,' Darlajane B. says.

'The older you get, the more neurone connections you grow,' the student says. He is wearing an expensive one-piece suit and is immaculately groomed – he is the first man Alex has met who has manicured fingernails. 'Civilization is very old, too. Many many connections. You are proof, Darlajane B., because you know many people.'

Darlajane B. passes the pipe and says, 'I knew twice as many when I was in Berlin, but half of them were Stasi informers. Now I choose more carefully who I talk to.'

Later, when the Muslims have gone, Darlajane B. suddenly doesn't seem stoned at all.

'They're assholes,' she tells Alex, 'and their community disowns what they do, but they're our assholes. They want to destroy the hatcheries, and every living doll, it's true, but they have access to raw materials I need to grow my chips. Besides, I like to use dolls which haven't yet been chipped, and so I want access to the hatcheries, too. Unchipped dolls are the best kind to turn into fairies, as routines are not worn into their brains. Routines are binding in everyone, little Alex.'

'I have routines, you mean.'

'You are a nesting type, Alex, but because of what you want, never can you live easy in one place. That I learned to give up long ago. I am not attached to these things.'

Darlajane B. gestures around her. Her room is low and windowless, a bunker with walls painted matt black. Dusty astroturf on the concrete floor. There are bubbling tanks with brightly coloured fish schooling through violet light, and a bank of television screens, some showing various views of the club, others flipping through the thousand-plus available TV channels, and one showing the night sky transmitted from the twenty centimetre reflector telescope on the roof.

Darlajane B. is reclining in a nest of cushions, a little old lady in black leather, with a five centimetre crest of glue-stiffened hair spikes running from front to back of her otherwise shaven skull, eyes kohled, fingers knobby with rings. She is playing Tarot patience, setting down the big, bright cards with decisive snaps.

She says, 'One day all this I will leave behind, and move on. If the bourgeoisie can live until two hundred years old in their hermetic cells, then so can I.'

'Are you saying I should move on too?'

'For two years you have been here. Have you forgotten your dark lady?'

Alex told Darlajane B. about Milena, and his own role in creating the first fairy, soon after he came to live above Zone Zone, although he's never sure how much she believes. He says, 'Perhaps she'll come to me.'

'Wish on a star.' Darlajane B. laughs her cracked, husky laugh. She had throat cancer two years ago, and although hunter-killer fembots destroyed every last trace, it scarred her vocal cords; she sounds like Marianne Faithfull after half a bottle of bourbon. She says, 'You are still wet behind the ears. The world you need to know if you are to survive on the fringe.'

'I don't intend staying here forever. I check out the Web every day. Sooner or later Milena will show herself.'

'Bah. You might as well look for portents in the belly of a dove.'

Alex says, earnestly, out of tender love for this cantankerous old woman, 'Teach me stuff, Darlajane. Show me this world. Share it with me. How long do I have to work for the liberationists before you trust me enough to let me know them?'

'Who says I work with anyone? I have contacts, it is true. But work with others? Pah. Besides, if you wanted to, you could find them yourself. They are everywhere. If they were just old punks like me, how easy it would be for the Peace Police to find us all. No, they dress like housewives, like students . . .' Darlajane B. laughs. 'Really, you do not get it, do you? Such a child of your times, you are. Very literal, very linear, self-sufficient to the point of autism. That is the disease of this new Millennium. Obsession with self-image, obsession with estranging technologies. Happier you'd be to have a one room efficiency in a ribbon arcology outside Munich or Paris.'

'What's in my future?'

Darlajane B. fans the remaining cards in her hands, and Alex chooses one:

A man, dressed in the parti-coloured tights, jerkin and cap and bells of a court jester of the Middle Ages, is about to step over the edge of a cliff into bright blue sunlit air. He holds a rose up to the sun, rests his other hand on one end of a stout staff which is balanced on his shoulder. At the other end of the staff is a leather satchel, its flap engraved with the eye and pyramid of the Gnostics. A dog attacks the fringes of the man's floppy boots, but the man seems unaware of this, and instead is intent on a sulphur-yellow butterfly that hangs before his face. Darlajane B. tilts the card and the figures in the laminated surface seem to move. The dog shakes its head to and fro; the butterfly flaps its wings, revealing human eyes on their undersides; the man smiles and starts to complete his last step, the beginning of his fall.

Darlajane B. tells Alex that he is this figure, the wise Fool, the vagabond who lives on the edge of society, despised, believed mad, yet the genius who carries the spark that will change that society. He is the pure impulse that is neither evil nor good, open to all the wonders of the world and heedless of its dangers; but he is also the Joker, who continually seeks extravagant amusements, heedless of the chaos his search causes because he is lost in the joy of the moment.

Alex says that it sounds more like Darlajane B. than himself. He isn't much taken with this reduction of the spectrum of human behaviour to a handful of Jungian archetypes, although he also feels, with a needle of unease, that there's some truth in what she tells him. After all, he did help Milena bring the first fairy into the world. He insisted on it, and now look.

Darlajane B. says that in a way he is right, that's why she tolerates him.

'But I am at the end of my journey, and you are at the beginning. The meaning is very different.'

'What does it mean to you?'

'For me the card is reversed. Problems rising from impulsive, reckless actions it foretells. For you, it suggests an unexpected influence that will force an important change.'

Later, when all is lost and he is homeless again, Alex will think she's wrong. Everything seems clearer in hindsight because you only remember what's important: the brain always finds patterns, and even if they're untrue, they're all that's left of the past.

Perhaps he remembers that conversation because of the microscopic intensity of the hash, or perhaps because, two weeks later, the Peace Police raid the club and arrest him. The doll dormitories of a chemical refinery in the east of the Czech Republic have been firebombed; the Muslim Jihad has claimed responsibility; Darlajane B. has disappeared.

Alex has been down this road before. Now he knows why Darlajane B. was reluctant to tell him anything, and also why she let him meet the two Muslims. He knows almost nothing about the plot, but he can give them up to the Peace Police. After six weeks he's released at the border, his visa cancelled. He's happy to leave the Czech Republic; he's pretty sure that what's left of the Jihad will be looking for him.

Alex doesn't see Darlajane B. again, although seven years later he comes close to finding her. Ironically, his arrest gives him cachet amongst the liberationists. He spends five years moving from group to group through France and Spain, making batches of thyrotropic hormone, learning all there is to learn about making dolls over into fairies. In Barcelona, he falls briefly in love with a young, brilliant neurologist who is flirting with the radical fringe. Alex learns much from her, but she soon grows impatient with him. She wants to change the world, and he is beginning to think that he has done enough of that.

In all this time, he finds no clue, no trace, of Milena.

After Alex breaks up with his lover, he breaks with the liberationists, too, although it's hard to escape them entirely. He has gained a certain notoriety which is transmuted to near-legendary status once he gives up regular contact. He takes up with a grey market biolab, but when he's in Albania, field-testing psychotropic viruses designed to disorientate troops, his driver makes a wrong turning. He spends two months as prisoner of war in Macedonia, in a little village in a valley high in the mountains.

Summer, the brown grasses noisy with insects, the smell of thyme drugging the blue and gold days. His captors are shepherds whose families have lived there for three thousand years, wiry old men with deeply wrinkled faces, quick to laugh, quick to anger, as slow to forgive as glaciers. There are no young people in the village: the men are away fighting or are dead; the children and young women, targets for ransom or rape or revenge killings, are hiding in the hills and won't come down until winter's forced truce.

Alex, fitted with a cuff which lets him roam no more than a hundred metres beyond the tumbledown, closely built stone houses, has plenty of time to think about the course of his life. When he is finally ransomed, for a ridiculously small sum, he works out his contract with the biolab and drifts to Amsterdam, where he finds Dr Dieter Luther running a sex arcade which exclusively features surgically modified dolls, with a lucrative and absolutely legal sideline in snuff sex.

Dr Luther pretends not to recognize Alex at first, but it turns out that he has been looking for Milena, too, and with no more success. Alex learns about what happened to Dr Luther's last assistant, a zek who fell under fairy glamour. There's a new kind of fairy community, and what it is doing has Milena's stamp.

Then Alex hears that Darlajane B. has been working in a zek hostel just down the coast at Scheveningen. Although she's gone by the time he gets there, he stumbles on to the beginning of Milena's new plan to change the world. A rumour of a changeling boy who for a few weeks ruled the auditing of a virtuality club, the Permanent Floating Wave, that's almost next door to Darlajane B.'s zek hostel; rumours of a new kind of fembot that love bombs people into permanent rapture.

Alex thinks that he has found Milena at last, but barely escapes with his life when he tries to confront her fairy helpers. And then he hears about something new just outside Paris, a place where, for the first time, Fairyland has come into the light, no longer off the map, but rising into it, rising into history.

A decade after it went into receivership for the third and final time, the Magic Kingdom has come alive again.

2
The Last Chance Saloon

The Twins find Armand in Frontierland. He's hiding behind the wreck of an upright pianola in a fast food outlet done up as an old-time Wild West saloon. He's been hiding there for most of the morning, ever since the rats came back. As their pheromones spread through the nest, Armand woke from a bad dream knowing that another changeling had been located, ripe for harvest, and he immediately went to ground.

It's cold in the gutted saloon, but although there's plenty of wood lying around, even if it is mostly rotten plastic-veneered chipboard, Armand doesn't want to light a fire. The Twins will find him, they always do, but he always tries his best to hide from them as long as possible.

Armand feels as if a thunderstorm is building all around him. Something bad is going to happen. Mister Mike will be called out, and something bad always happens then. His tongue throbs, and scraps of light whirl and fade at the periphery of his attention, the tatters of fairyland. He needs soma badly, but that's how it always starts, after he is fed the special soma from the mouth of one of the Folk. Then Mister Mike rises out of dreams and his hunger burns everything away.

Armand can still feel the psychic texture of the dream from which he woke. He knows it will cling to him all day, like a hangover. Sometimes he thinks the dreams are just flashbacks from bad chemicals, using found imagery from news items about the wars in Somalia, Liberia, the Sudan, all those countries in Africa where they say the end times are happening twenty years into the new Millennium. The dreams are so real, though – and in the dreams he is always someone else. In his dreams, Armand remembers being Mister Mike.

Armand sits behind the wrecked pianola, trying to remember the dream, trying to understand. If he can understand Mister Mike through the dreams, maybe Armand can make Mister Mike go away. He can't be sure – he can't be sure of anything, these days – but he can hope. Hope is all he has.

He sits behind the pianola with his back against the wall, the collar of his grimy puffer jacket turned up around his ears, his hands shoved between his thighs for warmth. Remembering.

Remembering figures, running. The light funny, bronze and flaked steel. The air hot and wet as a steam bath. Columns of light moving, tangling, moving on. Light brushing across the wrecked street, where two storey mud-brick buildings have spilled down across the cracked concrete roadway. Store signs in French and Arabic. Something burning fiercely in the distance, throwing up shivering gouts of orange flame. Figures scampering through firelit shadows.

In the dream, Armand is up close, heart pounding, chest locked so tight he has to take great shuddering gasps to breathe. The figures dance, taunting. Things arc out of darkness, tumble through the columns of light and shatter and explode into flames on the road, on the rubble heaps. Armand feels a burst of anger and raises his gun, and then he's standing over a bundle of rags, firing into it, hosing it with bullets, and it dances as if the bullets are a wind, bloody chunks flying away, and it rolls over and shows a starved child's face, black skin stretched over the bones of its skull, lips stretched back from long teeth, its woolly hair turning red with the first stages of kwashiorkor.

Armand feels sick, remembering. If these are Mister Mike's memories, and not just nightmares, Mister Mike has done some terrible things, even worse than what he does now when he comes back into the world. Armand wipes his nose on his scarf – and freezes, because he hears light footsteps on the creaking floor. Two sets of footsteps. The Twins are here.

They always find him, no matter where he hides. It is uncanny. He always hides in a different place, and there are so many different places to hide, overground and underground, but the Twins always find him. Armand is scrunched behind the heavy pianola, at the back of the big dark room, quite out of sight, but the Twins track straight across the room, calling softly:

'Loup Loup Loup.'

'Loup Garou.'

'Loup Loup Loup.'

Two pairs of hands grip the top of the pianola. It tips forward and falls on its face with a tremendous discordant crash. Armand jumps up, choking on the rush of pungent dust.

The Twins look at him, turn and look at each other, and giggle as if at a secret shared thought. They are small and skinny, dressed in their customary ragged desert combat gear. Jackets and trousers that are too big for them, splotched with brown and grey, steel chains wrapped around and around their waists for belts, high-topped baseball boots. One pair pink, the other blue. It is the only way you can tell the Twins apart. They have identical feral faces half-hidden by shoulder-length black hair cut ragged. Their faces are painted blue, and their eyes flash with a startling whiteness under the solid bar of their eyebrows. Armand doesn't know their names – but it doesn't really matter, because they are never apart. The Twins are one mind in two bodies. They smile down at him, showing small white teeth in pale, pulpy gums.

'You're a bad boy,' one says.

'A very bad boy,' the other adds.

Armand puts his hands over his ears and starts to moan. He doesn't want to hear this, but the Twins only laugh and start to dance around and shout at him, growing more and more gleeful.

'Mister Mike is coming out—'

'Mister Mike is coming out to play—'

'She is only a little girl—'

'A poor little—'

'—sweet little—'

'—homeless little black girl—'

'—but Mister Mike will hurt her bad—'

'—hurt her bad nasty—'

'—if we let him. And we might let him—'

'—just this one time—'

'—we might let him—'

'—do what he wants, because you won't be a good boy—'

'—you won't love us—'

'—and that hurts us—'

'—so we're going to hurt you!'

The Twins aim kicks at Armand and chant:

'If you won't be good, no more soma!'

Armand scrambles up. No matter how he tries to stay calm, the Twins always goad him until he has to run. They like to chase him, and when they're tired of that, they send the goblins to make sure he's brought back.

Armand runs down Main Street towards the castle. Its blackened, pointy towers claw a grey sky. He runs past broken storefronts, past clapboard buildings, scabby with peeling paint. Drifts of wet, black leaves are piled up along the edge of the raised pavement. Graffiti everywhere, garish scribbles, the slogan *A bas le Mouche!* over and over, the swirling patterns of the Folk that Armand doesn't dare look at because they'll suck out his soul if he lets them.

The Twins call after him. He stops and turns, and sees that they have guns. Real guns: on the other side of the street, a window shivers to pieces and bits of rotten wood explode from a sagging post. The frightening thing is that the Twins are such bad shots they're more likely to kill him by mistake than by design.

The Twins shriek with laughter and pose for each other, blowing smoke from the barrels of their pistols. Armand runs on. They won't hurt him. They can't hurt him, or not badly, because they need Mister Mike. One day they'll kill him, but not yet.

It's no use hiding, but Armand runs on anyway, runs until he has to stop, sick at heart, a knife twisting in his side. No use hiding, but he goes to visit the Algerians who for the last year have been camped out in the dry basin of one of the lakes.

They live in the submarine that is forever stalled in its tracks. It's actually more like a tram than a submarine, with a row of windows down each side, although it does have saw-toothed fins and a conning tower complete with periscope. For some reason, the previous set of tenants, a bunch of aging ravers, painted it yellow. They've gone now; they fell from grace with the Folk. But Armand thinks the submarine looks cheerful, a tropical fruit nestled in the little concrete basin amongst faded plaster corals, fake giant clams and plastic seaweed.

There are about a dozen Algerians, although they are never all there at the same time. Like almost everyone who has fallen under the glamour of the Folk, they are fringers. Ineligible for the Universal Unearned Wage, they subsist on Red Cross handouts and their own wits. The Algerians make jewellery from scraps of copper and steel mined in the Magic Kingdom, and they travel into the city to sell it, although of course that's not the real reason for going into the city. They have been touched, changed. They are with the Folk, now.

Sometimes they are allowed to have a woman or two with them, but never for very long. They say wistfully that there are not enough women, because in their country boy babies are preferred. It is against Allah to determine a baby's sex, but there it is, everyone does it. But they are happy enough. The Folk compel them to be happy. They work at their jewellery and smoke kif, with a TV showing the broadcasts from the Saudi Makkah 2 satellite, or a little radio playing rai, the high voices of the singers twisting like fine silver wire. Sometimes, at night, the Algerians play drums for hours on end, and their piebald dogs howl along, echoing across the abandoned theme park.

The Algerians take Armand in, feed him stew from their perpetually simmering pot, serve him strong, sweetened coffee in a tiny copper cup. Armand has learned to take off his shoes before entering the cramped living space inside the submarine, to eat only with his right hand, to slurp his coffee to show his satisfaction, and to always drink more than one cup, even when he doesn't need it. He's a guest after all, he should behave in the expected way. It doesn't cost him anything, and the Algerians appreciate it.

Armand once had a special friend amongst the Algerians: Hassan, the youngest, with sad brown eyes and a thick drooping moustache. It was Hassan who told Armand that he had been in the Foreign Legion – the red dot on Armand's wrist is a military ID chip. Hassan, who liked to play around with electronics, used a modified supermarket scanner to read the chip's data into the Algerians' portable computer. But most of the data was corrupted; all the chip yielded was Armand's date and place of birth. He was born near Lyon, a town called Chambéry. He remembers nothing about it. And he is exactly as old as the new Millennium, one of Midnight's Children. Although, as Hassan pointed out, the real Millennium is almost five hundred years away, the Algerians still regard this coincidence as auspicious. Perhaps this, as much as Armand's politeness, is why they tolerate him. Hassan said that if he had better encryption facilities he might be able to recover more details – but then Hassan disappeared.

Armand misses Hassan. It's bad to miss people in the Magic Kingdom, they come and go so quickly, but Armand especially misses Hassan because he wants to know more. He remembers so little of his life before the Folk. He was ill once. He was living here. The woman came, bringing the Twins and gathering together the Folk. And now she is gone, and the Twins rule in her place.

After a while, having satisfied the rituals of hospitality, the Algerians get on with their work. Armand sleeps dreamlessly until he is woken by the howling of the Algerians' piebald dogs.

The oldest of the Algerians says, 'They come for you.' There is a white rat on the old man's shoulder. Its head darts from side to side as it sniffs the air; its claws are hooked into the red strands of the man's mesh jumper. Armand would like to take that rat and swing it by its tail and smash its head in. They are sneaks and tattle-tales, the rats.

'Afreets,' another Algerian says. He is smiling but at the same time trembling, and tears glisten on his cheeks. He says with an effort, still smiling his terrible fixed smile, 'We are grateful you came, Armand, but now you must go.'

Armand thanks the Algerians for their hospitality, and, sick at heart, climbs out of the conning tower. It is almost sunset. The dogs howl and bark amongst the lake coral and seaweed, straining at the limits of their tethers. They are barking at the figures ranged along the edge of the basin. The Folk have come for their warewolf.

3
Lost Children

The Mobile Aid Team hits the recyclers' Bidonville late in the winter afternoon, its half a dozen vans and cars wallowing down the deeply rutted track with sirens wailing and blue lights whirling. Dr Science has rigged up a couple of strobes on his ancient methane-powered Citroën 2CV, and their stuttering white light freeze-frames the children running towards this circus. As he pulls out at the edge of the Bidonville, Dr Science fires his flare gun through the 2CV's open sun roof and green light bursts high above in the darkening sky.

Morag Gray, climbing out of the back of the mobile dispensary, sees the flare and instinctively flinches. Flares in the night sky beyond the wired perimeter of the refugee camp almost always preceded bursts of gunfire, as border guards hunted down people infected with the loyalty plague who were trying to cross the river.

Children are already flocking around the members of the Team. Morag pushes lollipops into clutching starfish hands until the pockets of her ankle-length quilted coat are empty. The ragged children chatter excitedly, their breath puffing into the air. Dr Science, like a ginger-haired pirate in his sheepskin jacket and tight blue jeans, casts handfuls of boiled sweets left and right into the growing crowd as he strides towards the young priest who is waiting in the lighted doorway of the makeshift chapel.

Jules and Natalie run up the mobile dispensary's rear door and switch on the spots above it. Jules throws Morag a black bag, and together they set off down the narrow track that runs down the centre of the Bidonville.

Filthy water runs beneath duckboards patched together from scrap plastic. Shacks and hovels stand shoulder-to-shoulder, some sturdily built from packing cases and flattened chemical drums, some no more than sacking draped on rickety framing. Biolume lamps and candles frame scenes of shabby domesticity: a man hunched at a table, smoking a cigarette with a weary voluptuousness; a woman washing a naked toddler who stands shivering in a plastic bowl; children silhouetted by TV flicker.

And everywhere there are the signs of meme infection, the effluvia of a hundred cults and crazes codified in fembot form and acted out by infected refugees too poor to be able to afford the universal phage which protects against the pranks of meme hackers and the predation of cultists. There are shrines to the unborn Messiah and to the UFO corn cult; a shingle advertises E-metering; scribbled tags proclaim that *Elvis Lives!* or *Bob Knows!* (spray-painted on the wall of a shack, the top-hatted, heavy-jowled silhouette of Papa Zumi promotes a chill of recognition in Morag); the distant sound of a drumming circle.

The marsh stink of the nearby dumps permeates the cold air; scraps of paper blow everywhere. Bulldozers, engines bellowing and blowing clouds of black smoke, are working on a ridge of com-pacted rubbish that rears above the roofs of the shanty town. People walk backwards in advance of the bulldozers, raking quickly through the trash turned over by the blades. It's dangerous work. The bulldozer drivers, isolated in airconditioned cabs, won't stop if anyone stumbles. Last week, Morag helped amputate both legs of a fifteen-year-old boy who was run down by a tipper truck. Beyond the softly rounded ranges of the trash heaps, the towers of the Magic Kingdom prick the neon glow of the Interface, the free trade zone where the corporate scouts, the curious, the crazies and the grey marketeers hope to make something from scraps traded or dropped by fairies.

Morag and Jules split up, stopping wherever someone calls to them. Many of the people know them by names; some even want to pay what they can, and Morag always takes what's offered because it's important to their dignity. Most of the inhabitants of this Bidonville are originally from Africa; those who know that Morag worked in the Sudan joke that like her they made the mistake of coming here to escape the loyalty plague.

It's Sunday, and there's plenty of work to do. There are the usual childhood illnesses, the diabetics who will never be able to afford gene therapy, and those with cancer or full-blown AIDS, with tuberculosis or antibiotic-resistant cerebrospinal and blood infections. Eye and skin infections are common; so is asthma. There's a particularly intractable strain of viral TB going through the Bidonvilles, too, and one of Morag's tasks is to try and vaccinate every poor body in this shantytown, whether they want it or no.

It takes a lot of persuading in some cases. Psychotics believe that anything from a hypogun must be some kind of fembot that will scramble their brains – not actually unreasonable, given that there are plenty of meme hackers and love bombers who go around doing just that. Morag was hit by a love bomber a few weeks ago, soon after she arrived in Paris. She saw a golden sphere float down and engulf her in a swarm of lights and a feeling of overwhelming peace. The transient stimulation wore off after thirty seconds, leaving her with a dumb expression that no doubt caused the gowk who zapped her to cream his pants.

All this, and the Saturday night specials to deal with, too. Takings from begging are highest on Saturday, and as well as all the usual problems there are minor knife and gunshot wounds, broken bones, alcohol poisoning, the residues of bad trips, and neurological damage caused by meme infections gone wrong.

One teenage girl is suffering multiple fits because someone in the Interface hired her for sex and instead zapped her with a new kind of fembot, which is the Interface in a nutshell. Morag tags the girl and uses her phone to check the taxi-ambulance's schedule with its driver, a tall laconic Pole called Kristoff, tells the girl's mother that someone will be here to take her daughter to hospital in twenty minutes or so, and moves on.

It's dark now, and freezing mist mixed with smoke from cooking fires swirls between the shacks. As Morag steps outside, the mist parts like a curtain and she sees a little girl standing in the middle of the pathway.

'Someone woke me up,' the little girl says.

She's no more than three or four, with glossy black skin. Beads and washers and bits of circuitry are woven into her tightly braided hair. She clutches an orange welfare blanket around her shoulders.

'You had a dream,' Morag tells her.

The little girl shakes her head and says solemnly, 'I'm scared.'

'You had a dream,' Morag says. 'I'll take you back to your mother.'

'My father,' the little girl says stoutly. 'And there's Gabriel, too.'

'Let's find them,' Morag says, and takes the little girl's warm, sticky hand.

A young man with cropped hair sits on an upturned crate, looking up at the sky with an unblinking stare focused on infinity. He glances at Morag and the little girl, and says blissfully, 'They're here. I saw their lights.'

The little girl leads Morag to a low, burrow-like shack. There's a kind of trolley outside, stacked with neatly folded cardboard. Inside, the little girl's father is asleep in a nest of cardboard. He is fully clothed, even wearing his boots; trench foot is endemic in the Bidonvilles. A chubby little boy in a ragged grey jumper sleeps in the crook of his aim.

Morag wakes the man. He is drunk or drugged, and hardly knows where he is, but he gives up his ID card readily enough. He must be asked for it at least a dozen times a day, even more if the cops have decided to especially hassle the recyclers for need of anything else to do.

Morag swipes the man's ID through her reader and learns that the little girl's name is Grace; the little boy, Gabriel, is her twin brother. They are Tutsi refugees from the last but one coup in Burundi. The little girl's mother died last year. Morag settles the little girl beside her father and brother, tucks the blanket under her chin.

The little girl looks up at Morag solemnly. She whispers fiercely, 'They wanted me to go with them!'

'Who did, dear?'

'The fairies.'

Morag smiles. 'You were dreaming, dear.'

'They were like monkeys,' the little girl says, and yawns, showing white milk teeth in pink gums. 'They sent in rats first. Little white rats.'

'Then you really were dreaming, dear. There aren't any white rats here. Go back to sleep, now.'

Dream about cute white rats, with lively red eyes and adorable pink noses and neat wee paws. Dream of something nice.

Morag meets up with Jules an hour later, in a shack at the far edge of this part of shantytown. Jules, a raffish Algerian barely out of medical school, is stitching a wound in the scalp of the shack's owner, an old black man who believes he once ruled the world. It is a delusion spread by a meme that was very common last year.

The old man is sitting on a web chair and leafing through a copy of *Vogue* while Jules, working by the light of a penlight stuck in his headband, puts in close neat stitches. He doesn't like to leave a scar. It is a serious point of honour. The voices of advertisements whisper and sing as the old man flips the magazine's pages. There are stacks of glossy magazines in the shack, and bales of flattened foil tied with bright blue or yellow nylon tape. Apart from the chair, the only furniture is a bed of warped plywood on cinder blocks and a wall-hanging TV with no sound that is showing the latest pictures from the Mars Expedition. The long arrow of the ship hanging at a tangent above Phobos's sooty surface; a shot of the rosy, battered face of Mars; a gaunt crop-haired woman in coveralls turning from a bank of instruments, giving a slow-motion wave. The TV's plastic screen is badly scratched, and washes of solarization bleed from the edges of anything that moves.

A battered radio lying on the rumpled sleeping bag on the bed is playing some kind of rai dub. The old man taps his feet, keeping perfect time to the five over eight beat: to hustle a little change, he sometimes beats out complex rhythms on an old cardboard box beside the Métro entrance at Les Halles.

Morag knows better than to sit on the bed – lice – and instead squats in the doorway. She wants some of the coffee in her flask, but because there isn't enough to share with the old man, she'll wait until Jules is done.

The old man winces, and Jules says, 'Courage, my friend. This will not take long.'

'I could have gone to the hospital,' the old man grumbles. 'In the old days . . . But I forgive you, my son. I'll remember everyone who has helped me once I regain my sky-borne throne . . .'

'We are pleased to be of service for you,' Jules says, and winks at Morag. He never seems to get tired.

The old man jabs his finger at a picture of a woman with a graceful profile and a long, elegant neck, and says, 'She was my consort. We lived in a palace of marble and pearl amongst the clouds.'

It is a picture of Antoinette, the vironment supermodel who

two years ago was discovered living in a Bidonville less than half a kilometre away, who has given up her contract with InScape to pursue some vague political campaign. It was all across the networks six months ago, but little has been heard of her since.

'She's a pearl, all right. Dream queen of the dumps.' Jules ties off the black thread, pats the old man on the shoulder and tells him to sleep, and next time go to the hospital if he gets hurt in town.

'I hate queues,' the old man says. 'I passed a law, you know, to ban them, but my enemies overturned all my good works. Anyway, I knew you come here today.'

'Even a day here with an open wound is to risk getting it infected, my friend,' Jules says, and tells Morag, 'Kids mugged him for change. Can you believe it?'

The old man says, 'They were amateurs. All they stole was an hour's takings, they didn't even look for my stash. Next time I'll have a knife ready for them.'

'And what if they have a knife for you?' Jules says, serious now. 'My friend here will give you a shot, then we're done. We'll leave you to watch the expedition getting ready to step into history.'

'Is it real? I thought it was some movie.'

Outside, it's freezing now; Morag is glad of the thermal skins she wears under her jeans and quilted silver coat. The taste of the dumps is in her mouth. She rinses it out with lukewarm coffee from her flask and pushes aside the wish for a cigarette.

Jules has a flyer. He shakes it out, and its tinny speaker crackles the crude threat printed in French and Arabic on its shiny black surface in dripping red characters.

We give notice that the garbage will be cleared from the dumps within the week.

'Posted all over here Friday,' Jules says. 'The people tore most of them down. They say it's from the Interface, but how do you prove it?'

'Dr Science will tell the police, I suppose.'

'Of course, but the police probably distributed the fliers.'

Morag tells Jules about the girl who was zapped, and Jules shrugs. 'That's nothing new.'

'I suppose not.'

'They come in at night,' Jules says, 'and try out their latest ware on these poor people. And we get to clear up after them. The more complex the meme, the more distributed memory it parasitizes, and the more damage it causes. They come up with the cutest things. Last month, just before you arrived, I had this guy who was convinced that Paris was populated by dinosaurs.'

Morag says, 'My flatmate has one of those pet microsaurs.'

'You see them in the park sometimes,' Jules says. 'Kids get tired of them and let them go. But they need some kind of special food, and don't live long out in the world. Let's go back. You must be freezing.'

'It's not as cold as Edinburgh must be, but Africa has thinned my blood.'

Someone is standing and shouting in the middle of the street. Tendrils of smoke and mist swirl around him. At first, Morag thinks it is the UFO watcher, but no, it is the little girl's father, big as a bear in a black overcoat so stiff with dirt that it stands like a bell around him.

He sees Morag and shouts, 'Where are they?'

Jules says, 'Take it easy, guy.'

'My children,' the man says. His eyes are red-rimmed and bloodshot; a livid scar down the left side of his face twists the eyelid askew. His breath has a sharp acetone reek. 'My children,' he says again. 'You took them. You took my Grace and Gabriel. You give them back!'

People have come out to watch, shadows in the lighted door-ways of their shacks. One of them calls to the man, saying that these are good people, they do good here.

'They took my children,' the man says, but he sounds merely truculent now.

'Your little girl was having a bad dream,' Morag says, as much to Jules as to the man. 'I'll look for her. Perhaps she went sleepwalking and took her brother with her.'

'We'll all look for them,' Jules says, and takes the man's arm.

Morag doesn't yet feel panic: after all, the little girl and her brother can't have wandered far. But then the young, shaven-headed UFO watcher looms out of the mist and says, 'They've got them,' and points out towards the dumps and starts to laugh.

Morag and Jules exchange glances and run, leaving the man

stumbling amongst the shacks, bawling his children's names, shouting back at people who shout at him.

As she runs, Morag casts her torch wide, sending the beam dancing over furrows and piles of compacted trash in which bits of glass and metal glint and glitter like fugitive stars. She glimpses a shuffle of shadows, swings the torch back and sees small, far-off figures dart into darkness and smoke.

Jules is already running towards them. Morag follows, calling the little girl's name. Her long hair has come loose from its French braid, and whips around her face.

Although the trash has been compacted by bulldozers and tipper trucks, it is a treacherous, uneven surface. Morag flounders through shifting seams of rubbish, skids on a drift of loose plastic bags and tumbles into a soggy hollow that exhales a choking methane stench when she lands heavily on her back. She pushes up, hands sinking in something wet, flings greasy droplets from her fingertips. Ahead, two, four, six figures run in front of the glow cast by a heap of smouldering tyres. Then acrid black smoke whips around them and they're gone.

Jules says smugly, 'Need a hand?'

'Thanks,' Morag says, and grins when he recoils from her clammy grip.

'I saw them,' Jules says.

'Me too.'

'They could be trouble.'

'They have the children, Jules. Come on.'

There's a wire fence at the edge of the dumps, but Jules quickly finds a place where a section of mesh has been removed. Morag squeezes through ahead of Jules, and stumbles down the steep slope on to railway tracks.

It is the old RER line into the Magic Kingdom. Morag steps as quickly as she can between the concrete sleepers, swinging the torch-beam across two sets of gleaming rails. Ahead, the railway runs into a tunnel.

Morag waits until Jules catches up with her, and says, 'Perhaps they didn't come down here after all.'

'Perhaps we should call the cops.'

'Would they come for a couple of homeless kids, Jules?'

'What have we got to lose? Besides, a train is coming. Feel the breeze?'

A cold wind is blowing out of the tunnel. It smells of oil and electricity. Morag and Jules have actually turned to go back when they hear the scream. It is high and horrible. It doesn't sound human at all.

Morag starts to run towards it, into the tunnel. Jules is behind her. The light of her torch dances crazily over the litter-strewn tracks and greasy cables bundled along the tunnel's curving wall. Little mice run from the light, scurrying across yellow scraps of newspaper and wads of soggy leaves. A Coke can shines like a jewel.

Morag is running into a rising wind. Scraps of paper spin around her feet and whirl away. Jules catches her shoulder and pushes her against the wall as the train bursts out of the darkness, briefly lighting the tableau in the middle of the other track.

The train roars past, roars and roars in an endless flicker of empty lighted windows that tears away Morag's breath. She is screaming into its roar.

Noise unravels into mere wind. The train is gone.

Jules snaps on his own torch in time to catch the figures scattering from a bundle lying between the rails. Half a dozen children, and a man running after them. The children run with an odd hunched scampering gait. The man turns, his face white in the torchlight. Then there's a flat snap and something strikes sparks from a rail and whoops away down the tunnel.

Morag has heard enough gunfire to know what it is, and throws herself to the oily gravel between the tracks. Jules crouches beside her. He has switched off his torch. There's another shot, then a long silence.

'Nine millimetre semi,' whispers Jules, who grew up in La Gouette d'Or, in the middle of the block wars between gangs of the established Algerian population and the new wave of Algerian refugees fleeing the Jihad.

'We have to go and see,' Morag whispers back.

The bundle discarded between the rails is the body of the little girl. She's been stripped, and lies as if flung carelessly beneath a symbol daubed in white on the grimy concrete of the tunnel wall.

For a long moment this symbol holds Morag's attention. It's a kind of blot-shaped spider, an intricate collision between a pair of jagged mandalas that seems to swirl, contracting in on itself.

Morag forces herself to look away. The little girl's blanket is thrown over her head, and there's a bloody flower on her naked belly. Blood is spreading under her body, shiny and black in the semi-dark.

Jules starts in at heart massage and artificial respiration. Morag leaves him there under the spidery white sign and runs on. Her phone yields a crackling dial tone when she comes out of the far end of the tunnel. Breathlessly, she informs Dr Science about what's happened, gives him the location and tells him to call the cops.

The towers of the Magic Kingdom's fairytale castle claw the neon orange sky on one side of the railway line; on the other, the Interface is a curtain wall of light. Warm yellow rectangles of hotel windows, the jerky swarming pastels of corporate ads, the ghost-light of holographic logos. As she stumbles along the track, Morag can hear the distant screeching of dozens of competing sound systems and the continuous whitenoise roar of the huge blowers which create an air curtain screening the Interface from the Magic Kingdom's infested atmosphere.

Someone shouts at Morag. She pushes hair from her face and looks around, sees a man gesturing at her from the top of the embankment. As she climbs up the slope of long, wet grass, she shouts back, asking if he's seen people coming this way.

'With a little boy? You saw them?'

'I've been busy.' He's a tall skinny teenager, his face mostly hidden by a black mask and bulky goggles. He wears leather jeans and a black puffer jacket that makes him look like an unexploded hand grenade. A computer hooked to his belt is wired into his goggles. He's some kind of penetration jockey or perimeter peeper, a kid using stealth remotes to pry the fairies' defences, looking for a thrill, or for information he can sell on. Plenty try it, but none have made more than a hundred metres into the Magic Kingdom, not even the jockeys who work for the corporations. He peers at Morag through his goggles and says suspiciously, 'You security?'

'I'm looking for a little boy. Someone took him.'

'I wouldn't know about that. I was pretty far in, bearing past Big Thunder when I was trashed. Didn't see what hit, just this flashover—'

'You didn't see anyone with your gizmo?'

'I based it on the last generation of Mars rovers. It's way smaller, of course, but it can tackle forty degree slopes, can move fast on the flat, and has cockroach wiring for random evasion of moving shadows. Not fast enough, it turns out.'

Morag wants to shake him. 'But did anyone get through the perimeter?'

'No one can get through the perimeter, that's the point. Hey, you know, you shouldn't be here without a mask. Fembots drift over all the time, you could get your mind changed in an instant.' The peeper's goggles film over, like little mirrors, then clear. He says, 'Death Star guards on the way,' and runs off towards the lights of the Interface.

The security force intercepts Morag as she is making her way back down the slope. There are half a dozen of them, all masked like the peeper. They wear a variety of quasi-uniform tunics or jumpers and are armed with semi-automatics, tasers, gas canisters and tangletape aerosols, but don't possess a single identifying logo or insignia between them.

Morag flashes her paramedic identification and tries to explain that she's chasing fairies who have taken a little boy, but the guards aren't interested. They know all about it, they say. The police are on the way and the best she can do is go back and tell them her story. Morag, beside herself with frustration and anger, says that they should be looking for the fairies and not hassling her, and the only female guard says that she can walk back by herself or be taken in and held overnight, it's her choice.

Morag stares at the guards, one after the other. 'I'll know you again,' she says, 'despite those silly masks.'

'You get yourself scanned when you get home,' the woman guard tells her. 'There's all sorts of strange shit loose in the air here. Maybe you even just thought you saw all this.'

'There's a little girl lying dead on the railway tracks, you fascist bitch.'

'Bleeding heart liberal cunt. Fuck off home.'

It's a stand-off. The guards watch Morag walk back into the tunnel. Jules is spreadeagled on the track with an armed cop standing over him, and a second cop is taking the dead little girl's fingerprints.

4
The Nest

The little boy wants to go home. He wants his father. He wants to know where his sister is.

'She isn't here,' Armand says, for what feels like the fiftieth time. 'Don't worry about her. Look at all the pretty horses!'

The little boy doesn't care. He says that he hates horses, and anyway, those things aren't real horses.

'You're right,' Armand says. He feels so weak that he might at any moment pitch forward on his face. He tells the boy, in a desperate attempt to catch his interest and distract him from this situation, 'They're not horses at all. You see, they're unicorns!'

'They stink,' the little boy says. 'This whole place stinks. It stinks and it's cold. I want to go home.'

He sits down on the artificial grass and won't be moved. He seems to have the ability to increase his weight at will, and sits as stubbornly as a limpet. He is four years old, a chubby boy with shiny black skin, dressed in filthy corduroy trousers and a baggy jumper that falls to his knees. A transparent, filmy scarf is layered around his neck. His name is Gabriel. Armand took him away from the nest when he came out of Mister Mike's dreams, with blood under his fingernails and the smell of propellant on his fingers and a deep, bad, black sense that something awful happened last night. For the second time in two days, he is hiding from the Twins.

The little boy says, 'It's stinky and it's cold here. And I saw a rat.'

Armand feels sweat stand out on the skin of his face. 'No. No, you didn't.'

The only rats left in the Magic Kingdom are spies. The Folk

dealt with the wild population, along with the feral cats that lived on them.

'I did,' the little boy says, and starts to cry. Armand tries to comfort him, but the little boy just cries louder, and says that he wants to go home.

'There, there,' Armand says hopelessly. 'There, there.'

They are in a fairyland glade, at the end of the *It's a Small World* ride. Fairyland is the last in a chain of fake landscapes stretching from Australia (a gum tree with some kind of grey stuffed bear clinging to it standing in front of a painting of a clamshell building in a harbour, and black-skinned puppets carrying spears and boomerangs) to the USA (the Statue of Liberty, a boy puppet in baseball uniform, a girl puppet in cheerleader uniform). The place has seen better days. The unicorns are waterstained, and peek forlornly from a thicket of dusty plastic vegetation. Most of the stars have fallen from the dark blue vault of the roof, and someone has uprooted the bright red toadstools and set fire to the fairies that hang above the flower-strewn astroturf, perhaps the same person who lit a fire in the litter-choked canal through which chain-driven pleasure boats once rode.

Armand sits down beside the little boy. He is so very weak. Saliva keeps flooding his mouth, and he keeps swallowing. His stomach is swollen with saliva. The wrecked glade is dimly lit by a blade of grey light that pries through a crack in the roof. Things seem to Armand to keep turning into their own shadows. He has to watch everything carefully, and his head hurts from the effort of preventing reality from betraying him. Even the air seems grey and gritty, heavy on his skin.

The boy, Gabriel, looks at Armand. He says, 'I have a headache.'

It will be an after-effect of the drug the Folk give changelings to keep them docile. Now it is wearing off.

Armand says, 'It means you're getting better.'

'My father gives me water, with this fizzy stuff in it.'

'Aspirin,' Armand says.

'That's what I want.'

'I don't have any.'

'You're no good. You don't know how to look after your guests. A good person,' the little boy says self-righteously, 'would do what a guest asks.' With the delicate dignity of a dowager in a drawing room, he uses the end of his filmy scarf to wipe a bubble of snot from his nose.

'I am looking after you,' Armand says, 'Be quiet, or they'll find you.'

'Who?'

'Monsters,' Armand says.

'What kind?'

Gabriel doesn't remember how he was taken. Nor does Armand, of course. All Armand knows is that Mister Mike came out, and that something bad happened. He says, 'It doesn't matter. They're after you. They'll hurt you.'

Gabriel doesn't believe Armand, and tells him so in a loud voice. Then he remembers where he is and starts to cry again.

Armand lets the little boy cry himself to sleep. In one part of his mind, he believes that after dark he'll find some way of getting Gabriel out of the Magic Kingdom, then say he escaped. In another, he knows that it isn't possible. He'll go without the soma as long as he can, then face the music. But he has to try. Armand is lonely. He misses Hassan. He misses human company, and the little boy is still human.

Armand falls into a kind of stupor, jerks awake when he hears the sound of goblins squabbling somewhere outside. He creeps to the end of the ride and peeks out at the cold grey afternoon. Low clouds sag over decaying buildings and snag the jagged sharp peaks of Big Thunder. No sign of goblins, no sign of anything at all, but when Armand gets back to the little fairyland grotto the boy is gone.

With a sick weariness, Armand realizes who took the little boy, and knows that he must go back underground. An open hatchway behind the tattered scenery of the grotto leads into the tunnels that run everywhere under the Magic Kingdom. The tunnels are wide enough to drive a runabout through. Luminescent brackets of fungi, growing on bits of wood jammed into the pipes and cables, shed a cold blue glow. Rooms where employees once changed into their costumes are as quiet as tombs.

Armand goes as stealthily as he knows how, but the Folk soon find him. The first is a tracker. Its eyes are like little white stones under the shelf of its brow, but sight is the least important sense underground. Its snout is enlarged, and folded in a maze of wrinkles; little maggots live in the folds of blue skin. It comes straight for him, making a wet snuffling sound. Armand stands still and allows it to pat his face with its long cold fingers.

Two more of the Folk emerge from the gloom. They are naked, their slight bodies marked in swirling patterns of raised welts. One puts a finger in Armand's mouth, and its nail painfully scrapes his swollen tongue. It sticks the same finger in its own mouth, and grins. It can taste his need.

Armand's hands are taken. With one of the Folk on either side of him, he is led deeper into the maze. A warm moist wind blows in his face, rich in pheromones. There's a tunnel where the bodies of worker dolls hang from racks, webbed with plastic tubes through which a clear pinkish goo slowly pulses. Their bellies are enormously distended by the controlled malignancies which secrete soma. Other worker dolls ceaselessly clean these living vats with darting tongues, permanently high on the traces of raw soma secreted in their sweat. The air is thick with its piercingly sweet scent.

The air grows warmer. The cracked seams of the tunnel are so crammed with fragments of rotting wood that the cold glow seems as bright as day. Armand knows where he is now. The tunnel ends in the chamber at the heart of the nest.

When the Magic Kingdom was operational, it had its own emergency powerplant. It could have kept running while all of Paris was blacked out, its amniotronic robots moving through their routines, the elevators in the four hotels rising and falling, the billion lightbulbs and neon tubes glowing. The gas turbines were stripped out after the park went out of business, and when the Queen brought the Folk here, they made their nest where the turbines once lay.

Armand is led out on to a catwalk that runs across the middle of the flooded chamber. The ends of the struts which once supported four locomotive-sized turbines rise like paired fins out of the black water. Cables dangle from the ceiling like jungle vines. One of the Folk escorting Armand suddenly jumps to the rail of the catwalk, catches a cable with hands and feet and pushes off, hooting as it swings from cable to cable and disappears into a duct at the far side of the chamber.

Armand can taste the traces of processed soma in the moist air. His tongue tinglingly swells in anticipation, like a moist pillow cushioned between his teeth. Phosphenes scribble writhing lines across his sight, dispersing and reforming every time he blinks. He aches with need, has almost forgotten why he is here. His escort makes him climb down a ladder, pats at his face and turns him around.

The Twins grin at him.

'You've been a silly boy—'

'—a very bad silly boy.'

They are lounging on a pile of foam insulation stripped from coolant pipes. The little boy is lying at their feet, sleeping with his thumb in his mouth. Slabs of concrete shelve down into black water, and a dozen of the Folk lie tangled there, slowly moving over each other. One looks up at Armand, its face blind with rapture. Beyond, a bloated doll lounges in the shallows. Its laborious breathing whistles. Plastic tubing juts from crusted wounds in its belly. It is ripe with soma, and the clear viscous fluid dribbles from the tubes, streaking the swollen blue skin of the doll's flanks. Armand's mouth fills with saliva at the sight.

One of the Twins giggles. The other says, 'We won't hurt him, Armand. The Folk want him. He won't be difficult—'

'—not like you—'

'—he'll be one of us. Oh, poor Armand, how hungry—'

'—how very hungry you look. But you've been a bad boy and before that—'

'—before that, Mister Mike was here—'

'Mister Mike was very naughty—'

'She was only a little girl—'

'—a poor little—'

'—sweet little—'

'—poor little sweet little homeless little black girl—'

'—but Mister Mike hurt her bad—'

'—hurt her bad nasty—'

'—because he loves us.'

'And because he loves us, we're going to have babies—'

'—lots and lots of babies—'

'—and you're going to help us—'

'—you're going to help us by letting Mister Mike come back—'

'—come back and help us again—'

'—because he was seen doing the bad thing—'

'—and that isn't safe for us—'

'—and it isn't safe for you.'

'So you have to help—'

'—for all our sakes—'

'—you have to help us.'

Armand's escort lets go of his hand. It walks down the concrete slope and wades out to the doll, bends and sips from one of the plastic tubes in the doll's swollen belly. Armand is tempted to try and make a run for it, but there is nowhere to go. The fairy Folk are everywhere, a murmurous presence in the cavernous space, and the Twins can always find him. Besides, the need is truly upon him now.

His tongue is heavy in his mouth, and he splutters saliva when he says, 'You won't ever hurt me because you need Mister Mike. But one day I won't let him come. You'll see . . .'

The Twins laugh and nudge each other and set up their mocking chorus:

'Loup Loup Loup.'

'Loup Garou.'

'Loup Loup Loup.'

'She'll come back! Then you'll see! She'll punish us all for what we've done!'

'Poor Armand—'

'—poor silly Armand—'

'—she won't ever come back. Not now—'

'—now we rule—'

'—and we'll rule forever.'

The Twins look at each other and chorus, 'Now eat, and be thankful.'

Armand tingles with anticipation as the blue-skinned, bow-legged fairy walks back up the slope. Armand squats down, and the fairy takes his face in both its hands. Its hot breath feathers Armand's face; then it kisses him full on his lips. Its hot

143

muscular tongue darts forward, slides between Armand's parted teeth. Soma, activated by enzymes in the fairy's saliva, rushes into Armand's bloodstream and sweetly, sweetly, he is lost.

5
Aftermath and After

The police keep Morag and Jules hanging around the murder scene for two hours before finally taking their statements, no doubt because Morag is a resident alien, and Jules, although he is a third generation Parisian, is also a *noir*. The police really were about to arrest him when Morag returned to the scene of the murder and told them in her best icy Morningside manner to unhand her colleague. They only backed off when Dr Science arrived and gave them his shuffle and jive, but they insisted on taking Morag and Jules in anyway, for statements. They had already arrested the father, and the reason they were fingerprinting the little girl's body was to check her refugee status, as if one more refugee would make any difference, especially when she was dead.

Dr Science gets Morag and Jules released after only an hour, but there is an implicit agreement that they aren't to talk to the press about this. When Morag asks what the police are going to do about the little boy, Dr Science starts in with more of his jive, and Jules turns away, disgusted.

'We have to live with the cops,' Dr Science says. 'We can't tell them what to do—' he lowers his voice, drops a hand on Morag's shoulder—'even when we know they're fucking us over. That's the thing. The good of the many against the good of the one, and so on.'

Morag shrugs off his hand. She thinks that for the most part Dr Science is an insincere old fake. Maybe the instant charm, the honey he can squeeze out to keep things sweet, was part of his act once, but now the act has taken him over. Still, she agrees to keep quiet, and Jules agrees, too. What other choice do they have?

Morag sleeps badly that night, but feels better after telling her roommate, Nina, most of the horrible story over a very Parisian lunch of *boeuf gros sel* with leeks and *navets*, and a carafe of rough red wine. Repetition weakens the horror of it a little, and the Bidonvilles seem remote and far away, there in the familiar little neighbourhood restaurant where Nina has her own napkin ring stored in a pigeonhole rack, with conversation *à la cantonnade* making cheerful noise between the tables, and Raymonde, a large woman with very long, very blonde hair, bringing the food.

Nina listens with intent sympathy. She is a paramedic at l'Hôpital Saint-Louis, and has the knack of listening, of saying the right thing. When Morag gets to the part about the security guards, Nina lights her post-prandial cigarillo with a characteristic snap of her lighter and suggests that Morag sue the bastards. Nina is a small spiky woman recovering from a messy divorce that left her, as she puts it, financially embarrassed. She is twice Morag's age and about ten times as *chic*, slim in a blue sheath dress with lots of jewellery. Light falling through the plate glass window gilds her ash-blonde hair. She leans forward and says, 'I know the name of a good prosecutor, if you need one.'

'It wasn't their attitude towards me that hurt, it was their attitude about the little boy.'

'You're worried about him, aren't you?'

'You can't help being a little bit involved. You can try not to because it's easier to cope with the situation, but then you always wonder about yourself.'

'He's probably dead, isn't he?'

'I expect so. But that's not the point.'

'Of course not. The point is what do you want to do about it? Go to the press?'

'It would be a one-day wonder, if it even got out. The Interface is very political, isn't it?'

'European political, not French.'

'Of course, I didn't mean—'

'What's the worst that can happen if you do talk to the press?'

'I'll lose my job. But that isn't the point, is it?'

'Perhaps you should take some time off, dear. Go down to Normandy. Use the cottage there, God knows that when we were still married Kazimir and I didn't use it enough, and now they're grown the children won't go near the place. Walk on the beach, get

145

all the city filth out of your lungs, and stuff yourself with creamy country food. Then decide.'

Morag tells Nina that she'll think about it, but meanwhile she absolutely has to go out with the Team tonight.

'Or I won't be able to go back, ever.'

'Well, if you're sure, but this is the second hard time you've had to go through in less than a year.'

'Oh, this, this isn't so bad. Not as bad as the camps, and I've been debriefed, I've talked it through with all the other aid workers there, I've had counselling. I'm all right, Nina.'

'Of course you are. But there's no shame if you take a rest. Do think about it,' Nina says, and Morag assures her that she will.

Morag is on her way back to the apartment when her phone rings. It's Dr Science. He wants to see her to discuss, as he puts it, last night's unfortunate occurrence. He will be at the Mobile Aid Team's depot that afternoon, and expects to see her then.

'Damn,' Morag says aloud, in the middle of the busy street. Then she turns and heads for the nearest Métro station.

The depot is a disused light engineering factory that was put out of business by nanotechnology, in the flight path of Roissy–Charles de Gaulle airport. Only Gisele Gabin is there when Morag arrives. Gisele is putting a fresh weld on the frame of one of the Team's battered vans, stroking drooping falls of sparks from the racked-up van's chassis that make vivid orange light in the depot's cold, hangar-like space. She says that she hasn't seen Dr Science all day. What is the old bastard up to?

Morag wishes that she knew. Tired and on edge, she leaves Gisele to her work and wanders about, her hands in the deep pockets of her quilted coat, until Dr Science turns up, unapologetic and distracted. He doesn't offer to take Morag into his office but talks to her right there, amongst vehicles that, charging their batteries, make a mingled drone like bees warming a hive in winter.

Morag is part of the Team, Dr Science says, she understands how important the public image is. A thing like this, well, mud sticks, that is the problem. A thing like this could be used against the Team. He appreciates her input, and her dedication. It is rare, it is what is so rewarding about his job, working with such dedicated people. So if she really wants to be part of the Team, he has in mind a place where she could help. In any case, it is time she has a fuller appreciation of the Team's activities. Helping out in the clinic will be a generous act he won't forget. And at such a stressful time like this, it will be good therapy for her to get away from reminders of the unpleasantness.

'What? What is it you want me to do?'

Morag doesn't quite understand. She is tired, and a plane passed overhead half-way through Dr Science's speech, its rebreather jets making the angled roof hum on a single deep note.

'It's not such a hard placement, and really very much less dangerous than the Bidonvilles.'

Dr Science has a knack of crinkling the skin around his eyes, making them seem to twinkle behind his round gold-rimmed spectacles. He does that now. He is a big, bluff, grandfatherly man, with vigorous ginger hair tied back in a bushy ponytail. Rumour has it that he has a pig's heart backing up his own, but that might just be malice. He is the kind of geezer who seems to grow as he ages, taking up more and more of the world's energy.

He says, 'The police don't want you going anywhere near the Magic Kingdom for now. They say it's due legal process, that you should be separated from the community there in case you're prejudiced by the rumours flying around—'

Morag says, 'If those rumours are about fairies, then they aren't rumours.'

'I understand how you feel, but we do need the cooperation of the police.'

'What about the little boy?'

'The police are looking for him,' Dr Science says. 'You know, every time I send people into the Bidonvilles I worry about their safety. You have proved your courage over and over in Africa, Morag, you don't have to prove yourself to me. You deserve a break, and given your dedication this is the best I can do.'

Dr Science's words are under Morag's skin like hooks, a confusion of duty and expediency. He is leaning on her conscience to make his job easier, she knows, but she can't find a way to say this without seeming ungrateful.

'I'm supposed to go and work in the clinic in the—'

'I know I showed you around there, just after you joined. I know you'll do well. I've seen how you work, I don't need to check up on you, do I? No, I'm sure I won't need to. Be there a little before midnight; that's when the gates are locked. And you know you can talk to me any time,' Dr Science adds, and favours Morag with a judicious, twinkling grin before striding off between the recharging vehicles, shouting to Gisele, his voice making echoes under the high roof.

Morag returns to the apartment and dozes until early evening, waking from bad dreams she can't remember. She takes a long bath and washes her hair. Wrapped in a robe, wet hair done up in a towel, she drifts into the living area, and the apartment asks if she's all right. She has been living there for almost a month, long enough for its expert system to become sensitive to her body language. When she says that she's fine, it suggests that it could make her a cup of tea.

'Maybe.'

Nina's microsaur pads across the tiles and nuzzles Morag's ankles. It's a stegosaurus, no bigger than a cat, with white fur on its fat body and black fur on the diamond-shaped plates on its back. Morag tickles it under its tiny head and it vibrates with pleasure.

The apartment says, 'I like to help.'

Morag wonders if the apartment is jealous of the microsaur. 'That's my problem, too,' she says.

The apartment emits a soft bleep, indicating she's exceeded the response capacity of its expert system.

'Just make me that tea,' Morag says.

'Of course. By the way, there's a phone message for you.'

Morag runs it. A fat man says in English, 'Dr Gray? I'd like to talk to you. Call me back.'

Morag switches off the phone as he starts to give a number. Dr Science said that he had fixed the media, but the fat man looks to Morag very much like a tabloid reporter. If she is going to tell the press about the murder and the cover-up, what better than the English tabloids, which would run away with a scandal like this? She really is tempted to do it, after the way Dr Science blindsided her with emotional blackmail that afternoon, but it would be a very big step indeed. Morag wishes she could talk to her roommate, but Nina is working the night shift at the hospital, and it would be unprofessional to page her about a personal matter.

Holding her cup of cooling tea in both hands, Morag stands at the sliding glass door to the apartment's tiny balcony, staring out at the view. Necklace strands of streetlights are strewn over the mosaic of the darkening city, dwindling towards the floodlit, clustered towers of La Défense. The apartment building is in the twentieth arron-dissement, Belleville-Ménilmontant, where ribbons of apartment blocks, housing impoverished, rootless middle-class professionals and students of the City University, surround unreconstructed rural streets colonized by artists and counterculture freaks.

Morag likes the arrondissement's shabby gentility, its air of having missed the Millennium and the flight of most of the city's population to the ribbon arcologies. There are quiet neighbour-hood bars, traditional *boulangeries* with second Empire lettering over gleaming plate glass windows, the old-fashioned cinema where customers can petition for particular films by dropping a written note in a box, a Chinese café where Nina and her colleagues from the hospital have dim-sum on Sundays. Morag has not been here long, but she is beginning to feel that she has found a place where she could be happy.

No, she thinks, no, she won't be driven out, even by Dr Science. She's not angry at the cover-up, if that's what it is, she's angry because the bastard pushed her into a place where she couldn't say no without seeming ungrateful, disloyal. She shouldn't break her professional obligations out of spite. What it is, she thinks, is that she's in denial. The second stage of shock. There'll be grief, and then acceptance. She'll get on with her life. She'll not forget the terrible thing done to the little girl, the horrible mutilation, the missing ovaries, but it won't haunt her. She has to survive by absorbing the bad things and remembering the good.

Then Morag suddenly thinks of the poor little boy, and starts to cry and laugh at the same time. She's come away from a place where a million people committed suicide and she's greeting over one little refugee.

The tea has grown cold. She carefully rinses the cup, dries it, puts it away. She is doing everything carefully, she notices. As if the world is suddenly all eggshell.

She dries and braids her hair and dresses in jeans and a sweater, has the apartment zap a canister of three bean stew and heat some pitta bread, and eats with the TV murmuring in the living room to keep her company. She orders a taxi, a luxury she can ill-afford but one she badly needs. If she's been exiled to the Mobile Aid Team's remotest domain, at least she'll live it up a little.

All the news channels are filled with commentary and items on the Mars expedition. The astronauts are sleeping now, after working to deploy the lander. A mobot camera shows the landing site, a plain of red rocks half-buried in sand stretching away under an electric pink sky. Morag is watching this with no real interest when the TV beeps and announces that there's a news item about the Bidonvilles that might interest her.

'Show me.'

She expects to see a report on the murder, but instead it's a snippet about a march on the Interface by refugee activists. Long shots of people marching down a dark, overgrown street, holding up homemade banners. *Our bodies our selves. Keep your filthy hands off our minds. Childkillers!* A crowd milling behind a tanglewire barrier, lit by floodlights, riot police in coveralls and body armour on the other side of the wire. Stones falling out of the floodlit night and suddenly the police charging, led by half a dozen mounted officers on muscular gengineered combat horses armoured with chitinous plating on their heads and flanks. A brief commentary informs Morag that this happened about twenty minutes ago, that the crowd has now been dispersed.

Morag is surfing through the local channels, trying to catch more of the protest, when the apartment announces that the taxi has arrived. Reluctantly, she grabs her bag, puts on her quilted coat and goes down.

The fat man who telephoned earlier is waiting outside the apartment building's front door. As Morag tries to get around him, he says quickly, in London-accented English, 'I know what happened, Dr Gray. That's not what I'm interested in.'

'I don't,' Morag says, 'want to talk. You're breaking the law just being here, harassing me.'

Her heart is suddenly beating quickly. She is gripping the strap of her bag so tightly that her trimmed nails are digging into her palm. The fucking taxi is parked on the other side of the street.

'I'm not with the media,' the fat man says, following Morag as she hurries between parked runabouts. There are two kinds of fat men, those with huge behinds and those without. He's the first sort, his expensive charcoal-coloured wool suit can't hide that. A red scarf is knotted under his double chin and a black floppy-brimmed hat is pulled low on his forehead, so that his round flushed face looks like the Moon in eclipse. He says, 'Did you see who did it, Dr Gray? Looked like children, but not really children? They were fairies. Have you heard of fairies? If they saw you, you're in danger, and I want to help.'

Morag climbs into the taxi and slams the door in the man's face. He bends to shout through the glass as the taxi pulls away. 'Alex Sharkey! My name! Call me back!'

6
The Fat Man

Armand watches the fat man watch the taxi pull away. Armand is crouching uneasily amongst the tubs of shrubbery which flank the entrance of the apartment building. This part of the city, with its clean rows of apartment blocks, is not a place where he can easily pass unnoticed. His leather overcoat is torn at one shoulder, his hair is long and greasy, and he smells of woodsmoke. He has been too long in the fringe. He had trouble finding the address which the Twins gave him, and when he went into a café to ask for directions, the proprietor ordered him out and threatened to call the police.

At least Armand was able to recognize the woman straight away. The Folk took her picture from the police records computer – she is a foreigner, and has to be registered with the police. That's where they found her address, too, and the place where she works, but how was Armand to get close enough to the woman when she came straight out of the building and jumped into a taxi? And then there's the fat man. The Twins didn't say anything about any fat man.

Armand decides to follow him. The Twins don't know everything, and this might be important. Besides, although Mister Mike is standing at Armand's shoulder, Mister Mike can't come out until Armand gets close enough to the woman. And he doesn't want that, because then something bad will happen. Something bad always happens when Mister Mike comes out.

He walks quickly, this fat man. He knows where he's going. Armand follows at a discreet distance. The wide pavements are buckled and potholed, and there are potholes in the road, too, some big enough to swallow a runabout. People and money are flowing into the ribbon arcologies, and one day the rest of the world will be empty. It is a belief of the Folk. They will take the cities then. They will inherit the Earth.

Not many people about at this hour. They're all at home in their little boxes stacked into the sky, eating dinner, watching TV, pottering around the little fantasy worlds they've gardened up in VR, or lost in the prime-time interactive worlds of *Nova Prodigy* or *The Secret History of the Twentieth Century*. Armand has been there with the Twins, although he wasn't allowed to do anything, just watch. The Twins were contemptuous when he didn't understand why they were so interested in one particular virtuality character. *One day*, they said, *we'll walk wherever we want in that world, but not until she returns from it.*

An old woman walking a little dog gives Armand a look as he goes past. Armand flips her the finger and instantly regrets it. He should stay invisible. He knows that if you think you can't be seen, if you really *believe* you can't be seen, it can work.

He practises being invisible now, as the fat man walks past a little fenced-in park, its grass a vivid green under the biolume streetlights. There's a construction site beyond. One of the old apartment buildings is being refaced with architectural stromalith. Supervised by a bored cop, doll labourers are being marshalled into line by a couple of men in yellow safety helmets. A white van drives up, and the fat man stops to watch as two technician types get out.

Armand crosses the street to watch the fat man watching as, one by one, the dolls are led up to the technicians. One of the technicians holds a kind of lamp that flashes red light in the face of each doll; the other studies a handheld computer. All the while, the petrol motor of the white van idles, and its exhaust makes smoke in the cold night air. The blue-skinned faces of the dolls, each illuminated by a quick blink of light, are all the same, a thrusting muzzle, small eyes under a shelf of bone. It is the face shared by many of the first Folk, except that it is not animated by intelligence.

Armand hugs himself. His leather coat creaks in the cold. His tongue is swollen in his mouth, and he must keep swallowing the saliva that wells under it. He needs a fix. He needs to get back. But he also needs something to tell the Twins, needs to explain why he couldn't let Mister Mike do the woman at her apartment like he was supposed to.

Before the technicians have finished with the dolls, the fat man turns away and walks on. Armand follows as the fat man takes a road leading away uphill. The neighbourhood quickly changes. It is a narrow rural street, an old *pavé* with a shallow gutter down the middle to drain off water. Two and three storey houses with crumbling plaster façades shoulder for space on either side. Many have been boarded up.

Then the fat man disappears. Armand stops, puzzled, then walks slowly on up the hill and discovers an archway between two houses. Armand sidles in. There's a long courtyard running away into darkness. A rusting white Peugeot van is parked just inside the arch, glimmering in a blade of light from a lighted window above. Armand stands still until his eyes have adjusted, but except for the lighted window there's no sign of life. Mister Mike would go and explore, but Mister Mike is sleeping. Maybe he's dreaming he's Armand, freezing cold in this damp spooky courtyard.

Armand turns, and the fat man is standing there.

'Surprise,' the fat man says, and there's a faint hiss. Armand's face is enveloped in a brief fine mist of oily droplets. He blinks, and slow pulses of white light ignite in his eyes.

When Armand can see again, he is sitting down and looking up at the fat man, who is leaning against the side of the van. Armand feels a funny floating detachment. His soma thirst has receded. It's

153

still there, but feels a long way off, as if it belongs to someone else. He says, 'What did you do?'

The fat man opens his hand to show the little brushed aluminium aerosol spray, no longer than a finger. He says, 'You've been love bombed, friend. We can talk now, can't we? I hope we can.'

'Sure.'

'You were following me. Not to rob me though, I think.'

'Oh no. I wouldn't do that, not unless the Twins asked me.'

It is out before he knows it. This fat man, he is clever. Armand must be careful.

'No,' the fat man says, 'because if you were going to rob me you would have tried that before we climbed all the way up this hill. You were following me, eh? Since when, I wonder?'

'Oh, from the apartment block.'

'Of the woman. The paramedic?'

'I don't know about that.'

'Yet she's one thing we have in common, eh?'

The fat man's smile is just visible in the light from the window above his head. He has plenty of time, this fat man, but that doesn't matter to Armand. He's quite comfortable, almost happy. Eventually, the fat man says, 'We both know about fairies, don't we? Do you go to Fairyland, my friend?'

'I don't think you're my friend.'

'But they take you there, eh? When did you last get a taste? You look like you're hurting right now.'

'I can feel it, but it's OK.'

'I gave you a little dose of fembots. Just a temporary thing. That's why you feel good. Your need will come back when they die out, worse than ever. And they die out quickly. If you help me, I'll help you. I'll dose you up again. Would you like that?'

'I feel good.'

'But not always, eh? It's a hard life on the fringe. I know, I used to live there myself. Perhaps I still do, in a way. Tell me about your friends.'

'Hassan is my friend. He said I was in the Foreign Legion. He found out when I was born, from my chip.'

'Oh yes? Did your friend find out anything else?'

'Chambéry.'

'Go on.'

Armand smiles, because he has puzzled the fat man. Drool leaks from the corners of his mouth, and he wipes it away with his sleeve. He says, 'That's where I was born. Chambéry. Midnight's Child. That's what Hassan said.'

'You didn't know that, eh? You'd forgotten. Why were you following me?'

'So I could tell the Twins.'

'They're human, yes?'

'Maybe.'

'Not a woman? Name of Milena?'

'Just the Twins.'

'And they have their friends.'

'The Folk.'

'And the Folk take you to Fairyland. Where is that? Where do you go to get to Fairyland?'

Armand's tongue is pressed against his teeth and the ribbed roof of his mouth. He can't speak. Someone is at his back. He can see red earth stretching away, a dry tortured plain of red earth punctuated by columns of smoke unpacking themselves into the big sky. Things move between the columns, helicopters small as flies. The earth is shaking.

Mister Mike is here. He's weak because of the fembots, but he's still strong enough to laugh when the fat man jumps back and pulls out a taser, still strong enough to scream with laughter and run off in search of his prey.

7
The Beginning of a Great Adventure

On the taxi ride into the centre of Paris, Morag is reminded how much she loves this city, its wide boulevards, its grand buildings, its sights. A man in a full-length fur coat sitting at a café table under a haze of diffused laser light; an illuminated *pâtisserie*'s display like a horn of plenty spilling a golden heap of brioches; transvestite hookers gorgeous in skimpy skintight knickers and halter tops, hair piled high and eyes made up like peacock wings, working the traffic in the Boulevard La Villette; a file of dolls, equipped with remote viewing helmets, looking this way and that as they trot along behind an armed guide, each under control of a virtual tourist vicariously enjoying some *Paris by Night* jaunt.

There are always one or two of the splendid buildings of the last decade of the last century visible on the skyline, and when the taxi turns on to the Quai de la Mégisserie, Morag sees the great gothic cathedral, encased in light like an insect in amber, and the tops of the towers of the National Library shining beyond the Eiffel Tower. She asks the driver to let her off right there, she wants to walk.

'Don't you miss it,' the taxi driver says, when he hands back Morag's charge card. 'They're about down.'

Morag doesn't realize that he means the Mars astronauts until he has driven off. The city is gearing down towards the night. Volumes of cold air lift from the river: it feels like rain. Traffic is sparse, swishing past on the wet roads with a scared, lonely sound. Everyone locked away, sharing history by proxy. Morag passes the museum. A huge turning hologram of Mars's acned globe, bloodily luminous, hangs above the glass pyramid in the centre of the museum's big courtyard. Lines of black limos are drawn up in the street, engines idling, pouring vapour into the cold air as they wait for their passengers. The old rich flaunting their power. Morag, hunched inside her quilted coat, doesn't notice the children until one calls to her.

It is a cherubic little girl, no more than ten or eleven, with chestnut curls down around her face and a winning smile. She pushes something at Morag, some kind of book, and for a moment Morag almost takes it. Then she realizes what's happening – this is a proselytizing sweep of the Children's Crusade.

The book flops open when it falls to the pavement. Its voice, deep and slow and seductive, starts up in the middle of a sentence. The little girl deftly dips and picks up the book, shakes it to silence it, and tries to hand it to Morag again.

'Why don't you just ask for a couple of francs for a cup of coffee?' Morag says. The Crusade uses hormone therapy, and this frighteningly serious little girl is probably at least twice the age she seems to be.

'Please, mademoiselle,' the little girl says. She has seen something in Morag's face, a weakness, a hesitation. Her face shines, as if it has been scrubbed. Morag can't bear to look at it. 'Please, mademoiselle, I see you are kind-hearted. Let our love shine in your heart. Join us, and simplify your life.'

Morag manages to get past. There's a cluster of caped policemen by the museum entrance, but they don't seem to be troubled by the children who are wandering up and down the line of double-parked limos. After all, anyone who counts has been inoculated with universal phage to protect them against fembot-spread meme plagues.

But the thing that scares Morag is not the possibility of infection. It is what she saw in the little girl's eyes, in the *Gestalt* of her body language. Like the refugees infected with loyalty plague, the little girl is a hollow vessel inhabited by something alien and remote. Morag remembers the children of the camp with a special pity, their solemn yet bewildered expressions, the way they moved with a careful stiffness, like badly manipulated puppets. She walks a little faster, as if to escape her memories.

Even at this late hour, cars and runabouts swarm in tangled skeins around the Place de la Concorde. There's a big McDonald's open twenty-four hours a day opposite the entrance to the Métro station. A white van, its engine idling, is parked outside the brightly lit plate glass windows. A couple of men in white coveralls are guiding a line of dolls through a kind of door-sized frame, like a security metal detector. The dolls wear the check trousers and white shirts of service staff. Their blue prognathous faces are shadowed by the bills of their red caps. One by one, they pass through the detector frame under the guidance of one of the men, while the other watches a handheld computer.

At the Métro station, the homeless and the dispossessed are moving in to claim their space for the night. They are bedding down even as the last of the revellers stagger off the last train and hurry away up the stairs into the night. Unlike many major European cities, the Paris mass transit authority only allows the homeless in when the system closes down, at midnight. There are no permanent encampments in the Métro stations, so the paramedics and nurses of the clinic at the Place de la Concorde must necessarily work at night.

Morag is late, and the shift boss is waiting on the platform outside the clinic, ready to complain. Morag smiles and tells him that it was such a nice evening she just had to walk.

'Louis, isn't it? Dr Science told me about you.'

Louis is a sour, middle-aged man in a green gown and a white plastic apron. With his hairy arms folded above his considerable belly, he looks more like a truculent butcher than a paramedic. He says, 'Yeah? He told me about you and your friend, too. This is no rest home, let me make that clear. You two are going to work harder here than in that flying circus.'

'My friend?' Then Morag sees Jules, already gowned, talking to an old woman just inside the clinic's door, and she realizes that Dr Science has shafted them both.

The first part of the shift is busy: that helps. Around three in the morning, when the clinic is at last empty, Louis retires to sleep on a trolley in a curtained-off corner. It is his habit to catch up on his sleep once the post-midnight rush is over, he tells Morag and Jules. He doesn't expect to be disturbed except for a real emergency.

Jules and Morag sit side by side on plastic chairs in a corner of the clinic, sipping vile milky coffee under a poster for skiing in the French Alps, some healthy tanned eighty-year-old taking off in a cloud of artificial powder snow. They talk in whispers, aware of Louis behind his screen, the restless sleepers laid out along the platforms outside. They ask each other how they are, and Jules says he's pleased to see that Morag is bearing up so well.

'Because I should be weeping and wailing instead? Please, Jules. I've seen dead children before. In some parts of Africa you start to think children are dying or being killed more quickly than they're being born. Some rebel groups make them into soldiers at five or six years of age. Dose them with fembots that turn them into psychotic killers and turn them loose into the bush to hunt down and kill other children.'

'Hey. There's no need to be angry with me.'

'I'm not angry. I feel guilty. Did you see the march on the Interface?'

'Sure. That's not the first, either.'

'I should have been there, Jules. That's what I think.'

Morag finds her coffee has gone cold, and pours it into the sink. Not much of a waste: it is the same coffee that the clients get, milky and gritty, boiled and reboiled in a big aluminium urn. The clinic is a long, low-ceilinged room, its bare concrete walls shingled with a mixture of travel posters and health warnings, damp despite the space heater that murmurs to itself over the door. Green curtains on movable rails form makeshift cubicles. Apart from the sink and the steel medical supply cabinets with their big padlocks, the single locker and the coffee urn, there's little else. A TV hung high on one wall is showing the latest pictures from the Mars expedition. The face of Mars is the same furnace red as the African dirt.

Jules says, 'Let me tell you something. This isn't the first murder of its kind. I've a friend in a department of the Ministry of Technology who's been correlating reports. There have been a number of similar . . . incidents.'

'How many?'

Jules rubs his eyes. He's tired too. 'Six. Six that they know about. All involving little girls from the Bidonvilles close to the Magic Kingdom. In every case the victim's ovaries were taken.'

Morag sits down again. 'When did this start?'

'The first was almost exactly two months ago. And that bastard Dr Science knows about it, I'm sure.'

'Jules, perhaps this is not my place to say so, but you are taking this very personally.'

'Why wasn't this in the media, Morag? Six little girls, horribly mutilated. And it isn't the police, or vigilantes. My friend works in a section of the Ministry of Technology that monitors the effect of technology on social trends. You know what it is, it's the fucking Interface. Six little girls are an acceptable sacrifice as long as the goodies keep flowing out of it. And the little boy, too. Think what he—'

Morag says, 'Don't.'

Jules says in a fierce whisper, his dark eyes burning in bruised sockets, 'Why, because it might blow your fucking cool?'

'We all have ways of dealing with it. You know that.'

'Right,' Jules says bitterly, and grinds the heels of his hands into his eye sockets. Morag wants to comfort him, but she hesitates, and then the moment is gone.

Bloody cotton swabs are spilled on the floor around a big trashcan. Morag pulls on a pair of latex gloves and tidies it up. It takes a while, because she's always wary of needles. The clients don't always deposit them in the needle exchange bank outside the door. Many have odd, secretive habits, especially the disturbed ones. Morag can't blame them – so much of their lives are lived in the public eye. They eat and sleep in public, use public toilets, public washrooms. There is nowhere for them to retreat but inside their own heads – and even that can be arbitrarily violated at the whim of any teenage meme hacker or love bomber.

Jules sprawls in his chair, watching the TV. He's been talking about the Mars expedition for days now, and this is the night the astronauts are due to land. Morag sleeps a little, wakes with what feels like sand behind her eyes, and Jules tells her, 'They're nearly there.'

The TV is showing a ravelling mix of grainy reds and ochres with a brilliant dot in the centre. The dot is the Mars lander. It is firing its engine to slow it down and bring it out of orbit. The picture is being transmitted from the base camp established on Phobos.

Jules says, 'They've about four more orbits to make, and then they'll begin airbraking. They'll be down just after the end of our shift.'

Morag says that she has seen so much suffering in Africa that this seems irrelevant, and Jules shrugs. He's happier to talk about this: it's a refuge.

'There will always be suffering,' he says. 'I see this Mars landing as the forward point of progress, pulling the rest of humanity behind it.'

'Yes, and I remember the right wing economic theories of the last century, all that rubbish about creating a wealthy élite that would enrich the whole community. We're still living with the problems that caused. The whole world is. There would be no famines in Africa if its countries stopped exporting the grain they must export to finance their debts. And most of those debts are because of adventures in inappropriate technological projects, or because of massive arms purchases.'

'I agree that the world is old and tired. But here is a new one. Perhaps from that we get a perspective on this world's problems. Half the world is watching this. Six billion people.'

'And the other half don't have anywhere to live, let alone a TV set. We've enough troubles in this world, without starting on a new one,' Morag says. It sounds harsh, and she regrets it. She says, 'There is sometimes a whole hour when I don't think about the little girl, the little boy. I know that I shouldn't think about them at all. People die so easily, don't they? How many people died down here, this year?'

'Probably not more than twenty. I know what you mean. But it was very different, was it not? The way she was cut open . . . Alessi is frightened.'

Alessi is Jules's wife. Morag says, 'Oh, Jules, I'm sorry.'

'And the children sense something, too. And then this man came to the apartment this morning.'

'English? Very fat?'

'Ah. You know him.'

'He's a reporter, I think. Don't talk to him, Jules. Call the police if he comes back. I know his kind. He was harassing me this evening. Their kind would dwell lovingly on the mutilation, and not on the fact that this was a little girl living in a shack in the middle of Paris's rubbish tips.'

'We have our own way of dealing with things in La Gouette d'Or. Or at least, that's what I told him. I doubt that he'll be back.'

'You make an unlikely tough, Jules.'

Jules grins. It makes him look very young. 'It is a matter of attitude. Listen, I'm just going to check on a few patients. I won't be long.'

Morag smiles, knowing that Jules is also going out to smoke a cigarette. She needs one, too. She smoked all the time in Africa. Everyone did. But she doesn't want to start again, not now.

She dozes again, and wakes with a crick in her neck. The TV is showing half a dozen men and women talking around a table, with a vast blow-up of Mars in the background and a clock running backwards in a corner of the screen.

The coffee is a few degrees colder. Morag drinks it anyway, and goes outside to find Jules. At first she isn't alarmed when she can't see him. She walks up the platform, past the bedrolled sleepers, then back down to the other end.

A man is standing there, swaying from one foot to the other in the practised manner of those who must stand and wait out most of the day. An orange blanket is draped around his skinny frame. He has yellowing bruises around his eyes and fresh stitches in his scalp, the kind of thick black sutures that a public emergency room would put in. The skin around the raw wound is stained blue by antiseptic ointment.

The man favours Morag with a bleary gaze and says, 'I told him not to go down there. Train'll be along in a minute.'

'Jules!'

'I don't know his name. He said he saw children. He went down there.' The man, clutching the blanket to his throat with both hands, points by raising one elbow, points into the tunnel.

Morag presses the emergency button so hard she bruises her hand to the bone. She doesn't remember running back to the clinic, is so out of breath that, after she wakes Louis, it takes her a full minute to tell him what has happened. Outside, the first train of the morning roars through the station, and Morag screams into the noise.

Louis makes her sit down. He is gone a while. Morag looks at the TV screen. It is showing a close-up of jumbled, pitted red rocks. Things dumbly persist. Nothing seems changed. Her hands are shaking. She jams them together. She is feeling cold, colder and colder. She is going into shock, she thinks. Her peripheral blood system is shutting down to divert blood to major vessels, adrenalin is flooding her body. But the thought is remote from what is happening to her.

One by one, a few of the homeless enter the clinic. Timid as mice, they steal glances at Morag, then turn to look up at the TV. The view jerkily swivels to show a sweep of rocks of all sizes and then dunes saddling away, crimson under a salmon sky. The camera holds on this panorama for a few moments, then tracks sideways. A glittering segment swings down from somewhere off-screen. It is a ramp. One of the homeless has found the remote

162

control, and a man's voice suddenly blares in the clinic, explaining that the images shown are of what happened twenty-two minutes ago. We are, he says, already in a new historical era.

Louis comes back. He looks grim. The homeless briefly glance at him, turn back to the TV. Red light falls on their upturned faces. A shadow spills across the ramp, moves forward. It is someone in a bulky white pressure suit.

Louis kneels beside Morag and tells her that Jules is dead. Morag knows. It doesn't matter that she knows. Louis holds her cold hands. He won't say how Jules was killed.

'The police will be here soon,' he says. 'This is a terrible thing.'

'Someone saw him. A young guy with a shaven head. A wound, here.' Morag touches the back of her head. 'We must find him.'

'The station is open. Most of the people have left. Give his description, I'm sure the police can find him.'

'He might have killed Jules!'

'I don't think so,' Louis says.

'Hey,' one of the people watching the TV says, 'keep it quiet, eh? This is history.'

On the TV, the astronaut is standing amongst pitted red rocks at the foot of the ramp. The astronaut's gold-filmed helmet visor reflects the angular bulk of the lander, the two pressure-suited figures watching from the top of the ramp.

The commentator has fallen silent: the clinic is filled with the hiss of the carrier wave. Then the astronaut speaks. It is a woman, her voice surprisingly clear across the millions of kilometres of seething emptiness between the two worlds.

'This is the beginning,' she says, 'of a great adventure.'

8
The Poor Knight

Armand walks with the little boy through falls of soft saffron light, by crystal waters lapping a shore of ivory and pearl. He feels very calm, even though a voice is screaming in a corner of his mind. He is showing the little boy Fairyland. It is the little boy's first time, and he is confused. He wants to know where all the concrete has gone.

'This is real,' Armand says. 'The other was just a dream. There's all sorts of reality. Don't you watch TV?'

The little boy says that of course he watches TV. He likes something called Hopalong Frog, and, with the tireless, uncritical fanaticism of the very young, tells Armand about it at length. It is set in a pond in the American Wild West. Hopalong Frog is the sheriff.

'Things seem very real when you're watching them on TV. Better than the world, brighter, more real than the world. But you can't ever go there.'

'I go to sleep and see Hopalong Frog.'

'This is that dream. But the thing is, the dream is real. Don't you ever think that the people on TV might be watching you?'

The little boy says with stubborn logic, 'Hopalong Frog *does* watch me. He talks to me at the end of every show.'

Armand ignores this. He says, 'There's a switch in your head, like the switch on the TV that turns it on when you order it. What you've been given is like that switch. Now you can see things as they really are. It's a great gift. Most people live their lives without ever really seeing what the world is like.'

Armand feels strange. It is as if someone else is speaking through him, giving him these thoughts. The screaming voice is very far off, but it is very persistent. It doesn't let up because it doesn't need to gulp for breath and it can't wear its throat raw. It just screams and screams.

The little boy says, 'Will we see Hopalong Frog? Does he live here?'

'Perhaps,' Armand says.

The little boy is better now, no doubt about it. He had to be held down by Armand and one of the Twins while the other Twin laid the living communion on his tongue. But as soon as the thing had bonded, one of the Folk gave the boy his first taste of soma, and he calmed down right away. He saw.

Armand says, 'It's a huge and strange world, full of strange and wonderful people. I'm sure Hopalong Frog is out there somewhere, but I don't know where he'd be living.'

'I'm going to look for him!' The little boy lets go of Armand's hand and runs down the slope of living marble to the edge of the pool. One of the shy silken creatures that bathes there, startled, slips deeper into the crystalline water. Patterns of silvery light race across the pool, curving and multiplying and growing so bright that Armand has to look away. That's the thing about Fairyland. Its beauty is so intense that humans can't live in it all the time. Only the Folk can do that.

Armand can't see the boy any more – he's dissolved into the light. Instead, the Twins are walking towards him. Their shadows are like tunnels that lead back into the pearly glow, aping their every movement. How beautiful they are! They are clad in beauty. Their attendants scurry at their heels, clever faces aglow and bent towards their mistresses as Armand, their poor knight, receives their instructions on bended knee.

He must travel far. From the womb of light into the cold night, beyond the grim shadow of the castle, across a land where the fey fires of the fringers are scattered in the velvet dark like stars fallen to earth.

Armand hikes along a road. The lambent eyes of argosies cleave the dark, rushing onward on their own breath, glittering with little lights strung across their bulks. Their sonorous voices boom and howl, and again and again Armand staggers into the motorway ditch, clutching his ears, his clothes flapping around him in the backdraught of the hovertrucks. He can hear the screaming still. He can never travel far enough to escape it.

Frosted grass creaks beneath his boots. His breath makes cloudshapes before his face and the thin wind tugs the clouds away. At the station, he paces up and down the platform, shivering as he waits for the train that will come just before the dawn to take him into the strange and terrible city. The soma is wearing off, and the tired world of things is showing through. He recognizes the voice now, although it is growing fainter and fainter. It is Mister Mike. He is screaming in rage because he isn't in charge. Not yet. Not yet. Not until he finds the woman.

9
Conspiracy Theories

Everyone is drunk, grinning like apes around the table. They raise their glasses and toss down brandy, slam the glasses on the table so hard that the flames of the candles dance. Morag is as drunk as anyone in the back of the little neighbourhood bar. Brandy burns in her stomach, and her head is dizzily stuffed with fumes. It is the evening of the day that Jules was killed, and the off-duty members of the Mobile Aid Team are holding a wake.

Michel Guidon stands, holding on to the back of his chair with one hand as he slops brandy into his glass with the other. Candle flames are reflected in his wire-rimmed glasses. It is his turn to propose a toast. Many of the doctors and paramedics of the clinic have worked in Africa, where they picked up this habit from the local aid workers. They are mourning Jules by celebrating what he did, by what he meant to each of them.

'He played chess like a demon,' Michel Guidon says. 'I remember that on hot summer evenings, when he had finished working and it was still light, he would sometimes take me to this little café in the Jardin des Plantes. There are always old men there, playing chess, maybe drinking a little beer. I've seen Jules take on three at once, and trounce them all.'

'He used to play with the Poles,' someone else says.

'To Jules and his chess-playing,' they all shout and toss down another round of brandy.

It is Morag's turn. She has enough wit left to pour herself a shot of brandy before she gets up. The room tips towards her and she plants a hand on the wet table-top to steady herself. Everyone is looking at her.

'Space,' she says, after a moment's thought. They have talked about Jules's love of jazz, his children, his work in Africa, his fierce care for his patients, the way he would painstakingly stitch their wounds so as not to leave a scar. Now she says, 'He was watching the Mars landing. He was gone before he saw the woman step out, but there were people there who would not be alive to see it if not for Jules's care.'

They all rise around her and drink to this, they all sit down and drink some more. One of the other customers complains about the noise, and the proprietor tells the man to shut up or leave, this is in aid of a good friend. The man ends up joining the party, and so does everyone else in the bar. Michel Guidon plays jazz guitar, stumbling on the runs, while everyone claps time, and then Gisele Gabin sings several plaintive folk melodies. Somewhere in the middle of this, a taxi arrives for Morag. It's close to midnight, she's not the first to leave. She stumbles towards the door accompanied by the loud farewells of her friends.

The driver, a solidly built woman in a leather jacket, helps Morag into the taxi. Morag has reached that stage of drunkenness where one accepts whatever happens next with an amused dis-interest, as if the world is a virtuality set. She doesn't question why the driver lets another passenger climb in.

It is the fat man. Just as Morag recognizes him, and belatedly remembers that she never ordered a taxi, the fat man lifts some-thing to her face.

A cold spray pricks her skin. Freezing electricity crackles inside her skull. She feels instantly sober, but she can't coordinate her movements and only bangs her elbow hard when she tries to open the door. It is locked.

'You're in danger,' the fat man says, and flinches when Morag brandishes her taser.

But Morag has it the wrong way round, and the taxi driver closes a hand over hers.

'Easy, sweetie,' the woman says. 'We're out to save you. If we wanted you dead, I wouldn't even be talking to you.'

The woman's scalp is clean-shaven except for a strip of what looks like leopard fur growing down the centre. A string of tiny skulls carved from bone dangles from her right ear.

The fat man says, 'Don't frighten her, Kat. Just drive.'

'I know who you are,' Morag says. 'I won't talk. I told them I won't talk.'

'My name's Alex Sharkey. I'm not with the press, Dr Gray.'

'Not a doctor. A paramedic.'

The taxi driver – if she is a taxi driver – says, 'She won't talk,

Alex. She is in denial. I say dump her now, find some other way. There'll be another killing in – how long to the next full moon?'

'We don't know that it's cyclic.'

The woman says emphatically, 'Always it is cyclic.' She has a German accent.

Morag meets the woman's eyes in the rear view mirror. Morag says, 'Kat, what do you know about this?'

'That's Katrina to you, little bird. Only my friends call me Kat.'

'Patience,' the fat man, Alex Sharkey, says. 'Where do I begin? I don't have the time. Truly. Nor do you. What you saw has put you in danger, you must realize that. What you have to do is tell us what you saw, and then we can help you. I promise.'

The woman, Katrina, lights a cigarette and says, 'Tell her about the good fairies and the bad fairies.'

Morag says, 'How many murders have there been? Six?'

'Seven,' the fat man, Alex Sharkey, says.

'Seven. I forgot to count the one I was involved in. All of them little girls. My friend was killed, too. And you know who did it and haven't told the police?'

Alex leans forward (Morag thinks of a mountain shifting – he takes up two thirds of the space in the back). He tells Katrina, 'I want to drive by a sweep.'

'Just do her, Alex! We can't risk—'

'I think we can. There are plenty of fast food outlets up by Les Halles. Shut up and drive, Kat. That was the deal.'

Katrina turns round and tells Morag, 'Anything this fellow tells you about deals, don't listen.' Then she starts up the taxi and accelerates into the traffic with a screech of tyres.

Even at this late hour there are crowds milling up and down the rue Berger. The half-sunken, double curve of the Forum burns from within, lit by thousands of lights and mirrors. Katrina has to bat at the taxi's horn to make way through the strollers, tourists, prostitutes, pimps, pickpockets, dealers and junkies. Kids on scooters, their puffer jackets iridescent with shifting patterns, sinuously weave through the throng. The tireless workers of the Children's Crusade are busy, begging, handing out leaflets, love bombing passers-by with instant karma when the police aren't looking. At any given moment half a dozen people are transfixed as their selves dissolve in a sea of nirvana, while half a dozen more are looking for the little bastard who zapped them. Music booms from an ambient sound system someone has set up by the Fontaine des Innocents. A big news-screen casts Martian light over the heads of the crowd. It shows a couple of astronauts in white pressure suits posing at the edge of a vast sinuous valley that, except for the soft-edged craters, could be anywhere in Arizona.

There are restaurants along the rue Berger that stay open all night, popular with junkies who know there's nothing like an order of fries to deliver the fat they crave after a hit. Morag sees a couple of flics, one with an alert Alsatian on a short leash, but they are hassling a bunch of scooterists and only the dog looks at Morag as she raps at the window.

'There's a Vietnamese place along here serves soup with testicles in it,' Katrina says. 'Want a snack, Alex?'

'Just make a left here,' Alex says. He sounds infinitely patient.

A white van is parked outside a fast food arcade. Dolls in red and white uniforms are lined up. Katrina double parks the taxi, gives the finger to a scooterist who toots his horn as he swerves past.

'You've seen these, I suppose,' Alex says, 'but I doubt if you know what they are for.'

One by one, the dolls step up to the pair of technicians. One by one, prognathous blue faces flash into sudden clarity, wink out.

'It's a test,' Alex says. 'They're screening for fairies.'

'I saw something like this last night.' When Jules was still alive. 'Only they were walking the dolls through some kind of metal detector.'

'A magnetic resonance imaging frame. This is a bit cruder, but the idea's the same.'

'None of their tests are worth shit,' Katrina says. She lights another cigarette from the butt of the first and breathes a cloud of smoke into the taxi's windscreen.

Alex ignores her. 'A fairy is a doll with enhanced intelligence and free will. To make a doll over, you take out its chip, the one that controls it when it's doing whatever it was bought to do. You put in a different kind of chip, give its synapses a connectivity boost, give it hormone treatment. The hormones are mostly to firm up the musculature; fairies are sterile unless they have reconstructive surgery, and most liberationists don't go to that trouble. The thing is, in first generation fairies all this change is on the inside. They don't look too different from unmodified dolls. But now the authorities are panicking, because they're becoming aware of the scale of what's going on. This is the result. Those techs are scanning the implanted chip of each and every doll, checking it against spec.'

'It will do no good,' Katrina says again. She cranks down the window a centimetre, flicks her half-smoked cigarette through the gap, rolls the window back up again. 'She's seen it, Alex. Let's *go*.'

'In a moment,' Alex says. 'The thing is, Morag, that fairies don't mingle with dolls. That was the mistake of the liberationists – they thought that fairies would make over the rest of the dolls, that it would be an autocatalytic liberation movement. But fairies aren't like dolls. They aren't even much interested in dolls. That's why this sweep is doomed.'

'Why don't the authorities do something about the Magic Kingdom?'

'There are fairies,' Alex says, 'and then there are fairies. Most kinds are harmless, and so they don't attract attention. You've encountered a set whose lifestyle is not, let us say, invisible. They've come out, they're trading for their existence, and that's the problem. They've bought themselves protection.'

'They took the little boy and they killed his sister. They killed all the other little girls, too, didn't they? And Jules. The things killed Jules. And you know why, and you haven't told the police!'

Alex doesn't answer. He's looking at the techs processing the dolls in front of the fast food outlet.

Katrina says, 'You've said too much, you silly fucker. Why does she need to know anything?'

Morag says, 'Because if I tell you anything, I want to know why. I want to know if we can get the little boy back.'

'We don't need to bargain—'

'Kat,' Alex says sharply. Surprisingly, the woman is silent. 'We can't talk here,' Alex adds. 'Do you really want to know, Ms Gray?'

'Are you part of the underground? I thought that the liberationists disbanded years ago.'

'Mostly,' Alex says. 'Some were arrested, some just gave up, some were absorbed, as it were, by their own creations. But there are still evolutionary changes going on, and something is driving that.'

'You won't find her,' Katrina says, 'not after all this time.'

'Maybe not,' Alex says. 'Let's go, eh?'

Katrina pulls a U-turn right there in the street, sounding her horn as she noses through the crowds. A vagrant lurches forward and starts smearing a rag across the windscreen. Katrina snarls and punches a switch on the dash. Fat blue sparks snap at the vagrant's fingertips and he jumps back, swearing and shaking his burnt hand. Katrina puts her foot down and aims the taxi through a gap in the crowd.

Morag tries to keep track of where she's being driven. Somewhere in the north east, she thinks, which makes it easier, because that's where she lives. These people don't strike her as particularly dangerous, or even professional at what they are doing. They obviously know something about the liberationists – perhaps they are a remnant of some cell or other of the fabled movement that, in the second decade of the century, did threaten to change the status of dolls from enhanced animals to legally protected human beings. But the liberationists foundered as all revolutionary movements founder if they do not quickly force and win war against the state. They broke up because of attrition by police actions, because of disaffection and internecine squabbling, because of exhaustion. People grow older, lose their fervour. They get a job, get married and settle down, have children.

Morag feels that bourgeois gravity herself, from time to time, the tremendous inertia of doing what is expected, of disappearing beyond the eventual horizon of marriage. She knows that she fled Edinburgh because of it.

The taxi takes a bridge over the Canal Saint Martin into the serried ranks of apartment buildings of Belleville-Ménilmontant. They are perhaps a kilometre from where Morag lives. The fat man, Alex Sharkey, is fussily scrolling through a note pad. The tiny light that illuminates the slate strikes him under his chin, catches a spark in each of the lenses of the little round spectacles he has hooked over his ears. He reminds Morag of a portrait of James Boswell, not at all like a dangerous underground revolutionary. And for all her tough talk, Katrina is more like a louche punk than a coldly efficient hitperson.

They are a couple grown old together, Morag thinks, their squabbling an affectionate habit. With that thought, Morag discovers that she is not frightened. The dose of whatever it was that sobered her has left her weak and lightheaded, but she has been in worse situations than this.

In the camps that sheltered refugees infected with the government loyalty plague, there was the continual ominous presence of Papa Zumi's secret police, smart young men in video shades and crisp white shirts and black suits. Armed with machetes and machine pistols, they made random tests on men, women and children, and executed those who failed to measure up to their parameters. They didn't live in the camps, but every morning drove in, in Mercedes and BMWs, from the five star hotel in the nearby town. The aid workers had to negotiate with the secret police every day, and at least once a week Morag was threatened by one of them. Until the terrible day at the very end, their regime was marked by sudden, random acts of extreme violence.

And before that, there was the time when she was out in the bush treating children for river blindness, and a minor Somali warlord stopped her Land Rover and held her hostage for five days. He was charming, Oxford-educated, and never once made an overt threat. Morag was given her own room in his rambling compound, was well fed and could talk to his wives. And yet she was in a constant state of terror.

There was an oppressive feeling in the compound, as if the air was under pressure, and lacked about half the normal amount of oxygen. Look out of any window and there would be two or three men in ragged combat dress, toting Malaysian Kalashnikov copies, heavy machine guns, one-shot light antitank weapons. And there were the sounds at night, off beyond the compound's perimeter. Human screams, faint but vivid, single shots like whipcracks, a truck motor idling for half an hour before being abruptly switched off.

When Morag was released, after some high-powered manoeuvring of which she'd been completely unaware, and was actually allowed to drive off in her own Land Rover, she got about ten kilometres down the rutted red dirt road before she started shaking so violently she almost turned the Land Rover over, shivering as if from malaria, then attacked by vomiting and diarrhoea. She dosed herself with morphine and managed to make it to a checkpoint manned by government soldiers before collapsing.

That was fear. That was terror.

The taxi jounces up a steep street. Beyond bare trees, lights of apartment blocks are sharp in the cold night. There's a bridge over a railway line, and then the road gives out in a cobbled *impasse* where nineteenth century houses of six or seven storeys stand behind railings and overgrown gardens.

It is one of the little pockets of old Paris that escaped the grand redevelopments of the last quarter of the twentieth century, surviving the new regime like dowager princesses exiled in coldwater flats. Although Morag lives right here in the arrondissement, she has only a vague idea where she is now.

Katrina cuts the taxi's engine and lights, gets out and opens the door for Morag who, as she climbs out into cold damp air, feels a wave of nausea rise through every cell in her body. She falls to her knees and throws up luxuriantly into the gutter in the centre of the street.

When she stands, wiping chyme from her chin and blinking chill tears, Alex is unlocking a gate in a tall iron railing. Katrina gets a shoulder under Morag's arm, helps her along. There is hard muscle in the woman's arms and torso. She radiates heat and a peppery scent compounded of cigarette smoke and incense.

Inside the house, in a room with a creaking wooden floor muffled with ravelled Turkish carpets, Morag sits on a plastic folding chair and sips warm orange juice with a couple of spoonfuls of sugar stirred into it while Katrina lights clusters of candles set on a heavy oak sideboard. The buttery glow of the candle flames gleams on her shaven scalp either side of the strip of leopard fur – it is real fur, a genemod epidermal treatment.

There's a sleeping bag balled up in one corner of the room, mouldering piles of old paperback books stacked along one wall, a few more folding chairs, a computer deck with goggle and mitt attachments. The deck is jacked into a phone plug; a single red light indicates that it is active. The vinyl of the mitts is cracked, and patched with silvery duct tape.

Alex returns from somewhere deeper within the house, takes a bite from the pastry in his hand, and says around it, 'He's coming.'

'Who?' Morag asks.

'A friend,' Alex says. 'This is very convenient for us. Out of the way, not overlooked, and with the railway line in the cutting behind that's mostly used at night. Anyone who's ever taken a sleeper train out of the Gare du Nord has passed by this place, but hardly anyone bothers to look out the window.'

'It looks like you're camping here,' Morag says.

Alex sits, not on one of the folding chairs, which would probably have collapsed under his weight, but on the carpeted floor. He takes his time, breathing heavily. When he's comfortable, he says, 'I met up with Kat about three years ago, in Amsterdam. She helped with some unpleasantness there.'

Katrina says, 'You think she needs to know?'

'Kat's brother was taken by fairies,' Alex says. 'She was hunting them down. So was I, but for a different reason. I was looking for the woman who started it all, although I find it hard to think of her as a woman. I knew her in London, and she was only a little girl then, you wouldn't think anything to look at her. She made over a doll into the first fairy, and escaped with it. Others started doing it soon after, but she was the first. She spread the idea, and the chips and the nanotechnology necessary for it. I've been looking for her ever since.'

Katrina starts to hum a tune. 'That Old Black Magic.'

'Well, it's probably true,' Alex says. 'I think she did infect me with something to make me loyal. Glamour is like love, only deeper, at a cellular level. I've never found her, only traces, hints. But now I'm certain she's in Paris. Or at least she was, until recently. What do you know about these murders, Morag?'

'What will you tell me?'

'What do you want to know?'

'There are two things. I want to save the little boy.'

Alex looked at Katrina, then nods. 'OK.'

'You think he's dead.'

'No, not dead. Changed, perhaps. But he might be saved. They haven't had him long.'

'Bullshit,' Katrina says, and stalks out of the room, banging the door frame with her fists as she goes. Candle flames bob in her wake like boats on a black, stormy sea.

'It happened to her brother,' Alex says. He pulls a tin from a zippered pocket of his jerkin, pops its lid and uses two fingers to scoop beans and franks into his mouth. Chewing noisily, he adds, 'They took him when he was three, and we found him four years later. No hope.'

'But these things have only had the little boy a few days.'

'Fairies. Never think of them as things. They are living, breathing, autonomous creatures. They are fairies. She didn't call them that, you know. I think it might be my fault.'

'This girl. In London.' Morag has the sense of going around in a circle.

'The girl. In London.' Alex digs deep into the tin for the last of the beans, licks tomato sauce from his fingers. 'What was the other thing you wanted?'

'The police say that Jules . . .'

Alex waits, patient as a mountain.

At last, Morag is able to say, 'My friend who died at the clinic in the Métro station of the Place de la Concorde. The police say that he committed suicide.'

Alex says flatly, 'He didn't.'

'He wasn't the kind to commit suicide. I know he didn't.'

'He was murdered,' Alex says. 'They lured him into the tunnel, caught him, and knocked him out. The train did the rest. It's brutal, I know. But it's the truth.'

'And I suppose you know who murdered him.'

'Fairies. Them, and someone helping them. At least one human agent. They do have those, you know. Many are liberationists, others are crazy people, all have been seduced by the fairy glamour. He's been seen, moving here and there. I have at least two confirmations of sightings close to murders. I saw him myself, two nights ago, waiting near your apartment. We had a little talk, but then he got away.'

'What was he doing there? What did he say?'

Alex raises a finger to his lips, says, 'Information exchange, that's the way the world works. Tell me about the murder you saw.'

'We didn't see it. We heard her scream . . .'

Again, Alex waits until she can go on. He listens intently as she tells him about finding the little girl and taking her back to the shack, about the chase, about the discovery of the little girl's body under the strange graffito, about the perimeter peeper and the security guards.

'They know,' Morag says. 'They know what's going on there.'

'I understand, but there's no good in getting angry with hirelings.'

Morag takes a deep breath, then another. 'All right. Tell me why the fairies took the little girl's ovaries.'

'Because they want to make more changelings. They have experimented with making over very young children, but I think that now they want to start at the embryo stage. Sperm is no problem, they can always cast their glamour over some poor sucker out on the fringes. Obtaining human ova is a tougher problem. They could hold a woman, I suppose, jack her full of hormones to bring on menopause, then start up ovulation again. That way she'll produce many eggs at once, yes?'

'Yes. But it takes time, and I suppose it would be too risky.'

'I think they just can't be bothered,' Alex says. 'Instead they are taking immature ovaries. Freezing some, perhaps, bringing others to maturity with hormone treatment.'

'And why do they want changelings?'

'Why do we want dolls?'

'Oh.'

'Of course, it isn't quite that simple. Basically, there are three types of fairies. The fey, who live mostly solitary lives. The sensualists, who cast their glamour over humans, but only to collect sperm to fertilize artificial ova they make from their own cells, to make more of their own kind. And then there are the others. I think they are hers, her own special kind. I first became aware of them in Amsterdam. There was a report of a changeling boy found wandering on the beach there, although he had disappeared by the time I went to check it out. And I think that's where the Children's Crusade started.'

Morag laughs. She can't help it. It's just that this is the kind of all-embracing paranoid conspiracy theory that drug addicts on the fringe dream up, a magical world of hidden forces often built on right brain delusions or visions induced by meme infections. She's heard everything, in her short time with the Mobile Aid Team, from flying saucer kidnappings, usually featuring some famous dead media star, through mundane mind-ray plots involving hoovering up people's memories into a giant computer buried beneath Paris, to people who claim to be three thousand-year-old high priests of Atlantis.

'I'm sorry,' she says, although Alex doesn't seem to be upset by her laughter. 'We seem to have moved a long way from where we started, that's all.'

Alex says, 'What do you know about entoptic phenomena? Well, have you ever done psychoactive drugs?'

'Kif. It was easier to get in the Sudan than alcohol.'

'Entoptic phenomena are a range of luminous precepts, independent of an external light source because they are generated by the human nervous system. They are the basic stuff of visions and hallucinations.'

'Oh,' Morag said, 'you mean phosphenes.'

'They're called that, too. Some people call them form constants. Anyone who enters an altered state of consciousness is liable to see them. They are a set of basic geometric forms which the subject embellishes with all kinds of iconic significance. They are the grammar of visions, if you like, although in the final state people move away from entoptic forms towards more hallucinatory iconic imagery.

'The point is that entoptic phenomena are independent of cultural background. All humans share the same basic set of forms – grids, parallel lines, flecks, zigzag lines, nested curves and filigrees. You can even find them in cave paintings, if you know what to look for. Those Stone Age hunters were stoned when they did their murals. Entoptic phenomena are derived from the basic wiring of our brains, down in the limbic brain, the innermost and most primitive layer. You might say that the grammar of the way we perceive the world is hardwired. But the fembots used by the Children's Crusade to induce visions in their victims have a distinctive signature quite unlike human entoptic phenomena. I've done some research, and I've come up with quite a different set.'

Morag remembers the strange swirling spider-shape daubed on the tunnel wall, above the discarded body of the little girl.

'If you're right,' she says, 'I've seen one.'

'I saw it, too. I bribed the police recorder. It's disturbing, isn't it? Hypnotic, in a sinister sort of way. Have you ever been love bombed?'

'Yes, but never by the Children's Crusade.'

'I have examples stored right here, if you'd like to sample them.'

'I'd rather not.'

'They're quite safe. I've defused them, removed everything but the overt iconography. It's the stuff beneath the overlay that's damaging. I've learned,' Alex says, cocking his head at a sound somewhere in the house, 'to be something of a meme hacker. She started that, too, you know. The very first crude images.'

'Tell me about this man. The one you saw near my apartment. The human agent, you called him.'

'He is a very confused individual. He remembers very little of his former life, but he told me that he was one of Midnight's Children, born in Chambéry, on midnight January 1st 2000. I hacked into the town hall records. An Armand Puech was born there at the right time; the Foreign Legion has him missing in action in Djibouti. That's all I know. Not much, I know, but he'll surface again. I'm quite sure of that. He's looking for you. You saw something, or they think you saw something.'

'I can't think what.'

'That's a pity. It would be a great help if you did.'

Morag is just beginning to decide that this fat man is mostly harmless, an obsessive suffering from mild paranoid delusions to be sure, but not violent, not *evil*, when there is a creak behind her, a footfall on a loose floorboard.

She turns, and the doll smiles at her, showing a mouthful of teeth filed to points.

10
The Human Agent

Armand wakes slowly. Pieces of consciousness bump and whirl apart and bump together again like ice floes on the black waters of a flooded river. Night. It is night. He is lying on a cold, hard floor, his neck, his back, his legs stiff. An unfamiliar ceiling, an unfamiliar room. The green glow of streetlamps, fretted by the blades of a blind, drops across him. When he brings his hands to his face he discovers that they are scaled with dried blood. It isn't his.

Something bad has happened again.

The woman.

Mister Mike has killed the woman.

Armand sits up cautiously.

He is in an apartment. A couch is tipped over. Clear gel bulges from slashes in its fabric. There's blood spray on a wall, blood trails across rucked rugs on the floor leading to a door that, not quite closed, shows a segment of white bathroom tile beyond.

The blood looks black in the green light leaking through the blinds.

Armand hears a sound and turns, his heart suddenly pounding. There's a nest of cushions in one corner, under a big fern hanging in a rope basket. One of the Folk sits there, watching Armand with dark, liquid eyes. It holds a raw haunch ripped from some kind of furry animal.

Armand asks what happened, but the fairy puts a long forefinger to its mouth. It is wearing loose paper coveralls and plastic sandals.

Armand says that he doesn't understand. The fairy points to the bathroom, then rips off a hunk of meat with its sharp teeth and swallows it whole, fur and all. Armand doesn't want to go in there, not yet. Instead, he walks over to the moulded kitchen nook and meticulously washes his hands. Bloody water runs over cups and saucers piled in the sink. All of the kitchen accessories are blinking the same message, over and over in red or green letters:

System disengaged. Please call your service agent.

Armand finds half a stick of stale bread on the counter. He tears off a piece and chews on it as he paces around the apartment.

The fairy watches from its corner.

A wall-hung TV, a scatter of magazines on slick erasable paper, Turkish cushions, an intricate carved frieze of fish and seaweed. The wood of the frieze gives off a faint odour of roses. There are two small bedrooms off the short hallway. Each smells differently, one tidy, the other strewn with clothes. Something moves under the bed, but it is only a little cleaning mobot, the tropic kind that comes out to vacuum the floor when no one's around. A panel hangs askew by the door at the end of the hallway, a single burnhole punched through it. Behind the blinds in the main room a view across the nighttime city.

The TV's clock tells Armand it is ten past five in the morning. A holocube lights up when he touches it. He tilts it from face to face, and scenes come and go inside: a man smiles at him; the bright sunlit straws and ochres of a parched countryside; a house with a terracotta tile roof under a deep blue sky; a group of people standing on the roof of a tear-drop shaped runabout parked in the sun-speckled shade of a poplar tree. Fragments of a life. Armand holds the cube out to the fairy, who takes it and tosses it aside without looking at it.

Armand sits down to think it through. Mister Mike came out to play. Probably Mister Mike was let into the apartment by the fairy, killed the woman who saw the bad thing with the little girl. Armand feels a measure of relief. Well, at least it's over. Perhaps he can go home.

He asks the fairy if that's what it is, and this time the fairy jumps up and starts pushing Armand towards the bathroom.

'All right,' Armand says, 'all right.'

Bright white light inside, bouncing from white tile walls. Someone is huddled in the shower cubicle. A woman, blonde hair down over her face, her shirt soaked with blood. The fairy pads up behind Armand, hands him a flat photograph in a brushed aluminium frame. A different, younger woman in a lime-green scuba suit, looking directly at the camera, mask and snorkel pushed up on a wet tangle of long black hair, salt-white sand and blue water burning behind her.

This is the woman Mister Mike was supposed to kill, but she wasn't here, and her roommate was killed instead. The fairy explains this to Armand, and tells him he isn't ever again to do anything he isn't supposed to do. He's to stay here, he's not to take one step out of the apartment, until someone comes for him, the fairy adds, then kisses Armand full on the mouth. Before it leaves the apartment, it waits for the kiss to work, then repeats its instructions over and over until it is satisfied that Armand has fallen under its glamour.

The trace of soma bestowed by the kiss blurs the edge of things, but the light of their real selves is sunk deep in their dead casings. Alone in the apartment, Armand paces around some more, scared and sick and excited. He is free, and yet not. He could walk out the door, but he knows that he won't. He can't. A geas has been laid upon him.

Armand ransacks the fridge, collects together half a sugar melon, a pepper sausage, three anchovies, a watery cube of tofu. While he eats, he watches dawn lighten the sky. Necklaces of green streetlights dim as the grey streets and tower blocks resolve from shadows. The ribbon arcologies loom like thunderclouds at the city's horizon.

Armand switches on the TV for company, its sound muted. He rearranges rugs to cover the blood smears. He looks through the closets in the bedrooms, sniffing the clothes, growing excited. It isn't that he has forgotten about women, he just doesn't want to think about them because that part of him is too much like Mister Mike.

He lies on the unmade bed and breathes in woman-scent from the pillow, masturbates with a pair of panties wrapped around his cock. He comes almost immediately. When he can't manage a second time, he hunts down the little mobot that lurks under the bed and stamps on it until its ceramic shell shatters. He finds another mobot lurking under the blinds of the picture window in the living room, a thing like an etiolated spider that clings to the glass with suction cups. Armand snaps its fragile limbs one by one and drops it on its back, laughs as it feebly struggles to right itself.

Later, when he has to take a piss, the accusatory presence in the shower at first defeats him, but after he throws a towel over her head it's easy. He grins in the bathroom mirror, and Mister Mike grins back. He's ready.

11
First Rays of the New Rising Sun

The fairy's name is First Rays of the New Rising Sun; Alex calls him Ray. Although Ray has the blue skin and wiry, metre-high frame of a doll, he also has large, lambent eyes flecked with gold, and sharp, high cheekbones a model would spend a long day under the knife to get. Ray's prominent ears are pointed like Mr Spock's, and the points rise above the knitted watch cap he wears on his bald head. The ears twitch this way and that with independent life. Their margins are notched, and the left is strung with gold rings and clips.

Ray is a solitary fairy, a fey, made over five years ago in a warren just outside Amsterdam and now living on the fringe of the fringe. He has travelled down the coast of Europe to the tip of Spain and back again. Fingering knots in a long string wound around his waist, he says that more and more people on the fringe have become incorporated into the Children's Crusade. They call themselves the saved. They want every one they meet, human and fairy alike, to be part of their cause.

'They are sick in the head,' Ray says. He squats on the ragged Turkish carpet, speaking careful, precise French in a gravelly voice, grinning around the words, showing his sharp shark's teeth. 'I keep away from them. I know that they will change me with a look.'

'It's a fembot meme,' Alex explains to Morag. 'A set of beliefs transmitted by machine infection. Fairies are more susceptible than humans.'

'Many fairies are part of this,' Ray agrees, smiling at Morag. 'I find many living in a warren in an old civil defence bunker outside

Brest. Fairies and humans.' His grin widens. 'Humans serve fairies now. One change that is better.'

Morag feels surprisingly calm. Perhaps it is part of the drunk cure Alex zapped her with in the taxi. She doesn't find Ray at all threatening, despite his filed teeth. His face sometimes seems to be that of a beautiful woman, sometimes that of a preternaturally alert child, and yet he is none of these things. He is neither animal nor human, but a synthesis that transcends both. Morag has listened to his story without question, but now she asks, 'What does the Children's Crusade want?'

'They all know the same thing, but you only know what it is if you are one of them.' Ray shudders delicately at the thought.

Alex says, 'It's her. It's her religion.'

Katrina passes a hand over the strip of fur that grows on the crest of her skull. She says, 'Children. They like to take children. Just like these fucking fairies.'

Ray says guilelessly, 'It is best to take children because they learn so quickly. They have less to forget. Besides, you have so many, and you are so careless of them. I am never surprised that it is easy to murder human children.'

'You take them because they are helpless,' Katrina says. 'The weak prey on the weak.'

'He means no harm,' Alex tells her.

The fey smiles at Katrina. 'I walk alone,' he says.

Morag says, 'But you help these people.'

'People help me. I help them.'

Katrina says to Morag, 'This little shit passes on gossip to anyone who will pay for it. He is shameless.'

'It's true,' Ray says. His wide grin shows all his sharp teeth. 'It's how I make a living. I'm not an animal, not like some of my brothers. They eat whatever they catch. Babyflesh, succulent even when raw.'

'Fucker!' Katrina's chair falls over as she springs to her feet. She grabs Ray by the lapels of his jacket and lifts him into the air.

Ray dangles limply in her grip, smiling fiercely, looking into her eyes. He says, 'I rip out your throat. One bite. Watch you bleed to death. This is a comfortable life here, you grow soft. I live out there, all the time. Every day I survive it.'

Katrina makes a sound of disgust and drops Ray. He resumes his squat, unperturbed.

Morag says, 'Ray, you do know something, don't you? You know about the little boy.'

'I hear he's alive, but I hear bad things and I move on. I don't stop to take care of any little boy.'

Morag says, 'But you could take me there. Into the Magic Kingdom.'

Katrina says, 'I wouldn't trust him to lead me across the road.'

Alex says, 'It isn't just a case of walking in there. The place is a real warren, a ruin combed with tunnels and chambers. You'd either never see a single fairy, or they'd kill you before you got to the heart.'

'There are guards,' Ray says. 'Things you wouldn't like to meet.'

Morag remembers that the perimeter peeper said something about goblins. She says, 'But there's the little boy. And you said that you can go anywhere, Ray.'

Katrina says, 'You don't know what you're getting into. On the last raid I made on a warren I was attacked by something like a dog with a crocodile head. Fought my way through a booby-trapped maze and all I found were a few dead dolls. I never saw a single fairy for more than a moment.'

'We make ourselves invisible.' Ray says. 'It is a trick we have.'

'They always have ways of escape,' Alex says. 'For every way in, there are two out. They don't need to be invisible.'

Katrina says, 'The ones I killed when I got my brother back weren't invisible.'

'Maybe they weren't fairies,' Ray says.

'Maybe you aren't one.'

'Doll-fucker,' Ray says, with equanimity.

'You wish,' Katrina says.

Morag says, 'I just want help to get into this place. What about it, Ray? What will it cost for you to take me there?'

'He doesn't want money,' Alex says. 'He wants what I can give him.'

'It's true.'

'Certain drugs,' Alex says. 'Hormones. He trades them.'

'Alex number-one.'

184

'It's true I was the first, although at the time I didn't know what I was getting into. Morag, it really isn't a question of walking in there. It's more like conducting a small war. I want you to understand because we need your help.'

'Alex, this is a crazy idea,' Katrina says.

Morag says, 'You're a drugdealer.'

'In my time. Actually, I was more of a gene hacker, dealing in psychoactive retroviruses. Have you ever done Ghost? Well, I suppose that it was a few years ago, and viruses are out of fashion. I work with fembots now.'

'What do you want out of this?'

'Information, if I can get it. It's all linked, Morag. It all stems from one source. I want to trace her.'

'This woman.'

'Yes. Oh yes.'

Alex says it in such a hopeless, yearning way, like a spurned lover in an opera, that Morag has trouble keeping a straight face. Katrina gives him a level, quiet look that communicates a world of sympathy. They are both wounded in different ways, Morag thinks. They understand each other.

Morag says, 'And what am I supposed to do?'

'You're to be bait.'

Morag doesn't understand.

'We let their human agent come after you. Then we find out from him what we need to know to get inside.'

'You're crazy.'

Ray said, 'They are stone crazy. Loco. They want to know things man is never meant to know.'

Katrina says, 'They want children. More and more are taken every day. I've destroyed two of their nests so far, and the second time I went in I didn't have the right information. I nearly died. I'm going in there soon. You can help me survive it.'

Morag says to the fairy, 'What about you, Ray? I'm a paramedic. I can get drugs, if you want them.'

'Not the right kind,' Alex says.

'It's true,' Ray says.

'You had better stay here,' Alex tells Morag. 'The human agent will be looking for you, and you don't want to come on him unprepared. I've every reason to think he's dangerous.'

Morag has a long soak in an old enamelled tub with clawed feet, in a bare room with mould-blackened walls and a warped sash window that lets in gusts of icy air. The room fills with steam and she nearly falls asleep, so she climbs out of the bath and wraps a towel around herself and takes a little black wake-up pill. She knows from long experience that with a little chemical help she can go without sleep for a couple of days.

Her phone is still in her bag, and she uses it to call the apartment. There's no answer. Not even the apartment's house-keeper answers. Morag is suddenly all goosebumps, shivering violently in the cold, steamy room. She calls the hospital, gets through to the surgery station, and asks for Nina.

The receptionist says that Nina is on duty, that she cannot be contacted except in a genuine emergency. Morag starts to say that this *is* an emergency, and then a man overrides the machine and says that Nina hasn't checked in for her shift.

'I'm her roommate. I need to talk with her.'

'She isn't here,' the man says, and cuts the connection.

Morag quickly rubs herself dry and gets dressed, undoes her hair from its loose bun and brushes it out. She searches through the dark rambling house and finds Alex in the tiled kitchen. He is standing at the counter, picking at a cold croissant stuffed with cheese and ham.

Fear and amphetamine have dried Morag's mouth. She drinks a glass of water and asks if she's a prisoner here.

Alex bunks with sleepy surprise. 'Of course not. Do you want some breakfast?'

'I have an errand to run. Will you let me go? I won't tell the police anything.'

Alex looks at her, then says, 'It won't matter if you do. But be careful. You don't know what's out there. Kat—'

'I want to go on my own. I promise I'll be back.'

'That's OK. We know where you live.' Then: 'Hey, that was just a joke.'

'Too many people know where I live.'

Morag forces herself to walk, not run, out of the house. It doesn't occur to her that she should tell the two fringers that there's something wrong at the apartment. The fact is that she doesn't trust them. She will deal with this herself.

It is dawn, grey and cheerless. Lights show in a few of the tall houses along the *impasse*; more than half have been boarded up. A woman in a floral print dress, emptying an electric washer into the gutter by her door, bids Morag good morning. A slow goods train rumbles through the cutting as Morag crosses the bridge. After a few panicky minutes she has her bearings, and half an hour later she is at the apartment building.

The elevator takes an age to get down to the lobby, just as long to climb back up. People on the way to work or university are getting on at every floor. Morag calls the hospital, is still trying to get through to the aide in charge of Nina's ward when at last the elevator reaches her floor.

The door opens at her touch. The apartment is quiet. Morag immediately becomes hyperalert, because the apartment has learnt to greet her when she returns home. Then she sees the burnhole in the expert system's service panel and she knows she should run. But if she starts running now she figures she'll never stop.

Nerveless, stealthily, she goes down the little hallway. The TV is on, its sound turned down. The rugs have been moved, and there's stuff flecking the walls. With a shock, Morag realizes what the flecks are – and a man slams open the bathroom door and rushes at her. He skids wildly on a loose rug, and Morag runs straight out of the apartment and bangs the elevator call, bangs it again and turns and sees the man standing there in the doorway.

A tall, raw-boned, unshaven man in his early twenties, his jumper ragged at the hem, his combat trousers stiff with dirt. His eyes are looking all over the place, everywhere but at her.

'Help me,' he says. He takes a step forward, flinches and dances back. It's as if there's an invisible wire there, a boundary he can't cross. 'Help me,' he says again. 'I want to get out. Help me, please.'

'Are you working for Alex? Alex Sharkey? You know him? Is Nina in there? Nina!'

The man's smile is there and gone, but it tells Morag everything. The fucking elevator is still descending towards her, floor by floor. Morag shoulders through the swing door to the service stairs, goes down them as fast as she can. The concierge isn't in, and so Morag uses her own phone to call the police, then to order up a taxi.

She's hunched in a corner of the lobby, shivering, trying not to cry. A gaggle of students give her quick glances as they hurry out to classes. Then a doll dressed in maintenance coveralls comes through the door. It looks straight at Morag, and her nerve breaks. She runs out into the street and is almost knocked down by the taxi she ordered.

As the taxi pulls away, Morag tells the driver she's changed her mind, she doesn't want to go to the Mobile Aid Team's depot out by the airport, she wants to go into the city instead. The driver shrugs and pulls a U-turn right in front of the police cars that have drawn up in front of the apartment building.

Morag spends the ride with her hands clamped between her thighs, letting deep shivers work adrenalin out of her blood. She ran once, she's determined not to run again, but first she wants to know who she's up against. She can't go back to the two fringers, and she certainly can't ask Dr Science, but in her short time with the Mobile Aid Team she's already learned that there's one person who knows everything that happens on the streets.

Morag leans forward and tells the driver to take her to the Jardin des Plantes.

12
The Wild Hunt

Claude the Cook has a well-established beat, swinging in from the Bidonvilles beyond the ribbon arcologies, through the half-abandoned suburbs to the centre of the city, and then back out again. Most of the aid workers know where to find him on any given day. Today his Cook-Out Collective is set up in a tree-shaded corner of the Jardin des Plantes, at the foot of the hillock crowned by the cedar of Jussieu, which that gentleman brought to Paris from London as a seedling nestled in his three-cornered hat.

Claude is supervising the cooking pot, a big round iron cauldron smoking in the cold morning air over a wood fire. As always, it contains red beans and rice. About twenty men and women are eating breakfast from paper plates. Most hardly spare Morag a glance, but Claude greets her cheerfully.

He is always cheerful, a strong pot-bellied man with a wide smile creasing his weather-beaten face. He lost his left arm in the American civil war, and the sleeve of his flannel checked shirt is pinned to his chest. He isn't French, but a Cajun from the Louisiana bayous, and his name probably isn't Claude. Everyone in the Mobile Aid Team knows Claude the Cook, and he knows more about the fringe than anyone else in and around Paris.

Claude is especially happy today, because he's hustled a tonne of day-old bread. He's expecting a lot of people later on, after the bread is trucked over. Morag tells him who she's looking for, and while he thinks it over, she takes a turn at stirring the mess of beans and rice with a heavy, metre-long wooden paddle that's charred black along its edge.

At last, Claude says, 'I don't know the fellow, but Justin over there, he was in the Legion. He could know.'

Justin is a very young, very shy man, with raw wrists poking from the frayed cuffs of his filthy puffer jacket. He tells Morag that he used to hang out with a few guys from the Legion, and yes, one of them was called Armand.

'But I haven't seen him for a year now, a year at least.'

'You don't know where he went.'

Justin shrugs. 'Maybe he's dead. Maybe not. He left the Legion before it was ready for him to leave, so he has good reason to hide out.'

Morag asks if Justin can tell her anything else, and Justin thinks it over. 'I remember his combat tag. What he was known by when he was in action.'

'Like a nickname?'

'More than that. Do you know how it is, in the Legion? They put in a chip loaded with what they call a partial personality. It learns off you until it can take over in combat. Then the officers can boot your ware, turn you wolf. So, see, it isn't you fighting, doing that stuff you need to do to survive in intense situations. It's the partial.'

Justin wraps his arms around himself and rocks back and forth on his heels. He suddenly has a thousand metre stare.

'It's like, you aren't even there,' he says. 'The partial uses you. It hacks your meat, you understand? It has reflexes you haven't even learned to use, and no morals. A compulsive something or other.'

'Psychopath?'

Justin smiles. 'Sure.'

'I thought that soldiers were just given extra reflexes.'

'The partial has access to hardwired chip modes, shit like that, sure. But it puts you offline, too, so it isn't inhibited by all the socialization stuff you learn as a very young kid. It doesn't want your reflexes messing up its reflexes, so it just throws that big red switch in your head, boots the ware, and you're gone. When it's done, you come back, because the legion doesn't want crazy people running around who are crazy all the time. You don't remember what you did. That's what they say. Except, sometimes, you dream. You dream stuff, and it's mixed in with your normal life. That's hard.'

'I imagine.'

'You can fucking imagine,' Justin says evenly, 'but you can't ever know. When you're discharged, they flash your chip to strip its codes, so it's gone forever. I kind of slipped the net, but I made sure I got my chip flashed all the same. You don't want that kind of thing in your head longer than you need. Even if your chip is flashed and pulled, you know, you still dream.'

Morag meets this poor, haunted young man's stare and says, 'I'm sorry.'

'You wanted to know about Armand. There it is. He still alive?'

'I think so.'

'They called his partial Mister Mike. He was the communications operative, you understand. So he was called Mister Mike when his ware got booted. Know why I'm telling you this?'

'Go on.'

'Word is, old Armand turned warewolf. A rogue, you understand? Last time I saw him, his chip was still functional. He said he was too scared to have it flashed. Said that Mister Mike told him not to do it. Poor Armand, he was more mixed-up than most. You excuse me now, mademoiselle,' Justin says, and gets up abruptly and walks away. He doesn't look back when Morag calls out her thanks.

'Come back later,' Claude advises. 'I put the word out, find out more about this fucker.'

It's possible that the police caught him, but Morag seriously doubts it. She's sure that the doll – the fairy – had come to set him free. Even now he might be on her track.

For the first time since Africa, Morag buys a pack of cigarettes. The first tastes terrible, and the nicotine rush hits her so hard it makes her dizzy. The second is better. What the hell. It isn't as if they give you cancer any more.

She's in a little café, getting warm. Coffee and cigarettes. Who first stumbled on this blessed combination? They should make her a saint.

When she's calmed down, she calls Dr Science. It takes her twenty minutes to get through his screening service, and when Dr Science finally answers he at first refuses point blank to see her.

'I'll go to the press,' Morag says. There's a silence. She says into it, 'I mean it. This thing can't go on.'

'What thing is this, Morag?'

'Not over the phone. Will you come and talk to me?'

Dr Science suggests that she should come to the depot, and she tells him, no, and explains where she'll be instead. He agrees reluctantly, and this gives her a thin satisfaction, like a skim of ice over a deep black cold lake. At least she has gained a bit of control.

Dr Science arrives late, saying that he had trouble finding this dump, why couldn't they talk at the depot or at least a decent restaurant? The place Morag has chosen has unnerved him: good. It is a cheap café that serves the students of the nearby medical school, tucked away in a little rubbish-strewn alley in the centre of the Left Bank. The guillotine was perfected just around the corner, next door to Marat's printing press, but the Left Bank has been going downhill ever since the expensive shops moved out, and hardly any tourists come here any more. Even the café has an armed guard on the door.

191

Morag faces Dr Science across a trestle table they share with half a dozen students. Most of the noisy people around them are wearing white laboratory coats, and there's a tang of formaldehyde that cuts through the haze of cigarette smoke. Waitresses bang down plates and flasks of wine with studied carelessness, shout orders to the chef who works behind a folding screen.

'It isn't beefsteak,' Morag tells Dr Science, when the waitress slaps down their food. 'It's really horse.'

She is feeling a fine adrenalin high now. She's burning her bridges and it doesn't matter. Perhaps later she'll feel remorse, but right now she's feeling a kind of rapturous glee.

'So few places serve good horsemeat any more,' Dr Science says coolly.

His equanimity is returning, although he's still uneasy. His denim jacket with the Harley Davidson logo sewn on the back, his Roughrider jeans, his motorcycle boots, are all too new, too well-made. He has a scarlet handkerchief knotted at his throat that in his usual haunts would be a piece of studied carelessness, but here is an affectation. He's a fashionplate about half a century out of date, and to Morag he's never seemed so old as now.

Morag can't eat. She pushes food around on her plate, then she comes right out and asks for this one favour. She wants the truth about the murder to be known.

Dr Science rears back from her, says something she can't hear because of the noise. 'No,' he repeats. 'It is out of the question.' His eyes won't meet hers.

'It's not just the little girl's murder: her brother may still be alive. I can tell the police, they don't have to know where the information came from.'

'There are . . . compartments.' Dr Science shapes divisions in the air. 'Information in one cannot leak into another. It causes problems. I see you do not understand, but it's true. In order to help the people of the Bidonvilles, we have to work in a kind of vacuum. And we do help them, don't we?'

'At what cost?'

'Morag, you should try and take in the whole picture. You are just seeing a little part of it.'

'Fairies,' Morag says. 'A new kind of fairy. That's what took the little boy. That's what is killing the little girls.'

'You see? You should not know this.'

'Jules is dead. I think my roommate is dead. If I'm not careful that will be my fate, too. Tell me that you don't know anything about what goes on in the Magic Kingdom. Tell me that the companies working at the Interface don't know about it.'

'Let me explain, my dear. The effect of technology on social trends is very unpredictable. It is not an exact science, any more than weather prediction can be exact. The more you look at the detail, the fuzzier the data get. As for fairies, trying to apply human logic to them is like trying to predict the weather on Mars by extrapolating what you know about weather here. It is very difficult. For a long time it wasn't understood that the murders were a part of the changes that resulted in the Interface. Now that it is known, believe me, every effort is being made—'

'I've seen the white vans. But it isn't the feys who are doing this thing. It's the fairies in the Magic Kingdom.'

Dr Science throws up his hands. 'You just don't have all the information. You have some of it, but not all of it. It isn't for you to make judgements.'

'I've seen a fey. I've talked to him. This thing can't be hidden any more.'

Dr Science slices the last morsel of meat on his plate in two, eats first one half, then the other. He says, 'Perhaps if you come back to my office, I can do something.'

'I don't have the time.'

'Morag, you must trust me.'

Morag realizes that she doesn't trust him at all. With a sudden constricting dread, she feels that she is in the middle of some kind of ambush. She throws money on the table and pushes her way through the crowded café without looking to see if Dr Science is following her. Then she runs.

She takes the steps of the Odéon Métro two at a time and rides the train out to Les Invalides, where she walks around the cold, over-decorated spaces of the Église du Dôme until she feels calmer. A group of dolls controlled by virtual tourists are clustered in the ornate gallery around Napoléon's sunken tomb. For the first time,

Morag sees the dolls as slaves, jerked around at the whim of people who might be on the other side of the world. She watches them for so long that the armed guide who accompanies them comes over and asks her to move on.

It's growing dark by the time Morag returns to the Jardin des Plantes. There's a steady stream of people making their way into the park. It's popular with the homeless as a spot to bed down for the night, and as long as they strike camp at sun-up, the cops generally leave them alone.

People have set up pitches under lampposts along the paths, the poor selling to the poor everything from half-used food packs to brand new TVs. A group of hackers have taken over a phone booth and are offering line access at reduced prices. There's open dealing in drugs and fembot hits; users stagger across the grass, holding intense conversations with God or with aliens, or contemplate empty air with wonder, seeing cathedrals or angels, dragons or dead stars. In one part of the park, a group of people infected with the drumming meme have already set up, and their polyphonic rhythms rise and fall like distant surf.

It occurs to Morag, moving amongst the homeless, that she is homeless too.

The best pitches, under trees or against walls, have already been taken. Single men and women, sometimes whole families, are wandering about, looking for their own spot. Portable TVs murmur. Their flickering screens, most glowing with the red light of Mars, are like a field of stars has fallen across the park.

Claude the Cook and his helpers are busy, tending three big cauldrons and serving people as fast as they can. Firelight beating across trampled grass makes shadows move in the trees which lean out from the slope beyond. Cartons of processed bread are stacked head high. A couple of saxophone-playing buskers are giving a free performance; their wailing freeform scat twists into the night. When he's not bawling at his crew, Claude blows on a harmonica in crude counterpoint, holding the instrument entirely in his mouth to leave his one hand free. He beats time with a big wooden paddle, splattering rice and beans.

Morag smokes a cigarette and waits until Claude has time to

talk with her. When he comes over she offers him what she is dismayed to find is her last cigarette – how did she get through the pack so quickly?

'I gave up again,' Claude says, 'Can't have ash in the food, eh?'

'It's an amazing operation.'

'There's a couple of guys who go around making little gardens in patches of waste ground. Maybe you know of them?'

'I think I saw one in an old industrial estate. There was a pond, flowers, a packing case bench. Lots of ivy up a wall.'

'Right. You know where to look, you can find these little gardens all over. It keeps those guys sane, and it claims back little bits of the city. We're an invisible country that's all around you if you know how to look. There are signs and pathways and meeting places. There have always been drinking places, of course, and the junkies and thieves hang out together because that's what junkies and thieves do. But there are places where you can meet like-minded people to play chess, shoot the breeze, whatever. Those two guys playing sax are part of a collective who hold clinics and jam sessions where people can improve their skills. You know what I'm saying?'

'I've seen a little of it.'

Claude grins. He is sweating despite the cold. He smells powerfully of sweat and woodsmoke. A red bandanna is tied around his forehead, and he wears a white apron over his coveralls.

'We appreciate your work. That soup kitchen over by the main entrance – they mean well, too. But we have our own thing. I tried settling down once, holding a steady job. I really was a cook, but fuck that shit, being told what to do, working for the system. We have our own system.'

'I understand.'

'I put the word out. Told them it was someone from the Mobile Aid Team asking. There's a bunch of guys, Algerians, who sell jewellery on the street. The kind made out of scrap copper? They heard of this guy. Couple of them waiting up by the trees there, if you want to talk with them. Hey, give me that cigarette?'

Morag hands him the pack. Claude flips the cigarette out, holds it up, then crumbles it between his big fingers.

'Smoking's bad for you. Now I do you two favours.'

And he laughs and wanders off to shout at his helpers some more.

Morag introduces herself to the two Algerians, and the older man tells her, in a voice dry as dust, that yes, he knows this fellow well. He is well known to all the people who live in the Magic Kingdom.

'Say that again?'

'You know it,' the old man says. The hood of his jacket is pulled up around his face, so that only the end of his white beard can be seen.

'You live there?'

Morag is uncomfortably aware that the other Algerian is looking at her intently – but with a kind of wistfulness, not menace. She returns his gaze, and he says, 'The man you are looking for has a troubled mind, but he keeps the afreets away from us.'

'Afreets?' Morag is discovering that the more she knows, the less she understands. Then she says, 'Of course! Fairies!'

'Some call them that,' the older man says. Something moves inside the shadows of the hood around his face: it is a white rat. The whiskers on the end of its pink snout twitch as it snuffles the air.

Something the little girl told her comes back to Morag, and her entire skin prickles.

A helicopter is beating through the black air above the Jardin des Plantes. Its searchlight is a brilliant pencil of white light that flicks this way and that. The branches of the trees on the slope that rises above the cook-out shiver in the wake of the helicopter's downdraught as it passes overhead.

Morag asks, 'Did you ever hear the name Mister Mike?'

The second Algerian says quietly, 'They'll be here soon.'

'Who?'

But neither man replies.

The helicopter is coming back. It is flying low and very slowly, turning this way and that with abrupt insectile movements. The white spear of its laser spot strikes down, winks off, strikes down in another spot. All over the park, people are standing to watch it. Beyond the main gate of the park is the blue flicker of police vehicle lights.

Morag realizes that Dr Science has somehow set her up. The helicopter is drifting sideways above Claude's makeshift kitchen. Smoke from the cooking fires is driven out in all directions. Cartons tumble, scattering sheaves of bread like a sudden miracle. A spear of light stabs down, transfixes Claude in the act of defiantly shaking a wooden paddle above his head. The helicopter's down-draught makes his coveralls flutter and snap. He is shouting.

The light goes out, comes on again over a patch of trampled ground. It winks out, then illuminates the two Algerians. They are not looking at the helicopter: they are looking at Morag. The younger man is crying steadily. Tears glisten on his cheeks and drop silently from his chin. His mouth is open. His tongue curls and writhes tike a pinned snake, but he can't speak.

Morag walks backwards into the trees, then turns and runs. The helicopter rises above the slope. Its spot snaps on and off like light-ning amongst interlaced branches. Morag runs right through an encampment, narrowly avoids stepping on a woman swaddled in filthy blankets. She vaults a low fence, cutting her hands on its wire, and runs across the asphalted space at the top of the hill. The branches of the gracious old cedar tree doff as if in a storm, and a blizzard of fragrant needles blow around Morag.

Light stabs down, diffracted by foliage into a moire pattern. The helicopter is directly above. An amplified voice clatters, is cut short by an electronic blare. Morag runs around the tree and down the steep steps on the far side. A man looms out of the darkness and tries to catch her arm, but she shoves at him and runs past without breaking stride. He shouts after her, but she's already gone.

There's a little garden at the bottom of the steps, with a pond where the round leaves of water-lilies step across black water. Morag runs straight into the pond and throws herself forward, crying out with the shock of the freezing water.

She stands up, water streaming from her sodden clothes, then ducks underwater again as the helicopter passes overhead. Light strikes a dozen metres off, illuminating a white stone statue of a naked woman, winks out. The helicopter moves on.

Fembots. Somehow, Dr Science put fembot tracers on her. It doesn't take much. A touch can transfer thousands of tiny sound recorders, transmitters and single shot fisheye-lensed cameras whose digitized pictures can be recalled after retrieval. The water has washed them away, and the trace the helicopter was following has been destroyed.

Morag wades to the edge of the pond. Shivers strike to her bones as she clambers out. A man is standing by the statue of the woman. He seems to have materialized there, a spectre mixed up from shadow and the green glow of a nearby lamp. It is the hungry-looking man from the apartment. He holds up a pair of plastic grips and pulls them apart with a sharp, sudden motion. There's a humming twang, and Morag knows that he is the warewolf, that what he holds is a monofilament strangling cord.

'Armand,' she says, amazed that she can speak, she's so scared. 'Armand, don't. I can help.'

The warewolf grins and runs straight at her. Light explodes inside Morag's head. She's pinned to the ground. The warewolf grips her hair and pulls, trying to lift her head. She yells and twists, knowing that if he gets the monofilament around her neck he can sever the major blood vessels with a single twist.

And someone shouts a shrill cadence. 'Sirius! Sirius! Sirius!'

Morag's hair is released so suddenly she bangs her head on the ground. She lies there, stunned, as the man is lifted off her. Someone helps Morag up. It is Katrina. She is grinning like a fool.

The warewolf, Armand, sprawls on his back a couple of metres away. He's sobbing, making odd strangled noises. Alex Sharkey stoops over him and says awkwardly, 'There, there. There, there.'

Morag sees that she has been set up. They let her walk away and walk right into this. 'You fuckers,' she says furiously. 'You stupid fuckers.'

Katrina scratches at the strip of leopard fur on top of her skull. She is dressed in black leather jeans and a black leather blouson half zipped over a furry red liner. She says, 'It worked, didn't it?'

Morag kicks Katrina in the knee. The woman doubles over, and Morag gets in a couple of whacks around her head before Katrina grabs her wrist, spins her around and pulls one arm up behind her back.

'You might be more grateful,' Katrina says in Morag's ear. 'I mean, we just saved your ass.'

'Fuckers!' Morag shouts, so loudly that it hurts her throat. The echo comes back from the hillock.

Katrina laughs and lets Morag go. 'You're all right,' she says.

Morag flexes her hand. The knuckles hurt. She says, 'You have a rock for a skull.'

'Why are you so angry? You didn't do anything we asked you to do. You went ahead by yourself.'

Katrina's aggrieved tone ignites Morag's anger again. 'My roommate is dead. He killed her, he was waiting for me when I went back to the apartment. You knew what I was walking into, didn't you? You didn't tell me.'

'Well,' Katrina says reasonably, 'you didn't ask.'

Alex Sharkey says, 'I told you not to go home. I thought something like that might happen.'

Morag starts to walk away.

Alex says, 'The cops are still looking for you.'

Morag turns. 'Yes, and did you set that up?'

'Of course not. As a matter of fact, it's a considerable inconvenience. But if you want to leave the park without being arrested, you'll have to trust us.'

13
Information Flow

Katrina turns the taxi's heater up to full as she drives across the river. Wrapped in Alex Sharkey's overcoat, Morag crouches in the hot roar of the vents. Her shivers go bone deep, and she hardly notices where she's being taken. The back of her neck is especially cold; as part of the strategy to get Morag past the police checkpoint, Katrina gave her a quick but expert haircut. Morag keeps touching her hair. She hasn't worn it this short since she was at school.

Alex is in the back of the taxi with the warewolf, Armand. He tells Morag that he found the switch word, the command that officers use to cancel the ware in their soldiers' heads.

'If there's a command to throw the switch on, then there has to be one to reset it,' he says smugly. 'I got it off a node in the Web a while back. Someone hacked the Ministry of Defence and down-loaded the specs on warewolf chips, compressed them and put them on the Web. Nothing hackers like better than showing off the inside info they've cracked. The switch word was buried in the default commands. It worked like a charm, don't you think?'

Morag thinks he's behaving like the hackers he pretends to despise. She's warmed up enough to be able to start peeling away the pseudoderm gloves which gave her fingerprints to match the false ID they used at the checkpoint. The stuff clings stubbornly to her skin, and comes away in strips and patches.

'It worked like a magic spell,' Katrina says, and laughs her cracked laugh.

They stop outside a shuttered shop in a narrow street. A young woman lets them in. She's a pale nervous wraith with stringy blonde hair who, when Alex starts to explain, shrugs, takes Morag by the hand, and leads her past empty display cabinets to a tiny bathroom. The blonde gives Morag a big, threadbare towel, and drifts off without a word. The towel is purple, with yellow sea creatures printed on it.

Morag strips off Alex's overcoat and her own soaked clothes, and wraps herself in the towel. Her newly cut hair is merely damp now. Following the sound of voices, she climbs a spiral stair to what was once an open-plan office. Desks and angled partitions are still in place. Overhead, swags of cable loop between cracked ceiling tiles. The windows are covered with aluminium foil.

For a moment, Morag thinks she sees something drift around a pillar and spiral up into the hole behind a dangling air-conditioning vent. She blinks hard – it was a tiny fairy, with wings and a white dress and a star-pointed wand. It has left a trail of silvery motes which wink out one by one.

Behind Morag, Katrina says, 'Fetching outfit.'

Katrina has taken off her leather jacket and is doing vigorous one-handed chin-ups using an overhead pipe. There are dark sweatstains under the sleeves of her grey T-shirt. Behind her, the warewolf is lying on a desk with the complete muscular relaxation of the recently dead.

'We gave him a dose,' Katrina says cheerfully. She isn't even out of breath. 'The poor fucker was so zonked he wouldn't do anything but cry. You can do what you want, I won't say anything.'

Morag gathers the towel around herself more tightly. 'What do you have in mind?'

'Me,' Katrina says, swapping hands smoothly and chinning the pipe, 'I'd kick him in the balls to begin with. Then give him one or two in the kidneys perhaps, so he pisses blood for a couple of days. Beat on his ribs so it hurts when he breathes. It slows him down, too. Then I would think about some permanent damage.'

'It wasn't him. I mean, he was being controlled.'

'Shit, baby, what do you know? Soldiers start to confuse themselves with their ware personalities because a good part of the ware personality comes from them in the first place. Most of the rest is just preprogrammed routines and reflexes.'

'Even if it was him, I don't want to hurt him.'

'You would turn him over to the police, I suppose.'

Morag retorts, 'No. No, I wouldn't. Because he knows the way into the Magic Kingdom.'

Katrina pulls herself up with both hands, then shifts her grip on the pipe so that she can raise her body parallel to it. She looks down at Morag and says, 'Good idea, but Alex will tell you the bad news about that. Go on. I will not hurt your boyfriend.'

Morag can smell coffee. It goes right to her back brain. Clutching her towel, she follows the aroma to the middle of the open plan office's dusty maze. Lounging in a bartered, padded swivel chair, and lit by a vertical biolume tube that gives his jowly face a lizard tint, Alex is repeating his story to a man in a sky-blue djellabah who is perched on a tall stool.

On the desk behind the man, translucent shapes tumble and spin above a computer deck's holostage. A bundled monofilament fibreoptic cable, no thicker than a hair but capable of carrying more traffic than all the cables in this old office space, runs from the back of the computer and disappears into the ceiling. Half a dozen silver flasks stand inside a constant temperature waterbath, and a thermostatic stage is cycling through a programme with a staccato of clicks as its heater switches on and off. Beside the stage is a Braun coffee maker, its jug half full.

The man glances at Morag, then tells Alex, 'You're lucky the switch worked, dood.'

Alex blows steam from a brimming mug, sips, and tells the man, 'He was a deserter, and the chip was wiped. Whoever is using him hasn't bothered with the code or doesn't know how to change it.' He smiles at Morag.

'Give me some of that coffee,' Morag says.

'This is Max,' Alex says. 'It isn't his real name, of course.'

Max hands Morag a mug of coffee. He's no more than twenty, with nappy hair and very black skin. His pupils are beaten gold; he's wearing the kind of contact lenses that transmit images directly to the retina. Tribal scars, a pattern of little crescents, are incised in the skin over his cheekbones.

'You're a lucky lady,' Max says. 'There's no milk.'

'I drink it black. What would you be, another flake with a theory?'

There's a flash of silver at the edge of Morag's vision. The little fairy hovers right before her eyes, blows her a kiss, and vanishes in a puff of silver flakes.

Alex says, 'Max works in the visual arts.'

'He's a love bomber,' Morag says. 'You're growing fembots right here without protection. One of your creations just zapped me.'

Max smiles. 'Tinkerbell? She's no fembot.'

'A hologram then. Bounced on to my retinas by hidden projectors. Look, I'm not as stupid as both of you assume me to be. Don't patronize me. I'd as soon walk out of here, except you silly people seem to be at the centre of what I need to know.'

'There's no need to go to the police,' Alex says, hands up in a soothing gesture. 'We have our own way of dealing with this. Go with it, Morag. That way we'll all get what we want.'

'Except Jules and Nina. They're dead. And the poor little girl, all the poor little girls.' Tears prick Morag's eyes. 'Damn you all,' she says.

The washed-out blonde drifts up, Morag's clothes over her arm. They have been dried but not cleaned. She hands Max two squares of adhesive tape in a glassine envelope and says, 'Positive.'

'Now we'll see,' Max says.

'We found fembots on your clothes,' Alex tells Morag. 'Also on the warewolf.'

Morag sets down the coffee mug and wipes her eyes with the heel of her palm. 'Armand. His name is Armand, What are you going to do to him?'

'Pull his chip might be an idea. Will you help?'

'I thought he could lead us into the Magic Kingdom.'

'I can ask him, but I can't guarantee anything. The last time I tried some persuasion, it set off his chip. The ware personality surfaced and it tried to strangle Kat.'

Max says, 'The army doesn't like its soldiers to be interrogated, so attempts at forced questioning will bring out the worst in them.'

'Perhaps he'll help if we ask him.'

Alex says, 'Perhaps, but we really must pull the chip first. Even without the chip he's seriously disturbed, but at least we won't have to worry about setting off the ware personality. Will you help us draw his teeth?'

'If I don't?'

'Then we have to dispose of him,' Alex says. 'Really, I'd rather we didn't. Aside from the moral consideration, it's very expensive, and a waste of a resource.'

Morag wonders if Alex Sharkey has ever had a moral consideration in his life. He looks like a kind of anti-Buddha beaming benignly there in the swivel chair in his white suit and green and orange plaid shirt, his hands clasped over his considerable belly. Whatever he wants from this, it is more than the story he has fed her, the fairytale of being under the thrall of a mad genius who supposedly created the fairies single-handed, who even now is warping them to her own ends. He is as deeply involved in this as poor Armand, but his motives are well hidden. Morag isn't sure if he really is working against the Children's Crusade, or if he simply wants to rip them off in some unspecified way. What she is sure of is that she isn't going to give up. For Jules's sake she can't give up. She's pretty sure that Armand, or at least his warewolf alter ego, killed Jules and Nina, and killed the poor little girls, too. If Armand can't or won't help her, then at least she can hand him to the police at the first chance she gets.

Morag thinks all this as, behind one of the screens, she pulls on the stiff, matted sweater and creased trousers over damp under-wear. The fleece lining of her coat is badly stained, and dry mud lies in the seams of its silver quilting. But at least she's warm again.

Max has clamped one of the squares of tape, adhesive side up, in a tiny stainless steel frame. Now he feeds this into a scanning tunnelling microscope rig that's plugged into one of the computer's external sockets. The rig's vacuum pump whines, and then the shapes tumbling above the holostage fade to show a rumpled landscape in shades of glowing green, its hills and dales speckled with tiny, hard-edged lozenges. Max zooms in on one of the lozenges. Resolution grows fuzzier as the thing fills the stage. It is some kind of fembot, a trapezoid about a micron on each side, its top surface an array of light-collecting diodes patterned like a compound eye.

Max twiddles a ball to move the view to one of the edges of the microscopic machine, then increases the magnification until the screen is filled with a pattern of fuzzy spheres: the doped buckyball molecules which make up the fembot. At the bottom of the screen, a stack of red and pink lines shrink and grow, then stabilize.

'Germanium and gold,' Max says. 'This configuration is the type of readout port used by the cops. The bug takes a single random, time-stamped picture and stores it. The cops retrieve a population of bugs, a couple of million or so, and use heuristic techniques to recover a time sequence. Crude but effective.'

'They were watching your every move,' Alex tells Morag, as Max inserts the second square of adhesive tape. 'You knew about it, didn't you? It's why you jumped in the water.'

The second sample consists of a scattering of a different type of fembot, lumpy and amorphous like so many agglomerations of soap bubbles. Each has a slot in its leading edge where it can clamp on to host cell ribosomes and force them to make novel proteins, and paddle-like effectors that use fluctuations in charge for propulsion through fluid media.

'Cool stuff,' Max says, raptly scanning one fembot after the other, loading the images into the computer.

'Fairydust,' Alex tells Morag. 'Some of them seem to do nothing; others will change a person's mind permanently, if they're given a chance. Know how it works? Our memories are distributed through our brains in branching strings. These fembots find a memory string and rewrite it. You lose that memory and gain a belief. I think it happened to me, when I was much younger. Different clades of fembot transmit different memes. Some are very strong, like the loyalty plagues used in Africa—'

'I know how it works,' Morag says.

She suddenly has a clear vision of the refugee camps, a million men, women and children with a single, myriad-branched thread, spun by Papa Zumi's loyalty plague, connecting them all. The few people who broke or were spontaneously cured of the plague were hunted down and killed by government men in black suits and video shades. Those young men – they weren't infected. They had chosen to do it to themselves. That was what was so terrible and so sad. They had given up an essential part of themselves for their suits and shiny shoes and for their rooms in the five star hotels, for access to a hospitality bar and satellite TV. They were carriers of power, but it was not their power. When the time came, at the command of Papa Zumi's government in exile, they surrounded the clinics. When negotiations between the UN and the imperturbable Papa Zumi broke down, the young men moved in and marched all the aid workers out at gunpoint. The next day the young men were dead, along with a million refugees.

Alex gives her a shrewd look. 'The fairies in the Magic Kingdom are releasing thousands of different kinds of psychoactive viruses and fembots. We're pretty sure the fairies aren't designing them; they're evolving them at random, and selecting the ones that are most successful at whatever they're supposed to do. The Interface samples the air and tries to sort out those which may be useful from those which aren't. But these are airborne contaminants the warewolf picked up from inside. Some of them may be the fairies' own loyalty plague.'

'Most of them fall into the spectrum of Interface samples,' Max says, 'but there are significant outliers.'

Light flashes over the holostage, clears to show half a dozen slowly rotating lumpy shapes.

Alex says, 'Fairy and Crusader fembots are very different from the fembots used by meme hackers. For one thing, they are manufactured by assemblers capable of sexual reproduction. That's why there are so many different kinds of fembots associated with the Crusade. It's just like biological sex in simple organisms, in which the parents act as their own gametes. The assemblers fuse, randomly exchange discrete bits of genetic information – in this case, algorithms – and separate. I think there's a degree of induced mutation at this point, too. The two new assemblers are chimeras of the sum of the combined genetic information of both parents. The fittest offspring are those which can infect people and make fembots which turn them into Children's Crusaders most success-fully. It's artificial evolution—'

'Except,' Max says, 'We're not sure what the endpoint is.'

'We don't even know if there is an endpoint,' Alex says. 'The assemblers spread like HIV. Or worse, actually, since a kiss is enough to do it. But there aren't any assemblers here, only their products, and besides, these are all dead – they only work in serum. See how they're kind of collapsed?'

Alex smiles at Morag, but she isn't impressed by this technical garble. She says, 'We already know where he comes from.'

Max says, 'She thinks it's a show, chief. You should let her go.'

Alex says, 'What about it? You want to go?'

'Of course not. I don't think that this is a show at all. It's all too familiar.'

'Well, if you want to stay, you can help out,' Alex says. 'Have you ever taken out a control chip?'

Morag has, many times. During her paramedic training, she spent a month at the Leith parole clinic, where she inserted control chips into newly convicted zeks and took them out of zeks at the end of their sentence. Like little independent consciences, like so many copies of Pinocchio's Jiminy Cricket, control chips are forever alert for wrong-doing. They limit zeks' movements to proscribed areas and induce a cataleptic reaction if the zeks take any kind of psychoactive drug or become involved in proscribed situations.

The warewolf's chip seems no different from civilian parole models. It nestles in a sliver-thin terminal implanted in his right eyesocket. Morag anaesthetizes the eye muscles with a curarine spray, slightly displaces the eyeball, and plucks the chip using a microstage scaffold that fits itself to the contours of the warewolf's eyesocket. She can do nothing about the pseudoneurons that fembots will have spun to connect the chip's hardware to the neurons of the warewolf's own cortex, but without the control chip the wetware is inactivated. The chip is no bigger than a pin; Max scans it and announces that it's a genuine army device.

Alex prises open the man's jaws and squints at his tongue, but just shrugs when Morag asks what he's looking for. 'We'll bring him around,' he says. 'Maybe he can tell us something.'

'That'll be the day,' Katrina says.

She's right. Armand does nothing but shiver and weep for an hour or so, and then can only tell them what they already know. Max scrolls up a plan of the Magic Kingdom, but Armand says he doesn't know where the fairy nest is. Somewhere underground. Close questioning reveals that it is centred on a generator pit; Max locates one in the theme park itself, and a backup system under the resort hotel complex.

'Except that is still in use,' Max says.

They don't learn much else from Armand. By degrees, he is ingratiating, then stubbornly sullen, and then almost hysterical, denying everything.

Finally, he starts to flail out wildly. Katrina gets Armand's arms in a lock behind his neck and marches him into the maze of cubicle screens. Morag hears her shout that she'll whale the shit out of him if he doesn't calm down, then the meaty sound of a couple of blows, then silence.

'She needs to blow off steam,' Alex says, as if to mollify Morag.

But Morag feels little sympathy for the man. He's a kind of shell, eaten away from the inside, pathetically obsequious, devious, and violent. Something about him breathes his victim status – more than sympathy, you want to pitch him out of a window and have done with him.

Katrina returns and says she put the little fucker to sleep. It is late, past midnight. Morag makes a nest of bubblewrap in a corner, pillows her head on her folded coat. She falls into a light, uneasy sleep, waking from bad dreams to the half-light of the biolumes, the low mutter of conversation elsewhere in the room. The swags of cable seem ominously like snakes, the random pinhole speckles in the ceiling tiles a movement away from making some kind of sense, but Morag falls asleep again before they do.

She is shaken awake by the washed-out blonde woman, who puts a finger to her lips when Morag starts to ask why. It's cold and quiet. The overhead lights shed a timeless greenish glare on the cubicle partitions, the scarred desks, the dusty grey carpet tiles.

As Morag gets up, stiff with cold, there's a muffled hammering downstairs. 'Quickly,' the blonde says, and hurries away.

Max is gone, although all his equipment has been left switched on, humming and blinking like some electronic *Marie Celeste*. The lights are out in the rest of the building, and Morag must fumble her way down the spiral staircase. The blonde hisses that she must hurry, there's no time.

'No time?'

Just then the hammering stops.

'They're in,' the blonde says, and snatches up Morag's hand and pulls her along. 'Hurry!'

Alex Sharkey is waiting with Katrina in a tiny basement room. Armand is curled on its oily concrete floor. Alex grins at Morag and says, 'I was right all along. It's the Children's Crusade. It's *her*.'

Katrina has a little flatscreen TV. 'They're at the back now,' she says. 'A van there. That's where they'll be expecting to take us out.'

'She's come for us,' Alex says. 'I knew she would.'

The blonde closes what looks like a fire door. It has thick rubber flanges at top and bottom, along both sides. She dogs it shut with some effort, throwing three big levers one after the other.

'So we're locked in here,' Morag says. She's still half-asleep. It isn't quite real to her.

There are two big air cylinders strapped to the wall by the door. The blonde opens their valves, and a high-pitched whistle fills the little room.

Morag's ears hurt, then pop when she swallows. Now she understands. Positive pressure. She says, 'Max is a love bomber.'

Katrina, grinning like a wolf, flicks the little control ball on her flatscreen with exaggerated shifts of her shoulders and elbows as she scans between the building's surveillance cameras.

'They're through the front door,' she says. 'Right up the stairs.

Nice moves in the doorways. They keep low, they let their weapons look round corners first. These kids are wired. Interesting choice of weapons, too. Tangle spray, tasers. Looks like they want to take us alive. Ah, this is good, now we have them. They are looking around. They don't quite believe what is happening. Oh, now they do. They really do believe. Looks like a regular prayer meeting starts up there.'

The blonde stands with her back to the sealed door. She says in a small, flat voice, 'We did so much work here. This building doesn't even exist on any database, we were so thorough. I'm sorry to leave it.'

'Max would say never get attached,' Alex says.

'That's because he steals anything he wants,' the woman says. 'To him, the world is just a department store and we're mice living in the chinks. All he needs is his data.'

'He left his computer behind,' Morag says.

The blonde says, 'That's just a terminal. The data is all over the world, encrypted in Web servers and commercial nets. We were using half a per cent of the Russian Stock Exchange system at one time. That's a lot of processing power.'

Suddenly, the little fairy is hovering in front of Morag's nose. She swipes at it and it gives her the finger before flying up into the glare of the buzzing fluorescent circlet and vanishing in a pop of silvery falling flakes.

The blonde says flatly, 'We grew stuff all through the building, too. All wasted.'

Alex says, 'It's for the greater good.'

'Bullshit,' the blonde says flatly. 'This will cost you even if you don't get in.'

'Oh, absolutely.'

'Or we'll track you down.'

'Oh, you won't need to do that.'

Katrina says, 'Half the fuckers are actually praying. One poor fool is rushing around, clutching his head – maybe he never was a true believer after all.'

'Oh, they are all true believers,' Alex says.

'They're getting a righteous rush now,' Katrina says.

Morag asks, 'Who are they?'

Alex says, 'A unit of the Children's Crusade. I've finally caught her attention. But these are only foot soldiers. They're not what I want. Anyone outside, Kat?'

'Two on the roof opposite the front. We got everyone in the back.'

'It's a confined space,' the blonde says. She hands out clear plastic goggles, and little filter masks that fit over nose and mouth. 'The fembots can only get in via the mucosal membranes,' she tells Morag. 'The mask has a reactive filter, little effectors help push air through when you breathe in, flip-flop a charge that blows anything off when you breathe out. It won't clog, although it might grow a little warm if you use it too long. Take shallow breaths.'

The edges of the mask and of the goggles seem to slither and squirm as they make a tight seal with Morag's skin. Katrina has fitted goggles and a mask over Armand's face; now she picks him up in a fireman's carry as the blonde unclamps the door.

There are two children by the stairwell, and two more in the corridor leading to the loading bay at the back of the building. Murmuring and weeping, they fix thousand metre stares on thin air, as if looking right through the building at some terrible and glorious apparition.

Morag steps around them, breathing shallowly. There's no resistance in the little mask; only a band of pressure around her mouth and nose reassures her that there's a barrier between her nervous system and the billions of fembots swarming in the air, each one pregnant with a dazzling vision.

A van is backed up to the loading bay in the rear of the building. A padded floor and benches, straps dangling from the roof. Morag hangs on to a strap as Katrina drives off at speed into the grey early morning. Armand rolls back and forth on the cotton padding as Katrina takes a tight corner without slowing down. The back of his head keeps bumping against Morag's boots.

They drive for a few minutes, Katrina turning right and left at random, before the blonde says that time is up. She strips off her mask and goggles. There are red weals where the seals gripped her skin. 'It's all right,' she tells Morag. 'They don't multiply, and they have a suicide clock.'

Morag takes off her mask, and discovers that the back of the van smells of cheap incense. Katrina stops the van and jumps out. Alex opens the rear doors, and Katrina picks up Armand and carries him to her taxi, which is parked where they left it last night. The blonde jumps down and walks away down the street without looking back, even when Alex shouts after her that he'll keep his side of the deal and he expects Max to keep his. She turns a corner, is gone.

Morag says, 'What bargain?'

'Max is monitoring the Children's Crusade. He hacked into their communications. That's why we knew about the possibility of a raid.'

'And he ran away.'

'He has to set up a new node.'

'You like this, don't you? This stupid conspiracy.'

Alex says, 'I don't have much choice.'

'Let's go!' Katrina shouts.

A gang of children, all dressed in white T-shirts and blue denim coveralls, are running towards them. Morag climbs into the back of the taxi, beside Armand, and Alex heaves himself into the passenger seat as Katrina guns the taxi's engine.

There's a bang on the roof. A moment later, a child's face appears upside down at the windscreen. It is as vacuously pretty as a cherub, with a mop of golden curls and plump, rosy cheeks. Katrina punches; the switch that connects the taxi's battery into the bodywork. There's a blue flash. The child rolls sideways and falls on hands and knees beside the taxi, and Katrina drives away as fast as she can.

When the taxi arrives at the head of the *impasse*, Katrina cuffs Armand to the frame of the taxi's front passenger seat and tells Morag to wait there and watch him. But Morag isn't going to sit in the car with the warewolf, even if he is unconscious and she has taken his chip out herself, and in the bleak early morning light she follows Alex and Katrina over the railway bridge to their tall narrow house.

The door has been broken open. A looped infinity sign with a dependent cross has been scrawled in white above the frame. Inside the house, someone has pulled down the heavy curtains and tried to set fire to the Persian carpet, but water from pipes ripped from the walls has put out the flames, leaving a stench of wet char.

The computer deck is gone. Alex says that it was just a terminal, like Max's, that his data files are stored elsewhere. But he's lost something of his cheerfulness, and sits on a plastic chair and stares into the distance, ignoring Morag's questions, while Katrina rummages noisily through the house. When she comes back, she says there're signs all through.

'Fucking Ray fucked us over.'

Morag asks if it's fairies, but Alex says no, it's definitely the Children's Crusade.

'I think we have her attention now,' he says. 'Come on. They'll have sown monitors here and I can't trust my scavengers to find every one.'

Outside, Katrina says, 'That little fucker. I see his blue face and his stupid grin he's dead.'

Alex says, 'We don't know it was him.'

Katrina says, 'You are too trusting. The fucker is working both sides. As usual. He was her creature all along. She will know everything.'

'No, not everything. I think we still have a chance.'

'Without Ray?'

'Well, you didn't trust him, so it should make no difference to you. We have Bloch, and we have the warewolf. Last time it was just us.'

'Last time we nearly got fucking killed,' Katrina says. 'One more thing, I say we leave her here.'

'You try,' Morag tells her.

Katrina gives her a hard cold look.

'We made a deal,' Alex says. 'Don't give me a hard time over this, Katrina. We're in enough trouble as it is.'

Armand has woken up in the taxi, and has been trying to free himself. He reeks of sweat, and his wrists are raw where be has been pulling at his handcuffs. He glares at them through greasy hair that's flopped down over his starved face.

'You'll get yours,' he says. 'I have friends.'

He keeps this up on the drive out of the city, laughing when

Katrina reaches around to slap at him. 'You wait,' he says. 'You wait.'

Alex says, 'You're on your own, my friend. The killer in your head is gone, and without him your little friends won't have much use for you. Think about it.'

This shuts Armand up for a while. They stop at a transport café just off the motorway. Katrina stays in the taxi to keep an eye on Armand. Inside, Morag drinks nutmeg-flavoured coffee while Alex devours three cheeseburgers, one after the other.

'You should eat,' he says, speaking English, 'Keep your strength up.'

'I want to know what you're doing this for,' Morag says.

Alex dabs at his greasy lips with a napkin. He is uncomfortable and anxious, squeezed behind the fibrechip table in the little privacy booth. Now that he is committed to act, he realizes that he depends upon this determined but naïve young woman more than he can admit. And he can't possibly explain the glamour that was cast over him so long ago, that pulls at him still for all that he was used and then abandoned.

He says, 'There was this fellow I met in Amsterdam. I learnt something from him about the kind of fairies that have taken over the Magic Kingdom.'

'Was this when you met Katrina?'

'Just before. Dr Luther had a kind of brothel, and used zeks as assistants. You know how that works?'

'I worked in a parole clinic for a wee while.'

'Dr Luther had special requirements. He used zeks with medical training to help him convert dolls into sex toys, and he could get around the limitations of zek control chips. He also dealt with fairies, a kind of side business. One of his assistants got mixed up with the fairies, and they gave him a taste of something special.'

Morag makes a connection. 'Armand needs something, doesn't he? Something the fairies give him.'

'I've heard it called soma, but it certainly isn't much like the drug of the Rig-Veda. It transforms your perception of the world, and gives you an intense sense of well-being, but you remain functional. It's also very addictive. Someone once told me it strips away the veil, shows you the light of creation shining through base objects. She said it really does put you in Fairyland, But you don't just need the drug, you need to be infected with something that knits itself into the muscle of your tongue and grows up into your limbic system. And that's all I know.'

'People would pay for something like that?'

'Of course. Drugs tend to reflect the stresses of the times. Think of the craze for mood-altering drugs at the turn of the century, when people struggled to adjust themselves to an ideal. Now there's a reaction to the kind of mass psychosis prevalent in the late twentieth century. People want individual trips. They want to disappear inside themselves. Think of all those geezers and babush-kas in their little cells in the ribbon arcologies, with only the artificial intimacy of the Web to connect them to other human beings. They spend much of their lives inside their own heads. One of the things Max monitors is social trends. There are thousands of mobots scattered across the Moon and Mars which people can plug into any time they want to – soon there will be at least a million on Mars alone, because the astronauts are setting up a factory there. There's the self-replicating probe in Jupiter. People in the ribbon arcologies spend at least half their lives in virtuality or plugged into some machine that experiences the world for them.'

Morag thinks of the excursion dolls that march in obedient crocodile files through the streets and museums and monuments of Paris, each with a virtual tourist gazing through its eyes.

Alex says, 'The next step is to move across the mind-machine barrier. It's been possible for five years, although impossibly expensive. But it's what an increasing proportion of humanity want. This is an age of solipsists, and I used to cater to that. It's how I made my living. I started by making psychoactive viruses for ravers, and more recently I fell in with love bombers like Max. And there's even more extreme stuff out in the world than anything I've ever made. Even more extreme than soma, believe me.'

Morag says impatiently, 'What does this have to do with rescuing the poor wean?'

'Armand needs soma. It's physiologically addictive, and he'll be hurting bad pretty soon. We'll let him go and he'll lead us in. I have a contact in the Interface who will help. At a price.'

'And then what will you do?'

214

'We've done this before. Trust us.'

'As long as you find out how to make soma? That's what you're really after?'

'I told you what I'm after. The soma is just for finance.'

'This woman. I wish I could believe it was as simple as that.'

'Love is never simple,' Alex says.

14
The Interface

They drive into the Interface without any trouble. Alex pays the outrageous toll with a platinum credit chip, and the taxi is waved through into the big, mostly empty parking lot.

Armand is nodding out, sweating heavily and shivering. Morag recognizes the symptoms. He's going cold turkey, with vascular collapse a real possibility. She wants to get him stabilized, but Alex says that it won't be fatal, and Morag has to believe him. Still, she gets a little orange juice down Armand's throat before she leaves him in the taxi with Katrina and follows Alex across the parking lot.

The Interface has grown up around the ruins of the main gate of the Magic Kingdom and the biggest of the resort hotels. The hotel's original structure has platforms and towers bolted on to it, crowding up around each other like plants fighting for light, all turned towards the Magic Kingdom. There are even camera platforms suspended from tethered blimps. The plump, silvery blimps swivel and flash like pregnant guppies above the Interface's unregulated sprawl. Close by the perimeter of the Magic Kingdom, filter traps, like plantations of giant black sunflowers, hoover the air for fembots and gengineered microbes let loose by the fairies.

Corporate research teams rent space in the hotel itself, paying astronomical prices for any room with a glimpse of the Magic Kingdom. But much of the surveillance and sampling of the Magic Kingdom is carried out by freelances. They live and work and play in trailers and slab prefabs and inflated tents strung out along pot-holed roads or muddy tracks, and in houseboats floating on the long lake.

The Interface is an unplanned zone driven by the Invisible Hand of free enterprise. Like a nineteenth century gold rush camp, extremes of opulence and squalor sit side by side. There are a dozen different communications systems, and a web of competing powerlines and cableways is strung overhead. Walls are scribbled with spraytags and scaled with responsive posters: an unwary step can loose a spray of advertising meme carriers in your face. There are fast food stands and credit washrooms, and dozens of tiny bars. Holograms hang above trailers and the flat roofs of prefabs, from the sharp, tiny signs of one-person operations to the serene, towering icons of the megacorps. Virtuality, Sanyo, Sega-IBM, InScape: characters from electronic dreams loom into the sky as huge and insubstantial as gods, the luminous figures Morag sees every night as she works the Bidonvilles to the south and east of the Interface.

Alex leads Morag through this maze of narrow streets at a good pace for a man of his bulk. Concrete paving gives way to astroturf to trampled mud and back to paving again. A Japanese TV crew is taping an interview with some teenage scout, who, lounging in black jeans, black leather jacket and video shades, is irradiated in a hyperreal glow from floating lamps. One street is blocked by sawhorses strung with bio-hazard tape, and a crew in decontamination suits, looking like Mars astronauts, is working inside a bubble thrown up over a prefab.

'Things get out of hand sometimes,' Alex tells Morag.

He's excited by the palpable buzz of the Interface's runaway commercialism. His face is flushed, and his breathing is alarmingly stertorous.

'You should have seen it when it first set up,' he says. 'The big corporations have marginalized everyone else now, but in the beginning it was a scramble where anyone could come out a winner. Now most of the small outfits are trying to work up stuff from the discards of the bigger outfits, gleanings that aren't worth the trouble of screening. The fairies seem to be manufacturing their stuff by hyperfast Darwinian selection. They don't design anything, they just seed a tailored environment and sit back and wait for something to win out over everything else. As a result, there are a million varieties of fembot that don't seem to do anything, but which could turn out to possess some novel and commercially useful feature. A lot of the gengineered stuff is junk, too, and most of the rest is nothing but stripped homeoboxes, strings of DNA coding for sets of effector proteins, but without any kind of activator or regulator. People bolt on all kinds of transcription instructions, and most times it doesn't work. And when it does, most times it doesn't do anything, or starts replicating in futile cycles of junk DNA. And usually when you do get something to work, you don't want what it does. Containment is the only thing that is regulated here, but sometimes it breaks down. Or it is broken down.'

Morag has noticed that half the passers-by are wearing the same kind of goggles and mask that the blonde woman gave her when the Children's Crusade raided Max's place. There's not only the risk of fembots small as bacterial spores drifting across from the Magic Kingdom; there are the products of a thousand unlicensed bioware and nanotech labs to contend with. Every month, someone in the European Parliament calls for the shutdown of the world's biggest uncontrolled bioreactor, this century's Chernobyl or Sellafield in the making. Nothing blown out or released or traded by the fairies has ever been proved infective, but that doesn't mean that some gene hacker won't make it so, by design or by mistake. Or that one day the fairies will not release something that will make HIV or Ebola virus look like the common cold. But the simple fact is that Europe needs the money; the demands of its vast social infrastructure are outstripping its shrinking manufacturing base.

Anything is possible in the Interface, but even so Morag is amazed when they turn a corner and run into a Children's Crusade revival meeting. One moment she and Alex are walking down a muddy track between slab concrete walls; the next, they are in the middle of a holographic vision of a pastoral heaven out of the chiliastic paintings of John Martin, with a celestial city shining like golden soap bubbles beyond the gauzy distance of English meadows. Angels as vacuously handsome as soap opera stars rush towards them, and Alex grabs Morag's arm and hustles her back the way they came, out of range of the meeting's sensors.

'Anyone who can afford it can set up here,' Alex says. 'You

understand that the Children's Crusade has more reason than most.'

He leads Morag to a long lake where houseboats and rafts rub together, linked by pontoon causeways or simply strung in rows, so that you have to clamber from deck to deck to get where you are going. At the outer edge of this shabby archipelago is a bar built inside a steel barge grounded to its gunwales on the muddy bottom of the shallow lake. Its deck is a tottering cascade of platforms, some with little gardens, others bearing wire or dish aerials, one with a holographic miniature of Escher's paradoxical watermill, shining in bright colours on this grey day. On the tallest platform is a pay telescope of the kind that used to be found along every beachfront in Europe. It is pointed towards the distant towers of the Magic Kingdom. Skull and crossbone flags and banners fly from a skeletal microwave mast; the largest, in letters made of skulls and long bones, proclaims that this is the *Oncogene*.

The inside is done out in tacky red velour plush and industrial steel. Blue and bronze welds scar mirror-polished surfaces. At one end is a pool table, with black baize and balls patterned like monochrome Bridget Riley prints. At the other end is a bar counter backed by a huge TV showing, like the information screens at an airport, acronyms and number strings that continually scroll up line by line.

A bored bartender is watching a soap opera on a palm-sized TV. The only customer is a lanky man who sits crosslegged on a couch, scribbling on a slate. This is Alex's contact. His name is Pieter Bloch. He has a long, morose face, and a shock of grey hair like electrified wire wool. He squints at Morag, taking in her water-stained quilted coat, and says to Alex, 'You said nothing about this person. Where is Kat?'

'Things change,' Alex says affably. 'You know how it is.'

Morag returns Bloch's stare until the man looks away and says, 'I don't like sudden changes. First there was this mass release, and now you bring this strange woman I do not know.'

Alex says, 'What mass release?'

'You do not know?'

'Let's all have a beer,' Alex suggests. 'Then you can tell me about it.'

The bartender opens three Heinekens – Heineken, blond or dark, is all the bar serves – by knocking off the caps on the edge of the counter. Bloch takes a long swallow of beer, wipes his mouth, and tells Alex that huge numbers of a single type of fembot were discharged into the air above the Magic Kingdom just after dawn.

'There are plenty of rumours about what it's for, believe me, but no one yet knows. The consensus is that it is a meme carrier.'

'It got past the air curtains?'

'Of course it did. They never really work. Prevailing winds were towards Paris, too.'

Morag says, 'Is it dangerous?'

Bloch shrugs.

'So,' Alex says, 'the fairies love bombed Paris. It's an interesting coincidence.'

'You know it is not a coincidence. The Magic Kingdom is either breaking down or undergoing some drastic change. This release is a part of the situation. You have the human agent? Where is he being held?'

'He's safe enough.'

Morag feels a sudden spurt of anger. She is beginning to realize how much she has been used. This has all been planned, and now she has been used as bait for the warewolf there is no real part left for her to play.

'So we can go in tonight,' Alex says to Bloch.

'Don't worry about that side of things. It's in my hands now. Trust me.'

Morag, who doesn't trust either of them, says, 'What about the security here?'

Bloch makes a kind of snorting noise through his nose.

Alex says patiently, 'Anyone can try and penetrate the Magic Kingdom, but no one wants to destroy it. The big corporations are probing it all the time, but no one gets very far. Nor do they want to, as long as the fairies continue to produce the goods. The aim of security here is to prevent attacks on the Magic Kingdom and the infrastructure of the Interface, to keep the outside outside. That's why we need specialist help to be able to sneak in – centimetre for centimetre, the Magic Kingdom is probably the most heavily watched spot on the planet.'

Morag thinks of how quickly the security guards arrived, and realizes that the perimeter peeper wasn't running from them, he was running from her. Association by guilt. And then it really hits her. The murder – all the murders – must have been witnessed by dozens of cameras and surveillance devices.

She says, 'Tell me one thing. Was I part of your plans from the beginning? When you saw the little girl's murder, when you saw who did it, when you saw me, Jules and me, find the body, did you work it all up then? Or were you just waiting for something like this to happen?'

Alex says, 'The fairies have been taking ovaries from little girls for at least a year.'

'But we disturbed them, and they wanted to get rid of us. That's when you saw Armand, wasn't it? That's when you decided to use me as bait.'

Alex says, 'Even if that's so, what does it matter? We'll take you in. Don't worry.'

Bloch says, 'If the little boy is alive, I'll find him.'

Perhaps this is meant to reassure Morag, but the flip way he says it reveals that for him this is a trivial part of the operation.

'Pieter's a good scout,' Alex says. 'He was here from the beginning.'

'Not for much longer,' Bloch says. He glances at his slate, then erases it and puts it away in a pocket of his smock-like shirt. He says, 'This whole place is about played out. Nothing's come through for a while now. The little fuckers are just diddling with the corporations. They're bluffing. It's plain to see that they've run out of trade goods. Sooner or later someone is going to go in with force and that will be the end of it.'

'That's why we're going in now,' Alex tells Morag.

'Oh no,' Bloch says. 'That's why you're not going in, because if you do, every ragged-arse motherfucker will follow, and no one will get anything out of it. Sit down, Alex. You too, mademoiselle.'

Morag reaches the helical stair ahead of Alex. Bloch calls after them, 'Really, there is no place to run.'

Morag scrambles out into the cold, grey air. Four security guards are making their way across the houseboat moored along-side the *Oncogene*. They are led by the blonde woman who turned

220

Morag away three nights before. She isn't wearing a mask now, but Morag would recognize her anywhere. The woman points at Morag and shouts something that is torn away by the freezing wind that blows across the lake.

Morag runs for the *Oncogene*'s bow. She plunges straight through the Escher hologram and clambers around the struts of the microwave mast. Black water two metres below; the guard coming around the mast. Morag tears off her coat and the guard grabs for her and is left holding the silver quilted coat by one sleeve as Morag dives into the water.

15
Surfacing

Morag comes up beneath a floating pontoon, gasping for breath in a tiny space of black, foul air. Footsteps bang and rattle overhead, moving away. Morag pulls herself towards a little tent of grey light, ducks under the ice-cold water again, and surfaces between the sides of two houseboats amidst a floating litter of dead leaves, foodwrappers and bleached Coke cartons.

Cold has robbed her of any feeling in her hands, and the weight of her boots is dragging her down. She manages to loop an arm through a fender's rope and hangs there, simply breathing. Then Katrina leans out above, her shaven head silhouetted against the grey sky. She grips Morag under the armpits and hauls her up.

The houseboat is an empty dormitory. Katrina silences its alarm circuits, smashes a door panel, and drags Morag inside a long cabin lined with bunks. She finds a sheet, and leaves Morag to strip out of her soaked clothes and dry off. Morag is sitting wrapped in the sheet, trying to stop shivering, when Katrina returns carrying a set of orange coveralls with the InScape logo emblazoned on their back. They are oily and ripped, and at least two sizes too big, but they are dry.

Katrina opens a carton of tomato soup, and Morag holds it in her hands as it warms. The first sip scalds her tongue, but she eagerly drinks the rest as fast as she can.

Katrina explains that the security guards came for Armand. She set fire to the taxi and escaped while they were trying to put it out and rescue the warewolf. Then she followed them to the *Oncogene*.

Morag says, 'That man, Bloch, knew about it. He betrayed you. They have Alex.'

Katrina scratches at the strip of leopard fur on top of her shaven skull and says, 'Bloch must have made a deal with these people, or with the company they work for. I talked with Max, and that's what he thinks.'

'What will they do?'

Katrina lights a cigarette. 'What the fuck do you care? I said all along this isn't your business. You shouldn't be here.'

'Give me one of those.'

'I did not think you smoke.'

'I started again.'

The nicotine rush is much diminished, but after a few puffs Morag feels calmer. She says, 'I thought you could help me. You and Alex. Tell me about Bloch and his friends. What will they do with Alex?'

'Alex will look after himself. He will try and bargain with these people. He knows things they need.'

'They could turn him over to the police. And won't they be looking for us?'

'At worst they will hold Alex until they have gone in, and then they will release him. By then he can do no harm.'

'You seem very certain.'

Katrina says, with exaggerated patience, 'Security patrols are made up of employees of the three big corporations, one from each. They do not trust each other, you understand. It is like Berlin or Vienna after the Second World War. These people, though, were all from one company, or at least they all wore the same uniforms and were armed with the same model of taser. You have finished the soup?'

'What? Oh, yes.'

Katrina hands Morag a carton of coffee and opens another for herself. 'We will wait here two, three hours. You get warm. Then we will go. Do not be scared. We will be fine. I have arranged things.'

'Do you still want to break into the Magic Kingdom?'

'Of course. Max says the fuckers who took Alex will make their move tonight, in case we try to make new plans. There was a big release of fembots this morning. Things are breaking down.'

'I know. I mean, Bloch told Alex more or less the same thing. Katrina, we must get into the Magic Kingdom ahead of them.'

'I admire your spirit. I rescued you from the water because you have guts, jumping like that. You did not know they were not armed with anything more than tasers.'

'It was stupid. I didn't stop to think.'

'If you stop, you do not do it. Tell me, now we have time to talk, why do you want to stop them?'

'They won't care that they are risking the little boy's life. I think that if they go in, the fairies might threaten to kill the little boy, and I know these people won't care if they do.'

'Fairies don't think like that,' Katrina says. 'We rest now.'

Katrina lies down on one of the bunks and promptly falls asleep. Morag finds a mirror in the dormitory's bathroom and finger-combs her drastically shortened hair into some kind of shape, then sits by a window and smokes four of Katrina's cigarettes, one after the other, and watches the segment of the Intersection's skyline visible beyond the superstructure of the adjoining houseboat. Three giant holographic figures of vironment supermodels, caught in heroic gestures, slowly revolve in the sky. One is the saint of the Bidonvilles, Antoinette. Morag thinks she recognizes one of the others. Joey something. Santano, Serpico, something like that. The third, a ruggedly handsome white-haired man, she doesn't know at all. She doesn't have much time for the vironment sagas in which you can pull on the body of one of these heroes like a suit of clothes, but she would like to be able to do that right now. She would like to be strong and certain, not cold and scared, not intensely aware of her vulnerability. She has been on intimate terms with death too many times not to be scared of it.

The holographic figures seem to grow brighter as the sky darkens. At last Katrina's watch beeps, scaring the hell out of Morag. Katrina wakes at once, and says that it is time to go.

Katrina rents a secure phone line from a fat Dutch woman who runs an office service in a cramped room in one of the prefabs.

223

Morag waits outside the sealed booth, nervously watching everyone who goes past, her arms wrapped across her breasts. It's cold, and the heating circuit in the baggy coveralls is defective, scorching her back and not working anywhere else. At any moment Morag expects the gang of security guards to round a corner and descend on her.

Katrina is in the booth a long time. When she comes out she looks grim, and tells Morag to follow her.

'I talked with Max again. He has made arrangements. He sends a car for you.'

'You're going to do something, aren't you?'

'Alex made a deal with you, perhaps. But not with me. You walk away, no shame.'

'Not without the boy.'

Katrina says, 'You can't save everyone in the world. Yes, you see I know something about you. Go home. There is no shame.'

'You're saying that you won't help me?'

'For what reason do I help you?'

Morag stops. They are at the edge of the vast, dark, weed-grown and mostly empty parking lot. Only a few lights are working. The burnt-out hulk of the taxi sits under one, in a drying pool of white foam.

Morag says, very much on her dignity, 'I'll find these people and offer to go in with them. They will take what they want, and I will look for the little boy. It's exactly the same deal I made with you and Alex. I don't care about these silly games. Only the little boy and an end to the murders.'

'Except they will not agree to it. Why should they?'

'Perhaps not. But if you won't help me, then I'll have no other choice.'

Katrina says, 'You come with me. We think of something.'

'You're going to run away, aren't you?'

'Think what you like,' Katrina says, suddenly angry. 'You come with me or stay here and get fucked. I don't care.'

Katrina walks away, heading straight towards the main gate. Morag lets her do it. Katrina doesn't look back, and after a minute Morag turns and heads towards the prickly towers of the Magic Kingdom.

16
The Magic Kingdom

When they come for Armand, he tries to knock down one of the guards and make a run for it, but another guard gets in first with a rubber cosh and Armand falls, pain exploding in his right knee. They have to carry him into the elevator that takes them down to the service level of the big hotel, although he barely notices. He's so hungry for soma that everything, even the pain in his knee, seems to happen at a great distance in a cold, grey, flat world.

Harassed guards talking into headsets wave on the two men carrying Armand. A man in a one-piece suit trots behind, telling them to hurry. It's cold and dark outside the service entrance. A jeep is waiting there, and Armand isn't surprised to see the fat man sitting in the back seat. Armand has to sit beside the driver. His handcuffs are locked to the crash bar, and one of the guards, a big blonde woman, gets in behind him and says that if he gives any trouble she'll jam her taser so far up his ass he'll be spitting sparks.

Mister Mike will eat her liver, Armand thinks, and giggles to himself. They don't know that they haven't killed Mister Mike. He's coiled inside Armand's skull like a snake.

The fat man asks him how he's feeling, and Armand says defiantly, 'Never better.'

'What did they promise you?'

The blonde guard says sharply, 'You be quiet.'

'Let's move it out, people,' the man in the suit says. He is very young, with a shaven head and plucked eyebrows. Rouge dusts his cheekbones, giving him the hectic look of a tuberculosis victim. He says, 'The clock's running.'

'We don't need this fat fucker,' the blonde guard says. 'This is supposed to be a simple in and out, not a tourist trip. It's my ass on the line here.'

Armand realizes that they're going to take him into the Magic Kingdom, and grins to himself. Once he's there, the Folk will deal with these fools, and then everything will be all right.

'It's all of us,' the young man says. 'The whole team is riding with you.'

'I'm just here to help,' the fat man says mildly. 'I made my agreement with your bosses, not with you.'

The blonde guard pulls the young man to her, kisses him, then pushes him away. She says, 'I'm in charge now,' and tells the driver to move on.

It's a short drive from the Interface to the perimeter of the Magic Kingdom. The whole time the jeep never gets out of third gear. Armand watches everything with interest. He's never been in the Interface before. He looks up at the giant transparent figures hanging in the black air above the buildings, at the different people the jeep passes. He thinks he sees the woman he was supposed to kill, but when he turns around the blonde guard raps the side of his head with her taser.

She was probably a ghost, Armand thinks, but he can't get out of his head the way she stopped and looked right at him. She was wearing baggy orange coveralls. Her black hair had been cut short.

The jeep bumps over wide grills set in the road, air rushing up around it, drives on past plantations of tall, spindly filter traps, then pulls off the road. The blonde guard unfastens Armand from the crash bar, locks the cuff around her own wrist, and hustles him down a grass slope to the railway tracks just outside the tunnel. By the light of the guards' powerful torches, he sees the faint outline of one of the fairies' involuted signs. He grins, tasting Mister Mike's memory of bloodwork.

A man is waiting on the far side of the tracks, bulky in a stiff flak vest under an unfastened puffer jacket. His web belt is loaded with pouches and little bags. Black stuff is smeared on his cheeks and forehead. He's one of the people who fuck around at the edge of the Kingdom, one of the dirty little spies the fairies play tricks on when they can be bothered.

Like the blonde guard, this fool isn't pleased to see the fat man. The fat man says, 'I cut a deal with the suits, Bloch, just like you. Don't worry, you'll still get your percentage.'

Armand says, 'You're all dead, standing here.'

'You shut up,' the blonde guard says.

The fat man says, 'They'll kill you too, Armand. You're a broken weapon. You know what happens to those. Your only chance is to help us.'

It is what they kept telling Armand in the hotel room, after the technicians had taken blood samples and put his head in a frame and looked at false-colour sections of his brain on a TV. It is lies. The Folk will not let him down.

Armand says craftily, 'Let me go in with him—' pointing with his free hand to the fat man '—and we get you what you want.'

The fat man says, 'It's an idea.'

Bloch says, 'You would like that, wouldn't you?'

Armand says, 'I only help him. No one else.'

'You need the soma,' Bloch says. 'I see how hungry you are for soma. Once you get a whiff you'll help us, all right.'

'Shut up, all of you!'

The blonde guard touches her left ear. Armand sees that it's sealed with a flesh-coloured button.

She says, 'The surveillance worm is in the system, ready to go. Once it's activated we have ten minutes at most, but probably no more than six, to get past the perimeter. Human security will have their hands full with the protest marchers, but the AIs won't even blink. You two – you follow the plan. You're in our machine now. Fuck up and I deal with you on the spot.'

She seals a mask over her mouth, puts on goggles. So do the two men. Armand smiles. They're so weak that they don't even dare breathe the living air of Fairyland.

The blonde guard says, 'Before either of you get any cute ideas, remember that the worm diverts the feed from cameras, it doesn't destroy it. Anything funny and you'll be wasted on the way out.' She touches the button in her ear again. 'It's launched.'

There's a shallow scrape under the fence, and they roll under it one by one. Armand makes sure that the blonde guard has to pull him through, even though it hurts his wrist. Once inside, she draws a machine-pistol from inside her leather jacket.

'Hey,' Armand says, 'I know about those,' but no one is listening to him, they're too busy looking right and left.

A wide belt of tall dry grass stretches away, glimmering in the distant light of floodlamps. Bloch tells them to wait, and moves off through the grass in a snaky dance that will do him no good at all.

The fat man whispers to Armand, 'Where are your little friends?'

'All around us. They can hear us. They can smell your blood moving under your skin.'

Armand is excited. He has an erection. His entire skin quivers with little jolts of nervous electricity. He wants to run through the grass, run wild through the Magic Kingdom. Perhaps this time he can chase down the Twins. Perhaps he can scare them so bad they'll never again mock him, never again shoot at him. The Queen is gone, and perhaps he can rule. He could be King. He tips back his head and howls at the night and then he's down in the dry grass with the blonde guard pushing his face into cold dirt, telling him in a whisper muffled by her mask to shut the fuck up.

Bloch comes back and they move on until they reach the weed-grown narrow gauge railway tracks. Ahead, paths glimmer in the semi-darkness. The big mountain in the middle of the lake takes a black, ragged bite out of the neon glow of the Interface. For a moment, nothing stirs; then a cloud of small moths gusts around them, paper-dry wings batting at bare skin and leaving trails like pollen on goggles. Armand snaps at the moths, because they smell faintly of soma, but then Bloch sprays something from an aerosol and the moths disperse as suddenly as they arrived.

The fat man says, 'Is that a helicopter? Listen.'

Armand can hear it.

Bloch says, 'It's on the far side. Probably some news crew watching the protest march.'

Armand giggles. 'They're coming for you,' he says.

They ignore him. Bloch leads the way to the railway station, watching the screen of a little handheld motion detector. Armand used one in Africa, going from house to house clearing out snipers.

The station ticket office is just a brick shell over a frame of rough timber. Inside, it stinks of piss and the ashes of old fires. Bloch kicks dirt away from the access cover, sprays the lugs with penetrating oil and uses a crossbar key to unlatch them. He and the fat man lift the cover.

Red light flares in the small space. Far below, something makes a snarly kind of roar. Then the light is eclipsed, and the roar grows louder. Something is climbing up the shaft.

Armand tries to pull away from the blonde guard. There's a

guardian in the shaft, and guardians don't stop to find out if you're with the Folk or not.

Bloch slams down the cover, manages to get two of the lugs fastened before something slams into the cover from below with a tremendous hollow clang. Dust flies up and Bloch staggers back. 'Out,' he says, 'out, out!'

Outside, the blonde guard says, 'Three minutes, and then there's no guarantee the AIs won't have penetrated the worm's cloak.'

The fat man says, 'They'll only let us in if they want to, Bloch. You know that.'

'Frontierland,' Bloch says. 'There's a dozen ways in through the concession stores there.'

The blonde guard says, 'You were supposed to have scouted this out.'

'I think we've rung their bell,' the fat man says, and points at the mountain.

Figures, small and skinny as children, scurry here and there on its crags, or stand silhouetted against the sky glow.

Bloch says, 'They know we have their warewolf. They won't try anything.'

Armand can smell his sweat.

Bloch says, 'We'll go through the Frontierland storefronts.'

They move forward. The path is littered with bits of metal – parts of the machines sent in by spies and fools. Armand kicks at the litter until the blonde guard jerks on the cuffs. A bridge loops over an arm of the lake. Below its span, islands of foam stiff as beaten egg white drift and turn on the black water. On the far side, there's a short street of old Wild West buildings, a movie set made three dimensional with scrupulous fidelity to an ideal of what never was. The buildings shimmer faintly, as if dusted with silver phosphorescence. The signs of the fairies crawl like black snakes through the dim glow. Fairies stand in every doorway, look down from balconies and the flat roofs.

The fat man says, 'Lead us, Armand. Take us to her.'

Suddenly, two giants race down the street – or no, they are slim human children riding the broad stooped shoulders of squat, muscular dolls. The mounts are bridled, and slaver drips from their snaggle-toothed jaws as the riders turn them deftly to come to a halt before the four humans.

It is the Twins. They point at Armand and say as one:

'Mister Mike will do you slow and nasty.'

The blonde guard steps forward, dragging Armand with her. 'We've come to talk,' she says. 'Take us inside. Out here, everyone can see what's going on.'

Overhead, there is the noise of a helicopter, and then the blare of an amplified voice.

The guard shouts, 'Otherwise we'll kill him!'

'It's too late—'

'—too late to talk now the barbarians—'

'—the barbarians are at the gates.'

The Twins raise their hands above their heads in a grand gesture. In the doorways, on the balconies and roofs, the fairies step backwards into darkness.

The fat man says, 'It's not the protest, is it? It's her.'

'You silly—'

'—silly foolish—'

'—silly foolish vain man—'

'—we don't fear her—'

'—not in the way *you* fear her.'

'We've done all we need—'

'—everything we want—'

'—and now it's time to go.'

The Twins look at each other – their equivalent of a shrug – then laugh and spur their shambling mounts. The brutes wheel and scamper away, their riders jouncing on their shoulders. At the same time, a gang of naked, muscle-bound goblins rush out of the storefronts.

The blonde guard raises her machine-pistol, and Armand runs into her: the pistol's short, sharp burst smashes fragments from the concrete around their feet. Armand is buffeted by a blow to his head, and after that everything seems to happen with underwater slowness.

The blonde guard screams as she vanishes under a flurry of blue bodies. Armand is picked up by his arms and legs. Something wet hangs from his wrist; it is a severed hand, dangling in a ring of steel.

Upside down, he sees headlights glare across the lake. A mob of people races towards the bridges, but then the things carrying him run into a frame of darkness, down into the familiar maze of corridors sparely lit by nodes of blue phosphorescence. The goblins run quickly, hooting softly to each other. Heat and a musky stench rises from them. Claws prick Armand's biceps and calves. The goblins ignore Armand's attempts to reason with them, and when he starts to shout, one clamps a hard leathery paw over his mouth and nose until he almost passes out. He's never liked goblins. They are stupid creatures, loyal because they can only hold one idea at a time in their heads.

Swiftly, he is carried through a long, wide corridor he hasn't seen before. Cold air blows past, and suddenly they're outside, beyond the perimeter of the Magic Kingdom. Armand twists his head and sees that a group of fairies are waiting. But these aren't the Folk; they have the sharp, cruel, clever faces of feys, and they are carrying automatic weapons.

For a moment, the two groups regard each other. Then the goblins drop Armand and with growls rising in their throats rush forward. Armand presses himself flat on the cold ground as gunfire hammers briefly. While the rest of the feys cut off the ears of the goblins for trophies, their leader walks over to Armand and squats beside him.

Armand turns his head and looks into the fey's dark, liquid eyes. He is resigned to death.

The fey says, 'The Queen wants you. Come with us, if you want to live.'

17
The Fairy Queen

Morag sees Armand turn in his seat to stare at her as the jeep goes past, and she starts to run after it. Alex Sharkey is in the jeep too, sitting beside the security guard who ordered her away from the perimeter of the Magic Kingdom. The jeep turns a corner and disappears into the night. Morag goes on at a steady jog towards the only place it can have gone.

Other jeeps start to overtake her, all heading in the same direction. Morag sticks out her thumb, and almost at once one stops. She's so amazed she doesn't move until the driver shouts at her, and then she climbs into the back. Two other people in orange coveralls just like hers make room for her.

The jeep drives across the grills of the air curtain and picks up speed, racing around the perimeter road in the middle of a convoy of jeeps and trucks. The woman beside the driver is watching a flatscreen TV resting on her knees, and at one point she turns around and shouts, 'They're off the road! Off the road and heading for the perimeter!'

Then the jeep crosses the railway line and tops a rise, and Morag sees what is happening. People are marching across the gentle swales and hummocks of the dumps behind half a dozen bulldozers and earthmovers with their racks of lights blazing, moving towards the floodlit boundary of the Magic Kingdom. A helicopter clatters overhead, probing the crowd with a laser spot.

The jeep swerves to a halt beside two trucks parked end to end, and Morag jumps out with the others. People in orange coveralls are unloading reels of tanglewire. Beyond the trucks, activated reels jump and dance as they rearrange themselves, throwing out neat coils that climb over each other and shoot out clusters of razor-sharp spikes. People with tanks on their backs wield wand-like sprayers as they build up huge banks of stickyfoam.

Morag can hear the crowd now, howling as one in sharp percussive phrases, but she can't quite make out what it is they're shouting. The helicopter whirs lower. Its loudspeakers clatter, and then a voice like the voice of God tells the people to disperse.

The crowd reacts like a single organism. A forest of arms thrusts into the air and then the crowd surges forward. The bulldozers belch clouds of smoke as they accelerate and smash through the fence at the edge of the dumps. The lead bulldozer hits the tanglewire and keeps going, dragging a long vee of wire, until it smashes into the perimeter wall of the Magic Kingdom. It stalls, as if stunned, its blade buried under an avalanche of concrete blocks.

People run forward and hurl arcs of liquid at the banks of

stickyfoam, which promptly start to dissolve as exponentially multiplying fembots eat away the foam's cohesive bonds.

Two earthmovers dump mounds of trash on a section of tanglewire, and people start climbing this makeshift ramp.

Morag runs forward to meet them, grinning like a maniac, shouting that she's a friend, she's on their side. A man holds out his arms and catches her and whirls her around. It's one of the drivers from the Mobile Aid Team, Kristoff.

Together, they move forward in the middle of the crowd. 'This is her,' Kristoff keeps saying to people around him. 'This is her! This is Morag Gray! The woman on TV!'

And people smile and shake Morag's hand. They know her. An old lady dressed in about a dozen falling jumpers layered over each other kisses her on the cheek; a man offers her a drink of wine from an unlabelled carton. Kristoff tells her that the call went out across the Web a few hours ago, and then someone inserted a pirate loop in the cable feeds of most of the local TV stations. People from the Bidonvilles, homeless people coached in from Paris, radical fringers and ordinary citizens: all have come together. It's an instant protest, catching the police and the Interface's security forces unawares. Morag thinks of Max, then wonders how he could have organized even one tenth of this.

Kristoff says, 'It grew! It just grew. Spontaneous organization!'

A great cheer goes up around them. Morag realizes that they're inside the Magic Kingdom. A dozen women in a kind of uniform of fringed black leather jackets and white jeans suddenly run towards one of the bridges across the lake. People are spreading out in confused knots. Off to one side, the roof of a house in mock Carpenter Gothic style is suddenly burning, the flames reflected in the foam-flecked black waters of the lake. There are people everywhere, suddenly running free through the fantasy landscape.

Morag runs too. Somewhere beneath the Magic Kingdom is the little kidnapped boy, the fairy changeling. She runs towards the prickly towers of the great castle simply because it is in the centre. Flames from burning buildings send her shadow staggering ahead of her.

Someone is standing on the drawbridge that leads into the high forbidding grey walls.

It is the fey, First Rays of the New Rising Sun.

He waits while Morag gets her breath back. Her back is hot under the coveralls, the rest of her chill with undried sweat. At last she can say, 'I've come for the boy.'

Ray shows his mouthful of needle-point teeth. 'He's not mine to give. But come with me anyway. We find him.'

'If this is a trick I'll break your spine.'

'You are listening to the ideas of that crude woman. Trust me. I make a deal.'

'Why should I trust you?'

'Why not?'

Ray takes one of Morag's hands. His skin is dry and hot. Morag lets him lead her through the castle gate. The fey suddenly lets go of her hand and shouts into the darkness, 'This is the woman!'

Another fey jumps on Morag's back. She whirls around but the fey is clinging to her waist with its legs. Strong fingers pinch her nose shut until she must gasp for breath. A glob of something with the texture of raw liver is thrust inside and she tries to spit it out but it has dissolved into her tongue.

'She wants this!' Ray is shouting. 'She wants this! Not me!'

Then Morag is picked up and swung over a muscular shoulder. An animal's muzzle thrusts towards her face. Tusks pierce its cheeks. The tusks are capped with silver. Talons prick through the coveralls as the thing tightens its grip and carries her down through long perspectives lit by wedges of dim phosphorescence.

Morag is lying under the bare branches of a big tree, on a soft fur rug that generates an animal heat and ripples beneath her as she gets to her knees in the cold air. Strange blue faces swim in and out of flickering lights set in a wide circle around the tree. Long mournful faces with wide lipless mouths, faces with mouths crowded with crooked teeth, like old kitchen knives, or faces with a ruff of stiff quills standing around them, faces with snouts like pigs, or long morose muzzles, faces as round as the moon with tiny features centred in them. People, small, strange, blue-skinned people.

Fairies.

'It's about time,' Ray says.

Morag turns. Ray is standing beside a woman sitting on a plain, high-backed chair. The woman is cloaked in a long, fur-trimmed velvet coat. A fantasticated helmet fringed with spikes and horns covers her face. Instead of eyepieces, it has four faceted lenses the size of saucers, so that the woman seems to have the head of a mantis. A cable runs from the back of the helmet into a computer deck lying on the withered grass.

'I bring her,' Ray says, 'I am true to my word.'

The woman reaches up and lifts the helmet from her head. Her face, its profile as keen as a knife, is the face that, from posters and pages torn from magazines, from TV screens, from the air above the Interface, blesses with its presence every shack and hovel of the Paris Bidonvilles.

A fairy steps up and takes the helmet from the woman. She says to Ray, 'We would have taken her anyway.'

Ray shows his teeth. 'I do so much for you, besides her. We talk about this, you say you help me, help my people—'

The woman says coldly, looking at Morag rather than Ray, 'I don't do deals with feys. You helped me because you know what I am. You shouldn't expect anything in return.'

She makes a gesture, and a muscular, bandy-legged fairy steps forward. It smiles at Ray. Its teeth are fused in two jagged curves of ivory.

Ray looks at Morag with something like desperation, and Morag says, her heart beating quickly, 'I can't help you, Ray.'

Ray howls, and runs headfirst at the circle of fairies. There's a knife in his hand, and its black, crooked blade slashes left and right, but the fairies simply step aside and he runs on, howling, into the darkness.

The woman tells Morag, 'You see that I am not cruel.'

'You used Ray. I think you were using me, too, and Alex.'

'Of course.'

'I'll not judge you. But I don't think you're a kind woman.'

'You want the boy back, and you shall have him. He should not have been taken in the first place.'

'Alex said you called yourself Milena, but that isn't your real name, is it? I mean, no more than—'

'I've changed myself, and soon I'll change again. Soon it won't matter what I'm called. I have little time left here, but that's time enough for you to see what the boy will miss. It's only fair, after all.'

The woman points at a fairy and it steps forward and kneels before her, looking up expectantly. The woman produces a little plastic bottle half-full of a heavy, milky fluid which she drizzles into the mouth of the fairy. It crosses over to Morag, takes her face between its hot, dry hands, and kisses her. Morag kicks out and knocks it down, but not before the hot sweet taste of its tongue has entered hers. And then the violation doesn't matter, because Morag sees.

The night is alive with light, a river of stars carried by people with grave, beautiful, shuttered faces, endlessly rising from darkness and sinking away.

'Walk with me a little while,' the woman says, and picks up a slender, luminous wand. It lays a buttery gleam on the black skin of her face. The tree seems to reach down with its branches towards the light, as a man might warm his hands at a fire.

Morag can feel the tree's yearning for the light as they walk away; for a moment she thinks it might pull its roots from the ground and follow, no longer content to allow the world around it to fall into spring.

The woman says, 'I've sent my words on the wind, and those who recognize them will know where to go.'

'You want the Magic Kingdom destroyed, don't you?'

'It was a mistake to let it live beyond its usefulness to me. I indulged my daughters, and they betrayed me. Do you know who lived here before history?'

Morag says she doesn't. She has the floating feeling of walking in a dream.

'They were hairy, mostly, and lived in holes in the ground. When the first true people came here, with their axes of pure copper, the hairy ones would take babies. Sometimes the babies were rescued, but they never could be human. You can have the changeling my children took, with that warning. He will always be with me.'

They have been walking up a slope, and now they reach its crest. Beyond, a long procession winds across the land. From this vantage it seems endless, although Morag knows that can't be true, because otherwise it would have been marching since the beginning of time, or would have no destination but an end in itself, having swallowed its own tail. It marches away from a burning city where huge, palely luminous ghosts haunt the air and giant insects buzz and chatter. A huge castle rises out of the flames, clawing heavenward with twisting towers.

Morag knows that this is the true aspect of the Magic Kingdom. She also knows that this is a hallucination, but she doesn't care. She feels a scary giddy glee at the way in which the world has been transformed. Happy. Her fear has become happiness, and it is this which makes her scared.

'We walk into the future, as we always have, second by second, but time is so much richer now that every second compresses a whole sheaf of years into its tick or tock. Fairyland isn't a place,' the woman says, 'it's a hyperevolutionary potential. It is where we can dream ourselves into being. Remember to tell Alex that, if you see him.' She gestures towards the darkness. 'My children's poor king.'

A group of fairies, slender and beautiful, talking animatedly, climb the slope, bowing low as they pass the woman. Behind them trudges a tall, burly, one-eyed man, dressed in scraps of armour and leather rags. A poisonous snake wraps his left wrist, biting into swollen tender flesh. There are ivy leaves in his hair, and his ruined eye drips tears of blood that steam when they strike the frozen ground.

The woman bids him draw near. He kneels and says, 'I failed. Forgive me.'

'I forgive you because you failed,' the woman says. She touches his bleeding eyesocket with long white fingers. 'I can't heal you, and perhaps that's best.'

'It was the Twins,' the man says. 'They brought out Mister Mike.'

'Yes, yes,' the woman says with sharp impatience.

Morag knows now who the King is.

He says pleadingly, 'I didn't believe them when they said they would rule the world. But perhaps Mister Mike believed them, do you think?'

'My children may rule the world one day – who knows? But not here, not yet. Now be still.'

And the King becomes stone, except that a rill of bright blood trickles down his granite cheek and splashes his grey chest like a medal ribbon.

The woman turns to Morag and says, 'Do you know about slime moulds?'

Morag shakes her head. She can hardly remember who she is; her heart is beating so strongly in her chest that she feels that she might at any moment be overwhelmed by the force of her own blood.

'I suppose that basic biology is no longer a part of medical training. There's no need for you to know, except that you can tell Alex that there will be a great scattering, and a greater union to come. He'll plod along after me, my poor faithful Merlin. He might even guess what I'm going to do, but he'll be too late. I can do anything I like. No one government or corporation can stop me, and none will join together until it is too late. It is always the way. No one who counts takes the future seriously because no one can canvass the votes of those yet to be born, let alone benefit from them. And more and more, people live in the past, sheltered from the winds of the future. Well, one day, quite soon, we'll blow their house down. You see if we don't.'

'The boy,' Morag says, and then she is walking in a meadow drenched in sunlight. Snow-white bunny rabbits – or they might be mice, or rats, the light is too bright – peep from dew-spangled grass. Bluebirds soar and dip, bluer than the perfect blue sky. The little boy scampers ahead of her, laughing with delight.

The woman says, 'He is my grandchild, you know. They all are, and so I have been punished by the deaths of all the little girls.'

It is night again. Morag says slowly, 'They all lived near the Magic Kingdom. They were all born after the fairies arrived.'

'My own children took it upon themselves to make more sisters and, by accident, one brother. I should have known what they were doing, but I was . . . preoccupied. Living another life while I waited for my own plan to mature. They were very clever. They took nuclei from their own ova and implanted them into artificial spermatocytes. How they laughed to see the women conceive, made big-bellied by the wanton wind, et cetera, et cetera. That was four years ago, when we founded the Magic Kingdom. And then they harvested their half-sisters.'

'They killed them.'

'My children were brought up to survive. They thought that this was the way to do it. They took the ovaries of their daughters, and perhaps they would have raised a strange and terrible army against me. Part of their punishment is that I won't ask them, or let them explain. No more questions? That's good. I'm tired. Tired of questions.'

Morag realizes that the woman has been growing smaller – when she speaks her last word, she and her retinue are no higher than Morag's knees. Then Morag realizes that they are not shrinking, but flying from her. The speed of their passage makes their clothes flap and billow like banners around them. Only the grey King is unmoved. Morag goes down on her knees, on her belly, to watch them dwindle into unguessable distances, and then she is awake.

She is lying on a cold bleak hillside, the ground trampled to mud around the little island of rough grass where she lies. The tree stretching its net of branches against smudged grey light is just a tree. Lying between its roots, wrapped in an ordinary orange welfare blanket, is the little boy, sleeping soundly, sweetly, innocently. Saved.

18
Saved

Six months later, Morag receives a postcard from Alex. She is back in Edinburgh, staying with her parents in the familiar Morningside house in the familiar quiet, tree-shaded street. What little media blitz there was has died down – the story of the lost little boy was swiftly borne away on the flood of speculation about the cause of the end of the Magic Kingdom and the crash of the Interface.

Morag left a message for Alex on the Web as soon as she could. If it didn't find him, perhaps someone in his circle of conspiracy theorists would pass it on. The message wasn't much more than what the woman told her, and she didn't expect a reply.

Meanwhile, she was given extended fembot therapy to remove the thing that bonded into the muscles of her tongue and extended its pseudoneurons into her limbic system. The doctors wanted to test it before removing it, but she insisted that it was taken away at once. The little boy still had his, after all, and his father was selling his story to the newschannels, and no doubt would be pleased to sell the research rights, too.

That is what hurts most, if Morag will let it, although she should have expected no less. In a way, the little boy's rather is right. She took it upon herself to rescue his son, unasked. She should look for no reward.

It was surprisingly easy to rejoin the aid programme. Her left arm aches from an injection of a clade of fembots that will specifically modify the helper T4 cells of her immune system, enabling them to recognize a broad spectrum of infective viruses and bacteria. She has already been through briefing. In a week she will be in Djibouti, where civil war between the two rival ethnic groups, Afars and Issas, has flared up again, forcing a million people to flee the capital.

One day, Morag returns from Tiso's with strong bush boots, a dozen T-shirts, and a hat with a mesh veil, her mother says that there's a postcard for her.

'Someone hand-delivered it. One of those young girls with the funny hair transplants.'

It is a picture of a sprawling fortress, white walls rising from grey limestone cliffs against a backdrop of snowcapped mountains. On the reverse, in cramped but neat handwriting, Alex has written, *Listen carefully.*

'Not hair,' her mother says, 'but a sort of cap of bright feathers. Like a hummingbird.'

'Did she say anything?'

'She said it was for you. She knew your name. Then she was off. Would you like some tea? There's still a smidgen of Earl Grey.'

Morag triggers the postcard's tiny voice. In accented English, it tells her that it is a picture of Gjirokastra citadel, one of the finest examples of a Byzantine and Ottoman fortress in the Balkans.

'. . . which has fascinated Western travellers since Byron and Edward Lear ventured here in the nineteenth century. Some claim that Berat fortress is a purer example of the Ottoman style, but Gjirokastra's dramatic situation against the Buret mountains . . .'

Morag holds the postcard to her ear and runs it again. The postcard's voice scratches on, and underneath it she hears Alex's London accent. He only says four words, and she has to hush her mother and listen to the postcard's spiel again before she understands his message.

'Still looking for Fairyland,' he says.

PART THREE

THE LIBRARY OF DREAMS

1
The Burning Man

'We're in,' Max tells Alex. 'Here, take a look.'

They are talking in Max's Home Room, a crystal-walled bubble that seems to float high above the sulphur-yellow cloud decks of Jupiter. The view is transmitted from an element of the European Space Agency von Neumann probe that is seeding copies of itself across the giant planet. Alex is lying on a couch: in real life he's lying on sunwarmed turf on a hillside, and orientation in a viron-ment at odds with reality makes him nauseous. While Max is present as himself, he has morphed Alex into the mad Roman emperor Caligula, with purple toga and a crown of laurel leaves. Their agents eye each other from opposite poles of the spherical room: Alex's scarlet daemon, with his pitchfork, horns and barbed tail; Max's green woman, her shape crammed with leaves, as if she's a window into some lost wood, her eyes cornflowers, her lips and nipples poppies, her hair delicate ferns.

Max opens a data window. Text scrolls up, is replaced by a glimpse of a burning figure running across a wide space floored with gold-veined marble. It leaves a trail of black footprints. Then more text, and row upon row of symbols. Max watches intently as they scroll up. Alex looks away. A lightning storm as big as a continent is flickering at the vast world's rim.

'Definitely fairy generated,' Max says, spearing an intricate moire pattern with a forefinger. 'Their entoptics underlie the primary image. See? Fuck, Alex, at least take a look. It took me thirty-six hours to strip out the codes.'

Alex looks. He asks, 'How did you get in?'

For years, cracking Glass's Library of Dreams has been a hacker grail.

'Some kid on a trawl found a backdoor,' Max says vaguely. He's more interested in what he's found than how he found it. 'I wonder what kind of computing power Glass has? Those flames must take up gigabytes of iterative calculations, even with anti-aliasing.'

'He has a lot,' Alex says. 'Especially a lot of Reality Engines. Otherwise Milena wouldn't have gone to him.'

'All that graphical power wasted on generating a mausoleum for one dead guy to wander around in. You do the Ultimate Hack, and you put yourself in a glass bottle when there's the whole world to explore.'

Alex asks, 'Don't you think it's a bit . . . suspicious that you've managed to hack into the Library of Dreams right at this moment?'

'Of course it's *suspicious*. It's all part of the game. The strange thing is, this burning guy leaves damage in the system. You saw those smoking footprints?'

'Where was that?'

'A copy of the Library of Congress, one of the lobbies between the stacks. It's not the generic portable Library, either. It's the fully integrated version universities use.'

'Why would Glass make something that damages his own system?'

'Maybe it's a watchdog, there to trash anything that logs in through the backdoor. The Peace Police will shit themselves if it gets into the Web.'

'Is that likely?'

'No one outside the circle knows about it. Not yet. But only because the kid who stumbled across this doesn't know exactly where he ended up. But he will, and then he'll tell his friends, and pretty soon half the world will want a look. There's enough bandwidth on the backdoor feed to allow it, too.'

Alex says, 'We need your help, Max. Don't forget that.'

'The burning man isn't some virus. Nothing can contain it, not even its host system. It can burn through the hardest security programs. It could burn out the whole Web. The more people start dicking around in here, the more likely it's going to get out.'

'You've already hacked the codes. We need a backdoor into his system, and I can't wait, Max. I'm out here in the real world, and its jaws are closing.'

'Yeah. Yeah, I know.'

246

'Split the problem up. Packet it. There are ten million bored wannabes out there. Give them something to do.'

'Don't teach me my job, Alex. I've already worked out an architecture for distributing the problem in a discrete way. All I have to do is press this button—' a bulging red button appears in the air before Max's forefinger, jiggling with barely controlled desire – 'and it's into the Web.'

'Sorry.'

'So, are you set to go?'

'Kat's out now, trying to make contact. Meanwhile, we have this local guy who says he can get us into the neutral zone. We don't trust him, but he's the only way through the army. Bribery isn't simple with these people; it's mixed up in some kind of ethical code. And then there're these mercenaries Glass's people have hired—'

Max says impatiently, 'I can find out about them. It's no big deal.'

'Perhaps we're wrong, Max. Perhaps we should just take everything we've got—'

'Yeah, and what? Tell the Peace Police? They'd love that. It would be perfect propaganda for their drive to send every fairy up a chimney before next Christmas.'

'I was thinking of the UN.'

Max looks scornful. 'One, they wouldn't believe us and, two, they think the Crusaders are, what . . . ?'

'Religious refugees.'

'Yeah, right. Listen, we're behind you, man. Every step. I'll distribute the problem. I estimate that twenty thousand people will try to hack it. Fuck, twenty thousand is a *minimum* number. My architecture will link them up. It will talk to them, drop hints. The thing will grow. I based it on the massive parallel distributive architecture of that three body solution hack the Princeton group organized ten years back. And that involved a million people. It's *under control.*'

'Sure, but I'm in the war zone, and you're . . . where? Where are you, Max? How's your girlfriend?'

'What the fuck does it matter, as long as we can talk? But if there are more of these fuckers—'

Max stabs at the data window, and there's the burning man again, running out of nowhere into nowhere and leaving behind his smoking footprints.

'If there are *enough* of those things and they cross over every time a lurker takes a peek into Glass's fabled Library of Dreams, then they'll burn out the Web, bit by bit.'

'And no one can squirt them with a fire extinguisher.'

'If we knew what to squirt them with it wouldn't be a bad idea. But don't think we're not trying. Maybe we'll get lucky. But if not . . .'

Lightning flashes all around Jupiter's horizon.

'Very dramatic, Max.'

'I'm good, aren't I? Call me when you know something, Sharkey.'

Max's agent spreads her arms. Max kicks away from the data window and, falling upwards, passes through her shape. For a moment, Alex sees him walking away between trees in some sunlit wood, and then the agent blows away in a scattering of leaves. Alex tells his own agent to shut down the connection and strips off his goggles and sits up in the real world, blinking in bright sunlight on a grassy slope that drops away to the red and grey roofs of Gjirokastra.

2
Cheap Holidays in Other People's Misery

The Holiday Inn in Tirana was Albania's first high rise structure, the Hotel Tirana, built all the way back in 1979. Despite extensive remodelling, including a spiky façade of architectural stromalith, nanotech tunnelled hyperconnectivity, and responsive environmental microconditioning, the hotel still retains the concrete bones of the original, starkly functional architecture. And although it is semi-intelligent, and generates its own power from wind stress and temperature differences, in these troubled times the elevators often aren't running and the water supply is, at best, erratic.

Todd Hart has been given a room overlooking Skanderbeg Square – by no means as good as it seems, because the room is in clear view of the mountains. That's where the pro-Greek rebels are, and currently they're winning Albania's latest civil war. Half an hour ago, Todd was up on the roof with Spike Weaver, his cameraman, watching tracer rounds swoop towards the city's dark rooftops like lines of incandescent hummingbirds. The bombardment seemed to be concentrated on the eastern suburbs, an extensive maze of unmetalled streets and flat-roofed single storey mud-brick houses. Nothing much, Spike said, and it was true, none of the other journalists had bothered to leave the bar to take a look. Spike is in the bar now, talking over old wars and actions, refusing offers of cheap sex and drugs from the artificially tanned whores, and generally ignoring the flatterers and hangers-on who buy the reporters drinks in the hope that this will persuade them to part with a few ecus in return for dubious nuggets of information.

If Todd had any sense he would be getting drunk with the others, exchanging gossip and plugging into the old baloney factory. God knows he had no luck with either the US consul or the UN press officer. The consul was a young and stunningly naïve Yale graduate with a doctorate in Southern Mediterranean Paleo-Christian archaeology; the press officer the usual time-serving bureaucratic reptile who didn't try very hard to give the impression that the UN was actually doing something other than watching the civil war from the sidelines. Not only did he try to stop Todd's overflight of the Children's Crusade, he also tried to have Todd arrested afterwards. Todd and Spike spent a long two hours in a bare room in the UN compound, without air-conditioning or access to the soft drinks machine humming just outside the door, before someone with a smidgen of public relations *savoir-faire* realized it might not be a good idea to piss off an accredited member of the US media.

Todd is looking forward to getting wrecked, but first he must file his report. He's been here three days, now, and he's on the sharp end of an unfavourable stringer's contract, the only way he could get accreditation and enter the country legally. He has to feed a few stories to the system and be a good boy until he's out of the capital and on his way up-country on his own business.

So Todd is in his room, lights off and the heavy curtains drawn (snipers have a habit of shooting at lit hotel windows), sitting in an overstuffed easy chair with his deck in his lap. Its parasitic patch cable, snaking out of a hole in the window frame Todd made with his portable diamond-bit drill (the window doesn't open because of the responsive environmental microconditioning), has found a connection with the main trunk that climbs the side of the hotel to the dishes on the roof. Todd is waiting for the deck to upload the footage he and Spike shot of the Children's Crusade that afternoon. The Crusade is old news, falling through the ratings net, but not many people go in for close-ups, and it will show the network that at least he's trying.

Todd remembers his first sighting of the Crusade from the hired copter. It wound across the dry, brown countryside about fifty kilometres south of Tirana like a column of army ants. Todd remembers the way the copter's cabin was filled with sunlight as it tipped down towards the column, remembers how dry his throat was when he started his speech with the Crusade ambling past in the background, down on the ground in the heat and whirling dust, and a powder-blue UN copter buzzing overhead.

Todd needed three takes to get his little speech off pat – that's what the deck is uploading, along with establishing shots and footage of Todd's brief forays into the column itself. Once the big squirt of fractally compressed pictures has been transmitted, Todd puts on goggles and mitts, and across the desk that's suddenly there, his editor asks him what he's got. Todd tells him, and the editor thinks about it, then shrugs.

'It's your show, kid. But I expected the Wild Man of Atlanta to come up with something more original.'

That tag has been around Todd's neck for twelve years, and although he's shamelessly exploited it whenever he could, he's getting tired of it. He's forty next year and, unlike his legend, he can't hack a story with a babe on his arm and a bottle in his hand. The ride into Atlanta's firestorm was a freak of fate that's taken over his life. He says, 'In a few days I'll have something you won't believe.'

'I believe anything as long as I can verify it.'

The editor, Barry Fugikawa, wears the traditional white shirt with rolled-up sleeves, a green eye-shade, and a smouldering stogey drooping from his pendulous lower lip. He has a crumpled bulldog face borrowed from Walter Matthau in *The Front Page*. It is one of the vironment's default morphs. All the experienced hands use default morphs rather than uncool commercial or customized ones – Todd is morphed as a young, fresh-faced Robert Redford, circa *All the President's Men*.

Although they've interacted a dozen times in the Web, Todd doesn't know what Fugikawa looks like, or even where he is when he isn't virched into this simulacrum of a newspaper office, with its endless ranks of empty desks under a low ceiling, and late afternoon sunlight falling through the windows. No one ever bothers to look out of the windows, which show a real-time view of Washington DC. Here and there is a pool of light where one or two figures work at a desk like this one, with its screen you can reach into to manipulate text and pictures, its trash can, its memo tablet and rack of icons and tools floating above an honest-to-God leather-backed blotter.

'There's one thing,' Todd says. 'I nearly got arrested by this asshole of a UN rep.'

Fugikawa's desk is checking and then stripping the encryption codes which verify that the data Todd has uploaded are genuine and untampered. These days anyone with a cheap computer deck and a graphics program can hack an image of anything at all. The data-gathering equipment of accredited news agency field reporters embed verification codes in digitized images by changing the least significant bit of some of the millions of eight-bit numbers which define pixel colours. The codes are distributed through the image so that any manipulation by lazy or over-eager field reporters can be detected. Only the news agencies hold decryption keys, and they reserve the right to edit the raw footage.

The desk beeps, and Fugikawa looks up and says thoughtfully, 'Were you arrested?'

'Not exactly.'

'Well, next time get arrested. There's your story. UN repression of the news.'

'That's why they let me go. If all you want is stories about reporters, next time I'll get shot in the head. It isn't that difficult. Things have tightened up here. Or I'll get HIV or viral TB from one of the low rent whores in the hotel bar, and die a slow lingering death. You could make a series of it.'

Fugikawa tips a centimetre of white ash into the trash can. His prop cigar never grows any shorter, no matter how long he pretends to be smoking it. He says, 'You're the human interest, God save the mark. That's what the public wants from you. The Wild Man of Atlanta entangled in a situation. They don't need facts. There are enough facts in the world already.'

Fugikawa is overdoing the cynicism, Todd thinks. Perhaps it is part of the morphing package. He says, 'Maybe I'm on to a real story this time.'

'Don't flatter yourself,' Fugikawa says. 'Run the footage. Let's try and make something from it.'

The copter sets down Todd and his cameraman near the head of the Children's Crusade and dusts off before the UN copter trailing the column can get authorization to give chase.

The Crusaders move past within swirling clouds of white dust. They are of all ages, all made over as children, in mind if not in body, by fairy memes. Some hold hands. Some play panpipes or beat little drums or shake rattles, making a ragged beat that rises and falls but never falters. Some ride solar-powered trikes or scooters, but most walk, carrying nothing but a minimum of camping gear, the clothes on their backs, a credit card backed by the Crusade's account at Credit Lyonnaise, and the conviction that they are marching to save humanity as they steadily move across Albania at five kilometres an hour for up to eighteen hours a day.

Until a year ago, the Children's Crusade was only one of many meme-based cults spreading through the disenfranchized communities at the fringe of the European Union. Then almost all of them were spontaneously or deliberately cured, and a residual core of about a thousand met up at the Albanian border and began a march towards their promised land.

They walk out of white haze into white haze. This was once good agricultural land, but it was virus-bombed by government troops retreating from the rebels, and nothing at all grows there now. Dead corn plants crumble like ashen ghosts under the feet of the marchers.

After doing a couple of takes of his little set-up speech, Todd puts on a face-mask and wanders along the ragged edge of the column. Overhead, the UN copter buzzes back and forth like a furious bluebottle. Todd talks to about a dozen Crusaders. Only one, a middle-aged woman with pendulous grey jowls, makes any kind of sense, but she doesn't tell him anything new, and then, inevitably, she asks if he's been saved yet.

'One kiss,' she says. 'One kiss and you'll live forever. Live free.'

Several others around her take up the chant.

'Live free! Free! Live free!'

Todd makes his excuses and backs away. Once out of the column, he waves to the pilot of the UN copter as it dips low above him, and jogs up the slope to rejoin Spike.

'Did you get that last shot?'

Spike pushes up his tele-presence goggles. Their lenses are coated with fine talc. He says, 'Through a veil of dust. Why doesn't that fucker fuck off, or what?'

'He's waiting for clearance to land. Then he'll arrest us.'

'Let's hope so. I'm not walking back.'

Spike runs the playback for Todd, and tells him that he's lucky – six months ago the woman would have ripped off his face-mask and French-kissed him without a thought.

'The fuckers are learning,' Spike says. 'The locals don't take kindly to these things trying to convert them. Being Orthodox, and all that.'

Todd takes off his bush hat and mops a gruel of dust and sweat from the back of his neck. He's a tall, husky man with a cap of fine blond hair and a craggy, open face. He's beginning to sweat off his sunblock, and the tip of his nose is sunburnt. He tells Spike, 'The people who own these farms are mostly Muslims. The rebels are Greek Orthodox, remember? That's why Glass converted to Orthodoxy. Try and keep it straight.'

'Glass was an American Muslim before that,' Spike says, as if that explains everything.

Glass is the Web prophet who has sworn to give protection to the Children's Crusade. He started his career as Professor of Media Studies at some Midwestern arts college, then became a Web host, handling a dozen user groups at once, shaping debate from their endless chatter. He made a fortune with some kind of complexity research that enabled him to identify brief windows of pre-dictability in the seething World Markets, blew most of his money on all kinds of wild research, and moved to Greece, where he con-structed a legendary virtual environment he christened the Library of Dreams. A couple of months ago he very publically married Antoinette, one of the newest virtuality supermodels, and now he's promising to save the Children's Crusade and bring the Golden Age.

Todd's contact in Tirana claims he has contacts who can take Todd to Glass. An interview with Glass would earn Todd enough money to keep his creditors off his back for a few months. The latest is his daughter, who is suing him for alienation of affection. Violetta is only seven, for Christ's sake, and Todd is sure that his bitch of a third wife is behind it. Marcy got the court to stop his right of access, claiming his lifestyle was affecting Violetta's social-ization learning curve, and it's Marcy's style to twist the knife once she's planted it in his back. Even if he wins, Todd will still have to pay off both sets of lawyers, and he still owes fees from the right of access case.

Todd and Spike watch the Children's Crusade wind its way across the dusty fields. There are poplar trees on the far side of the fields, and a sluggish river beyond the trees, but despite the heat and the dust no one leaves the column.

Todd cracks open a carton of Diet Coke, takes a swig, and hands it to Spike. 'There's definitely a story in this. What does a hip guy like Glass want with a bunch of chiliastic brainburns?'

'Maybe Glass has burned out. Maybe he's desperate for publicity.'

Spike lights one of the local, loosely rolled cigarettes with a heavy lighter made from a bullet casing. He rubs at the red circles his tele-presence goggles have left around his eyes. He is from South London, tough and bandy-legged and doggedly pessimistic.

'They're like the Chinese,' Todd says, the glimmer of an angle coming to him.

Spike squints off into the distance, where, high above the dust, the lenses of his camera drone reflect flashes of sunlight. He's set it to dogging the UN copter's tail, to give its AI practice.

Todd says, 'The Long March. Chairman Mao. China.'

'Didn't we go to China, a couple of years back?'

'That was Tibet.'

'Same thing.'

'You know it isn't, you bastard.'

'I know it was where I got the worst case of shits in my life.'

Todd throws the empty Coke carton at Spike's head. 'You never get the shits. All you ever eat is McFood.'

'It must have been a yak burger.' Spike says. He adds reflectively, 'That was a good story, the one about the Buddhist underground.'

'It was a fucking sad story.'

'Yeah, well, it's a fucking sad world, boss.'

The Children's Crusade ambles past at a steady rate through the dusty haze. There are about a thousand people living in the arcology in Denver where Todd has a one room efficiency. In a false name, because three of his four ex-wives have a lien on everything he earns until the end of the century. He has never before thought of all those people around him, like grubs in cells in rotten wood. Here they are. Hot sunlight flares through the white dust. Off in the distance, a second powder-blue copter is making a wide loop over the virus-burned fields, coming in towards them.

'Here we go,' Spike says. He takes a final drag from his cigarette, pinches it out and thriftily tucks the fag-end in the breast pocket of his jacket.

Todd says, 'What would happen if they all scattered, started to make converts? No one thinks of that, right? I mean, how many people in Albania can afford to be on the universal phage programme?'

'Like vampires?' Spike pulls his goggles over his eyes. 'Been done to death, that one. Staked out at the crossroads, through the heart. Try out that speech about the Long March, maybe it'll be a good opener.'

Out above the column of the Children's Crusade, the camera

drone swoops and turns, racing in ahead of the chopper that will soon set down and arrest them.

Todd and Barry Fugikawa use the footage of Todd making the Long March simile with the column going by behind him, then shots of individuals in the crowd, some still recognizably human, others heavily modified by fairy fembots. Fugikawa pastes in library clips, stragglers crossing France and Germany and the little republics and monarchies of the Balkans, the gathering of the Crusade and the beginning of its final march at the Montenegran-Albanian border. A glimpse of a fairy's blue sharp-boned face, then a cut back to Todd asking where all these people were going, what was the single thought that drove them, and concluding that as yet no one knows. A shot of the UN copter coming in, with a running strip explaining that minutes after making that statement, Todd Hart was arrested.

Two minutes' worth of filler for the loop on the Rolling News Channel. No one will remember it tomorrow except the ten thousand or so fans of the never-ending civil wars in the Balkans. Still, in his hotel room, masked and gloved, Todd shivers with a silly burst of excited pride. Even when he's doing a fill-in job, there's always the thrill of passing on a revelation from the inside track.

Fugikawa says that the Long March thing is a cliché, but what the hell. 'No one much cares about this shit except the peepers, and even they don't really give a fuck.'

'They would if the meme plague broke out again,' Todd says, and the editor looks at him, weariness deep in his sad bulldog eyes, and asks if he has a lead.

'Maybe,' Todd says, and remembers to have his partial give Fugikawa's partial a wink. This plague idea is a stone lie, but news is an arena where lies are often the start of a twisty path to some truth or other.

The image of the old woman's face hangs in the desk's window. Fugikawa animates it, runs the little loop he's made of her asking over and over that Todd join her.

'Don't get too close,' Fugikawa says. 'You don't want to end up looking like that.'

For a moment, he isn't Walter Matthau any more, but a fat bald Buddha naked but for a loincloth, with a golden skin and pendulous ears, a third eye painted on his forehead and a white lotus blossom clasped in his folded hands.

Buddha says, 'Wait for the story to come to you,' and then he's Walter Matthau again. He taps his bulbous nose. 'In the old days they'd call you a stringer, and stringers never did last too long. Lighten up. This isn't the end of the world you're reporting here. Just the tag end of a fading cult.'

Todd says casually, 'Hey, how long have I been in the job?'

'Long enough to get a rep, and don't tell me you don't know it. Do some local colour stories. Let the execs worry about the big picture.'

'Thanks for the advice.'

'We don't like stringers bouncing around the field without guidelines. Even if that stringer is the Wild Man of Atlanta. Read your contract.'

'My agent read it. She said it was a piece of shit.'

'But you signed it.'

There's a knock at the door. Todd says, 'Gotta go. Maybe it's the President of Albania with a nightcap.'

It's Spike. 'Fairy hunt,' he says. 'Everyone's in. Loosen up, it'll do you good.'

So Todd spends the next hour chasing through gloomy corridors after a fairy the Reuters correspondent swears she saw going into the emergency stairwell. The other journalists are wrecked on local brandy and kif, and they make a lot of noise as they scamper down stairwells towards the basements and run through bare passageways and disused laundry rooms.

Todd sees a scrap of blue whisk around a corner, gives chase, and runs straight into a tall blue figure that collapses around him in a tangle of blue plastic sheeting and memory wire. The others laugh as he disentangles himself. A camera drone bumps the ceiling, its turret of lenses intent on the scene.

'You fuckers,' Todd says. 'Whose round is it?'

There are drinks, then more drinks. Someone buys the night manager a bottle of champagne to placate him, and he genially asks if any of them are feeling lonely. All the girls and boys are clean here, he says, he makes sure of it himself. The champagne is Bulgarian, and bitter as burnt oil.

Todd gets back to his room late. The deck is still connected, and he virches to the office. Barry Fugikawa is long gone – the newsroom is deserted, which is odd – but the loop they made is playing on the desk's screen. Todd watches it with what he likes to think is professional satisfaction, and is about to quit when a movement at the far end of the empty newsroom catches his eye. A burning man is standing on a desk. Flames clothe his skin, form a flickering spectral crown around his head. He points at Todd, and then he's gone.

Todd sends his partial to the spot, suspecting yet another prank. The desk on which the burning man stood is marked with two scorched footprints, and the memo pad is smouldering, its edges crawling with sparks that form and reform in patterns of strange hieroglyphs.

'Some trick, guys,' Todd says to the empty air. He sweeps the smouldering memo pad into the trash can, and goes to bed.

3
The Brides of Frankenstein

Alex hears Katrina coming up the hill long before she reaches him, first her calls rising faintly, and then a clattering of wooden bells as sheep scatter from her ascent. Alex is lying half-asleep on a steep slope of sunwarmed turf. Below is the town of Gjirokastra, its hills and pine trees and narrow streets, its whitewashed houses with their red and grey tile roofs, the cluster of concrete apartment blocks, pockmarked by last year's firefights, the minarets of its mosques like unlaunched rockets. Above, the sheer stone walls of the citadel rise from scree slopes. It once held political prisoners of the old communist regime; there are feys in there now, awaiting shipment to the processing camp on the coast at Vlora. Alex tries not to think about that, but it's hard.

While he's been waiting for contact, he has taken to coming up here every day, ostensibly to check his datarats and get the latest news from Max, in reality to escape the attentions of Mrs Powell, a formidable Englishwoman of an indeterminate age who believes, passionately, romantically, *completely*, in fairies. She came here after a session of dowsing with a map of Europe and a crystal as a pendulum weight, but she is neither stupid nor naïve. She has been to see the citadel commandant about the conditions in which the feys are held, and has protested to the UN about the display on the Kakavia road, all in vain. Since Alex is the only other English person in Gjirokastra, Mrs Powell has targeted him as a potential convert to her cause.

Alex is beginning to believe that it is a kind of divine retribution for his part in helping turn the first fairy. It's not that he doesn't like Mrs Powell – in some ways she reminds him of Darlajane B. – but she's *relentless*. If he finds Milena, and if she refuses to set him free of the geas she laid upon him so long ago, he'll set Mrs Powell on her.

Checking the datarats and the progress of the Children's Crusade doesn't take long. The computer deck grows an antenna across the turf, a tangle of iron monofilament threads thin as spider silk, and plugs into the Web via a UN low orbit spysat. Alex's daemon tells him that Max isn't online, but he's left a message. It isn't good news. Hackers have found the backdoor into the Library of Dreams, and while at the moment it's privileged knowledge, sooner or later someone will post it across the Web.

After signing off, what Alex mostly does is watch little brown butterflies flit above the flower-starred turf, or look out at the distant mountains that rise up in a kind of blue haze far beyond Gjirokastra. He watches the sheep scattered over the slope, lazily thinks about an algorithm that could describe the way they bunch and straggle. Sheep with shorter legs on one side would move quickly on a slope, but only in one direction. Around and around until they reach the top of the hill. Then roll down to the bottom, protected by thick fleece, and start over.

The sheep here are shorn, skinny creatures which share a single startled expression. As Katrina climbs towards Alex, they bolt with sudden, ungainly movements, then forget what they've just run from and return to nipping at dry grass.

Katrina is out of breath. Her face shines with sweat, and her scalp is sunburnt either side of the strip of genemod leopard fur. His lady death. She has nowhere else to use her sudden energies but with him, in a cause she hardly understands. She thinks he's crazy to even think of trying to find Milena.

'Get a cure,' she tells him. 'It's not real, it's a fembot thing.'

They had an argument about it yesterday morning, after Mr Avramites told them he had secured safe passage across the border for them, and Alex told her then, 'Everyone has to have one disease they're comfortable with.'

'Fuck that shit. I'm going to live forever.'

'You're in the wrong place for that.'

'You wait and see,' Kat said, and shook her fist in his face. The place where she lost two fingers on her right hand in the battle of the Magic Kingdom – after she drove a bulldozer through the perimeter wall, she grabbed the working end of a security guard's taser – is almost healed.

Now she stands over Alex, blocking the sunlight and breathing hard from the climb. 'You'll get cancer,' she says. 'You'll burn red and break out in big, bloody tumours.'

'It's an Englishman's privilege to behave like a mad dog and lie around in the midday sun.'

Katrina doesn't get the reference. She really does think he's crazy.

'How are you, Kat? How were the woods?'

Katrina says, 'Full of trees. Where is the Crusade?'

'About three days out from the old border.'

'And after that they're in the neutral zone and we're fucked. Anything else?'

Alex has set a swarm of self-replicating datarats loose in the Web. They're programmed to search for traces of Milena and return to their nest – Alex's mailbox on the University of Kansas a-life bulletin board – with any tasty tidbits. There must be more than ten thousand active now, but for the past few days there's been no report, which could mean that Milena isn't doing anything, or that some Web controller has set a ratcatcher. Alex must ask Max to check that possibility; it could upset their other activities.

Alex tells Katrina, 'It's very quiet. The burning man hasn't crossed over. Or if he has, no one has spotted him.'

Katrina says, 'Just as well I've got some real news.'

'You saw—'

'The little fucker has caught up with us, yes.'

Katrina has been off the day before scouting the road up the Drinos valley towards Kakavia. She camped out in the empty woods a few kilometres south of Gjirokastra, and she tells Alex as they make their way back to town that it was a spooky experience.

'There was always a dog barking off in the distance. One time I woke and saw something big moving off in the moonlight, through the trees. I found big round prints. Think they have elephants here?'

'But you saw—'

'That little fucker. He is like the counterfeit currency.'

'The bad penny.'

'Yeah. Always he turns up, with that attitude of his.'

'He's a survivor, and he's taking a huge risk coming here. He's on our side, now.'

'Only because he thinks we want to help his mistress.'

'She used him, Kat, just as she used us.'

'Also, he knows there will be recycling camps in the rest of Europe soon enough. He knows that the way things are going, there soon won't be any place to hide. He is out to save his ass, not that I blame him for it. Still, he told me something about these so-called aid workers. I think we must believe him.'

'I assume that they're not really aid workers. It did seem a bit too convenient, them just happening to be able to give us a ride in the direction we want to go.'

'That fucker Avramites has sold us out. Just like I told you.'

'I believed you then. I believe you now. But Mr Avramites is a necessary evil.'

Mr Avramites is a lawyer who, in the long tradition of interpreters of *fis*, the complex tribal laws and customs codified in the *Kanun of Lek*, arranges negotiations and trade-offs between different factions in the region. At the moment, Gjirokastra is in the hands of a pro-Greek warlord, and although the federal government of Greece does not officially recognize him, it does allow a certain amount of unofficial movement across the border. Mr Avramites has arranged transport for Alex and Katrina with a jeep convoy that brought medical supplies into the town. It just so happens, Mr Avramites says, that one of the Greek companies that sponsors the aid once employed Glass's team to hack a new distribution structure.

Katrina says stubbornly, 'We could walk in. I know you say that the border is lousy with UN sensors and traps. I know you say it is bandit country besides, but our little blue-skinned friend says he knows a way through.'

'Kat, do you trust him? Completely trust him?'

'You say he's on our side. I say I trust him as much as I trust Avramites.'

Alex can't help smiling. 'She's here, Kat! I know it! And she needs me. Why else would he be here?'

'I must deal with these fake aid workers when the time comes. Also, I should kill Avramites, but I suppose you won't let me. Do you really have to sit down again? I'm carrying your fucking deck, after all.'

But Alex has to stop and rest. It's a long way down, and it is very hot. Katrina, wired on something more than last night's adrenalin, can't sit still. She runs down a sheep and wrestles it on to its back, laughs, and lets it scramble up and run off.

Alex tells her, 'Good thing there are no shepherds around. They'd set the dogs on you.'

Shepherd dogs here are combat enhanced, with behaviour-mod chips, re-engineered jaws and ceramic teeth, to protect sheep from wolves in the high mountain pastures.

Katrina says, 'Let them. I'm ready.' She dusts her hands on her hips, strikes a defiant pose. 'I am so tired,' she says, 'of all this fucking waiting. Even if we die tomorrow, I would not care, so long as we leave this backwater.'

That evening, they meet Mr Avramites in one of the few restaurants still open for business in Gjirokastra. Alex argues with Katrina for an hour before she agrees to come along. He makes her promise not to say anything, and not to try and stab Mr Avramites with a fork.

'There'll be time for that later, perhaps, but right now he can be useful. Besides, when he tells us he can't come with us after all, then we'll know he's sold us out.'

'We already know that,' Katrina says in disgust.

They pay war-inflated prices for mutton stew and rough red wine. The professional classes still dress up for dinner in Gjirokastra, doctors and schoolteachers and local officials in clean, pressed suits, their wives in starched cotton dresses. Alex is wearing a crushed velvet poncho over a one piece suit that in truth is a bit too small for him. Katrina is in her leathers, kicking at the flagstones with her biker boots. The bourgeoisie look at them sidelong, muttering what are probably unflattering comments. Mercenaries aren't welcome here, and Alex and Katrina are clearly foreign mercenaries, even if they are friends of the local *fis* expert.

Mr Avramites looks more like a grizzled roadmender than a lawyer, with a floppy cloth cap on his balding head, his black jacket out at one elbow, and a red kerchief knotted at his throat. He puts on gold-rimmed spectacles to read out the terms of the pass he's obtained. It is in Greek and Albanian. Katrina grimaces at Alex, and Alex smiles back serenely. Actually, Alex likes Mr Avramites. The old man's greed is honest and open, and he likes to be your friend even as he is insinuating his hand deep into your pockets, or, as now, selling you behind your back to your enemies.

Mr Avramites is supposed to be coming with them; Alex has hired him as translator. He lost his family ten years ago, during the government reoccupation of Gjirokastra. With the rest of the Albanian-Greek men, Mr Avramites fled to continue the fight in the forests in the mountains. He paid for his wife and daughters to be sheltered in a cellar in Gjirokastra, but the family who said they'd do it reneged, and moved north long before the Greeks retook the town. No one knows exactly what happened to Mr Avramites's family, but they were probably shot early on in the occupation, and buried in one of the mass graves outside the town. Mr Avramites sometimes lapses into a mournful silence, thinking about this, but now he's cheerful enough – too cheerful for a man about to embark on a hazardous expedition, Alex thinks.

Mr Avramites folds up the stiff paper pass with its hologram seal and hands it to Alex. 'You will keep that safe, Mr Sharkey.'

So this is it. Alex can feel Katrina looking at him, but he keeps his eyes on Mr Avramites. 'Surely it would be better if you kept it?'

'Ah. Alas . . .' Mr Avramites makes a complex shrug that involves most of his body. 'I learn that the commander of the medical team has a fair English, and alas, I have business still in town . . . I will not, of course, expect the payment that you would have given me.'

'That's something,' Katrina says.

'Kat, do keep quiet.'

'You will be in safe hands, I am certain,' Mr Avramites says. 'An old man like me, I would be a trouble.'

'I'm sorry you choose not to come with us,' Alex says.

'Ah, but still we are here,' Mr Avramites says quickly, smoothing over a moment of awkward silence. 'We will celebrate your departure after such a long wait.'

With Alex's money, Mr Avramites buys a litre of raki – where they are going, he says, is only ouzo, and that is only drunk by men who aren't confident of their masculinity.

Katrina gives Alex a dark look. She says, 'Perhaps we should let Avramites get on with his business.'

Mr Avramites misses or pretends not to notice the sarcasm in Katrina's voice. He says serenely, 'Plenty of time for that. Tonight I am here for you.'

Alex says, 'Kat, why don't you tell Mr Avramites about the big animal you saw.'

Mr Avramites listens, then shrugs. 'Things from the war. Not good to know about them. Besides, a lot of stuff isn't real out there. The hills are full of ghosts. If you walk into one you might never walk out again. Lamia, they call them. You know the old story. A contemporary of Lord Byron, John Keats, wrote on the subject a moving poem.'

Byron is something of a hero to the Albanians. Even if he did side with the Greeks in the end, it was for all the right reasons, chiefly honour. Alex has found that Albanians expect the English to be intimately familiar with Byron and all his works, but all Alex knows is that he had something to do with *Bride of Frankenstein*, or some other ancient black-and-white horror movie.

Katrina bangs her tumbler on the table. The couple at the next table, who all evening have bent towards each other and talked in whispers, turn and blink slowly, as if coming awake. Katrina glares at them and says, 'This thing was no ghost. It was as big as a fucking elephant.'

'Perhaps it was a horse,' Mr Avramites says. 'They take horses and change them, in this war. Men too. The fairies like to do that.'

Katrina says defiantly, 'I heard voices, too. Like whispering. High in the air. It's a very Shakespearean wood, no?'

'I was in the forest an entire winter,' Mr Avramites says, with the intense gravity of the very drunk, 'and I never once saw a fairy. They had some dolls, in Tirana. In the tourist hotels there. For business entertainment, you understand. That kind. But they took them out and shot them last year, when the new government took power. One thing on which we Greeks and the Muslims agree is that fairies and dolls are an abomination in the sight of God. These fairies that are here now have come from other countries. Like your friend Mrs Powell. She does not understand that we must deal with them in our own way.'

Alex has been looking into the candle flame. Something seems to live in there, small and snaky, coiled around the burning wick, breathing the cool steady flame. He has been doing too much networking these past few days, trying to trace Milena's work, connecting with his allies out in the interstices of the Web. Hypnogogic visions bedevil him when he's tired.

He says mildly, 'Mrs Powell is no friend of mine. She believes in all the right things for all the wrong reasons.'

Mr Avramites shrugs. 'In the woods, you will be more concerned with bandits and Nationalist guerrillas, believe me. Fairies are nothing, not out here. Not any more. We have invented the solution.'

Alex thinks that the old man has a lot to learn. He says, 'That's not what Glass thinks.'

'We have to get past the fucking Nationalist border guards first,' Katrina says. 'We have to get out of this fucking country. I told you,' she says, pointing her ruined hand at Alex, 'that we started in the wrong place.'

'She's drunk,' Alex says. How did she manage to get so drunk?

Mr Avramites says, 'The Nationalists are a long way off. They have lost the south of the country. We control it now. You will go with this convoy, and you will have no trouble crossing the border. Bandits will not attack anything flying the Greek flag.'

Alex says, with as much sincerity as he can muster, 'I'm sure your Greek friends will see us safe.'

'Truly, you will not need me. They will look after you, I swear it.'

They fall silent, Katrina belligerent, Mr Avramites retreating inside himself, into the past, Alex trying to guess the future. They all know what has happened, betrayed and betrayer alike. They finish the raki, and the next morning, when he is woken before dawn in time to join the convoy out of the ancient hillside city, Alex has a terrible hangover.

4
Trouble in Tirana

While Todd Hart is waiting on the steps of the Holiday Inn for his contact to show up, he's witness to an assassination in the second-hand car market on the western side of Skanderbeg Square. Todd isn't looking for trouble. He's just had a shave and haircut in the hotel's barbershop, and he's wearing neatly pressed linen shorts and a fresh white T-shirt. His lightweight *faux* sharkskin jacket, iridescent with a million tiny, fembot-spun scales, weighted with his notepad, is slung over one shoulder; his bush hat, with its *faux* tigerskin band, is at a jaunty angle on his head. He's feeling pretty terrific. He did a little Serenity up in his room, and it's mellowing him out nicely; he isn't even worried that his contact is late.

It's early evening. People are promenading around the big square in the welcome coolness. Half a dozen open air cafés are set up in the shadow of the crumbling Palace of Culture, and their radios send up a mix of polka tunes, opera and Thai pop. Around the plinth on which once stood a colossal, gilded statue of the old dictator, hawkers sell bandwidth access to the Web, line rental on mobile phones, iced sherbet, lemonade and cigarettes. The money-changers are doing brisk business: many Albanians cherish the dream of making a fortune by judiciously playing the international money markets.

From his vantage point, Todd sees someone running out from the ranks of battered Mercedes and Peugeots on the far side of the square. The man runs in a desperate zig-zag scramble, waving his arms as if trying to swat something. People scatter – they know what's about to happen. The man has been targeted by a hornet, a small, self-powered micro-missile guided by scent to a specific target. All the foreign journalists take pills which alter the pheromone content of their sweat from day to day; hornets can be primed with an old sock, or a newspaper handled and carelessly set down. They are implacable assassination machines. Both sides in the civil war use them, and so do the ganglords who run the black market.

The man stops and starts to tear off his shirt – then there's a flash and he tumbles backward and lies still.

'Another debt repaid,' Eduard Marku says.

Marku must have arrived at the same time as the hornet reached its target. Not a comforting connection. He is a suave, sardonic man in his late forties. As always, he is wearing a crumpled black suit and chain smoking Italian Camels – a sign he has connections, because Camels, the favourite cigarette of Albanians, are not even available on the black market. Todd first met him three years ago. Like the city, Marku has grown embittered, closed in, and careless with threats. Todd remembers when Tirana was open and welcoming. Police would shake your hand when they learnt you were a journalist; they would invite you into their homes. Now they hang about in threes and fours, harassing passers-by, arresting journalists and letting them go after a few hours with vaguely threatening advice that foreigners should take especial care on the streets.

Back then, Marku worked for the last government's information service. He went to prison when that government fell, and was released in the amnesty for political prisoners declared on the present regime's first anniversary (the President was once an MTV advertising executive, and, if nothing else, is big on gesture and rhetoric). He is neither a reliable nor a particularly trustworthy informant, but Todd likes the man's style, and his sense of the macabre.

When Todd arrived back in Tirana, Marku told him that just a week ago a man was hacked to death in the lobby of the hotel. It was a revenge killing: forty years ago, in a northern village, the victim's father had killed his sister's fiancé. Marku insisted on showing Todd the exact spot of the murder.

'Blood has a curious effect on marble. They have an affinity for one another.'

They had to move a carpet and an armchair to see it. Todd took a couple of photographs to placate Marku, but it was embarrassing, and more than a little ghoulish. Something to do with it being in a hotel lobby, perhaps. He later learnt that most Albanian stringers insist that their employers take a look at the bloodstain – the murder for a debt of honour is bigger news than the civil war.

Marku says now, 'You want to report this assassination, I will find out all about it for you. We wait a few minutes and his relatives will come, shouting for revenge. They will tell us all. A little local colour for your report.'

Todd says, 'I haven't got that long. This meeting is more important.'

Marku exclaims, as if it is Todd's fault, 'Then why are we standing here, idly gossiping?'

As they walk, Marku says, 'You do understand why you can't bring your cameraman. They don't trust anyone. Even me.'

Todd says, 'Are you sympathetic with these people?'

Marku shrugs. 'They are dreamers. Like your Lord Byron. I hear you left the city today. You should be careful.'

'I don't take sides here.'

'Some people might say that if you live in the city, you shouldn't talk to people outside it. Especially the Crusade.'

'Do you believe that?'

Marku smiles and says, 'I just worry about your safety. No one in this country likes the Crusade. But it has protection and money, and my countrymen's hate and fear are directed on any associated with it.'

Todd doesn't trust that smile. He says, 'Well, I won't be going back. The UN arrested us for a while, in case we didn't get the point, and in any case this is the real story.'

'Ah, you are still the Wild Man of legend,' Marku says. 'It is an honour to work for you again.'

'Save the bullshit for the interview, Eduard. I've a feeling we might need all the charm we can slop on.'

'Do not worry. She wants to talk with you. She says you are the only journalist famous enough to carry her story.'

'Then she's fuller of bullshit than you. She could talk with *Vogue* or *Rolling Stone* any time she wants.'

'Ah, but she does not want some interview with an online journal, here today, gone tomorrow. She wishes to talk with the Wild Man of Atlanta.'

'You're getting a cheap thrill from this, Eduard. I'm not sure if that's flattering or disturbing.'

'I'm hoping to get some good money,' Marku says. 'I could do with getting out of this country. I have too many enemies.'

Todd and Marku cross a little canalized river, the Lanu, and pass the Enver Hoxha memorial, a strange structure like a huge concrete flying saucer poised for flight. Although Albanians still call the long-dead dictator the ugly one, and most curse his memory, in these troubled times some wish him back. He is becoming confused with the old hero, Skanderbeg, who drove back the Turks and united the country. It is said that he never died, but lies waiting for the call to arms to save Albania again.

Once he's satisfied that they aren't being followed, Marku steps out into the surging traffic, dodges a pedicab like a bull fighter, and flags down a Mercedes taxi. It has been converted from diesel to alcohol, and frequently misfires or stalls. It wallows along the poorly maintained roads at a speed that has Marku looking at his old-fashioned LED watch and haranguing the stolid driver.

This part of Tirana still hasn't been rebuilt after the earthquake of '09; there are whole blocks of tumbled roofless ruins. Refugees who fled the countryside ahead of the pro-Greek rebels camp out amongst weedy spills of brick. The air is blue with woodsmoke. Bats, roosting in shattered leafless trees lining the road, twitch like little leather suitcases about to unpack themselves. A skinny cow wanders into the road, and stands looking baffled as the taxi driver raps impatiently on his horn, until at last a small boy in a long ragged jumper drives it back with a stick.

'You can take the peasant out of the country,' Marku remarks, 'but not the country out of the peasant, eh?'

Marku's jacket has ridden up, and Todd notices that a pistol is tucked into the waistband of his trousers. Todd says, 'What kind of gun is that?'

Marku takes it out and shows Todd. It has a short, fat barrel and a floating breech mechanism. When Marku ejects the clip, the driver glances in the rear view mirror, looks away. Marku says, 'You like it? It is Russian. They make good automatics.'

'It's a pretty big gun, Eduard.'

'You want to stop a man, this will do it with one shot. Caseless hollowtips, a pop-out laser sight. It does the business.' Marku smiles, racks the clip, and tucks the thing away.

'Have you ever shot anyone?'

'You need a gun in this city,' Marku says. 'At home I have a Mac-10.'

Todd hunches forward in the sagging seat, looking through the dusty windshield at the ruins. Little groups of men stand smoking and drinking on street corners. Most of them have semi-automatic rifles slung upside down on their backs. The setting sun infuses everything with an apocalyptic light.

Marku says, 'Don't worry. It's safe until dark.'

'I've seen worse in New York,' Todd says. Mugging or kidnapping is the least of his worries. An edgy nervousness is beginning to cut through the benign glow of the Serenity. Todd is breaking an important precautionary rule by entering dangerous territory on his own. He adds, 'I thought we had safe passage.'

'Up to a point,' Marku says vaguely. He smells overpoweringly of cologne; sweat makes half moons under the arms of his linen jacket. It occurs to Todd that Marku is more frightened than he is.

The taxi leaves the boulevard and plunges into a maze of narrow streets that wind between two storey mud-walled houses packed so close together their overhanging tile roofs almost meet overhead. The taxi driver turns on his headlights, plays a restless *arpeggio* on his horn, and guns the Mercedes through every junction in a cloud of dust.

When the taxi finally pulls up, outside a house no different from any of the others, Marku talks rapidly to the driver and has Todd pay him fifty dollars.

'I tell him there's three times as much for him if he waits. He says he will.'

'This had better be worth it,' Todd says.

'You will be amazed,' Marku says.

Armed soldiers lounge just inside an arched gate at the side of the house. They are young, smooth-skinned, muscular giants, adolescents given growth and muscle enhancement treatments and fembot-spun nerve nets. Capturing the enemy's young male children and turning them into short-lived killers is a recent trend in the hundred or so civil wars and insurrections around the world. The treatments will give these young supermen marrow and liver cancer, by and by, and make them prone to pseudo-Parkinson's, and *grand mal* seizures, but most don't live long enough for the side-effects to become a problem. They are armed with snub-barrelled high velocity rifles that fire caseless ammunition, mostly memorywire needles that expand and sprout spikes on impact. One soldier has something that might have started off as an Alsatian on a chain leash. Its over-muscled jaws make its head look like some diseased tree root dug up from the earth.

Like basketball players in a fast-forwarded video, the tall soldiers bounce and jostle around Todd and Marku. They wear the death's head badge of the Nationalist government. When Todd points this out, Marku tells Todd that they are hired for the occasion.

'There's no loyalty in the city these days. It makes my job very interesting, as you can imagine.'

Todd and Marku are patted down – Todd has to show the soldiers how the notepad works, to convince them it isn't some kind of bomb – irradiated with low energy microwaves to inactivate any hitch-hiking fembots, and finally allowed into a paved courtyard where lamps burn amidst lemon trees and orange trees growing in tubs. Fairy lights are strung on the high walls around the courtyard. A tall, slim woman in combat jacket and trousers and high-topped boots sits on a canvas camping chair within a circle of light. The two soldiers standing behind her are real: she isn't.

Antoinette. Her image has a fine faint luminescent shimmer, as if coated with oil. She seems to be abstracted from a more perfect world, where even light is finer and purer.

Todd has seen plenty of pictures of Glass's consort, but she is even more beautiful than they suggest. Until a year ago, she was a vironment supermodel, plucked from a Bidonville outside Paris. Hers is a rags-to-riches fairytale that burnt a brief predictable arc through the information-saturated mediaverse, terminating in a contract with InScape which she famously broke after six months. After issuing a single page manifesto calling for the deconstruction of male and female rôles within all vironments (which one commentator compared unfavourably to an earlier Antoinette's pronouncement, saying that at least France's last Queen offered cake, while this opinionated *gamine* offered nothing but rhetoric), she vanished and then reappeared in Glass's stronghold.

Todd has her figured as either a poor little rich girl looking for a strong father figure, or an incredibly clever manipulator of media image. Either way, she's his way to Glass. And, yes, she is beautiful, even allowing for subtle morphing of her image. She has the deep black skin, long neck and swelling, bicephalic skull of a Pharaonic princess. Her hair is done in tight cornrows caught with silicon tags that flash intermittent constellations of little white lights. Her eyes are beaten gold; her eyebrows are a solid bar above these eyes, a single flaw that simply makes her more beautiful than mere perfection. Her smile is slow and lazy and very wide in her generous mouth. It is a lioness's smile.

One of the tall soldiers sets out a bottle of Johnny Walker Black Label and a flask of cloudy raki. Todd can't help noting the faint tremor in the boy's hand, the sweat standing on his brow. His cheeks are stippled with steroid-induced acne.

Marku introduces Todd, pours a shot of whisky and carefully toasts Antoinette's image. '*Jete te Gjate.*' May you have a long life. Todd follows suit, and Marku repeats the toast, this time with raki. Todd downs a glass of the stuff, too. He's already beginning to feel woozy, but at least he isn't scared any more.

Antoinette's image finally stirs, and her voice comes from the

272

air above their heads. She tells Todd how much she admires his broadcast about the Children's Crusade. 'It is always useful to have a new perspective on that particular problem,' she says.

She has a British accent. Todd remembers that she claims to have learned her English from BBC news broadcasts.

He counters, 'I was hoping you'd tell me about the Crusade.'

Antoinette smiles her slow, predatory smile. Her gaze is precisely centred on Todd: the remote sensing equipment she's using is very good, although he expects nothing less.

She says, 'The Crusade has some interests in common with our cause, but many that are not. We wouldn't have it any other way, of course. After all, the Web is an arena of accelerated discourse. "All things exist within it, and all possible configurations of things."' It is a quote from one of Glass's rants.

Todd says, 'A woman in the Crusade asked if I'd join.'

Antoinette dismisses that with a flick of her hand. Her palms are dyed red. She says, 'That's irrelevant now.'

Todd says, 'You quoted Glass just now. Are quotes all you have for me?'

'This is a story in itself, is it not?'

'Very much so,' Marku says.

Todd says, 'It isn't a story without my cameraman.'

'We will supply you with a record of this meeting.'

'It would have to go out with a disclaimer.'

'So be it.'

'How many questions can I ask? Three?' Todd realizes that he's more than a little drunk. Maybe it wasn't a good idea to drop that dose of Serenity. Still, he has a gut feeling that an aggressive line of questioning may let him learn something useful, and besides, he's no good at the PR sycophancy which media stars expect.

Antoinette says, 'It's a strange restriction for an ambitious man.'

'I hear it's traditional,' Todd says. 'Tell me something new about the Crusade.'

'The Children's Crusade is dangerous not because of what it believes, but because of what it is. In the wrong hands, it could change everything.'

'But not in the way you want things changed?'

Antoinette responds by quoting Glass again. ' "The meta-environment of the Web, which contains all possible vironments, is real and unbounded; nations are no more than fictions glued together by common delusions. Democracy is a fiction within a fiction. It is only a special case of the human experience. In the Web, everything is possible, because everything is allowed." '

'I can get this stuff from any archive. Why has Glass made an alliance with the Crusade?'

Antoinette says, 'We offered the Crusade a haven. You know that, Mr Hart. Everyone knows it. We offer it no more than that; it is all we can offer. You say, Mr Hart, that it still wants to gather more and more to itself. I'd know more about that.'

'The woman was pretty old, and she looked like an elephant's asshole. She wanted to kiss me, I guess. She wanted to turn me on. I got out of there before she tried.'

'There's no need to be ashamed,' Antoinette says. 'Sexual panic is a natural reaction when certain men feel they've lost control of a situation.'

Todd is touched by anger. It burns through the heat of the alcohol in his blood. He says, 'I tell it the way I see it. You read into it what you will. I don't even know if you're real.'

'Of course I'm not real.'

'I mean if you're the real Antoinette, not some expert system manipulating a morphed image.'

'Does it matter so much to you? You could be useful to us, Mr Hart. We could be useful to you. Would you like to know more?'

'That's why I'm here.'

'You're there because you're being followed, and your hotel room is bugged.'

'All the rooms in the Holiday Inn are bugged.'

'Parasitizing the hotel multimedia cabling isn't a very good idea. All your traffic is being monitored.'

'Which is why I want to talk with Glass face to face. How about it?'

Antoinette laughs, and then her image shrinks into itself, condensing into a dot of white light that hovers for a moment before rising into the darkening air above the little courtyard. The two soldiers move forward. They have drawn their pistols, and are deaf to Todd's protests.

'Shouting will do no good,' Marku says, as they are marched out of the courtyard. He seems resigned to this turn.

'I don't think they'll kill us, or they'd have done it in the courtyard, right?'

Marku says grimly, 'The river is considered to be a convenient place for that sort of thing.'

'Maybe they'll take us to Glass. Is that it, boys? I do want to see him, but I have to pack my bags first, and I need my cameraman. So how about if we go back to the hotel first? Get a meal, have a drink, it won't take so long. I mean,' Todd says, as he's hustled into the dark street, 'what's the rush?'

The taxi has gone. The two soldiers keep hold of Todd and Marku while one of their fellows talks into a radio and is answered by an angry burst of speech. He closes his fist over the little transceiver, says something to his companions.

'They are waiting for someone.' Marku says, when Todd asks what's going on.

Then all the soldiers whirl as, with the scream of an overpressed engine and a dazzle of headlights, an army truck roars at them down the narrow street. The soldiers stand their ground and start to shoot. The truck's windscreen turns to lace and blows away. Its engine coughs a geyser of hot sparks and it slews to a halt in a shower of scraped mud-brick fragments. More gunfire, unbearably loud in the confined space. Shots are coming from the roofline and the soldiers fling themselves into doorways and return fire. Marku, caught in the crossfire, is thrown against a wall. Todd is grabbed by a soldier, turned, lifted – and the soldier shudders and collapses on top of him.

For a horrible moment Todd thinks he's been hit too, but the blood is only the soldier's blood. He kicks and kicks, losing his bush hat and a shoe but getting clear of the soldier's dead weight, and runs back into the courtyard. There's a door. It's unlocked. Todd bruises his shoulder and hip as he slams through it.

He runs across an empty room, kicks open another door and falls into a narrow passageway, picks himself up and then simply runs. He doesn't see the hornet until it slaps into his chest. The sharp pain makes him think he's having a heart attack, but then he sees the little machine clutching his T-shirt with its eight wire-thin legs. He beats it off, but the thing circles back and stabs him in the neck. He manages to run a few more steps but then has to sit down on a doorstep, which is where, after they have killed the ambushers and set fire to the army truck, the surviving soldiers find him.

5
Across the Border

The commander of the medical relief team is not pleased to find Alex waiting by himself in the chilly pre-dawn light outside the hotel. When the two jeeps arrive and Alex goes forward to meet them, the commander looks around the empty square and asks severely, 'Where is your woman?'

It's something Alex would like to know. He and Katrina had another big row last night, but she did at last agree to his plan.

'For now,' she said. 'But if the fuckers start acting funny, that's it.'

'At the moment, that's the least of our worries.'

'I will deal with this ersatz medical team. But even if I don't, the worst that happens is that we're taken to Glass and your precious dark lady.'

'Yes, but I don't want to go there empty-handed. Ray says he needs our help, not hers, and I believe him.'

'That little bastard. He sold us out in Paris, and he will do it again.'

'Things have changed,' Alex said, but Katrina was not convinced. She went out two hours before sunrise, and now the medical relief team is here and she is not.

Now, Alex tells the commander, 'She had to run a little errand. She'll meet up with us, I'm sure.'

'This isn't in the arrangements.'

'Well, you can always go without me.'

'Of course not. Is that all you have?'

Alex has brought his computer deck and a small kitbag. He lets one of the men stow his stuff away and then, with difficulty, he climbs up beside the commander.

They take the Kakavia road. Katrina is waiting a kilometre outside town, sitting amongst dry roadside weeds upwind of the gallows where a shrivelled, crow-pecked fairy corpse hangs. Mr Avramites isn't with her. Alex has a bad feeling about that, but now isn't the time to ask.

The two jeeps of the medical relief team are semi-intelligent models equipped with fat mesh wheels that conform closely to the rough contours of the ruined road as it swings through the high pass. The little convoy moves at a steady fifty kph, ahead of a rolling tail of dust. The sun strikes down from a white sky. Alex, sweating into the back of his shirt, is glad of his big black hat. Behind him, Katrina is sprawled in the jeep's narrow loadbed, seeming to sleep, biding her time.

The commander of the medical relief team is a straight-backed muscular young man with a neatly trimmed pencil moustache and a grasp of English that slips at convenient moments. Alex tells him of the time he was held captive in Macedonia, and the commander shrugs and says they are crazy wild people up there.

'They claim that they have lived there three thousand years, and why not? Men like that could have fought off the Spartans, believe me. They are like wolves.'

'Because they know the moon rides before the sun,' Alex says.

The commander pretends that he doesn't understand. He stares ahead, sweating into his many-pocketed blouson and running a finger along his moustache. The other five members of the team, all men, wear pressed camo trousers and white T-shirts. They might as well be in uniform. Alex wonders when the guns will be pulled out.

After an hour, a small black shape, jiggling in the heat rising from the road, appears ahead of the little convoy. As the shape grows nearer, Alex sees that it is Mrs Powell, riding sidesaddle on a skinny donkey. She is wearing a hunting jacket and twill trousers, and has rigged a lacy parasol to shade herself from the brutal sun. She waves to Alex as the jeeps sweep past, and Katrina wakes up when Alex tries and fails to make the commander stop.

'She went past me while I was waiting for you,' Katrina says. 'She seemed happy enough.'

'This is bandit country. We can't let her roam around alone.'

'You are our only passengers,' the commander says.

'One more won't make any difference,' Alex says, but the commander only shrugs.

The little convoy turns off the road and zig-zags up steep, overgrown pastureland, making a long detour to avoid the border town of Kakavia. The town's ruins shine on the far hillside, white as bone. It's a haunt, the commander says. Warewolves, giants, mantids, many other kinds of bad creatures. Alex would ask more – he's professionally interested in the uses insurgents and fairies have found for gengineering and fembot morphing – but the commander won't talk about it.

'They eat human flesh,' he says, and touches the knuckle of his thumb to his lips, the sign of warding evil. It gives Alex an idea he knows Katrina will like.

They cross the border just before noon, rejoining the road near the burned-out remains of the old Albanian and Greek border gates and customs buildings. Half a kilometre beyond is a bunker, half-buried behind a berm and capped with a ceramic blast shield like a bleached tortoise shell. A mast studded with microwave relay dishes rises above the trees that grow right up to the border fence. A few refugees are camping there, and naked children chase around the jeeps when they draw up at the steel gates. Alex buys a carton of Coke from an old woman and tries to pay no attention to the handful of Nationalist soldiers who amble out of the bunker. No one seems to be in charge. One soldier barely glances at the sheaf of IDs the team commander offers; another unlocks the gates; the two jeeps are waved through.

There's a new road across the border, of carbon fibre mesh laid on vitrified rock. It roars and roars under the jeeps' wide wheels. The open oak woods have been burned back a hundred metres on either side; the jeeps space out, in case of ambush.

After crossing a slender bridge that arches over a deep gorge, the two jeeps stop beside an extensive swathe of trees killed by some post-Great Climatic Overturn syndrome. At the turn of the century, before weather systems stabilized in a new pattern of colder, wetter winters and hotter, drier summers, it rained almost continuously for three years along the European coast of the

Mediterranean. The white skeletons of the trees, long ago stripped of bark, rise out of banks of dusty fern.

There's an anxious moment when the commander takes out his pistol. Alex thinks that Katrina might try to take it from the young man, but she meekly submits to being cuffed with plastic bracelets. The commander says that Alex will be spared this indignity, as will the life of his woman, provided they both cooperate. He tells Alex more or less what Alex and Katrina have already guessed, that the relief team is in fact part of Glass's small security force.

Katrina, to her credit, gives a believable performance. She curses the commander, and, with her hands cuffed behind her back, manages to get to her feet and make a run at him. One of the men trips her up. Amidst much laughter, the commander tells her, 'We were told to take care of the man, but nothing was said about you. Keep quiet, or we will leave you here.'

Katrina gets to her knees. Her nose is bleeding. She says thickly, 'I fight anyone who has the balls to go against me hand to hand. You let us go if I win.'

'Shut up, Kat.' Alex's blood is singing.

'Fuck you, Sharkey. I give these fuckers a chance at a fair fight. Their problem if they refuse.'

'Maybe later we play games with you,' the commander says. 'For now be quiet. We give you something to eat, something to drink. It is eight hours more to travel, over rough roads.'

The security guards break out their rations. They don't set a perimeter watch, Alex notices. They aren't soldiers.

The food is reconstituted but good. After he feeds Katrina, Alex eats enough for two men, especially savouring the sickly sweet honey cakes.

'Two minutes,' Katrina says.

It is very hot. Crickets make noise in the ferns. Some of the men are napping. The commander is virched up, masked in state-of-the-art video shades and manipulating the air with gloved hands as he conducts an apparently one-sided conversation.

Alex inserts filters into Katrina's nostrils, then into his own. There's a thump behind them as the gas canister explodes. Katrina hid it in the empty canvas sacks in the loadbed of the lead jeep, and sacks, some on fire, are blown high into the air. The commander

279

pitches forward. Only one man was outside the spreading boundary of the narcotic gas, but now he runs towards his fallen comrades and collapses. The gas stings Alex's eyes. The filters clog his nostrils, and it is an effort not to breathe through his mouth.

'Fish in a barrel,' Katrina says, as Alex unlocks the cuffs with the key he found in the breast pocket of the commander's blouson. She takes the cross the commander wears around his neck and puts it around her own.

'I'm not entirely sure if that's appropriate,' Alex says. 'All things considered.'

'It isn't meant to be a sign of allegiance. Maybe it will protect me against vampires.'

'That's bad semiotics,' Alex says.

'Fuck you, Sharkey. You never could take a joke.'

Katrina finds a machine-pistol and shoots out the brains of one of the jeeps. She hunches over his computer deck in goggles and mitts, negotiating with the other jeep. Alex collects up the rest of the team's weapons and throws them into the gorge, then turns the unconscious men on their sides, so that if the gas makes them throw up they won't choke on their vomit.

'You should shoot them all in the head,' Katrina says. She has taken off her goggles. The jeep isn't cooperating.

'I don't think they'll follow us,' Alex says. 'They're not what you'd call real soldiers. And even if they do follow us, there is something we can do to make sure they don't get very far.'

He tells Katrina his idea, and she smiles and says it's the dumbest thing she's ever heard.

'I thought you'd like it. What did you do with Mr Avramites, by the way?'

'What do you think I did?'

'It was stupid, Kat. You should stop and think. We can't go back, now.'

'Good.'

'We have to agree on what we do.'

'What else could I do? The old fucker sold us out.'

'Of course he did. Everyone is for sale in a war. Can't you get that thing to obey you? The gas doesn't last forever.'

'We should shoot them all in the head,' Katrina says again. 'Then we'd know they wouldn't come after us.'

'But their friends would. She wants me, Kat. Don't you see?'

'She wants you in a cell, out of the way. That is, if these fuckers are working for her. Which we don't know.'

'The commander said he was working for Glass.'

'That's not the same thing.'

'But I was right, wasn't I? Morag Gray saw truly, back in the Magic Kingdom. All that time she was hiding in plain sight—'

'Wait a minute,' Katrina says. 'Who the fuck is that?'

Someone is coming across the bridge. After a moment, Alex laughs. It is Mrs Powell.

'Shit,' Katrina says. 'Tell me we're not taking her along.'

'She must have ridden straight through that haunted town. She isn't as superstitious as our friends here.'

Mrs Powell hallos them and vigorously shakes the donkey's reins, which makes no difference at all to its ambling gait. Despite the parasol, her fleshy face has been burned by the sun to an even brick red. When she reaches Alex and Katrina, she looks down at the sleeping men and says, 'I see you have had a difference of opinion.'

Alex says, because he has always wanted to say it, 'I was misinformed.'

'My late husband always said that he'd as soon trust a shark as a lawyer. Oh, do forgive me, Mr Sharkey. I didn't mean anything by it.'

'No offence taken, Mrs Powell.'

'I must say that the pass Mr Avramites sold me did work, although the bribe was considerably larger than I had been led to expect. I was wondering if you could perhaps give me a lift. This donkey is rather less than ideally comfortable.'

Katrina says, 'We're not going anywhere you want to go.'

'I have no particular destination in mind,' Mrs Powell says, 'so your destination will be as good as any.'

While Katrina works on the jeep, Alex shares out the last of the security guards' food with Mrs Powell. Alex thinks that, for all Mrs Powell's vapourhead belief in a cosy, ecologically and politically correct fairyland, she has resources that may prove useful. She may be a hippy chick who has never grown up, but she has made it this far. It says something for her stamina, if nothing else.

'You know something about the wild fairies,' she says to Alex. 'I can tell that you do, Mr Sharkey.'

'That's what I'm here to find out.'

'And so am I. We have a joint interest. I knew it as soon as I learned who you were. Ghost, wasn't it?'

Alex is surprised and flattered. 'That was a long time ago.'

'Such an interesting drug. It's a pity no one does that kind of work any more. Fembots are so inelegant, don't you think?'

'You're trying to flatter me, Mrs Powell.'

'I don't try and flatter everyone, Mr Sharkey.'

Finally, Katrina whoops and punches the air, then strips off mitts and goggles. She has won over the jeep. Its ceramic motor whirrs into life; she unclips the computer deck and takes the wheel.

They drive two kilometres down the road, and find, as promised, a little side road running away into the forest. It hasn't been used in a long time, and the jeep leaves a trail of broken pioneer saplings that a blind man could follow. After about three kilometres they stop and unload their gear. The jeep makes a careful three-point turn before moving away at not much more than walking pace.

Katrina tells Mrs Powell, 'It'll reach those fools just about night fall. I fucked over the other jeep, so they'll be glad to jump on that one and get out of warewolf country before moonrise.' She throws back her head and howls.

'I don't think you should do that, dear,' Mrs Powell says. 'It isn't a good idea to mock the Powers.'

Alex says, 'I was wondering how you got through Kakavia. Our friends wouldn't go near it.'

'Let's say that the Powers are not capricious,' Mrs Powell tells him. 'At least, not by day. By day, we're little more than dreams to them.'

Katrina says, 'That's the first true thing you've said. As for dreams, we have some of our own.'

She staples a little infrared source to the trunk of a tree, and fixes the sensor and the little projector to another tree on the other side of the road. It takes no more than a minute.

Alex tells Mrs Powell, 'Anyone following us will trigger a hologram. A little clip from an old horror movie.'

Katrina howls again, just to make Mrs Powell wince.

Around them, widely spaced oak trees rise into the late afternoon sunlight. It is cool and shadowy beneath their thick canopy. Their mossy roots grip lichen-spattered boulders. Katrina's howl has been absolutely absorbed into the intent silence of trees drinking sunlight and exhaling water and oxygen.

Then, faintly, distantly, a howl rises in answer.

Mrs Powell shivers. Katrina grins and shakes the little silver cross she took from the commander.

Mrs Powell says, 'I don't think that will do much good. The Powers are so much older than that, after all. Would I be right in thinking we've disturbed a warewolf?'

'As you said, they only come out at night.' Katrina pats the stock of the machine-pistol she liberated. 'Besides, I'm better armed.'

'Not necessarily,' Mrs Powell says. 'I believe they have been getting weapons from the Muslims. When I was living in the woods I saw many things. I once saw a troll—'

'Trolls aren't anything,' Katrina says. 'They suffer from fused joints, and are as stupid as a bunch of rocks because of hormone imbalances.'

'This one was armed with a grenade launcher, dear. The automatic kind with the big magazine.'

It takes them two hours to walk the rest of the way. Mrs Powell matches Katrina's steady, unforgiving pace more easily than Alex. The overgrown road dips down into a narrow valley and makes a tight turn around an outcrop, and then one side of the valley drops away.

Mrs Powell claps her hands with girlish delight.

The ruined shrine stands in a kind of hollow or grove. It is no more than a line of truncated, badly weathered pillars and the knee-high remnants of walls of rough, unmortared stones, shaggy with weeds. The turf between the walls has been kept down by rabbits, although the black and white mosaic floor for which the shrine is famous (although no tourists have dared come here since the turn of the century) is now overgrown with creeping grass. There is a wall of naked rock to one side, and a steep tree-covered slope falling away to the other.

As the three people enter the ruins, something bolts away on the far side of the line of broken pillars. Alex glimpses the white deer as it leaps through a shaft of sunlight: then it is gone. Katrina throws off her pack, but Alex tells her to let it go.

'It might be one of theirs. Remember what happened to Actaeon.'

'I try not to think about all that bullshit,' Katrina says. 'In any case, we'll need some kind of sacrifice. The little fucker enjoyed giving me precise instructions.'

Mrs Powell looks at her, but says nothing.

'It's merely a token of good intent,' Alex says, and sits down on a large stone.

The walk has left him breathless and drenched with sweat. There's sweat in his hair and eyebrows, and he must keep blinking away pearls of sweat that gather on his eyelashes. He feels a watery weariness in his knees, and his pulse is pounding behind his eyes. He is too old and too fat for this kind of adventure. Wiry, hyperactive Max should be here, while Alex watches over all from the Web. Except Max would never modify his immune system. For all their affected disdain for their bodies, for the meat that anchors their minds, hackers are surprisingly squeamish when it comes to gengineering.

Katrina says, 'There are many deer here, despite the war. Or perhaps because of it, for now men hunt men instead of animals. There are wild boar and chamois also. I'll get what we need.'

'Perhaps we should have brought my donkey,' Mrs Powell says. 'Although I think it would be too tough for even a warewolf.'

'We'll need something,' Alex says, 'and it had better be bigger than a rabbit.'

'Anything you say, boss,' Katrina says, and then she is crashing away downslope.

Mrs Powell takes off her straw sunhat and elaborately pats her brow with a white handkerchief. 'I'm pleased you brought me with you,' she says. 'I can still be of much help.'

'Perhaps,' Alex says.

'I'll find out about this place,' Mrs Powell says, and ambles off amongst the weedy stones, scrolling through her pocket guide.

Alex smokes a cigarette, letting the old woman discover the remnants of the altar, and the spring running from the little cliff that backs the shrine. He stretches out on crisp, sun-warmed turf and wakes with a start when Mrs Powell returns.

'My guide tells me this place was sacred to Asklepios, the god of the Illyrian coastal town of Butrini,' Mrs Powell says. 'A beautiful town, Mr Sharkey. You should visit it. I have been to Butrini, to protest about the use of slave labour in the docks.'

Alex lights a cigarette and says, 'I admire you, Mrs Powell.'

'They were once intelligent creatures,' Mrs Powell says. 'The butchers at Butrini turn fairies back into dolls. Worse than dolls, for they do not live long, and suffer terribly. What else could I do, in all conscience?'

Alex says 'What does Butrini have to do with the shrine?'

Mrs Powell says, 'Butrini was a Roman colony, and perhaps two thousand years ago this was an outpost of that colony. It has exactly the same vibrations, you know. Vibrations do persist if they are undisturbed. They are faint here, but quite unmistakable.'

'Before then, it was sacred to the triple goddess,' Alex says. 'You'll find a grove of laurel further along, the tree sacred to Daphne.'

'You're interested in the old stories.' Mrs Powell waves at the midges that dance around her head. 'Very few are, these days.'

Alex is pleased to show off the results of his research. 'Her real name was Daphoene, the bloody one. The Maenads, her priestesses, were supposed to chew laurel leaves to help them achieve an orgiastic frenzy. In Africa they called her Ngame; in Libya, Neith. She is also Hecate, and Graves's White Goddess of Pelion, Keats's *Belle Dame sans Merci*, and Mab, Thomas the Rhymer's Fairy Queen. Apollo tried to rape her, and when she turned into a laurel, he made a wreath of her leaves as consolation. We still remember that, every four years; but perhaps we forget that she never died.' He looks at Mrs Powell. 'I hope that we're going to meet someone who claims her place, soon enough.'

'I *knew* it,' Mrs Powell says. 'I must say that you are a dark horse, Mr Sharkey. Who do you really hope to meet here? You never did tell me.'

Alex says, 'The people who took us over the border were anxious to move on before darkness. Humans only rule by day. This is no-man's land, quite literally.'

'Quite dangerous,' Mrs Powell says. 'So I'm told. Mr Avramites let slip that you are interested in the Children's Crusade.'

'Mr Avramites let rather too much slip for his own good.'

'Mr Avramites said that the Children's Crusade will not be allowed across the border.'

'Oh, it will. That's the problem. It will cross from Albania into the neutral zone, but if I'm right, it will not survive to cross the border into Greece. That is why we have to meet it. I think Glass's girlfriend wants something from it, and so we have a chance to bargain, her and me.'

Mrs Powell says, with a shrewdness that surprises Alex, 'Then this *is* about the woman you knew so long ago. Perhaps you will tell me about her? I see you as the parfit gentil knight, seeking your long lost love.'

Alex smiles. He's happy here, in the quiet, immemorial ruins. He has only just realized it.

He says, 'Who is she? She wants to be thought of as a lineal descendant of Daphoene, the huntress of the moon, the triple goddess of air, earth and the secret waters of death. It's symbolic that the stones here were raised in triumph by men over a site originally sacred to women. They overran the goddess's shrines, killed her Pythons, and shackled her sacred horses to their war chariots. They cut down the laurel groves, too, but the laurel has grown back.'

'Oh yes,' Mrs Powell murmurs, her eyes half closed. 'It's true enough.'

Alex says, really getting into it now, 'The Age of Reason was almost a fatal blow to the triple goddess, but in its ending is her new beginning. For the last century saw the deposition of the paternal God who was set on the throne of Zeus, which was once *her* throne. The Age of Theocracy in the West was already in decline when in our country Cromwell forcefully rejected the ceremonies that obscured the godhead from the common man.

He couldn't see that the Age of Reason, in which every man was entitled to read and interpret the scriptures, would bring about the death of the idea of God. The god of science and reason, Apollo, was raised up in His place, and at either side of Apollo were Pluto and Mercury. I worshipped Apollo and Mercury when I was young, but it is Pluto who is in the ascendant now. Pluto, the hoarder, god of the geezers and the babushkas, god of all the people who hide away in the ribbon arcologies and in virtuality, jealous of the young and denying death, for that would mean losing all they've accumulated.

'But I think Apollo will have his revenge. The last spurt of technology engendered the dolls, the slaves without souls, animals become like men. The woman I'm seeking – although she was only a crazy clever little girl then – raised them up, gave them souls. And I think that now she wants them to worship her. She believes she is the triple goddess returned. In Catholic countries the triple goddess never quite went away, for the cult of Mary was little more than a dilution of her own cult. Crusaders brought back a version of this story to Britain, although Mary quickly became Marian, the companion of that Jack-in-the-Green, Robin Hood. She is waiting, a seed in the bitter earth.'

'Some of us never lost our faith,' Mrs Powell says.

'Of course. At the end of the twentieth century it was thought that a new goddess was raised up: Gaia, the Earth herself. But Gaia is the world, not the meaning of the world. Gaia existed before us, and will exist after. She needs no worship, for we are already part of her. It is the triple goddess who interceded with Gaia on our behalf. It was she who ordered the lives of our ancestors. Without her there was no sacrifice of the temporary kings; without her no seasons, no harvest. And here she is again, incarnated as the self-appointed queen of the fairies. She marked me, you know. Long ago, when she was making her first fairy. I've been trying to understand ever since. I think I'm beginning to understand. I think I know what she wants to bring back, and I don't like it, or the way she's trying to do it.

'I think that the Children's Crusade was a first step. A test to see if she could spread a religious meme. But she doesn't own the fairies. They've grown beyond her control. Strange things live again, not just because of the war, but because they can. Fairies can remake things at will. They can directly control the fembots that course through their blood. I believe that Glass wants to make use of that ability for his own ends, and that's why he made his offer of sanctuary to the Children's Crusade. But I'm not so sure that he should. I don't think he has the right.'

Mrs Powell says, 'We really do have a lot in common.'

Alex says, 'Not really. You believe that's the literal truth. I believe it's a metaphor my dark lady has been playing with. Now she's lost control, and has enlisted the help of this technocrat.'

'And will you wage war on the Children's Crusade all by yourself? I would like nothing better than to help. The existence of the Crusade is used as an excuse to justify the hunting down and destruction of fairies.'

'I only want to defuse the Crusade, not destroy it. The human component isn't important. It's what's changed them that's important. I do have help. That's why we're here. But perhaps you can help, too.'

Mrs Powell says, 'I thought I saw something. It is watching us from behind those pillars.'

Alex looks carefully, but sunlight dancing through leaf-laden oak boughs dazzles his eyes. He tells Mrs Powell that she has the better eye-sight.

'I bought new corneas on the grey market five years ago,' Mrs Powell says. 'For what I paid, I should not see things that aren't there.'

She has been squinting into the bright sunlight, at the line of broken pillars that stand amongst the weed-grown stone walls. Now she looks at Alex and says, 'If she wants to be the fairy goddess, what are you, Mr Sharkey?'

'She called me her Merlin, once upon a time. We were much younger then, but perhaps there's a grain of truth to it. Well, if I'm Merlin, then she's Nimue. I've given her my secrets, and she's left me locked in the cave of my skull. I suppose I've come here to be freed, but I'm not without gifts, or allies. I fully intend to live through this, but it will be dangerous.'

'You're trying to tell me that I could walk away. It's well meant, but I'm so thrilled to be here, Mr Sharkey. I'll do all I can. I think

I'll take a reading of this place. It is absolutely throbbing with energy.'

Alex unpacks his computer and, while it extrudes its ferrite antenna, eats a bar of chocolate and smokes another cigarette. Then he sends a one line message to Max, confirming that all is well, and checks on the progress of the Children's Crusade. It is right where it is supposed to be, just to the north of Corovoda, no more than two days' forced march from the border. There is only one way it can go now, up the Vjoses valley towards the abandoned town of Leskoviku and then across the wild Grammos Mountains. Katrina will be pissed: Ray was telling the truth.

Mrs Powell is taking her time setting up a series of dowsing rods – bits of wire bent over at the top, with a thread weighted by a crystal teardrop – and adjusting a laser diffractometer to measure the crystals' movements. Alex dozes in the warm sunlight of this late afternoon, and dreams of Milena as she once was, although he's chasing her through the wreckage of the Magic Kingdom while fairies, blue-skinned, red-eyed, nip at his heels. It's a silly, trivial dream, but its claustrophobic urgency is real enough. Time's running out.

6
In Trouble Again

Todd Hart wakes, headachy and dry-mouthed, in hot darkness that's filled with the noise and vibration of engines. From their laboured rumble, and the way the ribbed steel floor cants beneath him, Todd realizes that he's in some kind of vehicle climbing a long slope. The mountains – but which ones? There are so many mountains in Albania, and it's surrounded by mountains, too. Christ, if he's being taken across the border then he's either truly fucked, or on his way to the biggest story in his life. Either way, he feels as if he's fallen over a cliff.

Todd makes the bad mistake of sitting up. It appears that someone has cut off the top of his head and fixed it back on with a bunch of nine inch nails. He can't help groaning. Close by in the noisy darkness, a familiar gloomy, gritty voice says, 'Welcome to the shittiest taxi service in the world.'

It is Spike Weaver. He was taken at gunpoint from the hotel, he says, and put in the back of an armoured personnel carrier with Todd already lying unconscious on its floor. He has his watch; it is just past nine in the evening. They've been travelling about two hours.

Todd checks his jacket pockets, then goes through them again in a kind of panic when he realizes that his wallet with his accreditation, and his notepad, which contains all the information he needs, as well as an expert system translator, a historian and a travel guide, are gone. And he's lost his bush hat and one shoe – he remembers the firelight in the narrow street, and struggling out from under the dead soldier's weight. He tells Spike what happened when he talked with Antoinette, and Spike says that he mostly figured it out already.

'The thing is, I don't even know it was her,' Todd says. He has to shout to be heard above the clamour of the engines, which does nothing for his headache. 'It could have been anyone morphed to look like her. Well, I guess we're in trouble again.'

Spike grunts. 'I think we're in a shit-load of trouble. The only thing that makes me feel hopeful is that I have my drone.'

'Good. If we keep calm we won't blow this. We'll get our story. Meanwhile, let's have some light in here.'

'I was saving the batteries,' Spike says, but tells the drone to switch on a single light at low gain.

They are in a steel can. A ribbed steel floor, bulkheads of riveted steel, a braced ceiling of steel plate about a hundred and fifty centimetres above the floor.

'Fuck,' Spike says, staring at Todd, 'are you hurt bad?'

The front of Todd's jacket is stiff with dry blood. 'Someone else,' he says, taking it off. 'I was knocked out by a hornet.'

Spike has a bad cut on his cheekbone, and a lump on the back of his head. They weren't subtle when they took him. 'Worse things happen at sea,' he says mysteriously. He almost seems to be enjoying this. It confirms his belief that the world is a shit-storm, and happiness can be found only in those moments when someone isn't actually dumping a load on your head.

When Todd mentions his headache, Spike produces a couple of paracetamol from one of the zippered pockets of the flakjacket he wears every waking hour of the day – Todd believes he sleeps in it, too. There's a chemical toilet in the corner, with a spigot and a chained steel cup beside it. The water is flat and warm and tastes of metal, but after a while the paracetamol kicks in and Todd feels a little better, even a little hopeful. Maybe he really is riding towards his old-fashioned exclusive scoop.

Spike isn't so sure, and Todd tries to talk him round. 'She trusts me,' he says, at the end. 'That's the point. She chose me. That makes us safe, doesn't it?'

'You're the only journalist in town that isn't from Europe, and the only one sniffing after Glass. Of course you were chosen. People like that still think the States count for something. And you do have a reputation. Maybe she's a fan.'

'There's a story here, Spike. Be positive. I can feel it.'

Todd has Spike shoot some footage, a quick impressionistic account of why he's locked in this steel coffin of a personnel carrier that's labouring its way up some godforsaken mountain to an unknown destination. Illuminated by light bounced off blued steel, with the rumble of the engines and the lurching ride, it will be crudely and urgently realistic. Todd tries to emphasize the urgency and hide his fear, and does it in a single take.

'Not bad,' Spike says. He tries to patch into the vehicle's systems, and at last the drone's parasitic cable finds a place where it can interface with the inertial navigation system and, through that, one of the navstar satellites. Ten seconds later, the report is in the Web, a coded squirt worming its way from node to node until it can download itself into the editor's desk.

After that, Spike turns off the light, and they sit in the clamorous, swaying dark. Spike lights a cigarette. Its acrid smoke quickly saturates the air conditioning, and when Todd complains, Spike says that he should try one. 'It'll calm you down. You have to be calm around these trigger-happy hyped-up goons.'

'I'd rather deal with whoever's giving the orders.'

'If anyone is.'

'Someone wants us, Spike. We can work with that.'

'They better not touch my fucking gear. That's all I ask.'

Spike draws on his cigarette. Its glowing tip briefly illuminates his booze-reddened nose and sets a tiny star in each of his spaniel eyes. In the jouncing roaring dark, he explains his theory that as long as he's behind a camera, he's invulnerable.

'This old dead bloke, Isherwood, had it right. You become like a disembodied observer. You aren't part of the scene. Shit only happens when you lose concentration. It's like a zen thing.'

'Give me one of those cigarettes.'

'There you go,' Spike says, lighting two in a brief scratch of flame and passing one over. 'It's not as if they give you cancer. The thing is, when you're in an intense situation, you have to relax into it, sort of thing.'

But it's hard to find any comfort, on cold steel, in the noisy darkness. When the armoured personnel carrier finally stops, and switches off its engines, their roaring runs on inside Todd's skull. It's as if he's become part of the machine, the idea of the machine travelling on forever.

The hatch is opened with a hydraulic thump, and a trio of giant adolescent soldiers rout out Todd and Spike. Spike starts to swear at them, saying they're not to touch the drone, he'll fucking take on the first fucker who fucks with his drone. The armoured personnel carrier squats under a row of arc lights like a toad constructed of angles. Its black skin absorbs light and gives nothing back. Volumes of air blow out of the night and move through gnarled trees. There's a crashing noise, an endless falling roar – slowly, Todd realizes it's the sea.

The trees are olive trees. The APC is parked on a road with groves of olive trees on one side and a sheer drop to the sea on the other. There are other vehicles parked here and there, and their headlights add to the general glare. A half-moon is tipped high above. The tall soldiers march Spike and Todd, who's half-shod and limping, away from the APC. They go past a jeep with the UN symbol on its hood, and then Todd sees soldiers wearing powder-blue berets and shouts to them.

'American! I'm American!'

One of the UN soldiers, an officer, turns. His mahogany skin gleams under the arc lights.

'American reporter! I've been kidnapped!' Todd struggles as a soldier buffets him with quick hard taps, trying to turn him away. 'American reporter! CNN. ABC. CBfuckingS.'

The officer says, 'As I understand it, this is a local thing.'

Todd feels a surge of righteous anger. The UN is supposed to protect people, and he wants protection. 'I'm a reporter! CNN! You make them let me go!'

But the UN officer shakes his head and walks away. Todd swears at him, and the tall soldiers laugh. They know American swear words. One tells Todd, 'That man no good. Stay with us. Give us cigarettes.'

'The UN is operating within local restrictions,' Spike says. 'What can you expect?'

'Light me. I'm doing a field report right here!'

'Fuck off. These people are nervous enough as it is. Let it go.'

'That fucking Marku. He set me up!'

'Of course he did,' Spike says, 'but don't take it out on me.'

The soldier who has a little English runs a finger across his throat. 'We kill Marku dead. Try and sell us out. We kill him dead. We look after you.'

Todd kicks off his remaining shoe. He says, 'Are you working for Antoinette?'

The soldier shrugs.

'The woman I was talking with? That's who told you to kidnap us?'

Spike offers around his cigarettes. 'Where are you boys taking us?'

The soldiers grin and nudge each other, happy to be smoking these fine imported Camels. They are like eager nervous colts, their skins quivering with internal lightnings, their eyes rolling at sounds Todd can't hear. Their hands never leave the stocks of their Kalashnikov Mark Vs. Swollen nail-bitten fingers tap at taped stocks, the worn guards of filed-down triggers. They keep glancing up at the black night sky.

'Come on,' Todd says, 'it's just a harmless question. Who's your boss?'

The soldier who speaks English holds out his hand, and Spike gives him the rest of the cigarettes. 'Rich Greek fucker buy us. One day. Bring you here. Here you are. We *good*.'

293

'Glass,' Todd says. He feels a measure of relief. 'It *is* Glass. I told you, Spike. Was there a woman with him?'

But the soldiers aren't listening to him. Todd looks up, and sees the helicopter swinging towards them out of the night.

7
The Angry Ones

When Alex wakes, the light is fading and there's a chill edge to the air. It's fifteen hundred metres above sea level here, high in the immemorial mountains of what was once called Illyria, and the summer nights are cold. Alex checks his watch, a single dot and two lines generated by a chip implanted under the skin of his wrist. The effects of the narcotic gas should have worn off about an hour ago, time enough for Glass's security guards to have followed the trail to the shrine. Alex feels a lifting of pressure. They aren't here. They probably took the jeep and made a run for it. He begins to think that this might actually work out.

There's no sign of Katrina, but that doesn't worry Alex. She can look after herself. Mrs Powell is sitting with her back against the low remains of a wall, talking softly with her guide book. The laser diffractometer ticks at her feet, firing threads of red light at each of the dowsing rods in turn. She looks up when Alex stirs, and tells him that the shrine is absolutely packed with energy.

'But it's so calm. Nothing has disturbed this place for a long time.'

Alex goes to the spring to wash his face, and that's when the fairy steps out from behind a low ruined wall.

It is First Rays of the New Rising Sun, jaunty as ever. He has a new jacket, a cut-down camo affair with zippered pockets and slithery green and brown blotches that continually change shape. It glitters with dozens of talismans, and there's a big pistol tucked into its cinch belt.

'Long time no see,' Ray says.

Alex holds out his right hand, and Ray slaps it. The fey's sharp nails prick Alex's palm.

Ray says, 'You got away from those creeps. I knew you would.'

'Were they Glass's men?'

'That's for you to find out, big man.'

'Maybe I should have gone with you.'

'I had things to do.'

'How was your journey?'

Ray shrugs, setting his talismans all a-jangle. 'Wolves chase me, one day, two days gone. I hid in a tree. It is no problem. I piss in their faces and they run away.'

'Really?'

Ray grins his sharp-toothed grin. 'They are warewolf wolves, big man. Wolves with human bodies and military imperatives. I dose them with something that blows their chips.'

'It's the real humans you should be afraid of.' Alex kneels and splashes his face with some of the cold water that trickles down the slick rockface.

Ray observes, 'You take a risk, big man. That there is a sacred spring.'

'The sacred spring vanished long ago. Some earthquake sealed it up, and another earthquake opened up this one, by and by.'

'Everything is sacred here, because it is on sacred ground. You should watch out.' Ray shows his teeth. They are all the same size, and filed to sharp points. He's lost nothing of his quick sense of malicious mischief. 'Who's the old fart? She the sacrifice? I see her thumping around in the woods by Gjirokastra. I warn off a troll getting ready to eat her.'

'She believes in fairies. She'll be thrilled to meet you, but don't let it go to your head. How are you, Ray? We never said goodbye properly, in Paris.'

'I fool you there,' Ray says, grinning.

'That you did. You played both ends against each other.'

'I'm fooled, too. She plays me like I play you. She uses me and I run away. She makes slaves of us all, if she can.'

There's one question Alex wants desperately to ask, but this isn't quite the moment. If he asks about Milena now, Ray will lie, or turn it into a joke. With their strong survival instincts and fragile sense of self, fairies can fall into rage or fugue with very little provocation. Their consciousness is in no way equivalent to that of

295

humans. It's a vulnerable affair built on partial personalities, and generated by implanted chips, which interact across a highly connected neuron net. Their memory is not distributed, but is discrete and linear – the long knotted string that Ray wears looped around his waist is an externalization of the integrated memories which bind his selves. It is his life-line. Fairies can marshall vast amounts of processing power but lack the sudden insights of humans, whom they think of as disturbingly capricious, unbound creatures.

'Well,' Alex says, instead of asking his question, 'here we are, back together again.'

'We knew you'd rise to the bait, big man.' One of Ray's large, pointed ears flicks. 'She's coming,' he says, and scampers away.

A moment later there's a faint breathy scream. Mrs Powell has seen her first real wild fey. When Alex follows Ray across the ruins, he finds Mrs Powell sitting quite still, staring at Ray with her hands clasped before her mouth. Her book lies at her feet like a wounded bird, talking to itself in a ravelling whisper.

Katrina walks up out of the trees on the far side of the ruined shrine. A mostly headless, bristle-coated piglet is slung around her shoulders. She doesn't seem surprised to see Ray. She drops the corpse on the turf and says, 'The little blue-skinned fucker fucked off when it came to carry this back.'

Ray says, 'Without me you never catch it.' He stamps around on the grass, looks over his shoulder at Katrina and laughs. 'You have heavy feet.'

'What I have is a smart Glock semi-automatic machine pistol that fires Glaser loads at a hundred rounds a minute. It did the job, not your fancy tracking, or that cannon tucked in your jacket.'

'This is a good gun,' Ray says, brandishing it.

'Make sure the fucking safety's on,' Katrina says.

Alex says, 'What kind is it, Ray?'

'A good American gun. A .357 Colt Python. You see it.'

Ray proudly displays the weapon. Intricate self-engulfing fairy entoptic forms are chased into the barrel.

Ray says, 'It fires magic bullets.'

'It better had,' Katrina says, 'because you can't shoot for shit.'

'She blows off the pig's head,' Ray tells Alex. 'We bleed it out so she can carry it. It is no way to hunt. Feys run down deer, and drink their blood until they fall from exhaustion. That's hunting. Hunting people is the best fun of all, but I tell you nothing of that. Perhaps I hunt you one day.'

'Bite your tongue and bleed to death,' Katrina advises Ray.

'Don't worry, I kill you quick if it comes to it,' Ray says. 'But you're safe, big man. Your blood tastes of vinegar and piss, and no one wants to drink it.'

'You might have to drink it all the same,' Alex says.

'I know it. You better eat much sugar food, sweeten it up.'

This joke does not disguise Ray's profound unease. Fairies drink each other's blood during sex, when they exchange clades of fembots, or after fighting, when the victor takes away a part of the loser. Drinking Alex's blood will be necessary, but even so it is a deep perversion.

Mrs Powell draws herself up and says, 'You must introduce us, Mr Sharkey.'

'Oh, of course. Mrs Powell, this is First Rays of the New Rising Sun. Ray, you put away pistol and meet Mrs Powell. Mrs Powell will probably have plenty of questions later on, when we've time.'

Katrina says, 'With luck there won't be time.'

Alex says to the fey, 'Then they will come for us?'

Ray grins. He's enjoying this. 'Maybe soon. Maybe not.'

Katrina starts dressing the piglet. Alex tells Mrs Powell, 'We should gather fuel.'

Once they have walked far enough back down the trail to be out of even Ray's earshot, he adds, 'Ray isn't like most feys.'

'You don't have to apologize,' Mrs Powell says.

'It's a warning, not an apology. Ray's a flirt. He's a little shit with a tremendous ego who wants to be the coolest free agent around. He got badly burned when he tried to change sides, and he's determined to erase that humiliation. We can exploit his attitude so he'll help us, but other feys aren't as human as he is. Don't ever make one angry. Ray talks about killing humans – and I think it's mostly talk. Other feys would do it without blinking, if they felt their honour was hurt. Very big with the feys, honour. It took me a long time to get them to agree to this. They have to think they're more important than we are.'

'Perhaps they are,' Mrs Powell says.

'It'll soon be dark, so we really should collect some wood. There must be an offering. It's only polite. Politeness is what will save us.'

They collect armfuls of dead, crumbling wood, and pile it neatly in a shallow pit Katrina has dug in the turf using her hunting knife. Ray brings boughs of wild rosemary. Katrina stuffs these inside the chest cavity of the gutted piglet, then coats the carcass in a slather of clay.

Once the fire is burning well, the clay casing around the piglet starts to crack. Little yellow stars of fat pop and flare in the flames. Alex sprays an entire canister of pheromones into the rising smoke, just to be sure. The smell of roasting meat fills his mouth with saliva. He tells the others that in Italy pork roast with rosemary is called *aristo*. 'It's a funeral meat.'

'Rosemary for remembrance,' Mrs Powell says.

They sit in the light of the fire. Little biting insects zip around their heads. Mrs Powell hands around a repellant spray. Ray sniffs it and sneezes, like a cat. While Alex gazes sleepily into the fire, nibbling a bar of piercingly sweet emergency chocolate, Katrina watches the dark forest. She's very tense, but pretending to be cool. Alex knows better than to say anything to her. Silently, they all wait and watch.

At last, Ray says, 'They're coming.'

Alex hears the feys before he sees them. They call out of the darkness to each other. High voices merge in a chant that chills the blood.

Euan! Euan! Eu-oi-oi-oi!

Katrina jumps to her feet, cradling the machine pistol. Alex tells her to put it away. She hesitates before she fits it inside her leather jacket. She says to Ray, 'You fucker. You didn't tell us it was the Angry Ones who'd come to us.'

'You didn't ask,' Ray says, with a sharp, toothy smile.

Mrs Powell says, 'It is the song the drunken hill shepherds sing. That's all.'

'Let's hope so,' Alex says. He is trying not to show his fear. Ray promised that he'd gather together the wild and secretive feys who haunt this land. The Angry Ones are a very different proposition.

'Still,' Mrs Powell says doubtfully, 'it's a very *old* song.' For the first time her indomitable spirit of inquiry seems to be weakening.

'Feys borrow what they need,' Alex says. 'The Angry Ones are hedonists, living only for the day, for pleasure. They're on a permanent trip. If they were the traditional followers of Bacchus, like the pack which killed Orpheus, they'd be running on wine, or beer laced with ivy, or raw *Amanita muscaria*, depending which theory you believe. The Angry Ones infect themselves with nanoware effectors that induce production of psychoactive chemicals in specific neurons. Actually, I have quite a nostalgia for the method. I—'

'Let's hope they've heard of us,' Katrina says. 'Let's hope they've heard of what we did in Amsterdam. They do, we'll get all the respect we want.'

'No killing,' Alex tells her. 'You promised. It will all come to an end with killing.'

'I didn't know this kind of shit was about to happen,' Katrina hisses. 'This fucker has suckered us in and sold us out. For the second time.'

Katrina lapses into this kind of tough guy dialogue when she's stressed – she learned English from virtual shoot-'em-ups. Firelight flatters her face. She looks young and fierce and alert, a warrior-princess from the sagas in a black leather jacket, buckled biker boots and black leggings. All she lacks are mirrorshades.

Ray says, 'I always fool you.'

'You've fooled yourself this time,' Katrina says. 'The Angry Ones won't be any use in this thing. Where are the other feys? Even two or three would be better than this bunch.'

'This thing is a fey thing,' Ray says, showing his teeth. 'We decide.'

Slowly, figures become visible in the flickering shadows at the edges of the firelight. Mrs Powell looks around as the feys' high voices call out, first from one side of the clearing, and then the other. Katrina watches Ray with an unforgiving stare. Alex looks straight ahead, his heart beating fast. There is a tremor in his hands. He can't stop them shaking, and at last puts them between his heavy thighs.

Faces appear and disappear in the flickering dark. Sharp foxy faces, snouted pig faces, the long mournful faces of horses. The feys are masked and mostly naked. True feys despise clothes as a human affectation, although some wear animal pelts, cast over their shoulders and knotted around their hips. Some have wound ivy in their long hair. Some have dabbed their bare blue skin with blotches of red – ivy sap and urine make a dye the colour of lake. The blotches look black in the firelight.

Memes, Alex thinks. Milena buried them deep, but they will always show themselves in the right circumstances. These feys are not as wild and free as they like to think they are. The psychoactive fembots liberate the old stories locked inside their heads.

One of the feys, masked with a tragic human face, carries a bear cub that's barely old enough to have opened its eyes. It stands in front of the humans and watches them while its brothers slowly advance towards the fire and the roasting piglet.

Katrina slips her hand inside her leather jacket, and Alex whispers, 'Easy.'

With a sudden rush, the feys knock the roast piglet from the fire, shatter its casing, dismember it with their knives, and retreat to devour the portions they have taken. In the darkness, something large moves forward. It is a small mammoth, not much bigger than a horse but more solidly built, and covered in coarse long red hair. Between curving tusks capped with steel, its trunk weaves back and forth, snuffling the air. On its back is a wooden platform with a single piece of carved wood for a seat.

Alex gets to his feet. Mrs Powell has taken out her camera, but one of the feys snatches it from her. The others watch Ray through their masks as he goes to the mammoth and taps its trunk firmly. It kneels, and raises its trunk above its domed head. Ray turns and tells the humans triumphantly, 'It's time!'

8
Welcome to the Pleasure Dome

The arc-lit olive groves drop away as the helicopter swings out to sea. The helicopter's pilot, small as a child, is masked with a black glass helmet and wrapped in an effector cocoon. He won't or can't answer Todd's questions; nor will the one soldier who came along, a tall boy who must hunch with his knees around his ears to fit in one of the jump seats in the copter's tiny cabin. The soldier rolls his eyes nervously, and strokes the barrel of his Kalashnikov. He has a teddy bear fastened to his webbing belt. This is a war of children.

The helicopter is swift and light and responsive. It makes a long curve across the sea, canting above moonlit whitecaps, then swings back towards the black shore and suddenly is travelling barely a metre above treetops, rising and falling in an endless switchback ride.

'That fucker's not human,' Spike says, meaning the pilot.

The black forest drops away. There is a moonlit lake like a shining silver shield ahead, with a kind of necklace of lights heaped carelessly at the far end. As the helicopter skims in, Todd realizes that the lights are those of a long, low building. It is a series of interconnected single storey hexagons and pentagons, grown from architectural stromalith and cantilevered out over the rocky lake shore, a retro gesture to the Arizona buildings of Frank Lloyd Wright's last, late burst of creativity. A hundred narrow windows blaze with light. Todd hears the thready pulse of Moroccan pop above the flutter of the helicopter's fan-blades as it turns on its axis above a flat roof and delicately lowers itself towards a cross limned in flecks of red light.

A man in full butler's rig – black frockcoat and grey trousers, starched white shirt and bowtie and white gloves – opens the copter's hatch and lowers the steps. The boy soldier swiftly unpacks himself, jumps down, and covers Todd and Spike with his rifle as they clamber out.

'That won't be necessary,' the butler says. The tall soldier stares at him wide-eyed. The butler sighs and says something in Albanian which makes the soldier shrug, smile, and put up his weapon.

'That's so much better,' the butler says. He's about sixty, his long silver hair caught in a ponytail that reaches halfway down his back. He says to Todd, 'I do hope you had a good journey. I understand that doll pilots are very capable, although I wouldn't trust myself to one. Please do follow me.'

Spike slings the harnessed camera drone over his shoulder, and they go down a winding stair towards a wide, freeform terrace scattered with tubs of geraniums that look stark and unreal under bright lights. Todd tells the butler, 'I'm here to see Glass.'

'Of course you are.'

'Or Antoinette. I've already talked to her, although not in the flesh.'

'Oh, she's about. Somewhere or other. The truth is, we're having a bit of a crisis. A little local difficulty with some former employees.'

'We were brought here at gunpoint,' Spike says. He seems to resent the man's supercilious tone. Todd wonders if it is some kind of British class thing.

The butler says, 'I daresay you were, but there's no need for that now. We're inside a very tight security perimeter.'

'I think Antoinette is expecting me.' By now Todd is only fifty per cent sure that it really was Antoinette that he spoke to, in that dusty little courtyard in Tirana.

'Then I daresay she'll find you, sir.'

Spike laughs. 'He's a fucking card, this one. Where are you from, mate? I bet you didn't start off with that fucking cutglass accent.'

'I'm Ralph,' the butler says.

Steps at the end of the terrace descend to a gravel path that snakes across a cactus garden. Concealed lights illuminate tall saguaros and barrel-shaped mammillarias. Todd treads carefully, feeling every sharp stone through the thin material of his silk socks. It is warmer here than by the sea. Crickets stitch the night with pulses of insect code. Beyond the cactus garden is the noise of a party, the babble of many voices rising over thready pop music.

The butler, Ralph, says, 'This part of the complex is an open house. It's best not to ask about political matters. The people here aren't interested in them. Other than that, please do enjoy the party.'

'Don't you worry,' Spike says.

He lopes forward, the snout of his camera drone jogging at his shoulder, and vanishes into the crowd. Most of the men and women are wearing the bright splash prints that are fashionable this year, a dazzle of shifting reds and greens and golds that look like a gaggle of ongoing attempts at solving the four colour map problem. Most of them are older than the butler, too.

Spike comes back and hands Todd a sweating, woman-shaped carton of Asahi beer. Todd takes a swig of the ice-cold raspberry-flavoured stuff and looks around. The urbane, silver-haired butler and the boy soldier have vanished.

'I'm having a weird day,' Todd tells Spike. 'Maybe we should do a number here. No one will believe it otherwise. This is supposed to be in the middle of the fucking neutral zone.'

'That would be rude,' Spike says. 'It's a nice party. There's food over there.'

Sushi, yellow and red and black caviars, and fanned slivers of smoked salmon are displayed on shaved ice around a melting ice sculpture of a fish standing on its curled tail. While Spike gorges himself on caviar, Todd watches the crowd slowly move around itself. They are baby boomers, geezers and babushkas in their late seventies who, thanks to fembot therapy, hormone replacement and microsurgery, appear half their age. Todd sees a woman he vaguely remembers from hype shows; escorted through the throng by a tall, white-haired man in a dinner jacket, she's dressed in a mu-mu, and coloured glowing rods are spiked through her spire of jet black hair. On the far side of the terrace, big screens endlessly cycle through satellite channels, five second slices tumbling past in a flicker of crazy light. Dolls in satin peach uniforms move amongst the people with trays of drinks; one doll has a hairless head shaped like an anvil, and lines of white powder streak the flat plate of its blue scalp. Every now and then someone bends to it and takes a toot. Spike wonders aloud if they grew the doll that way, or did it have surgery.

Todd says, 'This is weird, Spike. Deeply, badly weird.'

'It's good caviar, this. You should try some while you have the chance.'

Todd scoops up a mound of soft grains with his thumb. It *is* good. He says, 'I'm going to ask around. Maybe we'll do some set-ups later. Save some caviar for me.'

'No worries,' Spike says.

Most of the people Todd tries to question don't or won't speak English. There's something glazed about them. Most don't even seem to hear him, but finally he finds a man who listens politely, and then explains that all this is for Glass.

'We're here to cheer him up. It's a splendid party, isn't it?'

'Oh, it's something all right.'

With his deeply tanned, creviced face, shock of grizzled grey hair, and scarlet, gold-trimmed robe, the man looks like a pirate king. He says, 'It's old-fashioned of us, I know, but actually being here is important. It's what counts with us.'

Todd says, 'I have business with Glass. And with Antoinette.'

'He will be enjoying the party. Watching over us all.' The man takes in Todd's blood-stained jacket, his lack of shoes. 'Where are you from, young man?'

'Albania.'

'How lucky that you're here, then.'

'I was sort of kidnapped. Is Glass really here?'

'We came here for Glass,' the man says. For a moment, his gaze becomes unfocused, and then he blinks and says, 'What were we talking about?'

Todd sees that the man is about to turn away. He says, 'What is it, between Antoinette and Glass?'

That gets the man's attention. He smiles and says, 'If he's John F. Kennedy, she's Marilyn Monroe.'

'Except this is the twenty-first century,' someone else says. He's a skinny man about Todd's age, with the unhealthy pallor of a cave-dwelling animal.

'Of course it is,' the older man says. 'And such a wonderful time to be alive, don't you think? Now I simply must talk to a very dear friend who won't forgive me if I continue to ignore her. You must forgive me, Mr . . . ah . . .'

'Hart. Todd Hart.'

But the man has already turned away. In his place is a tall, pale wraith dressed entirely in black, with a dead white face and a mop of pale hair. His eyes are masked by little round landscape mirror-shades. This apparition grins at Todd, exposing discoloured teeth set crookedly in pale gums. 'You'll have to excuse the way we wired up the Eurotrash,' he says, and shoves his hand forward. He wears memory rings on every finger, the kind that are accessed through a secondary nervous system grown through the epidermis by fembots. 'I'm Frodo, Frodo McHale. I can't talk long. Security is amazingly poor here, but eventually they'll catch my morphing program and I'll no longer be the Invisible Man.'

Todd shakes Frodo McHale's hand. 'Glass has some strange friends. Who are they?'

'Don't you worry about them. They're getting kind of worn out, and besides, they never were much more than burnt-out pre-millennial cases. Still think possessions count, still hooked on the money fetish. They want to live forever, freeze themselves in their ideal images. They reject *change*, reject *diversity*, reject *freedom*. They can't learn what Glass teaches.'

'How is Glass?'

'He's a mystery. A riddle wrapped in an enigma. He's himself. That's what you have to accept. Good, bad, that's a human thing. A duality created by split-brains joined at the animal level. Our work will transcend that.'

'I accept I was brought here at gunpoint. I thought I was here to talk with Antoinette.'

'That fucking bitch,' Frodo McHale says evenly. 'You don't know how it's been here. She seduced Glass, stopped us from talking to him, threw us off the project. But we're going to get it back. Stick around and you'll see. Sooner than she thinks you'll see. Then her agenda will be history, believe me. I came here to warn you.'

Todd asks, 'Can you tell me where she is? Or how to speak with Glass? I'll be honest with you, I'm not in any kind of mood for a debate on post-human ethics.' He's wondering what kind of work a virtuality supermodel could be doing here. Brazilian callisthenics for the troops perhaps, or presenting the publicity package. Every rebel gang and freedom fighter group, even one as small and obscure as Glass's – *especially* one as small and obscure as Glass's – has some kind of mixed media data set ready for upload. It would make a change from earnest, stilted voice-overs in fractured English and slow, unfocused tracking shots of comrades doing drill with scarves over most of their faces.

Frodo McHale shows his bad teeth. One incisor in there is totally green. 'Speak, and he'll hear you. The place is his skin. His presence is everywhere. She's put her spell on him, but he's wiser than she knows. You look around while you can. Pretty soon we'll talk some more. I got to fade now, get back to our side of the wire. Outside, can you believe that, after all we did? But she can't keep us out forever.'

Frodo McHale turns and pushes away through the crowd. Todd goes in the other direction, thinking that a little reconnaissance wouldn't be a bad idea. He takes a bottle of Metaxa and explores a series of open plan rooms which lead one into the other, all exquisitely furnished, all uninhabited. In a corner of one room, he finds a computer deck on a Louis Quinze secretaire. There are disposable goggles and mitts in one of the secretaire's fragile drawers.

Todd plugs in and addresses himself to the network's editing suite. It scrolls up around him, but every desk is dark, and when Todd tries to leave a message explaining where he is, the note-pad doesn't respond and the phone doesn't work. He has his partial jump to another desk – the same problem. Even stranger, the computer deck won't address itself anywhere else.

There's a flicker of movement and Todd swings around and sees the burning man standing on the far side of the room. At first it seems that he's clothed in blue flame, as if he's been doused in brandy and set alight. Then Todd realizes that he can see through this apparition – the burning man is nothing but flames, fire contained within a human shape. He just stands there, looking at Todd.

Todd has his partial make the jump across the editing suite, but the burning man is gone. Todd strips off goggles and mitts, and drops them in a wastepaper basket that imitates an elephant's foot. The big room is in semi-darkness. The noise of the party like surf in the distance. African masks on the walls, vat-cultured lion skins on the long sofas, fake zebra skin rugs. At least, he supposes these things are fake, but with the geezer generation you don't know. Some of them used to wear fur coats. He takes a long swig of Metaxa and shivers. He's lost in this strange land, and it seems the next move is his captor's.

9
The Wild Hunt

Alex wakes with a start to find Ray straddling his chest. In the moonlight, the fey's small, close-set eyes look like the holes of a mask. He says, 'They find us.'

'Who's found us, Ray?'

'Big trouble,' Ray says, and Alex realizes that the fey is afraid.

'I'm getting up,' Alex says, but Ray catches his face in both hands. The fey's sharp nails prick his jowls.

'Listen,' the fey says.

Far out in the dark forest, something blows a long mournful bugle note that rises in pitch as it fades away.

'It's started,' the fey says, and scampers away to wake Mrs Powell.

The stones of the shrine shine like bones in the bright moonlight. The night sky is filled with a harvest of stars. The Angry Ones have disappeared. The sacrificial fire is out. On the far side of the clearing, the pygmy mammoth shifts uneasily from foot to foot.

The mournful bugle note sounds again – and the pygmy mammoth raises its trunk and answers.

Ray grins at Alex. 'You think there is more than one? This is the home of the oldest population of feys in the world. They are here from the first. Their children are many and strange, in the forest.'

Feys don't distinguish between the dolls they've made over and the creatures they gengineer.

Alex says, 'Are you scared, Ray? I need to know the truth.'

'No games, big man,' the fey says. 'We're surrounded. They have the numbers, and at least one warewolf. I think they outgun us, too. The feys here make do with what they find, and they find a lot, because you humans are fighting so much. But their ammunition supply is patchy, and these others bring stuff with them from outside. Bad karma.'

Someone runs down the grassy aisle of the ruined shrine towards them. It is Katrina. She has stripped to her T-shirt and leather jeans, and has smeared her face and bare arms with night camouflage. She wears padded protective bands on her knees and elbows. A tiny infrared torch is slung beneath the muzzle of her machine-pistol, and night-sight goggles are pushed up on her forehead.

'They've broken through,' she says, 'If we're lucky, it's just a scouting group, but I don't know how many are out there. Fucking Avramites set these fuckers on us, I swear.'

'You change the air for leagues around,' Ray says.

Alex tells Katrina, 'We need one of them. Dead or alive it doesn't matter. Just the chip and a few millilitres of blood, if you can't bring the body, but the body would be better.'

'They turn us,' Ray says. 'They have strong glamour.'

'They won't turn you, Ray,' Alex says. 'Your glamour is just as strong.'

'Well, that's true,' Ray says, and draws his pistol. 'And I have these magic bullets.'

Alex says, 'If I get a chip and some blood, then maybe we can think about turning *them*. Or at least shut them down.'

'They'll be at the perimeter in two minutes,' Katrina says.

She sprints back the way she has come, twisting this way and that, doubled low. A moment after she disappears into the trees there's a quick burst of automatic fire. The hard sounds echo from the cliffs behind the ruined temple.

Mrs Powell says, 'What can I do, Mr Sharkey? I'm not entirely useless, you know. If there's to be a fight, I have first aid. I once worked with a flying doctor in Africa.'

'Then start making bandages,' Alex says.

He finds his pack and straps on night-sight goggles. The moon-lit clearing intensifies into a startling chiaroscuro. He can see little shapes running this way and that amongst the trees downslope, but even with false-colour enhancement he can't tell which are the Angry Ones and which are the enemy. There are very few gun shots; fairies prefer to fight face-to-face, saving their human-made weapons for truly desperate situations. Just as well, because most fairy bullets are hollow tipped, containing fembots that swarm through their victim's bloodstream and eat away major vessels. The spaced bursts of fire are probably Katrina's.

Alex pulls his brace of air pistols from his pack and loads them with hollow-tipped feathered fléchettes.

Mrs Powell says, 'I am a fair shot, Mr Sharkey.'

Alex gives her one of the pistols. 'That's good, because I'm bloody awful. These are soporific darts. Don't touch the tips. One will bring down a fairy, two a man or a warewolf, a dozen the little mammoth there. I want something alive, if I can. Try not to shoot it in the head, either. If I can get a chip, perhaps I can find out the control codes. Usually, chip codes can be accessed through visual input – the right pattern of light pulses can shut them down. You stay here. I'll do a little hunting of my own.'

Mrs Powell looks at him. Half a dozen shots light up the trees downslope, but she doesn't flinch.

'You wouldn't last a minute out there,' Alex says.

'I know what they are, Mr Sharkey.'

'No, you don't. Even I don't know what they've done. Fairies can instruct their fembots to make specific changes in the gene-plasm of creatures they infect. Like the pygmy mammoth there, or the troll you saw.'

'I know all about their magic. I know the creatures of the woods. I've studied them for a very long time. I know they've made real dragons, for instance.'

'No one uses dragons in a fight like this. When it's all over, I'll explain why. Don't be surprised by anything that comes at you. Just shoot it. And look after the pack. It has all *my* magics in it.'

Ray tags along as Alex carefully makes his way between gnarled oak trees towards the fierce, short-lived trajectories and collisions. Alex feels powerful and quick and excited. He feels as if he's floating through the sharp night air. The eerie thing about the fairy battle is that there's so little sound. No shouts or cries of pain: only a few spaced shots, quick flurries of footsteps, and shocked cries quickly stifled.

Ray touches his arm, and Alex turns and sees a dead fairy sprawled in a bower of dry ferns.

'One of the Angry Ones,' Ray whispers.

Tenderly, Ray turns the body over. The eyes are blinded by thick mucus; the throat has been torn out. Ray looks around, then says, 'Three more over there.'

But they are all Angry Ones, too.

Alex tells Ray they might as well wait until the fight comes to them. He takes shelter between the roots of a riven oak. The night-sight goggles reveal in false colour details his merely human eyes would entirely miss. About a hundred metres off, something is chasing something else through a bramble thicket. There's a brief, fierce commotion, and after a minute's quiet a single stooped figure runs off. Alex tracks it with the sight of his air pistol, but it is already out of range, and quickly disappears downslope.

Ray impatiently makes a little foray to one side of Alex's hide, circles back to quarter in the other direction. That's when he's attacked.

Something long and lithe springs at him, and they go down in a tangle. Alex fires a dart into the ground, momentarily distracting the thing, and Ray rolls clear. He jumps up and fires his big pistol, and the recoil knocks him backwards. The thing springs at him again, and this time Alex gets a clear shot. It thumps down, bites at its flank, and subsides.

It is a fox, but a fox with huge ears and a wrinkled, elongated snout. Enlarged glands like wattles depend from its lower jaw – poison sacs, Alex guesses, but Ray shakes his head, and lifts the thing's lips to reveal the hollow front teeth. It is a vampire, able to inject fembots from its wattle-like storage sacs.

'Half my people are made over by things like this,' Ray says.

Alex puts on disposable gloves and uses a hypodermic straw to draw milky fluid from the vampire fox's sacs. He sticks the straw in a test kit, notes the red light that indicates the presence of fembots. No point testing further – if Ray is right, Alex knows what kind of fembots they will be, mapping closely if not exactly to the clades infecting the Children's Crusade. The fox has tiny eyes sealed with a thick callus of epidermis; it is not chipped.

'At least we can use its blood,' Alex says.

Ray lifts his head, his big ears twitching. Alex glimpses something throwing itself into cover behind the swollen bole of a grandfather oak. Something else is crawling beneath a cloak that matches the coloration and heat signature of the forest floor. Alex puts a dart through the cloak and the fairy underneath bolts out from under it. Alex misses with his second shot and turns and sees another fairy not twenty metres away. Very tall and very thin, it makes an impossibly quick sinuous toss of its head and a gob of thick saliva blinds Alex's goggles – the stuff burns his fingers when he tries to wipe it off.

Ray's gun goes off as Alex strips away the goggles. The venom-spitting fairy has gone, but even by mere moonlight, Alex can see that more are moving towards him between the trees. A human figure stands amongst them. It seems to bear the antlers of a deer, and is perhaps three metres tall.

Alex and Ray retreat, abandoning the body of the vampire fox. Alex fires off a dart wherever Ray points, but he doesn't seem to hit anything, and has exhausted the magazine by the time they reach the shrine.

Katrina and the surviving Angry Ones are already there. There are not many of them. Mrs Powell is wrapping a bandage around the head of one – the creature snaps at her, and she slaps its face and calmly finishes her task.

Katrina, breathing so hard she's almost hyperventilating, tells Alex that she made a couple of sure kills, but one was dragged off and the other was a head shot.

'But you brought it anyway, I hope,' Alex says.

'It's over there.'

It is a squat thing, naked and covered in quills, with long heavily muscled arms that, when it was alive, would have dragged on the ground. Its skin is as tough as badgerhide, and Alex has trouble finding a vein. He tests for fembots, then squirts the rest of the blood into a little plastic beaker and drinks it straight down. It is cold and tastes vile, but although he gags he keeps it down.

Ray says, 'How long? How long for our turn?'

'Half a day, perhaps less,' Alex says. He feels cold, then hot. He's committed now. The fairy fembots will be crossing his mucous membranes into the backwaters of his capillaries, making their way into veins and then to the heart. Within minutes their presence will activate his rejigged immune system. Or at least, that's the plan.

Something rockets through the canopy of the dark trees and bursts overhead, shedding a blue radiance that fills the ruins with light and shifting shadows. Everyone looks up.

'This is no scouting group,' Katrina says. 'It is a full war party.'

Ray runs across to the pygmy mammoth and whispers to it, then runs back and tells Alex in an excited babble, 'We go, meet up again. You ride, big man. Just tell him what to do. His name is Hannibal. It's safe. He knows humans.'

The mammoth proves this by crooking one foreleg to make a kind of step when Alex approaches. With some difficulty, resisting the urge to pull himself up using the beast's long, coarse hair, Alex climbs into the curved wooden seat on the mammoth's back. Sitting there, on something more like a stool than a saddle, with only strips of leather to hold on to, it seems a long way to the ground.

Ray hands up Alex's pack and says, 'Put your legs out in front of you, it's more comfortable. Don't worry, Hannibal knows the way.' He leans close and adds quietly, 'We leave the old fart, eh? Not much meat on her bones, but they are grateful for anything they get.'

The blue flare is guttering out as it floats lower. A pall of sweet-smelling smoke drifts from it. Its failing light throws Ray's shadow halfway across the clearing.

'We're all going together,' Alex says. 'I'm not travelling on my own.'

'Ray's right,' Katrina says. 'You're the only one of us who can disarm the Crusade. Get away now, we'll catch up.'

'I'm supposed to ride a hairy elephant across thirty kilometres of rough terrain, while fairy fembots cook away inside me?'

'We'll meet up by morning,' Katrina says firmly. 'No problem. You look after your fat ass, Sharkey. Get the fuck out of here.'

Alex tells Ray, 'You'll look after Mrs Powell. I mean it.'

'OK, big man. I won't eat her.'

'And make sure Kat doesn't go and do something stupidly heroic and get herself killed.'

There's a howl from the dark woods. A muscular, half-naked man rushes out of the trees into the moonlight. Half a dozen Angry Ones try to bring him down, but he scatters them with sweeps of a long staff. Lightnings flash from the staff's metal tips, starting little fires in the dry grass.

'Warewolf,' Ray cries. Suddenly, he's perched on the pygmy mammoth's back, cowering behind Alex.

The man howls again, and flings his arms wide in triumph. Katrina steps forward and calmly shoots him in the head. The warewolf drops in its tracks, but now two fairy-sized things swoop across the clearing on wide, membranous wings. Fire from the ground downs one; the other does a half-roll and drops into the shifting shadows under the trees. Ray whacks at Hannibal's hairy flank and springs to the ground with a whoop.

The pygmy mammoth takes off, running with a surprisingly quick and even gait. It's like being in a boat speeding over a light chop; the waves are the muscles working under the mammoth's hairy hide. Alex clings to the leather strips on either side of the seat until at last Hannibal slows to a trot. A great musty heat comes up from it. Alex gets his breath back, puffs out his cheeks. Hoo! He feels as if he has been running as fast as the mammoth.

Then, as the mammoth passes under the spread branches of an oak, a fairy ambushes Alex.

It lands on Alex's back, catches hold of his hair and pulls back his head so that it can lay the edge of its knife blade against his throat. Prehensile toes claw at his flanks. Its head snakes around on a long neck and grins into Alex's face. It has too many needle-pointed teeth in a narrow jaw, eyes that in the moonlight are no more than black holes under the boney shelf of its brow.

'Surrender,' it says.

Alex says slowly, feeling the edge of the knife with every syllable, 'Take me to your leader.'

The fairy laughs, a spitting, sputtering sound like a kettle boiling dry. 'Bad man,' it says. 'S-s-s-spy.'

'No!' Alex cries, thinking that the thing will cut his throat just for the fun of it. The fairy laughs again – and then a bubble of colour blooms around them. A man in black rushes towards them, hands raised in clutching claws, a black cloak lined with blood-red silk sustained behind him. He has a white face and burning eyes. It is the ghost Katrina set up to scare anyone who followed them.

Hannibal starts running, panicked by the apparition. Alex grabs the fairy's arm. It is lithe and strong, but Alex is bigger and heavier and can exert more leverage. The knife falls. The fairy makes a wild lunge for it and Alex quickly shifts his grip and snaps its neck.

The dead fairy still clings to him; the secondary nervous system spun by its fembots has locked its muscles. As Alex tries to pry it loose, the fembots he's ingested begin to work on him. Slowly, like an old-fashioned TV warming up, a new layer of reality is worked into his sight. The air is alive with bright motes that slant through the night, each as individual as a snowflake. It is as if every tree, every branch and every leaf, is coated with a frost of photons. Ahead, a glorious music rises in a neverending harmonic.

'Welcome to our land,' the fairy croaks. Its head lolls on its broken neck. Its eyes are points of red flame. Lines of golden light make arcane maps under its blue skin.

Alex is not afraid. It is as if the child who once stood with its mother on the shabby balcony of a highrise council flat, surveying the skeins of London's lights, the child who somehow, by a strange and subtle transformation, became him, is now once again looking through his eyes.

He hears Lexis say, quite distinctly, 'Fairyland!' as Hannibal trots into a clearing at a bend in the overgrown road.

Everything is so clear, so bright. A wash of huge, blurry stars arches overhead. The glow of the half-moon that hangs above the treeline seems to be focused into a kind of temple of vaporous illumination in the middle of the road. Within that distilled light, a host of fairies and other creatures flank the two figures sitting on high-backed spiky chairs fretted from thin white spars that might be the bones of extinct birds.

A fairy runs forward and loops a silver thread over one of Hannibal's tusks, draws him to the two seated figures.

'My Ladies,' the fairy at Alex's back says in its flat, dead voice. 'Here he is at last.'

Then its muscles finally give way to death, and it falls at their feet. As one, they look up at Alex, their faces pale in the moonlight, and with a shock he sees that they both have the face of Milena, as she was when he first met her.

10
Antoinette

At dawn, Spike finds Todd sleeping in a reclining chair, at the edge of a triangular terrace that angles out over the water. The lake stretches away under a brightening blue sky. A motorboat crewed by two dolls sits a little way offshore, rocking on the gentle swell.

When Spike shakes his shoulder, Todd comes awake thrashing, out of bad dreams of chases through obscure streets. His head still hurts, and he gratefully accepts Spike's offer of a beer.

'Hair of the dog,' Spike says. 'By the way, there's a hole in your sock. The left one.'

'Just call me Barefoot Joe.'

Todd downs the beer in two swallows, crushes the stressed plastic carton, and drops it into a tub of geraniums that are already beginning to drop their red petals in the brassy morning heat.

'Oh man. Put a raw egg in the next one. And a dash of tabasco.' Todd grinds the heels of his palms into his eyes. 'I finished this bottle of Metaxa, and I think I swallowed the worm.'

'Beer was all I could find,' Spike says. He's leaning on the iron rail, looking out at the lake. 'I was talking with this Web cowboy last night. He claimed he was working for Glass, but there's something bloody strange about him. I was in Afghanistan this one time—'

The butler, Ralph, walks out of the open French windows on to the terrace. He's exchanged his butler's rig for a brushed suede jacket and blue jeans. A big pistol is holstered at his hip. He wears video shades and an earplug. Behind him, half a dozen dolls cradle fat-barrelled M10 pulse rifles.

Todd says, 'Spike—'

'—and there were cowboys like that guy, working on some kind of scam—'

'Spike, just get—'

'—to bring down the Moscow stock exchange. Fucking long memories, the Mujahadeen. Anyway—'

'—your fucking drone, OK?'

'There's no need, gentlemen,' Ralph says. 'Everything is recorded here.'

He claps his hands, and dolls carry a table covered with heavy white linen on to the terrace. Chairs are brought, silverware laid in flashing patterns. A large-screen TV is placed at one end of the table. The dolls offer fruit and herbal teas, and look confused when Todd asks for coffee. Their sly blue faces peek from beneath powdered wigs. They have white gloves, peach-coloured silk jackets and puffed breeches, and buckled shoes of shiny patent leather.

Once Spike and Todd are seated, the TV comes on. Antoinette says, 'I'm sorry that I couldn't see you last night. Things are reaching a climax.'

She is standing in a white room. Behind her, sunlight falls through a window. She wears a white silk robe that puddles around her feet. Her hair is piled into an asymmetrical layered cone of tightly packed charcoal-coloured curls, slashed by a vivid white streak.

Todd says, 'This would be something to do with a guy called Frodo McHale?'

Spike says, 'That's the cowboy I was telling you about. He—'

'Shut up, Spike,' Todd says.

Antoinette says, 'Manufacturing a permanent cocktail party was Glass's way, when we first met, of showing me that he could also change the hearts and minds of people. It is not a very good joke, but I love him deeply, and I don't have the heart to let them go. They'll be sleeping now, like so many vampires. At night, their fembot personality constructs stir, and they live again. As for this place, it's become a mausoleum. Glass was researching—'

'Something to do with the ultimate in virtual reality,' Todd says.

On the TV, Antoinette walks over to the sunlit window. A breeze sustains long white curtains around her. She says, 'Glass wanted immortality. He was on his third heart and his second pair of lungs and was weary of the flesh. He was to be the first human to cross the mind-machine barrier. But you know that, Mr Hart. You were allowed to find that out.'

'I was? Listen, if this is all some kind of PR stunt it's frankly not in very good taste. Perhaps I better—'

'Sit down,' the butler, Ralph, says.

'Sure. You're the one with the gun. You and these little blue suckers here. Are dolls allowed to bear arms, by the way? I thought there was some kind of UN treaty about that.'

'We're in the neutral zone,' Ralph says. 'Besides, they aren't exactly dolls.'

Todd leans on the table, fitting his elbows amongst a clutter of chased silver cutlery and translucent porcelain. 'Tell me about this fabulous experiment. Did it work?'

The view on the TV zooms into close-up as Antoinette returns Todd's stare. Her eyes have pupils of beaten copper.

'Glass was translated six months ago. His functions are active, but he isn't talking. That will change.'

'And the computers are here.'

'This is his research institute, the heart of what Glass calls the Library of Dreams, but Glass isn't exactly here. He's everywhere and nowhere.'

'Did you tick the no publicity box?'

Antoinette blinks.

'I mean, I'm not learning very much here. I haven't even met you, in the flesh.'

'I believe you've already been in the Library of Dreams, Mr Hart. You used one of the decks last night. They access only the Library.'

'I tried to get hold of my office. They'll be looking for me.'

'They know you're on a field investigation. What you accessed was not your network's node, but a simulation. Among other things, the Library of Dreams has mapped a version of the Web into itself, for its own purposes. It is contiguous with the Web, but it is not topologically connected with it.'

'A simulation of the Web? What kind of computing power does Glass have?'

'The Library of Dreams isn't a simulation of the Web. It takes what it needs and uses it to generate the world where Glass first awakened. It is a little like a pocket universe.'

'I saw someone there,' Todd says. 'A burning man, a man on fire. Or made of fire. Was that Glass?'

'What you saw wasn't Glass. That's a creature derived from the Children's Crusade. The horned King in the real world, what you call the burning man when he crosses over. His nervous system has been rebuilt by Frodo McHale and his acolytes. You might say he is the first real astronaut of the Web. Or he would be, if he could escape from the Library of Dreams. You met Frodo McHale last night. I think he wants to make sure that I know he's back.'

'You don't like him.'

'He wants to kill me, Mr Hart.'

'He has hired mercenaries,' the butler says. 'They reached the other side of the lake two days ago.'

'I expect they're watching you have breakfast,' Antoinette says. 'Frodo McHale wants to use the Children's Crusade for his own ends. Glass and I want to neutralize it.'

'That's a very emotive word. Does it mean what it implies?'

'I want to destroy the fairies who created the Children's Crusade, too. Does that shock you?'

'I thought they were destroyed. There was that thing just outside Paris—'

'The Peace Police claim to have solved the problem of the fairies, but although the Magic Kingdom is dispersed, it lives on. Frodo McHale wants the Children's Crusade, and I want to finish it. It's out of control. With creatures like the burning man, it threatens to spread to the Web, and I can't allow that.'

Now Todd knows what Antoinette's white-streaked pile of hair reminds him of. Elsa Lanchester. *Bride of Frankenstein*.

He says, 'That stuff's out of date. I can't make any kind of pitch with it. No one wants to hear fright stories about Frankenstein running around out of control.'

'The monster,' Spike says.

Todd looks at him.

'The monster,' Spike says again. He takes a bite of sweet pastry and says around it, 'It was the monster that ran off. Frankenstein was the scientist who made it. It didn't have a name.'

Antoinette says, 'These days monster and scientist, creator and created, are often the same. You see, Mr Hart, the problem I have. I am not a storyteller. I am not a journalist.'

'You want me to tell your story. I have to tell you it's a pretty good story, by the way.'

'I tried to escape what I had been, and I lost control of what I made. Now the burning man is loose in the Library of Dreams, and soon he'll cross over into the Web, him and hundreds like him. They'll saturate the Web with fairy memes. Perhaps they will deny the Web to us. And what then?'

'Why is this important to you?'

'Because I'm going to join my dear lover, and live forever. You're the only American journalist I could reach. Glass has a story

318

to tell, and because he's still a US citizen it's best told to a US audience. Seventy per cent of the Web's computing power is located in the States, after all.' The TV flickers, shows Antoinette in medium shot. She holds out her hands as if to reach through the glass and says, 'Can I trust you, Mr Hart?'

Spike laughs.

'Shut up, Spike,' Todd says.

There's a noise far out across the lake. It is the flat thump of a mortar round.

Todd is on his feet, torn between running and diving under the table. The motorboat is making a run in towards the shore, zig-zagging this way and that. It is pursued by a small, slow, smart missile. The motorboat's engines roar as it makes a last desperate turn. The missile leaps forward and the motorboat disappears in a rising plume of white water. Spike grabs Todd's arm, points. Another missile is skimming across the lake, heading towards the southern wing of the complex. Its slim body and flat stabilizing vanes are marked with a red and white chequerboard pattern, vivid against the blue water.

On the table, the TV is showing nothing but static snow. The butler is at the glass doors, standing to one side as the dolls trot past him. He says, 'My contract has just terminated. Good luck, gentlemen.'

He steps inside and the doors slide shut.

11
Fever

In the dark, in the cage in the dark, in the cage in the dark beneath the trees, the fembot fever slowly leaves Alex. A brief war has been waged in his body, and now it is almost spent.

His rejigged immune system has manufactured millions of microscopic predators to pursue the fairy-grown fembots through the tides and backwaters of his bloodstream. Each predator has a slightly different set of receptors, so that at least one will bind to any invading fembot and immobilize it. Binding releases a signal which stimulates manufacture of more of the right kind of predator. Unlike the totipotent immune systems which protect the affluent, these predators strip the invaders of their codes, which are transformed within assembler libraries in the marrow of Alex's long bones, but he can no more alter the codes than he can change his own DNA. Only the feys can use the libraries to make an antidote to the Crusade's memes.

Slowly, copies of the library of fairy fembot code are written into tangled buckyball strings, which are delivered to Alex's T-lymphocytes within protein coats derived from modified HIV virus.

Slowly, he is cured of the fairy calenture.

Slowly, his blood becomes a book.

The bars of the cage no longer seem like living serpents, but merely green branches tightly woven with memory wire into a kind of basket. The cage is scarcely bigger than Alex, and he must choose between squatting or standing in a kind of stoop, and is constantly squirming to try and find relief from the aching of his poor joints and the jab of the untrimmed branches.

The radiant creatures that strut beyond Alex's cage dwindle to mere fairies that are scarcely different from the dolls they once were. These are not like the wild feys, with their sharp, fine-boned faces and lithe bodies, but are squat creatures with small eyes glinting under prognathous brows. They are mostly naked, and armed with little more than knives. Paradoxically, as Alex's fever clears, they become less easy to see in the predawn darkness, for they no longer seem to trail streams of sparkling motes as they scurry to and fro.

A little way off is a pack of gengineered wolves, with ruffs of carbon-fibre spines, forequarters so over-muscled that they look humpbacked, and long crocodile jaws filled with triangular shark's teeth. The wolves are staked out so that they cannot reach each other. They rest their long heads on heavy pads, and watch their fairy masters with half-closed yellow eyes. The pygmy mammoth, Hannibal, is tethered at the far end of the clearing. His trunk switches back and forth, and every now and then he tugs at the iron fetter around his right foreleg.

By the luminescent dots of Alex's tattooed watch, there's an hour or so before dawn (he wonders if he can trust his watch – there are strains of fembots which can rebuild biomechanisms). His mechanical watch and every other piece of metal, including the tags of the zips of his trousers and his jacket, have been removed by the fairies. They even searched the inside of his mouth. No doubt they scanned him for fembot-constructed nervous system aids, too, but the assemblers are hidden inside his bone marrow cells, and the predators are in themselves little different from the fembots that anyone who has undergone totipotent immune system treatment would have in their blood.

He must be patient. He has delivered himself into the hands of his enemies. They will come to him, in their own good time.

Alex dozes, and wakes, swoony with sleep- and sugar-lack, to find a man staring at him. The man is tall and burly, and squats on his haunches a good distance away from the cage. Scraps of grey sky are caught amongst the branches of the trees. As he watches Alex by this faint dawn light, the man absently caresses the ears of one of the gengineered wolves – the thing is attentive as a cat to the man's touch, its red tongue lolling from jaws that could take off his arm with a single bite.

Alex returns the man's stare. Branching horns of buckyball data storage wires sprout from the man's temples, and carbon whisker aerials from the base of his skull, and his body is thickened with either grafted muscles or sub-dermal plating – perhaps both. Alex wonders what all that extra-cranial capacity is for, but knows better than to ask.

Behind him, a young girl's voice says, 'We've met before.' Alex hunches around in his cage, and is filled with a wild mixture of despair and hope.

His first thought is that it's Milena.

His second is that she's far too young.

He has to look twice to be sure, because he was expecting to meet his old love at last. But it isn't her. He'd know her anywhere, no matter how well she disguised herself, how much she had changed, or been changed.

And then a second little girl steps from behind her sister. Alex saw them last night, and thought then that they were a fever dream. They are identical twins, dressed in cut-down camo gear.

Although they are both blue-skinned and shaven-headed, they are astonishingly like Milena – their cocked-hip careless poses identical to that of Alex's vivid, love-lorn memory of the brilliant, crazy little girl who picked up his life and threw it away, who left the void in his memory that is still there, still unhealed, the white room where something strange and wonderful and terrible happened to him. These little twin girls aren't much younger than Milena was then, Alex realizes. They are the little girls from the Magic Kingdom.

The Twins look at Alex with a sly mixture of amusement and contempt. The blue on their faces is some kind of greasepaint.

'You're the one that helped wreck—'

'—helped *destroy*—'

'—our nest.'

They both laugh. It isn't a nice sound.

'I expected to find you with the Children's Crusade.'

Alex is trying to stay calm. It's happening at last. He cannot let himself become excited, or it might fail.

'Oh, they're on their way—'

'—and we're near—'

'—closer than you think.'

'It's already breaking up,' Alex says. 'It's individuating. That's the way with any kind of movement. Even those bound together by infection with fairy memes.'

The Twins smile suddenly, sly and amused and knowing, and then the doubled smile is gone.

'You think the changes are bad—'

'—a bad thing. You're wrong—'

'—very wrong.'

'You're angry because of the fall of the Magic Kingdom. I understand.'

The Twins shrug inside their overlarge jackets. How old are they? Eight? Nine? No more than that, surely. Milena must have managed the miracle of parthenogenesis so very quickly after she fled with that first fairy. How far they've come! Alex feels heavy with history.

The Twins say, 'Oh, the Magic Kingdom was fun—'

'—we had fun for a while—'

'—but we knew it couldn't last. It was an exponential thing—'

'—it had to grow and grow. The people around it—'

'—the ones who wanted the little toys our people made—'

'—they grew too greedy.'

'Do you know why I'm here?'

'You're all alone in your cage, Mister Alex—'

'—that *is* your name—'

'—but we'll bring you the heads of your friends, one by one—'

'—by one. We'll put them on stakes—'

'—stakes around your cage—'

'—we'll feed you the manna of Fairyland. Then you can talk with them—'

'—you can talk, but you won't like what you'll hear. The dead don't lie—'

'—and they'll be very very dead.'

'I can help you.'

'Oh, you'll help us—'

'—and the woman, when we catch her—'

'—Katrina, she calls herself—'

'—Katrina, but her real name is Dania—'

'—Dania Haessig. Ah, you didn't know—'

'—*we* knew—'

'—but *he* didn't.'

'Names aren't so important. Where is Milena?'

'But names *are* important, Mister Alex. We have to know who someone is—'

'—we have to know their *name*—'

'—before we can kill her.'

The little blue-painted girls say this with chilling matter-of-factness. One adds, brightly, 'What do you think of our king?'

'He's interesting. More complicated than the warewolf.'

'Mister Mike had his uses—'

'—but our king is something else.'

'His capacity looks very impressive. I hope you haven't filled him up.'

'His time will come—'

'—because we have plans—'

'—we have plans for him.'

'Where is Milena? Or whatever she calls herself these days?'

'She interfered,' the Twins say in unison. They are suddenly indignant.

'She left us—'

'—all alone—'

'—and then she came back and interfered. But we have—'

'—we have other friends—'

'—friends who give us gifts.'

The Twins turn and walk away. 'Beware of Greek gifts,' Alex says, but they don't look back. The horned man follows them into the trees.

No one else comes near Alex for a long while.

Slowly, it grows lighter. Sun strikes under the trees; the hot, sticky air is rich with the tang of pine resin. Alex soon gives up trying to swat the flies that land on him to sip his sweat. He changes his position in the cramped cage, favouring first one leg, then the other. Fairies come and go. One leads away the wolves. Another throws a bucket of water over the cage, drenching Alex. He wrings water from his shirt and drinks that, but he's soon thirsty again. His gut is loose with fear and hunger – pretty soon he'll have to take a shit.

Slowly, Alex becomes aware that a man is watching him. The man is dressed in black. The toes of his shiny winkle-picker boots are so long that they must be held up by chains that loop around his ankles. When he sees that Alex has noticed him, he struts over. He's tall and thin, pale as paper under a rumpled cap of dirty blond hair. He wears little round landscape mirror-shades, the kind that can overlay your sight with fossil martian dunes or a coral grotto. He squats on his heels, a respectable distance from the cage, and asks Alex how he's doing.

'Not too good. Can you let me out?'

The man is amused by this. 'That's good. Yeah, that's good.'

Alex licks his lips. He is infernally thirsty, but when he asks for water, the man just shakes his head.

'I wish I could do it. But this is part of the process.'

'I came here to see Milena.'

The man shrugs.

'The mother of the little girls.'

'They have a mother? Hard to believe.'

The man says this too casually. He knows, all right. He's a Web cowboy, no doubt about it, and there's only one reason why he would be out here in the wild wood.

Alex says, 'Are you one of Glass's people? When did he go over to the fairies?'

'He never did. He was betrayed. His mind was clouded, his head was turned. But in the end it won't matter. He's beyond all that good and bad stuff now. He's beyond *sides*. Where he is, it isn't relevant.'

'Where I am, believe me, it's relevant. Will you take me to see him?'

'I can't do that, man. See, we're out here in the world, but for Glass the world is not the case any more. All this nature, the evolution of matter, it's over. It's finished. More species became extinct in the last fifty years than when the dinosaurs were knocked down by the comet. There isn't a place on Earth we haven't touched. There's no nature any more. So we've transcended that. We're looking for the next step.'

'Is that what Glass says?'

'That's what I say.'

'It's a lot of bullshit.'

The man nods solemnly. 'You've still got a sense of humour. That's good. That's important. You're gonna need it.'

Alex says, 'If I can't talk with Glass, then perhaps I can talk with Milena.'

The man touches his lips with a forefinger. He wears a silver skull ring, with ruby flecks for eyes. He says, 'You should be careful, friend. Dropping the right name in the wrong place can be dangerous. If you're relying on the harlot, you're in deeper shit than you can know. I've taken her out of the picture. I own it all now. You want to do deals or look for help, then you talk with me. I'm all there is, here in the world.'

'What's your name?'

'Frodo. Frodo McHale.'

The man stands up and walks away. Alex has plenty of time to think about what he said. He wonders what plans Frodo McHale has for the fairies, and for Milena's daughters. He wonders what plans Frodo McHale has for him.

325

12
For Your Own Safety

Before Todd and Spike are taken to see the leader of the mercenaries, Captain Spiromilos, they are forced to strip at gunpoint and take a shower. Their guard, a young man with brush-cut hair, his black, one-piece leather suit unzipped down his triangular bodybuilder's chest, explains that Captain Spiromilos is paranoid about fembot contamination. He picks his teeth with the point of a knife and watches as Todd and Spike put on the loose-fitting orange jumpsuits and shower sandals he has provided. The guard's name is Kemmel. He says, 'Captain Spiromilos thinks that Antoinette wants to change his mind in a radical way.'

'We heard that,' Todd says. He pushes back his wet hair. 'You guys are scared of her, right? I don't blame you. She's a scary lady.'

'Believe me,' Kemmel says, 'she is not a problem.'

He pulls on disposable latex gloves, and has Todd and Spike each prick the ball of their thumb with a lancet and express a drop of blood into a plastic straw. He inserts the straws into an analyser and studies the readout.

'We do this every day,' Kemmel says. 'It is a loyalty test. You're clean. You can see the Captain now.'

Captain Spiromilos has set up his command post on the highest part of the sprawling complex, beside the helicopter pad. As Todd and Spike follow Kemmel, they can see that the wrecked southern wing is still smouldering. A cluster of dish antennae hang over the scorched hole punched by the missile. Broken stromalith slumps to the water's edge. The mercenaries are still combing the complex, searching for Antoinette. There has been remarkably little resistance to their assault. The bodies of half a dozen dolls lie at the edge of the cactus garden, and twenty more in peach satin uniforms sit docilely, watched by a bored mercenary.

Captain Spiromilos is sitting in a canvas chair in the shadow of the black helicopter, watching a rack of TV screens. He is a stern, upright man in his early forties, with a kind of clenched, held-in look. The sort of guy, Todd thinks, who wears a corset and can count change with his asshole. He wears a flakjacket over a neatly pressed blouson with a red cravat peeking at its open neck. The sleeves of the blouson are rolled up past his elbows; a blue eagle is tattooed on his left forearm.

Near the edge of the flat roof, a teenage kid in baggy jeans and a wrinkled sweatshirt is virched into a computer deck holstered at his skinny hip. He pecks and slashes at the air with gloved mitts: it looks like he's doing blindfold karate. His goggles are half-hidden by a fall of unwashed hair. Another kid jumps out of the helicopter and says he's turned the pilot, nothing to it.

Captain Spiromilos says, 'It is your life if you're wrong.'

'Hey, fuck you, man. I know my job, OK?' The kid is wearing a loose red sweatshirt and bright red leggings. A ripped seam at his thigh reveals a length of white flesh. He glances at Todd and Spike. 'What about the assholes in orange? Want me to do them, too?'

'They're clean,' Kemmel says.

'They are my guests,' Captain Spiromilos says.

'Oh sure,' the kid says, as he climbs back inside the helicopter, 'the journalists.'

Spike and Todd are offered drinks. Spike takes Chivas Regal; Todd Jack Daniel's. Captain Spiromilos expresses his regrets for having held Todd and Spike prisoner for most of the day.

'It was for your own safety, gentlemen. But we have secured this place now, and we're ready to move on.'

Captain Spiromilos has a soft voice with a hint of a lisp. His English is very good.

Todd sips his Jack Daniel's. No ice, but you can't have everything in a war zone. He knows better than to start complaining about being held at gunpoint. Captain Spiromilos will explain what's going on in his own good time. Guys like this always like to string you along. They like to have an edge on you, even if it doesn't mean anything.

Todd says, 'I expected to see Frodo McHale here. I mean, you are working for him.'

'We have an agreement.'

'Does that include trying to kill Antoinette?'

'We believe that she killed herself.'

'That's pretty hard to believe. I was talking to her just before you started in here.'

The teenage kid at the edge of the pad slashes his hand through the air and says, 'She's not exactly dead, dood. Just translated. She did the Ultimate Hack.'

Captain Spiromilos says, 'The civilians were supposed to prevent that. They failed.'

Todd realizes what they're talking about. 'Jesus. She went where Glass is. She crossed over.'

Captain Spiromilos says, 'It's a minor concern.'

'But it sure is irritating, isn't it?'

The kid pushes up his goggles and shucks his mitts. His eyes are as pale as milk. 'We'll get her, dood. She's hiding, but we'll flush her out. It's no big deal.'

Captain Spiromilos says, 'I believe she talked to you about Fairyland.'

'As a matter of fact, she didn't. What is this, an interrogation? Come on, Captain, what do I know about this? No more than what you'll tell me.'

But Todd is beginning to suspect that Antoinette isn't finished with him. She didn't go to the considerable trouble of bringing him here only to have him captured by mercenaries, unless that was just what she wanted to happen. Why else would she have had him and Spike locked on the terrace?

Captain Spiromilos says, 'We are all friends here. Have another drink, gentlemen. Relax. We have a long ride ahead of us.'

'You don't indulge, Captain. From your accent I put you somewhere near Boston, and that's a good drinking town.'

'Ah. I thought I had lost my accent.'

'You should lose the tattoo, too. Only American citizens can serve in the Marines.'

Captain Spiromilos says, 'I know you were in Atlanta, Mr Hart, after the Christers used their nuke. That was a famous atrocity, but there were others. I was in the advance guard that retook Des Moines. We found fifty thousand people dead. Mass suicide. You news reporters were wandering around with handkerchiefs soaked in whisky over your noses and mouths, filming the swollen corpses. I knew then that America was finished. I never regretted leaving when my time was up.

'My grandfather emigrated to America at the end of the Second

World War, when the communists took power in Albania. He came from a small town, Himara. It's about a hundred kilometres from here, where my family had considerable influence. By birthright I am Archigôs, the leader of the Council of Elders of Himara. My family always kept alive the hope that we would regain our country. It's up to me to do it.'

'You want your own country?'

'I have my own country,' Captain Spiromilos says. 'The communists took it away, and I will take it back.'

'It's kind of cool,' the kid says, 'Not big. Not much more than a fishing town. But it's a real once-upon-a-time country. Countries are an outmoded nineteenth century concept, but they can still do things that companies can't. Put people to death, issue money, set up data havens. Things like that.'

'So you're recruiting the Children's Crusade to help you?'

Captain Spiromilos says, 'I'm a Christian, and I believe fairies are soulless beasts of the field, don't let anyone tell you different. The Crusaders have destroyed their souls by embracing the fairy creed. By using them, as you put it, we may in fact redeem them.'

'I understand you have fairies working for you.'

'They're decontaminated. The way the Albanians do it. We run them now, like puppets, from a command computer. Once we're done, they'll be discarded. We're not doing anything more here than the Peace Police are doing in the EU. This is an alien plague we're dealing with, and I intend to play my part in seeing it's dealt with.'

The kid says, 'There's what the Captain wants, and what we want, and there's a way we can both get what we want. It's kind of neat.'

'We risk our lives,' Captain Spiromilos says, 'and they sit here playing with their toys.'

The kid says, 'No one said life is fair. And Frodo—'

'Frodo McHale is on his own business.'

It's interesting to watch Captain Spiromilos suppress his natural inclination to snap the kid's grubby pencil-thin neck.

He turns to Todd and says, 'You'll be the first to report the re-establishment of Himara's sovereignty, but the rest of your pack in their expense account hotel will be there as soon as your pictures hit the Web. You will thank me for this.'

Todd and Spike get back their clothes, and Spike is given his camera drone. By now it's growing dark. Floodlights come on in the cactus garden, where a couple of mercenaries move amongst Antoinette's doll servants, shooting each one in the head. Spike manages to snatch a few seconds' footage while pretending to examine his drone.

'No good for fighting,' Kemmel explains.

Todd wonders what will happen to Glass's zombie cocktail party, but this isn't the place to ask delicate questions.

The helicopter takes off, heading north. To pick up a couple of Antoinette's accomplices, Captain Spiromilos says. In the service area of the complex, fairies are climbing one by one into the back of a truck. They look like blue-skinned, starved children in army drag. They have teeth filed to points – one has actual tusks growing through its upper lip. Most are no more than a metre high. They are armed with short-barrelled plastic rifles with swollen over-and-under magazines, the kind made in Israel that fire subsonic rubber bullets.

'Those were fairies once,' Kemmel explains. 'No longer. They have been—' The mercenary makes a chopping motion at his crotch.

Captain Spiromilos leads his men in a brief moment of prayer. The mercenaries bare their heads and bow their necks meekly enough, then scatter to their vehicles. Todd and Spike are put in a jeep driven by a shaven-headed man who grins when he sees their orange coveralls. Kemmel roars past on a motorcycle, to take up a position as outrider. Someone toots on a tinny bugle, and then the convoy moves off, headlights glaring, into the road that runs north along the lake shore and into the forest.

13
Not a Rescue

Alex wakes with something sharp prodding his belly. It's near dark. He looks up, expecting to see a fairy, and a familiar voice says, 'Dear me, Mr Sharkey. You are in a pickle.'

'Mrs Powell.'

Alex finds he isn't surprised. Nothing about Mrs Powell can surprise him. She is a locus of improbability.

Mrs Powell smiles. Her hair-do is coming apart, grey strands hanging around her flushed face like Medusa's locks, but otherwise she looks as if she has been on a light stroll. She emanates a stifling jasmine fragrance. She is carrying her parasol – that was what she woke him with – and now she straps it to the top of her daypack.

'Mrs Powell, you amaze me. I assume you aren't captured. Or have you changed sides?'

'That doesn't become you, Mr Sharkey. No doubt your temper is not improved by being shut in this cage.'

'No doubt. I don't suppose you have a cigarette?'

Mrs Powell says, 'First Rays of the New Rising Sun knew where you were. And as for transport, we rode here on mules. It took most of the day. I must say I was disappointed. I expected something . . .'

'More exotic?'

'More romantic. We're close to the border, Mr Sharkey. The Children's Crusade is almost here. I must say, you do look uncomfortable in there. Shrink-wrapped, as it were.'

'I've been in this cage for some time, Mrs Powell.'

Alex's gut loosened a few hours ago; although he heaped dirt over the pile of shit, the smell is awful. But he refuses to be embarrassed by his predicament. He has never apologized about his weight, or his life. If he started, he feels he would never stop. Besides, apologize once to Mrs Powell and she'll never let you forget it.

Mrs Powell fastens the straps of the daypack around her shoulders. The handle of the parasol sticks out on one side of her head.

'It was a terrible battle, and something of a rout for our side,' Mrs Powell says, and adds, with dreamy rapture, 'I wanted to fight. And I would have fought, if I hadn't been busy tending the wounded.'

'They've worked their glamour on you,' Alex says. He wonders what she has been infected with. He doesn't have a database on the clades of fembots manufactured by the feys. No one has, or can. Change proceeds at too fast a pace. The feys, like the Children's Crusade, evolve fembots rather than design them: the outcome is never predictable, and often there are many radically different solutions to one problem.

'It's a glorious adventure,' Mrs Powell says.

'If you think that, you're going to get yourself killed.'

'I only meant that your friends fought so bravely,' Mrs Powell says.

'The Angry Ones and the rest of the feys are fighting for their survival against the things which created the Children's Crusade. Neither side is much concerned about us. They aren't subtle, or kind, or noble. Those are human attributes.'

'You should not have run off, Mr Sharkey. You missed all the fun.'

'It really would help if you could get me out of here. There's memory wire lacing under these branches, but if you can find my pack, there's a torch in one of the side pockets. It's a ruby laser. Dial down the focus and there's enough power in the battery for three or four high energy pulses. Enough to cut a way out.'

'I'm afraid that I wouldn't know where to begin looking for your pack, Mr Sharkey.'

'Where's Kat? She has a torch, too.'

'I really don't think she likes me, Mr Sharkey. Even though I bandaged her. Please don't worry, it was only a flesh wound.'

'A bite?'

'No, a little cut from a knife. She isn't infected, but I did learn some very colourful language. Should I ever find myself in Germany, I can certainly shock the good citizens.'

'Mrs Powell, I really need to get out of here. You may not have noticed, but we are in the middle of a camp of the enemy. A rescue is not a rescue until you free someone.'

'They are not here,' Mrs Powell said. 'Except for one poor guard. I'm still not reconciled to the killing, you know. A blow to the head would suffice, but—'

'Get me out!'

Mrs Powell points and says, 'Don't be impatient. Help is on the way.'

Alex turns awkwardly, and scrapes the pile of faeces with the heel of one boot. In the last of the daylight, he sees the little figure digging at the stake which tethers the pygmy mammoth. It is Ray. Alex's heart leaps at the sight. He asks Mrs Powell, 'Where exactly is Kat?'

'On the way to a rendezvous. Or that's what Ray said she was doing. She won't talk to me at all, no matter what I say. Very rude, if you don't mind me saying.'

'It's just her way, Mrs Powell.'

Ray scrambles on to the back of the pygmy mammoth and leans forward to whisper in Hannibal's ear. The mammoth ambles over, and delicately inserts a curved tusk through the lattice work of the cage. Hannibal jerks his head. The edge of the cage tears free with a ripping noise, showering Alex with dirt.

Ray jumps down and starts trying to pull Alex through the gap, and lights come on all around the perimeter of the clearing. The lights are biolume lamps, held up by more than a hundred fairies. The greenish light of the lamps makes their skins look unnaturally blue. A single ogre towers at the back, three times the height of ordinary fairies, its tusked mouth working. Hannibal steps about uneasily.

'Oh dear,' Mrs Powell says.

Alex squints into the greenish glare of the lamps, then looks at Ray.

The fey shows its sharp teeth. 'Not ours, big man.'

'I suppose,' Mrs Powell whispers fiercely, 'that fighting our way free is out of the question.'

Ray says, 'Is she crazy?'

'What do you think, Ray?'

'I think I should have left you.'

Mrs Powell says, 'How much trouble are we in, Mr Sharkey?'

'I wish I knew, Mrs Powell.'

Alex is heartsick to realize that he was used as caged bait. While Katrina's still free there's still a faint hope that the Children's Crusade can be turned, but without the library in his bones and the link to Max it isn't much of a hope.

Three human figures walk through the circle of light: the Twins and the Web cowboy, Frodo McHale. The fairies part to allow their horned king to follow. His carbon whisker antennae splay out around his head like a spiky corona. A slick of saliva glistens on his chin.

'Oh dear,' Mrs Powell says again.

Overhead, somewhere in the night beyond the lights, is the sound of a helicopter coming in to land.

14
In Another Part of the Forest

The narrow, steep-sided little valley where the fairies ambush Captain Spiromilos's mercenaries is full of roses. Thousands of white blooms as big as cabbages flower on thorny canes, forming dense drifts between the pine trees on either side of the road. The warm night air is thick with their perfume.

Ever since nightfall there have been flickering lights moving far off in the dark woods, sometimes keeping pace with the convoy for as much as a kilometre. When the mercenaries started to take potshots, Captain Spiromilos passed the word that they should save their ammunition; the lights were no more than a diversionary tactic of the enemy. But suddenly, as the convoy starts the switch-back climb out of the rose-filled valley, there is a line of lights on the sinuous ridge ahead.

In the jeep that brings up the rear of the convoy, Todd peers through borrowed night-glasses and sees that the lights are held by very active child-sized figures. All are misshapen in some way. Some are horned, others have spurs on elbows or knees, or tusks, or fan-fold ears. Their actions don't seem hostile, or even directed at the convoy. In fact, Todd has the distinct and disturbing impression that they are dancing.

Then an explosion lights the night ahead of the convoy. A hail of splinters is punched into the air, rattling through the trees and rose thickets. Tall pines, their bases blown away, thrash and topple across the road. Trucks and jeeps slew to a halt in a flaring necklace of brakelights.

After a moment, the mercenaries' guns open up, spraying drifts of tracer across the ridge – but the figures are already plunging downslope towards the convoy. Most are cut down in less than five minutes. Heavy gunfire smashes through the rose thickets, scattering white petals like snow. A figure twice the height of a man stands on the ridge, wielding a grenade launcher in one hand and beating its chest with the other. A wireguided mini-missile takes it out in a plume of smoky red fire.

After that there are only individual shots as sharpshooters with infrared sights and motion detectors finish off the surviving attackers. It's over in ten minutes, so quickly that Spike is still cursing the driver of the jeep for not letting him use the camera drone. It is so one-sided that it is more of a massacre than a fight. And the horrible thing is that the mercenaries are really buzzed by their easy victory, whooping and shouting, passing around bottles and snap ampoules, and loosing tracer fire into the sky like Fourth of July fireworks until Captain Spiromilos gets on his amplifier and tells them in a voice like the voice of God to quit fucking around and clear the roadblock.

As mercenaries set to work with chainsaws to cut away the fallen trees, Captain Spiromilos walks back along the line of vehicles. Struts would be more like it, Todd thinks. The man even exchanges high-fives with some of his men. When he reaches the end of the convoy he is grinning like a Hallowe'en pumpkin.

'How did you like the fight, Mr Hart?'

'It was pretty one-sided. Is that why you didn't want us to record it?'

'There'll be plenty of time to use your camera, but I suggest you don't try it in combat. Your drone might be mistaken for a weapon of the enemy.'

Spike says, 'Is that a threat?'

'Shut up, Spike,' Todd says. He doesn't want to antagonize

Spiromilos. The man might just take it into his head to shoot them both and make his own arrangements for publicity.

Captain Spiromilos says, 'It's a pragmatic warning. We can supply footage if you need it, but defeat of the fairies is a minor part of this.'

Todd says, 'That's fine, but the agencies won't touch footage that isn't encrypted with a key they can verify. It's too easy to fake stuff these days.'

Captain Spiromilos ignores this. He takes out a slate and says, 'Let me show you where we're going. We did a flyby yesterday, using our own drone.'

Todd looks at the montage of aerial views of a small, ruined town. Marooned amidst dark forests, it is bounded on one side by a wide irregular lake that gleams like ice.

Captain Spiromilos says, 'We're about a kilometre away. The Crusade will come through there, at dawn. By then, we'll have taken the town. It's an unChristian place full of ware-wolves and worse, but they lack discipline.'

'With a force like yours, I'm surprised you don't try exorcism.'

'In time I will, Mr Hart.' There's a sly edge to Captain Spiromilos's voice. 'In good time all of this country will get the cleansing it needs.'

'There's that word again.'

'They used to grow good grapes down there, make the grapes into wine and brandy, and drink what they made. It was about all they did, because they lost their lands to the Greeks just before the First World War. Then they started to grow gengineered sunflowers. The sunflower seeds were rich in opium, and supplied half of Europe's heroin trade. But a rival cartel bombed out the fields in the last civil war, just before the UN established the neutral zone.'

'It doesn't look too damaged.'

'It was bombed with nanotech stuff,' Captain Spiromilos says. 'That's why the land east of it shines. That's the remains of thousands of hectares of plants. Their cellulose was transformed into a polymer that flooded out across the fields and formed a deep lake before it hardened. The enemy has changed the town since then, but nothing in the way of what you might call defences. We can punch right through. The Crusade will come up the old road, towards the pass, and that's where we'll meet them.'

Captain Spiromilos's Turkish second-in-command, Kemmel, rides his motorbike along the edge of the convoy. His passenger is the pale-eyed Web cowboy. When Kemmel slews the bike to a halt, the cowboy says, 'Nothing's moving out there.'

Todd glances at Spike and says, 'Maybe we could go up on the ridge and shoot some footage of the convoy.'

The cowboy says, 'There're more than a hundred semi-autonomous probes out there. If a beetle farts, we'll record it in stereo.'

Todd explains all over again about the need for encryption.

'Guy,' the kid says, 'that's nothing more than some kind of fingerprinted bitmapped image deal. We can hack that in no time, put authentic codes in whatever you want. You should lose these no-hopers, Spiro, I can give you anything they can.'

Captain Spiromilos looks at the kid for a long moment, and then says, 'Maybe the journalist is right.' He tells Todd, 'I want you to get all you need. It's good for me, and it'll be good for you. We'll be ready to roll in about twenty minutes. Kemmel, you take them up there in this jeep, make sure they don't get into any trouble.'

The jeep is smart and quick and agile. Its big segmented wheels have independent universally jointed suspensions and are each driven by a separate motor, controlled by a hardwired nervous system. Kemmel lets the jeep find its own way, and it moves up the rocky slope like a bug on a griddle, dodging amongst trees and crashing through rose thickets.

Spike has already unshipped the camera drone, which follows the jeep like a pilot fish surfing the wake of a whale. The red light above its lens turret blinks calmly. Kemmel grins and gives it the thumbs-up, happy to be a prime-time star.

Todd hangs on to the crash bar and leans forward and says to Kemmel, 'Are you happy? It's not exactly real fighting.'

'Plenty of action soon,' Kemmel says. 'In the town it is quiet, but that does not mean it is unpopulated. They wait for us, I think.'

Todd says, 'What I mean is, I didn't come out here to record a meaningless firefight, or an equally meaningless massacre.'

Kemmel says, 'But you'll still use what you get.'

The sick thing is that the mercenary's right, but Todd can't admit that. He says, 'You've been around, Kemmel. So have I. Let's be men and agree that much. What are you getting out of this?'

'I get paid. I get to see action. I get to grease as many monkeys as I can. Why do you think I'm here?'

'Don't be an asshole, Kemmel. Spiromilos is a crazy man, we both know it.'

'Maybe so, but he knows how to hustle.'

'He'll run out of luck sooner or later.'

Kemmel shrugs. 'Not yet. This high enough for you?'

The jeep has climbed out of the trees, and is scrabbling and sliding up the beginning of a steep field of scree with dogged determination. Below, the lights of the convoy glimmer amongst dark trees. The ripping sound of chainsaws drifts up.

Todd says, 'Do him, Spike!'

The drone swerves sideways and rushes forward. Kemmel sees what's happening and has time to raise an arm in front of his face before the drone smashes into him. His head cracks against the jeep's windscreen with enough force to star the glass.

The jeep registers the problem and stops, and together Todd and Spike heave Kemmel on to the scree. The mercenary's face is masked in blood, but he's still breathing.

Todd is trying to figure out how to override the jeep's AI when something lands on the hood and levels a pistol at him. He shouts, 'American! American journalist!' before he sees that the thing is a doll – no, a fairy, barechested in cut-down camo breeches, with nipple rings and a mouthful of pointed teeth. A pair of crooked tusks, yellow as ivory, grow through its cheeks. The tusks are tipped with steel.

'Come with me,' it says in a thick voice, 'if you want to live.'

15
Milena's Last Gift

'We took this from your dark lady,' Frodo McHale says. 'So now you get to ride into battle in style, and on the winning side.'

The cowboy, grinning like a fool, is standing in the aisle of the helicopter's little passenger compartment, holding on to the head-rests of the seats in which Alex and Mrs Powell are fastened. His little round landscape glasses are like black holes in his long white face. Another cowboy, a kid in red, crouches up front. He's wearing goggles and mitts, and his computer deck is jacked into the pilot's cocoon. Ray lies beside the pilot, his wrists shackled to his ankles. The fey's eyes are open, staring into infinity. He lies so still that he might already be dead.

Alex watches the green-lit clearing drop away as the helicopter rises above the trees. Its searchlight comes on, probing the dusk as it turns northwards, towards the abandoned town of Leskoviku. They're going to meet the mercenaries with whom Frodo McHale's cowboys have formed an alliance, and then intercept the Children's Crusade.

Frodo McHale tells Alex, 'As your friend Katrina might say, for you the war is over. In fact, it never really began, did it? Our little trap might not have caught everyone, but we have the leader of the feys.'

'You don't know much about feys, do you?'

Frodo McHale isn't listening. 'We'll have to kill it, of course, once we've taken everything it has in its blood. If you cooperate, Alex, we won't have to do the same to you.'

'Let Mrs Powell go. She has nothing to do with this.'

'The old woman? Why not? She's harmless. She can go when this is over. We wouldn't want the British Embassy making noises, would we?'

'Young man,' Mrs Powell says, 'I shall certainly be making noises about this.'

Frodo McHale ignores her. He leans close to Alex and whispers, 'By the way, Alex, there's something you should know about your dark lady. She—'

That's when the helicopter tilts sideways. In the cockpit, the kid's goggles suddenly blaze with light, and he screams and claws them off.

The helicopter tilts the other way. Its nose goes down, and Frodo McHale falls backwards. As he starts to get up, Mrs Powell whacks him on the top of his head with the carved handle of her parasol. He falls to his knees and puts up a hand to protect himself, and Alex distinctly hears two of the cowboy's fingers break when Mrs Powell hits him again and lays him out as flat as a landed fish. Ray suddenly twists and bites into the cowboy's throat.

Alex shouts, 'Don't kill him!' and pops his seat harness. The vibrating deck yaws violently. Beyond the canopy, in the cone of the searchlight, the air is filled with a blizzard of wood fragments as the helicopter drops through the forest canopy.

Although it is a controlled crash-landing, the impact knocks Alex on to his back. Frodo McHale is arched, his weight supported by his heels and the back of his head as he claws at his spouting throat.

Ray turns his head and spits a wet mouthful on to the deck. He says thickly, 'No words there.'

Frodo kicks out and then relaxes. His black clothes are wet with his own blood.

'I think we have an angel on our side,' Mrs Powell says.

Crouched by the pilot's cocoon, the kid is pressing bunched fingers into his streaming eyes and howling that he's blind. His face is underlit by the light pouring from the goggles he has dropped.

Then the light starts to pulse.

Ray says, 'She wants to talk with you, big man.'

The blinded cowboy won't stop wailing, so Mrs Powell gives him a sedative shot and takes him outside. Alex jacks his own computer deck into the pilot's cocoon. He pulls on his mitts, fits the goggles over his eyes, takes a breath, and punches the space bar of the keyboard that appears in front of him.

And his eyes are filled with white light.

Gradually, like a developing photograph, lines and perspective emerge from the light. It is a room, a white-painted room with bleached wooden floorboards. The white shades at the two windows are luminous with sunlight. Between the windows, a yellow canary in a cage is singing its heart out. Although in real life it was a mechanical toy, here in virtuality it appears to be alive, its eyes bright, its yellow breast heaving and its head turning back and forth as it looses a cascade of trills.

For a moment the canary is the only spot of colour in the room, but then something moves against the wall, and Alex sees a woman in a long white dress standing there. Her dark eyes burn through the white hair that shrouds her face.

Alex immediately thinks of the virtual ghosts in the Ladies' Smoking Room of the Grand Midland Hotel at St Pancras, for the woman *is* a ghost. She is Nanny Greystoke. Then she is Milena as Alex remembers her, the little girl with the calm wise face, her thick black hair woven into a French braid. She is wearing the same white T-shirt and green shorts that Alex recalls from the second time they met, in the Pizza Express in Soho.

Alex stands up, and Ray asks him what is happening. Alex ignores the fey. The raw stench of Frodo McHale's blood, the hot oil smell of the crash-landed helicopter, the sounds it makes as it settles in its canted bed of smashed tree branches: all falls away. Alex is deep in virtuality, registering only what he sees and hears through the link.

He says, 'Is this what happened after I rang your doorbell? Is this what I've forgotten?'

'This isn't what happened, Alex. Does it matter?'

'All these years—'

'You were looking for me because—' The single line of Milena's eyebrows dents in the middle. Then she laughs. 'Oh Alex! You are such a romantic!'

'You never did understand people too well.'

'I was never interested in details. Nothing's lost, Alex, if you know where to look.'

There are toys scattered across the floor. A couple of racing cars circle each other and then zoom off towards opposite corners of the white room. A clown beats a drum and a redcoat soldier blows on a tiny, tinny bugle. A teddy bear clumps up to Milena, its unjointed arms held out in mute entreaty. She picks it up and cradles it.

'You came back,' the teddy bear says in its gruff, growly voice. 'I knew you would come back.'

Milena says, 'I found this room in the archives of the company that owned me. They were very meticulous about recording the circumstances of my disappearance.'

'I remember that. I found your daughters in Paris, Milena, but I just missed finding you.'

'They aren't my daughters. You know that, Alex.'

341

'You cloned yourself, when? It must have been soon after you left London.'

'Dr Luther helped me. Curiously, although I gave him the technique – I stole it from my company – he used it only to make his sex toys.'

'I saw Dr Luther last year, but he never told me that.'

They are like old, former lovers, Alex realizes, talking over past times and lost friends.

Milena says, 'Despite his interests, or perhaps because of them, Dr Luther has a very Victorian sense of honour. He gave me his word that he would not divulge what he had done. I'm pleased to see that he kept to it. But you, Alex. You're something of a disappointment to me. You keep bad company. That impossibly crude vigilante, and the silly old woman with the romantic ideas. Siding with the feys. It doesn't become you. I thought you were smarter than that.'

'Cleverness isn't everything.'

'No?' Milena sets the teddy bear on the floor, and it vanishes along with the rest of the toys.

'I'm here—'

'Please, Alex. Spare me the speeches. I know why you're here.'

'The feys—'

'It got out of control, I admit, but I have made arrangements.'

One of the window shades rolls up, and sunlight floods the room. It's so bright that Milena seems to dissolve into it. Her voice says, 'I have made a fairyland. Look.'

With no sense of transition, Alex is standing at the window. Outside is not the little street – he's forgotten its name, although he remembers double yellow lines on heat-softened tarmac, high brick walls, and service entrances – but a verdant, summery countryside. Green hills saddle away under a bright blue sky towards a horizon where, like a storm, or the battlements of a walled city, a vast forest looms. There are meadows starred with poppies, and copses of oaks and elm. In the middle distance, a little pavilion, its walls creamy silk, its conical roof pink, is pitched in a daisy-starred meadow. A white horse grazes beside it. The horse has a spiral, nacreous horn as long as a man's arm growing from its forehead.

Antoinette says, 'Fairyland.'

Alex isn't surprised at the change. He is surprised to see that Antoinette is naked, with raw sutures around the top of her shapely, shaven head. He says, 'It's a bit of an anti-climax, frankly.'

A disneyfied bluebird flies up to the window. Its brown, human eyes, with coy, fluttering lashes, stare into Alex's. It chirps a merry song, and then swoops away across the sunny meadows.

Antoinette says, 'It can be anything you like. The window is a metaphor for a very special buffer. You're not seeing it the way the fairies see it. The way, Alex, that I can see it.'

'Who did your body, by the way? Not Dr Luther, I take it.'

'He does tend to overstate the attributes of his sex toys, doesn't he? He's a great believer in the lordotic response, which is why he exaggerates secondary sexual characteristics. Oh, some of the work was done in Thailand, and some of it was done in the old-fashioned way, diet and exercise. It was Glass's idea, and we had so much fun planning it. We made up a whole other life, faked our way into InScape's auditions and rigged the selection. We even created an agent which did all its business over phone lines. It made my transition so much easier, because InScape had done all the physical and reactive profiling already, and of course I had access to the back-doors in their Reality Engines. We borrowed a lot of their codes to build the foundations of the Library of Dreams.'

'Are the stitches a fashion statement, or another of your metaphors? Are you getting ready to follow Glass? You may be disappointed. It isn't over yet, Milena. Not until the Children's Crusade crosses the border.'

'You're too late, dear Alex. You worked some of it out, but you were too slow.'

'We can still stop them,' Alex says, but he's uncertain now. He has the free-falling feeling that Milena has outsmarted him again.

'Of course. But only with my help. And that's all you can do.'

Alex understands. The sutures. The playfulness. He would never have expected Milena to be playful, not in the real world.

He says, 'You really did it, didn't you?'

'Three days ago. Frodo McHale made an alliance, but I out-manoeuvred him.'

'He's dead.'

'I know. The pilot was always mine, Alex.'

'You can't go back?'

'A bush robot with ten million fembot-sized scanning and recording arms stripped my cortex neurone by neurone. It took no more than a hundred seconds, and at the end of it my original was dead. I'm not a copy but a simulation of that original, built up from the bush robot's measurements and six months' sampling and recording of cortical activity. Everything I remember of my original's life was built into a cross-reference data-base, and a heuristic program does its best to fill in the gaps. Frankly, it's not recording and simulating the activity of a mind that's the problem. It's the interface between the simulation and its environment.'

Alex says, 'We could still turn you off.'

'I'm not in the Library of Dreams. It was useful, but I've spread out. I'm distributed across the Web, Alex. I use a maximum of about point nought nought nought five per cent of its capacity, but only when fully recalculating Fairyland, and that last happened when the curtain went up for you. If you want to hurt me, you'll have to switch off most of the Web. I'm not anywhere any more, I'm everywhere. You're still blundering about with those ridiculous goggles on. You have to plug in. But I'm *here* . . .'

'What's it like? Really. I'd like to know,'

'It hurts. I'm feeling so much that it hurts. I'm using every one of the receptors that were mapped across, and half of those are pain receptors. But that will pass, I'm told. I'll adapt. The inputs should slowly change the output of the receptors.'

'And if it doesn't?'

'Then I can accept the pain.'

Alex tries to imagine it. Like instantly being flayed alive, and that instant lasting forever, never dulling from its peak intensity of raw white-hot agony.

He says, 'It must be like Hell, Milena.'

'I'm going to live forever, Alex. What's a little pain?'

'You haven't changed. You always were . . . unique.'

'I knew you'd understand, Alex. After Glass, you understand me best.'

'When I was much younger, I'd've taken that as a compliment. Where is Glass?'

Antoinette hands Alex a little brass spyglass. It allows him to

344

look through the walls of the silk pavilion and see the old man sleeping inside a glass coffin.

'He passed through before the codes derived from the Children's Crusade were available. I'll wake him soon. Then we'll be together forever.'

'You love him.'

'It's not exactly love, Alex.'

'It's more than understanding.'

'He's nearly as brilliant as I am, Alex. And as alone. We were fated to be either lovers or mortal enemies.'

'You were using the Children's Crusade all along, weren't you? And even after your daughters turned against you, you were still using them.'

'I admit certain aspects got out of hand, but side-effects are inevitable in a project this size. My daughters interfered, it's true. They were very naughty, but they didn't really know that what they were doing was wrong. Besides, the world won't mourn a few little girls who would have grown up only to die of violence or a fatal disease after breeding more of their kind. In a way, you know, they were my true daughters.'

'I know you're not human, Milena. But you needn't pretend to be a monster. It isn't you.'

'But I'm no longer the Milena you knew. The mapping isn't even remotely precise, but that doesn't matter. No one remains the same. We all map and remap ourselves.'

'I'm not out to destroy the Children's Crusade, Milena. That never was my intention.'

'And that's why you are a fool. My daughters may want to use the Crusade to change the world, but that was never *my* intention. The Crusade is my laboratory. I used it as a self-organizing system to evolve fembot interfaces by artificial evolution, driven by the requirement to translate fairy entoptics as efficiently as possible. The codes used by the fembots are the only way to directly interface with virtuality . . .'

Alex turns as her voice fades. She is Milena again, the little girl with the glossy black hair, the white T-shirt, the knee-length green shorts. She says, 'You're still here.'

'You were explaining what you did. That's why I'm here, isn't it?'

'I thought I had explained.'

'I'm still human, Milena. I have to proceed one bit at a time.'

'I don't move any faster, Alex. Each of my sub-selves must be recalculated in parallel, or one would begin to dominate the others. I would suffer a psychosis.'

Alex prompts, 'You used the Children's Crusade.'

'I used it as a laboratory, a space to evolve fembot interfaces. The evolution was driven by the requirement to perform translation of fairy entoptics. Fairies can live in unbuffered virtuality. They can make their own worlds in it, because their entoptics are the same as those of information space. I should know – I designed them that way. The Crusaders marching towards the neutral zone are only a small part of those who were infected by the fairies. They are those in whom the pseudo-sexual combination and recombination of the best assembler codes produced something close to what I wanted. The fact that they responded to my call shows how closely the codes fit to my ideal. The rest, all the other people infected by Crusader memes, I freed.

'The remainder are too dangerous, because what they carry could be used by others. In them I found what I wanted, and I took it. Assemblers in their blood make very fast and very compact interfaces between the human nervous system and artificial realities. I sampled over a thousand different types to build a library of source code for the interface which allows me to directly immerse myself in virtuality. I made my selection in Paris, by the way, while you were scrabbling in the bowels of that dreary little pleasure park. Do you really think I'd allow such a precious cargo to make its way on foot through a war zone? In fact, I hoped they wouldn't make it this far, because it would save us the trouble of neutralizing them. The Crusade reached its end long before it began its final march.'

Alex remembers her precocious interest in a-life. 'You planned well, Milena.'

'I intend to live forever, and I long ago learned the spider's art of patience. When I met you I had already been planning my escape for years, and I have been planning this apotheosis for almost as long. I'll be a saint, you know. The saint of the Web cowboys. For I have shed my burden of flesh, and how they long to do likewise! Except, poor children, they'll never manage it unless they start my work over.'

'And you'll destroy all the Crusade and the feys and the other fairies, because otherwise the cowboys just might use what's in their blood to follow you. You don't have the right, Milena.'

'Dolls are destroyed by their creators every day, thousands and thousands of them. In a way, fairies are less than dolls – they exist only because of radical neurosurgery. Pull their chips, and they become of less use than they were when they were dolls.'

'They are a new thing, Milena. You may have created them, but you don't know what you have created.'

'I know exactly what I did, Alex. I always knew what I was doing, every step of the way. My daughters were a little *too* like me, perhaps. They have devised a way to control the last remnants of the Children's Crusade. But you already know of the burning man, and even that small trouble will be smoothed away. Despite your interference, I might add.'

'And that wasn't part of your plans.'

Milena smiles. 'Perhaps it was, perhaps not. But you have to admit we both want the same thing. We want the Crusade neutralized. We both know that it is too dangerous to be allowed to continue in any form, especially if it falls into the hands of Frodo McHale and his mercenaries. You have no choice but to help me, if you want to save the feys.'

'I do want to save them. That's the difference between you and me. You want to destroy the fairies because they can come after you.'

'There are forces out to destroy the fairies that have nothing to do with me, Alex. The fairies have had their time, and now people know that the fairies can change people just as people changed them, that time will soon be over. I hardly need to do anything. You hope otherwise, so you do not believe me.'

'You have a moral responsibility. Not only for the fairies, but for the people you changed, too. The people of the Children's Crusade you used as incubation chambers.'

'Most are already freed of the glamour which held them. The remainder, a tiny minority, are too dangerous to be allowed to live.

347

You know it. Not because of what they are, but because of what they carry in their blood. Because they are the ones in which the interface codes evolved most successfully. Even the UN has recognized that they are dangerous. You're just as dangerous, Alex. Infecting yourself that way, turning yourself into a breeding ground . . . You're a fat man, I know, but you shouldn't abuse your body.'

'Frankly, I didn't plan my life to take this path.'

'I know. Sometimes I wish that I could feel sorry for you.'

Milena walks over to the other window. She is fading. Alex can see the white-painted Adam fireplace through her shape. She says, 'There is one more thing,' and unhooks the window shade with one ghostly finger – or perhaps the shade itself has become ghostly, the shade of a shade. Cold yellow Jupiter light falls through the window, which looks into Max's virtuality Home Room. The view of Jupiter's cloudscape seems more real than the white room, which like Milena is becoming transparent.

'Come here,' she says.

And Alex is there.

'I'll give you a last gift,' Milena tells him. 'It will help you neutralize the Crusade, if you choose to use it.'

Her ghostly form suddenly shrinks into itself, gaining mass and definition and light. Apart from Alex and the two windows, one on to Jupiter, the other on to Fairyland, she is the only real thing in the room. She hovers in midair, small as a butterfly, with gauzy wings and a dress like an inverted tulip, and shining silver hair done up in a lazy coil. She wrinkles her pert nose, throws a nebular scattering of sparkling dust at Alex, and zooms off, passing through the ghostly glass of the window into Fairyland, tracing a rising contrail of luminous dust as she soars into its vast, perfect blue sky.

Which vanishes. There is only the window on to Jupiter, now. A seethe of nothingness presses at Alex's back. He could take off his goggles, of course, but instead he makes a step and is in Max's Home Room, with Max suddenly turning to look at him, startled, then puzzled.

'Now, what the hell? I thought that I was the only one who knew about that backdoor.'

'I had help.'

'This wouldn't be something to do with the codes that were just dumped into my buffer, would it? It's the strangest thing, but I've just found the way into the burning man.'

Max reaches up and pulls a data window out of the air.

Alex says, 'Don't use it. It's her gift. It's from Milena.'

'He's got to be destroyed.'

'Yes, but not yet. She did the Ultimate Hack, Max. Her and Glass. She wants to pull the door in with her, and the burning man is a key to that door. He's our way into the Crusade.'

Max looks off at the ochre cloudscapes of Jupiter. Light from the dense lines of code glowing in the data window is caught in his nappy hair like scraps of brass. At last, he says, 'It's the Web or her. Wannabes and lurkers are beginning to sniff around the backdoor to the Library of Dreams. I sent out a cancelbot, but assholes are posting the address faster than it can cope, and anyway I can't do anything about word of mouth. We've got to *close* it, Alex, or someone will hack it permanently open.'

'You've got to trust me on this, Max. We need to use the burning man to stop the Crusade.'

'What do you know?' Max says, suddenly challenging. 'Tell me what you know.'

'I was caught by fairies, Max. The same ones that were in the Magic Kingdom. They're allied with some of Glass's hackers—'

'Yeah, I know. And these mercenaries, I promised I would find out about them? They're led by someone—' Max pulls down another window '—name of Captain Spiromilos. Used to be in the US Marines. Claims he's Archigôs of Himara, whatever the fuck that is. Before this he was working freelance for the Peepers, hunting down feys in Slovakia. That's where I got most of the information.'

'Can you give it to me? I mean right now?'

'Consider it done. Why are you in a helicopter, by the way?'

'It's a long story. The important thing is that Milena wants us to use the burning man to stop the Crusade's march. She says it's the only way, and I'm beginning to believe her. So we can't destroy him, or not yet. Not until the Crusade is stopped, because if we can't stop it, how can we begin to try and cure the Crusaders? And we have to cure them before they reach the mercenaries and Frodo McHale's hackers.'

'You know, I could destroy him right now,' Max says, and Alex feels a measure of relief, like a drink of cold pure water, because he knows Max won't. Not yet.

'A little longer is all I ask.'

'I just bet she plays chess. This is your classic knight fork. We have to choose to sacrifice something because we don't have time to chase after Milena *and* to stop the Crusade. And because we have to stop the Crusade to begin to cure it, we must choose between destroying the burning man or using him to try and access where Milena has gone, and risk letting copies spread into the Web. A little longer is all you've got. The Crusade is almost at the border. It's on half the news channels.'

The data window flickers with a cascade of aerial shots of a long column of people marching down a forest road.

'The UN is letting them through,' Max says. 'They'll cross the border tomorrow. When that happens I pull that flame-filled fucker's plug.'

'There are more than a thousand Crusaders. We can't kill them, not all of them, Max. We need—'

'That's it, Alex. I'm running out of thumbs here.'

'Thumbs?'

'To plug the dike. Lots of luck, dood.'

The bubble vanishes, and Alex, his sight and hearing filled with white noise, almost falls over before he remembers to strip off the goggles.

Green light fills the helicopter's cabin. Ray turns from the open hatch and says, 'They've caught up with us.'

The Twins are standing at the edge of the swathe of broken foliage cut by the helicopter's abrupt descent. The horned man stands behind them. Green lamps held by the fairies make a scattered constellation in the dark trees beyond.

Mrs Powell is standing under the helicopter's hatch, her hands on the shoulders of the blinded cowboy.

Alex tries to reassure her. 'We've something to talk about now. We've something we can agree on.'

The blinded cowboy says, 'They'll kill you, you fat fuck.'

Ray says, 'Just say the word, big man. I drink his blood.'

'Let him be,' Alex says. 'He never was very important, and he's nothing now.'

The truth is that Alex feels sorry for the young cowboy – he's another one of Milena's dupes. They should form a club, and Alex could be president.

Alex walks towards the Twins, holding out his hands. They glare at him from beneath matted fringes. He says, 'She's left you here,' because he doesn't know *what* they call Milena. Not mother, he's certain of that, at least. He says, 'I can help you, but you must help me, too. Otherwise she'll win, and you'll have nothing left.'

'We already have friends—'

'—friends who can do more for us than you can.'

Alex says, 'These kids are nothing to you; they hired mercenaries, and the mercenaries would rather kill fairies than serve them. In a minute, I'll prove it to you. Forget the promises made to you. You know about me. You know what I did in Amsterdam. I'm offering an alliance.'

The Twins look at each other, look at Alex.

'You don't know us—'

'—you don't *understand* us—'

'—you can *never* understand us.'

'I know. I never understood her, completely, even from the first.'

'We know all about you, fat man—'

'—about how you loved—'

'—how desperately you loved—'

'—and lost and never won—'

'—never *could* win.'

'I helped her, from the first. She's gone. She's left you. You know that. Now let me help you. She gave me the way to destroy your king. So far, I've spared him.'

'Leave them, big man,' Ray says.

Alex ignores the fey, even when Ray's nails close around his wrist.

The Twins look at each other again. 'You want us to help—'

'—to help *them*—'

351

'—to help the feys?'

'You and the feys all want the same thing. You all will lose the same thing if you don't cooperate. Frodo McHale and the other cowboys hired mercenaries who were hunting fairies for a living. They're only your allies for as long as they need you. After that, they'll destroy you.'

'Prove it,' the Twins say, and Alex knows he's won.

16
Leskoviku

Flares rise up and burst in the black sky as Todd and Spike slog their way across the polymer lake behind the fairy guide, and the ruins of Leskoviku are suddenly pinned under their stark white light. The little town has been changed by fembots. Clusters of fantastic, organic-looking spires rise out of shells of buildings eaten away to stone lace. The buttresses and spines, encrusted cliffs and fluted towers, as richly complex and colourful as a coral reef, resemble nothing so much as the post-apocalyptic organic geologies of Max Ernst's decalcomanian paintings.

Above, Spike's camera drone turns to take in all of this. Spike has been recording ever since they came down the far side of the ridge and started to cross the polymer lake. Because Spike is using mitts and tele-presence goggles to control the drone, Todd must help him over the glazed ground.

The polymer is humped and rippled, a quick-frozen sea. It refracts the flare-light around the dark shadows of the things suspended within it. Some of the things are bodies, inhabitants of the town caught in the wave of their transformed crop. The face of a bearded man looks up at Todd through a few centimetres of glaze. His body is perfectly preserved, like a bug in a resin paperweight, except that one arm reaches up through the surface: the hand is gone, not even the bones left.

'Hurry!' the fairy says. 'Or kill you here.'

This is its constant refrain.

Todd says, for maybe the twentieth time, 'Who are you with?' but the fairy only glares at him before scurrying on.

The combined light of the flares, falling lower and swaying under their chutes, moves over the spires; shadows move, too, making everything seem to shift and melt. Spike punches Todd's shoulder and points. Above them, the camera drone turns to point in the same direction.

Two, ten, twenty figures unfurl from the needle-tip tops of the tallest cluster of spires and fall through the white glare and shifting shadows of the flares, gliding on membranous wings. They look a little like bats, but must be bigger than men. All at once, three of them flare with red light and fall from the sky. A spire cracks apart in a molten spray, its tip plunging down amidst burning wreckage. Someone has just used a one shot pinch fusion laser. From the ridge overlooking the town, tracer fire loops in towards the other flyers, which swoop back into the ruins.

Captain Spiromilos's mercenaries have arrived.

As Todd and Spike stumble into the outskirts of the transmogrified town, a long line of flames roars up behind them like a curtain, and heat and lurid light beats across the ground. The flames are ten metres high, and send up dense black smoke and an acrid kerosene stench.

Shallow ridges and whorls of rotten concrete, depleted by fembots and fragile as snow crust or termite-eaten wood, crunch under Todd's boots. He and Spike leave a trail of centimetre deep prints.

The fairy, Todd notes, leaves no footprints at all. There are others here, scampering this way and that and firing at random through the curtain of flames in the general direction of the mercenaries' convoy. Some hoot and jabber, jumping about on ruined walls and squeezing off single shots; others run up and down, firing short bursts and falling back, their place taken by others. The clamour is tremendous. The curtain of fire roars and roars: the heat and light are apocalyptic.

Todd hunkers down beside Spike, who is calmly recording as much as he can. Firelight reflects in the gold-filmed lenses of his tele-presence glasses; he slashes and cuts at me air with his hands.

Out above the polymer lake the drone bobs and turns, drinking everything in.

'This is fucking marvellous,' Spike yells gleefully.

'Five more minutes. Then we find some cover.'

'I don't care! I'm a fucking point of view!'

The mercenaries appear to have spread out along the ridge above the town, and are returning fire. Despite the heat searing his skin, Todd feels a chill shiver at his core. Adrenalin wearing off. Things seem to be happening in discrete intervals: drooping fans of tracer fire sweeping across the night air with eerie precision; the slow collapse of a filigree siding from the wall of a house at the edge of the town; a yellow belch of flame purling upwards from the far end of the wall of fire; a fairy running out across the polymer lake in long leaping bounds, taking a hit and dropping down in the unstrung way of the suddenly dead.

'Some fun,' Spike says out of the side of his mouth. Then he adds, 'Jesus Christ,' because lights have come on all through the transformed ruins. Strings and loops and lines of lights, yellow and green and blue and red, blinking and stuttering and pulsing.

Todd turns to look at this, and a fairy, naked and lithe, its blue skin gleaming with sweat, lays its gun on him. It isn't any kind of gun Todd has ever seen before: a swollen barrel with a tiny aperture, and what looks like a cylinder of compressed gas slung underneath. The fairy is no bigger than a child. It grins, showing teeth all exactly the same size, all filed to points. Its big, pointed ears are studded with gold clips.

Todd raises his hands and shouts, 'American journalist! American journalist!'

A woman's voice says, 'Leave him be, you little fucker.'

The fairy sticks out a long, black, pointed tongue and is gone. The woman crouches beside Todd and lights a cigarette. She's in her forties, hefty in leather jacket and trousers. There's a strip of leopard fur like a cropped mohawk on the top of her shaved skull. She carries a machine pistol fitted with a flash suppressor.

Todd says, 'You're in charge? I'm an American, an American reporter. This is my cameraman. You should keep these soldiers of yours under control. Someone could get killed here.'

'Someone will kill that drone if you leave it up there,' the woman says. She has a German accent. She emits a powerful smell compounded of woodsmoke and old sweat.

Without looking around, Spike says, 'No shit.'

Todd says, 'We need to record all this. Please. Are you in charge?'

The woman laughs. 'In charge? No one is in charge here.'

Todd starts to explain that he escaped from Captain Spiromilos's mercenaries, but the woman cuts him off and says, 'Did this Spiromilos have any other prisoners?'

'I didn't see any.'

The woman tells them that her name is Katrina; she's the only human here. 'You come with me, I'll show you a safe place.'

Katrina leads them through the centre of the town, past spires and struts and soaring buttresses. The old paving is as fragile as pumice, mined by fembots for material used to reconstruct the ruins. At the far side of the little town, Todd and Spike follow Katrina up a stairway untouched by fembots. There's a long room, its floor dense with stalagmite growths, its walls covered with crawling veins of stone like petrified veins. Todd crouches beside a window and finds that he can see past the curtain of fire to the polymer lake and the terraced slope rising to the forest edge, where the mercenaries have established their position.

Katrina tells Spike, 'Will you keep that fucking drone down! It's drawing fire!'

Todd no longer feels afraid, although his mouth is bone dry and his heart is pounding and the big muscles in his thighs keep jerking. He tells Spike, 'Let's not put ourselves out of business.'

'The point is that Spiromilos wouldn't fire at the drone,' Spike says, but it dips down all the same.

There's a stutter of gunfire along the ridge overlooking the town. Something tears the air with a heavy rumble like a freight train. Todd has been in enough war zones to recognize heavy ordnance, and ducks down as a level plane of fire guillotines two of the fragile towers. The tops of the towers, burning but otherwise intact, plummet straight down, turning to dust before they hit the ground.

'TDX,' Katrina says. 'Gravity polarized explosive.'

Todd says, for his own reassurance as much as anything else, 'It isn't much of a force. There are more fairies than men.'

Katrina nods. 'All we have is fairies. Look at the silly fuckers.'

The fairies have been stirred up by the explosion. Spilling around the ends of the curtain of flames, they rush forward to the edge of the polymer lake, fire towards me mercenaries' position, and rush back to rejoin their fellows.

Todd says, 'I saw some of them flying.'

Katrina says, 'The flyers are as much against us as for us. Like the warewolves, they believe this is their place. They are no allies. One reason why the fairies lit the fire is to keep the warewolves from coming back out of the forest and attacking their asses.'

'And it fucks up the thermal imaging, too.'

Katrina shrugs. 'I doubt they think of that.'

'You don't think much of the fairies, do you?'

'These are feys. The Angry Ones. They fight for their lives. You did not know a prisoner of Spiromilos? Or perhaps of Glass, or of Glass's woman? His name is Alex Sharkey. Perhaps there was also an old woman, and a fairy.'

'Spiromilos brought us along. No one else.'

'Then he is dead, or the Twins have him,' the woman says. 'In that case, we have lost. Unfortunately, the Angry Ones will not believe me. They will fight to the death.'

Another mortar round takes out a big tower. It falls slantwise, like a tree, taking a score of lesser towers with it. The sound, more like breaking glass than fractured stone, is incredibly loud.

'The Angry Ones found a fuel store,' Katrina says. 'They filled a trench with fuel oil, set it alight. Sent mobile lights crawling over the building. Things like beetles. They space themselves out, react to each other. I don't know what crazy kinds of ideas the fairies have, but I do know they know nothing of warfare.'

'You really don't like them.'

'They're not rational.'

Spike points and says, 'Spiromilos is sending out his dolls.'

'Maybe not Spiromilos,' Todd says. 'I think those Web cowboys have got some sort of tele-presence control. As far as they're concerned, this is just like a fucking arcade game.'

The dolls come down in a line, running fast and without

discipline, so that the line soon breaks up into discrete individuals. They are carrying their plastic riot control rifles, and fire short bursts as they run.

The fairies defending the ruined town rush out to meet the attacking dolls. The two ragged lines meet in the middle of the expanse of polymer and dissolve into knots of furious turbulence. Todd watches in amazement. In real war, you hardly ever see the other side; the only time the infantry use their rifles and sidearms is when they harass civilians. Even in Somalia and Mozambique they had mortars and rockets, tanks and helicopter gunships. Here, there are only distant figures running and struggling on a slick, flat plain. It's almost exactly like the shoot-'em-up combat games you can play in the Rotterdam arenas.

Suddenly, the dolls turn and run. The fairies chase after them until the mercenaries lay down covering fire that winnows both fairies and dolls like wheat in a storm. Fairies dance in triumph like their ape ancestors. The harsh red light of the wall of flames at their backs casts their capering shadows far across the polymer lake.

Katrina says, 'The Angry Ones are crazy fuckers. All life is cheap to them. Their lives and our lives. They were born in pain out of incomprehension, and so they don't fear death.'

Todd says, 'Say that again when things are quieter. We'll use it in one of our clips.'

Katrina says, 'No one will want to see this madness.'

Spike says, 'You'd be fucking surprised.'

Todd says, 'We can put this kind of thing out across fifty or sixty subscription newsgroups. If you help us we'll cut you in on, say, two per cent of the residuals?'

Katrina gives him a hard look.

'OK, OK, maybe three per cent. It doesn't sound like much, but the potential audience is huge.'

'I do not think you understand why I'm here.'

'We'll interview you later. Listen, they won't kill us. They'll kill the fairies, that's what they do for a living, but not us.'

'Don't be too sure,' Katrina says, and turns to watch the battle.

Spiromilos's men start up the bombardment again. Half a dozen mortar rounds walk back from the centre of the ruined town, and the last scatters air-fuel bomblets that ignite in a blast of white fire and knock down almost every tower and spire.

Todd is on his knees, half-blinded and half-deaf, his face scorched. For a moment, he's back in the firestorm of Atlanta. It was all a dumb mistake really, or dumb luck. His driver misread the map, and they ended up two kilometres closer to the centre of the groundburst than they should have been, on the outer edge of the suburbs of Hell. The driver and cameraman would have turned back, but Todd, young and foolish, persuaded them that this was the scoop of the decade. They put on breathing masks and protective suits and drove in as far as they could, their Blazer rocking in the tremendous winds which were rushing in to fuel the fires that stretched from horizon to horizon. With the camera running, Todd kept up a ceaseless commentary, not even knowing if it was going out on the air. They stopped on a flyover of the Interstate, above blocks of ordinary houses burning in unison. Only when the Blazer's tyres burst because of the scorching heat did they turn back. They were arrested and put in hospital for decontamination treatment; Todd was having his second change of blood in twenty-four hours when his editor finally got a message through. His coverage of the agony of Atlanta had spanned the networks, pushing aside scheduled programmes. He was famous.

Katrina is shouting into Todd's face, asking if he can hear, if he can see. Todd opens his eyes. The long room is full of dust; part of the ceiling has collapsed. Todd and Spike and Katrina beat out smouldering fragments that have lodged in each other's clothes. Spike is still running the camera drone; it's at its ceiling now, riding at the western edge of the town, waiting to capture the mercenaries' final push.

But things quieten down after the airburst. The fire curtain has been blown out. Grey light slowly spreads along the eastern rim of the sky. Only single shots from Spiromilos's position now, at annoyingly irregular intervals. Spike brings down the drone and goes to sleep.

Todd must have slept, too, because he wakes to find a fairy grinning in his face. When it sees that he's awake, it turns to

Katrina and says, 'Tell him we win. Tell him they want to surrender.'

'They want you to give in,' Katrina says, with weary disgust. There's enough light to see the bruised skin around her eyes.

The fairy shrugs. 'We kill them all. Kill them dead. They come down, they're dead.'

It is taller and burlier than most of the fairies. Bloody claw marks stripe the blue skin of its shoulders and hairless chest. It has a kind of belt or bandolier of ears slung over its right shoulder. They are like fleshy leaves, each as big as one of Todd's hands.

Katrina says, 'You should run for the hills.'

'We're the Angry Ones!'

Todd says, 'What does that mean?'

Katrina says, 'They take drugs together.'

'We share blood.' The fairy fingers the knotted string around its waist. 'Many are one. The enemy knows we cannot be defeated. The enemy wants to talk.' It points to Todd. 'Talk to you.'

The fairies have a shortwave transceiver. They were using it to shriek defiance at the mercenaries after the air-fuel explosion, but when they started to wind down, Captain Spiromilos got a message through. The fairy, which calls itself Eater of the Sun, tells Todd it will be all right, no one will shoot him, but Todd feels a tingling across his whole skin as, in his scorched orange coveralls and shower sandals, followed at a discreet distance by the camera drone, he walks out across the polymer lake. He's dropped a tab of Serenity, but it isn't helping much.

Fairy and doll bodies are strewn across the slick, undulating surface of the polymer lake. A few are still alive. A doll that seems able to use only one arm and a fairy with a bloody gash where its eyes should be are trying to strangle each other. They writhe like maggots in a hollow where their own blood has collected in a shallow pool.

Walking around them, Todd feels a certain detachment, just as he did in the burned-out church in that little mountain village in Somalia on his first foreign assignment. The church was filled with the charred bodies of children. Some had been shot, but most had been burned alive. He stood there in the stench and heat, big, bronze flies loud around him, racked with the dry heaves yet recording, recording. It is what you do. You record. You show the world its underside, the forgotten overlooked deaths. The death dispensed by men who think nothing of death.

Todd stops at the far side of the polymer lake, beside a telegraph pole that cants out of the slick surface at a steep angle. It's warm and a soft dawn wind is blowing from the east. Todd can hear the noise the wind makes in the trees at the top of the ridge, where the mercenaries are.

Presently, Kemmel's motorcycle roars out of the trees and ploughs its way down the eroded terraces. He brakes the bike next to Todd in a flashy slide that gouges the polymer. His forehead is lividly bruised, and there's a bandage across the bridge of his nose.

He says, 'You're on the wrong side, journalist.'

'I don't take sides.'

'That's not how it seems to Captain Spiromilos.'

'He never was a real Captain, Kemmel. He promoted himself. The hell with him. Are you having fun? I'm sorry about knocking you out back there.'

'This kind of mess isn't my idea of a good time, but it's weakened the enemy. Not many left alive, eh?'

'But I guess there are still too many for Spiromilos to risk a frontal assault. Or I wouldn't be talking to you right now.'

Kemmel looks at Todd with a pretty good imitation of contempt. 'You go back to that side, dig yourself a big hole. Better still you get the fuck out of there.'

'I'm right, aren't I? Spiromilos underestimated the fairies.'

'We're coming through that place.'

'Is that your message?'

'Oh no,' Kemmel says, showing a lot of white teeth. 'You tell those blue-skinned fucks to run away or face up to their makers.'

'I don't think they're going to run away.'

'If they stay, they're going to be killed. I don't mind that, but if they run we'll just do what we came here to do, no more, no less.'

'You're looking forward to that, Kemmel? A turkey-shoot involving over a thousand people?

'We aren't going to shoot them,' Kemmel says. 'We're going to process them. There's a difference. It's a necessary thing.'

'That's what Spiromilos tells you? You believe that? It's murder, whatever you call it.'

'Now you take sides again,' Kemmel says. 'You make the fairies pull back, and Captain Spiromilos might be more friendly towards you.'

'The fairies won't listen to me.'

'Listen, journalist, the fairies are nothing more than dolls with a different kind of control chip. They were made to obey people. You find the right way of telling them, they'll listen. You don't, it will be bad for them, and worse for you.'

Kemmel revs the motorcycle engine, rides a tight circle around Todd, and yells, 'You better run, motherfucker. I think Spiromilos wants to kill you personally. And I want a piece of you, too.'

Then he's gone in a cloud of blue smoke, his bike leaving deep tracks as it slithers across the polymer, then gaining traction and roaring away up the slope.

Todd walks back. The entwined fairy and doll seem to have settled deeper in the polymer. The legs of the blinded fairy are encased in a bloody sheath. It has its teeth in the throat of its one-armed opponent, but seems too enfeebled to be able to complete the gesture.

Todd lifts his shower-sandalled feet, one after the other, frowns, then walks as quickly as he can, followed by the little camera drone. He walks past the burned-out trench and walks through the blackened ruins of the little town, fembot-stuff crunching and crumbling under his feet.

Spike and Katrina and most of the surviving fairies, about fifty of them, have retreated to the far side of the town, at the edge of dusty, weed-grown fields. They are sitting around a crater made by an overshot mortar round. The reeking earth in the bottom of the crater is still smouldering, and the acrid fumes catch at the back of Todd's throat as he repeats Kemmel's message to Eater of the Sun.

'Then we all die,' Eater of the Sun says. It doesn't look too disappointed.

Katrina tells Todd that he can leave if he wants. 'No one here will stop you.'

Todd says, 'What about you, Spike?'

'You're staying, right? I'm not leaving you here alone. You can't be trusted to look after yourself.'

The clear blue sky is brightening above the sawtoothed line of the forest. It is noticeably warmer. Todd says, 'Is this polymer stuff thermostable?'

Katrina shrugs.

'Kemmel's motorcycle left tracks. And I left footprints, but they started to fill in.'

Neither Katrina nor Spike hear him. They are looking west, down the overgrown road that leads out of the town. All the fairies are looking that way, too, their big, pointed ears cupped forward.

The camera drone rises up, turning as it rises, its turret of lenses flashing. Spike hands a monitor slate to Todd and says, 'There are people coming this way. A lot of people.'

Now Todd hears something, faint but distinct. It is the sound of human voices singing in close harmony. It is the Children's Crusade.

17
The Horned Man

Someone says, 'It's the Children's Crusade.'

And someone else: 'Look at the town! They're destroying Fairyland!'

Alex sways on the wooden chair on the back of the pygmy mammoth. He is burning with fever. Unless he pays close attention, things start to move at the edge of his vision. His computer deck has spread an aerial through the coarse hair of Hannibal's flanks, and the spider's web of filaments seems to spin and glitter. Dully, he watches as the fairies run off, scattering into the forest. The horned man lumbers after them and the Twins chase him, shouting in frustration. The horned man isn't completely cured – Alex still needs to use his hardware – but he's no longer entirely under the Twins' control.

Ray, who is leading Hannibal, says again, 'The Children's Crusade. Listen. I can hear them.'

Mrs Powell comes up behind Ray. She is crying, yet her coarse, sun-reddened face is full of wonder. 'How do you feel, Mr Sharkey?'

'Like shit. I think I drank too much blood back there.'

Out along the ridge, something arches up from the trees. Trailing thick white smoke, it plunges into the little town, and a section of the fragile towers rises into the air, shedding scrolls of fine debris. Skirts of dust billow out as the sound of the explosion, like a door closing, reaches Alex.

Mrs Powell says, 'It's all being wrecked. We must do something, Mr Sharkey.'

Alex gathers his thoughts. His head seems to be packed with cotton wool. His mouth and sinuses burn with a dry febrile heat. At last he says, 'The town isn't important.'

But Mrs Powell is still upset. She has been looking for Fairyland for so long now, and here is Leskoviku, made over by fembots into a semblance of a fairytale castle with shining turrets and minarets as fragile as icing sugar, under bombardment by Spiromilos's mercenaries.

As a cloud of dust spreads across the deep lake of polymer where the drug fields once were, the mercenaries begin to lay down a pattern of small arms fire.

'They can build the town again if they want,' Alex tells Mrs Powell. 'Let Spiromilos waste his time pounding it.'

The Twins come back, driving the horned man through the dense ferns at the edge of the forest. The horned man stumbles along with both hands pressed to his head, and when he trips and sprawls headlong the Twins start to kick him in frustration.

Mrs Powell chases them off, using her parasol like a stave.

'Wicked wicked children!'

The Twins run from her fury, then turn and shout their defiance.

'You're a silly old woman—'

'—very silly very foolish—'

'—you should be down there—'

'—down there, marching towards slaughter—'

'—marching with a song in your heart and nothing—'

'—nothing in your head.'

'She changed you, too,' Mrs Powell says. She helps the horned man sit up, and turns his head and holds his forehead as he groans and spews a thin gruel.

The horned man's name is Thodhorakis, but he can't remember much more than that. The modifications run deep, and appear to have erased whole blocks of his memory. He may have been a soldier or a bandit, caught during some incursion into the neutral zone, or perhaps an innocent shepherd. He can't remember. His excursions into the inner space of the Library of Dreams are more vivid than memories of his life before he was changed.

The horned man, Thodhorakis, lifts his head and says, 'I can't see too good.'

Mrs Powell gingerly touches the carbon whisker aerials that sprout in a rigid fan through crusted skin at the base of Thodhorakis's skull. She says, 'If you can remove these things, Mr Sharkey, you should do so at once.'

'We still need his hardware,' Alex says. 'But he can ride up with me.'

'Better to walk,' Thodhorakis says.

'Good for you! If you don't mind me saying so, Mr Sharkey,' Mrs Powell adds, 'you need attention yourself.'

'You'll need to draw more blood soon,' Alex says.

He has already drunk a measure of blood from each of the Twins, and from the horned man. Once his modified immune system processed the exotic fembots, Mrs Powell drew off a litre of his own blood for distribution amongst the Twins' fairies. It was one of them that effected the partial cure of the horned man, with a kiss. The surviving Angry Ones will also need to taste Alex's blood, assimilate the T-lymphocytes with their libraries of defused Crusade fembot codes, and use them to build fembot vectors which can strip the Crusade assemblers and fembots from the Crusaders' nervous systems.

The Twins take a couple of uncertain steps towards Mrs Powell, their eyes searching her face, trying to figure out whether they should trust her or try to trick her.

'Give him to us—'

'—we can help him—'

'—we know how to help him.'

Alex feels sorry for the Twins. They have been hard used by Milena. Although they are as intelligent as she is, they have always been dependent on her. She even found a way to profit from their rebellion. They do not acknowledge that they have lost, but they know that they've been playing in a game where the rules are very different from what they supposed. It has taken the heart from them.

Alex says, 'This will be over soon, one way or another. You can help us or you can leave.'

The Twins look at each other, then flop down amongst the ferns, arms around each other's shoulders. More and more they look like two ordinary, frightened little girls.

The mercenaries' gunfire peters out. In the hush, something in the undergrowth sings, an open-throated cascade of notes. Alex looks down and sees a small lizard on a lichen-spattered boulder close by Hannibal. It has a ragged covering of feathers, a skinny elongated neck, and a bulging belly. Ray tries to stalk it, but it belches a lick of flame at his fingers and springs away into the ferns.

'That's what I meant about the dragons,' Alex says to Mrs Powell. 'They're very small, mostly, and live in holes in the ground. They ferment vegetation in a crop and store hydrogen in throat sacs. They only use it for defence.'

But Mrs Powell isn't listening. Perhaps, in his fever, Alex only imagined he spoke. Instead, she has risen to her feet, is pointing like the statue of victory towards the little town. She cries out: 'They're here! Oh, they're here!'

Ray stands beside her, looking at Alex over his shoulder and baring his teeth. He is ready to fight.

A straggling column is moving up the road on the far side of the town. From this distance it looks like a single organism, a ragged snake uncertainly probing this way and that.

With fingers made clumsy by fever, Alex fits goggles over his eyes and inserts the foam button of the speaker in his ear. White noise, grey light. Then Max says, 'Can't you give me a visual feed?'

Alex finds that he seems to be floating in midair. He feels a lurch of nausea, as if at any minute he might plunge through Max's crystal sphere and endlessly fall through Jupiter's decks of poison clouds.

'You don't need to see anything,' Alex says. 'It's about time.'

'I could perhaps tap into the visual feed,' Max says. He's sitting cross-legged in the air before the data screen. His fingers move on the ghostly keyboard that floats in front of him.

'The poor guy is fucked up already. You take away his sight and he might just run out over a cliff.'

'I could ghost the feed,' Max says.

'You're already trying that, aren't you?'

'I want to see what's going on. We all do.'

'Most of all, we need to stop the Crusade.'

Alex makes his partial frown, and Max gets the point. He says, 'Don't worry. It's done.'

'Like that?'

'You saw me do it. It wasn't hard, once I got into the guy's backpack computer. There's about fifteen hundred cowboys and wannabes helping out. Half the Virtuality Labs at MIT are in on it, too. We're using huge amounts of bandwidth on this problem. More than half just hiding what's going on from the Web monitors. Just don't lose the link, or I'll have to reestablish the networking system, and that will take time. Is it working?'

Alex takes off his goggles.

He tells the empty air, 'It's working.'

Ray looks up and says, 'Now they are ours. It is our time.'

Alex says, 'You let us handle this—'

The Twins are laughing.

Ray insists, 'This is our place. Our time. This is the place of the knot. Now it is cut.'

And out along the ridge, there's the sound of gunfire and revving motors.

18
Wise Blood

'He did it,' Katrina says. She hugs the slate to her breasts and rock back and forth on the heels of her biker boots. 'The fat fucke actually went and did it.'

'What is it?' Todd says. Something's happened, he can feel it in the air, but he can't work out what it is.

Eater of the Sun, its bandolier of ear trophies flapping at its chest, scampers up the side of a ruined wall. Lacy stonework crumbles under its clawed toes. At the top, it raises itself to its full height and beats its chest. Something cracks past in the air and Katrina shouts at it to come down, but the fairy puffs up its cheeks and hoots in noisy defiance.

Spike has the camera drone far out, over the Children's Crusade. He says, 'Jesus fuck!'

Todd says, 'What is it? Has Spiromilos—'

Katrina says, 'Spiromilos doesn't matter now.'

'—attacked the Crusade?'

'It's nothing like that,' Spike says. 'What it is, they've stopped.'

Todd starts to run. Spike calls after him, but he runs on, across dry, weed-grown fields towards the road and the Children's Crusade.

The road that runs out of the forest is raised above the fields on a gently sloping embankment. The long procession of the Children's Crusade has stopped halfway between the forest and the town. It is breaking up. More and more people are wandering away from it into the fields. They move with the slow uncertain deliberation of sleepwalkers, their wide eyes starry with unshed tears. Some beat at their foreheads with their fists; others press the heels of their hands into their eyes: all share the same goofy, wondering grin.

Todd runs from person to person, waving his arms and shouting, trying to grab their attention. They have had a hard time of it since he last saw them. They have lost or abandoned their camping gear, their solar-powered trikes and scooters. They are gaunt with hunger and red-eyed from lack of sleep, and their ragged clothes are heavy with dirt and dust. A young man carries an old woman on his back. Others carry young children in their arms. Many are barefoot; the stony ground cuts their feet and they leave bloody prints amongst the dry weeds.

Todd whirls amongst the Crusaders as they scatter across the fields. None of them pays him any attention. They are listening to something only they can hear, stare through him towards some invisible glory.

His wonderful story is disintegrating around him, foundering like a well-appointed cruise liner that, on course for its string of exotic ports, suddenly runs on to an uncharted reef. When a young girl, naked but for an even coating of talc-like dust, stumbles into him, he grabs her and shakes her and shouts into her face, 'What is it! Tell me what you see!'

She blinks and says, 'Fairyland,' and suddenly throws her arms around him and kisses him on the mouth.

Todd, electrified with fear, pushes her away. He spits, tries to spit again and chokes on a mouthful of dust. All around him, the Crusaders have stopped. They are all looking in the same direction, turning to stare towards the ridge beyond the town, just as a field of sunflowers turns towards the sun. They begin to murmur the same word, over and over – *fairyland, fairyland, fairyland* – and a sudden wave of motion spreads through them. Along the road and the embankment, across the brown, weedy fields, they are sitting down.

In a minute, Todd is the only person standing. Frustrated and heartsick, he turns and runs back the way he has come.

Katrina says, 'They think they've arrived.'

Todd gargles a mouthful of water and spits it out. He is frightened that the girl has infected him. His hair is full of dust, and he has a stitch in his side. He wipes his mouth with the back of his hand and says, 'Where did they think they were going?'

'Fairyland, of course. Or so they believed. In truth they were walking to their own deaths, although I hope they did not know that. If they did, she is more cruel than even I think she is. But we have saved them!'

Todd says, 'Antoinette did this?'

'Now she calls herself that. Before that she called herself Milena, and that was not her real name either. We never knew her real true name, Max couldn't find it . . .'

'Names are important, huh?'

'Names are power. But if she drew the Children's Crusade here, it was someone else who stopped it.'

Katrina turns away and looks through field-glasses at the ridge that rises above the ruined town. She says, 'I think something has infiltrated the mercenaries' line up there. Make your thing, your camera platform, fly over it.'

'Do it, Spike,' Todd says.

'And get it shot down?'

'Now you worry about that.'

Spike sends the drone up to its ceiling of two hundred metres. The view on the data slate is crystal sharp, looking down on vehicles beginning to move around each other. Muzzle flashes blink and stutter amongst the trucks and jeeps. A jerky jump of magnification shows naked, blue-skinned figures flitting to and fro amongst the trees and dense stands of dry bracken at the edge of the forest.

Todd sees Kemmel's motorbike crest the ridge. Jeeps and then the trucks follow, running abreast in a ragged line. Some of the mercenaries are laying down smoke and the rest are firing through it as they accelerate towards the ruined town. Orange muzzle flashes punch through the bank of dense white smoke that's rolling down the terraced slope, and then the vehicles outrun the smoke and spread across the polymer lake . . . and begin to slow down.

Katrina is whooping for all the world like a triumphant fairy, and all around the surviving fairies are hooting and drumming.

The mercenaries' vehicles are sinking. The heavy trucks are going nose-down. The jeeps are trying to turn back, but their balloon tyres only churn up gouts of semi-liquid polymer as they subside. It's over in a matter of minutes. Some of the mercenaries keep firing right until the end. A few gain the cab roof of a truck, but then the truck tilts sideways and they must jump into the liquefied polymer.

Then there's only the white smoke, dispersing into the brightening morning air above the polymer lake. Fairies stand along the ridge, calling to their fellows in the ruins of the town below.

Katrina grips Todd's arm and says over and over, 'Wise blood. They have wise blood.'

Spike is still masked with his tele-presence goggles, still recording. He says, 'There's someone coming down on a little hairy elephant. That wouldn't be a friend of yours, would it?'

369

19
Fairyland

Ray says, 'This day and the night. You go. You all go.'

Katrina says, 'You're an ungrateful little fucker.'

Ray looks up at her and strikes an attitude. 'I can hurt you bad nasty, but I don't. You thank me for that.'

'Alex nearly gave his life for you. Me also. Fuck, you are only here because someone made over a worthless doll labourer.'

'You ask to be born?'

Ray is grinning now, and Katrina takes a step back.

Alex raises himself up and says, 'I've always been grateful to my mother, Ray. My father, I never knew my father, but I knew my mother.'

Alex is lying on a deep litter of pine branches. The fever that has burned through his blood for most of the day is subsiding. He feels tired and heavy, as heavy as if he were on Jupiter, and cold despite the silvery blanket Mrs Powell has tucked around him, despite the hot sweet tea she made him, despite the rich sweet chocolate he's eaten, a whole half kilo. His heart is flopping around in his chest; he's frightened it might burst.

He has donated another litre of blood rich in T-lymphocytes. The surviving Angry Ones wander up one by one, scoop a dripping handful of his blood from a communal bowl, drink and turn away, licking their long fingers. Drink this, my blood. My wise, quickened blood. They'll use the libraries of code sequestered inside the T-lymphocytes to make clades of anti-Crusade vectors, pass them on with a kiss to each of the remaining uncured Crusaders who sit or sprawl in the weedy fields to the west of the ruined town.

The fairies from the Twins' entourage, quickly grown bored with changing humans, have slipped away. The Twins disappeared at the same time. Alex had to ask Ray what happened to the two little girls. Suddenly, he's dependent on Ray. They all are. Most of the feys won't talk to the humans; most of the rest will only talk nonsense. There's one, a big fellow hung with grisly trophies, who talks as if the humans are pets or slaves. Katrina came near to shooting him, before Ray interceded.

The few surviving Angry Ones are still here, drumming and drumming amongst the shelled ruins, and solitary, wood-wise feys are slipping in from the forest. Some have brought food, haunches of deer or wild pig, or skinned and gutted rabbits. The dazed Crusaders accept a portion of this bounty as their due, and are roasting the meat on little fires that haze their casual encampment with blue smoke.

Ray tells Alex that the Twins know only Fairyland. It would be cruel to take them away from that. He says that the Twins will help the feys. There will always be a need for human agents. Alex thinks that Ray is indifferent to the danger that the Twins might once again try and turn the feys to their own use, but you can't talk to Ray or any of the feys about what might happen. There is only what is, the present moment pregnant with the past.

Ray says now, 'My mother a breeding thing. A doll. My father a woman who wants me to be her child. I leave her long ago, far away.'

Alex says, 'You remember who quickened you?' He's interested; Ray has never before spoken about his past.

Ray is fingering the loops of knotted string that hang from his belt, telling his coded memories. After a while, he says with a shrug, 'I cut that knot.'

Mrs Powell says, 'You should rest, Mr Sharkey. Sleep, and tomorrow you can think about these things.'

'I'm not ill, Mrs Powell. Exhausted, that's all.'

'You are ill, Mr Sharkey. You're just too stubborn to admit it.'

Mrs Powell is tending the only surviving mercenary, a woman who speaks neither English nor French nor Greek nor German. She had to be cut from the hardening polymer, and has suffered multiple fractures of both her legs. Chunks of hardened polymer bonded to her skin will have to be surgically removed. She is in a lot of pain. Mrs Powell has given her a shot of morphine and now is making sure she doesn't slip into shock. The other mercenaries are drowned and buried, locked within the polymer that the fairies phase-changed with their own wise blood.

Ray says again, 'This day and the night, and you go.'

Alex sleeps a little. When he wakes it's night. The feys are still drumming. He can hear the crackling of the polymer lake as it hardens, and the tiny, stealthy noises, a billion minute raspings and creakings, as the towers and spires and arches of the little town are rebuilt, molecule by molecule, by a myriad microscopic tireless toilers. Little lights twinklingly outline those few spires which survived the bombardment. The lights are slowly crawling around each other, like the fragments of shattered moons that make up Saturn's rings.

'Fairyland,' Alex says, and feels a moment of pure intense happiness as he accesses some simple childlike part of himself, a buried mote of memory that flares with the brief intensity of a meteor.

Fairyland.

Lexis says, 'It's all around you, Alex. You only have to open your eyes to it.'

He smells the harsh sweet smell of hash – but Lexis is dead, she died last year. He got a letter from Leroy six months after the funeral. Poste restante. He remembers standing there in the central post office of Tirana with a stunned look on his race and the crumpled piece of blue paper, its address half-obliterated by official stamps and frankings, in his hand.

Mrs Powell holds out the joint, and Alex takes a long drag.

'Nature's analgesic,' Mrs Powell says. 'Go back to sleep, Mr Sharkey.'

'I think I've been sleeping ever since I left Gjirokastra.'

Katrina is asleep, and so is the cameraman; his sleek black drone hovers three metres above him, its fans murmuring quietly in the warm night air. The American journalist, Todd Hart, is masked and gloved, using Alex's deck to access his news agency. Farther off, Hannibal stamps at his tether, his trunk twitching between his up-curved tusks. The pygmy mammoth is made uneasy by the drumming of the fairies, and the occasional shrieks as disputes break out amongst them.

'Look,' Mrs Powell says, 'there goes one of the fliers.'

They watch it soar across the face of the setting moon into the night.

'I can die happily now,' Mrs Powell says, 'although I'm sorr that I can't stay here a little longer.'

'That will go when you're cured. I can have Ray do it right now

Mrs Powell says. 'Oh no, Mr Sharkey. That wouldn't be right. I want to live all of it, the wonder of it, and the sadness of it too.'

'You amaze me, Mrs Powell.'

'Oh, I'm just an ordinary woman, Mr Sharkey,' Mrs Powell says. 'I've had my adventures, it's true, but who hasn't, in these troubled times?'

'Most people of your age have settled for their arcology efficiencies, their multimedia links. For safety and a long life.'

'They,' Mrs Powell says, 'are already dead, and don't know it. Besides, they are only a small part of humanity. I was in Africa, remember, and although there are arcologies in South Africa and Egypt, most people have yet to be touched by the nanotechnology revolution. There are still a few wild places on the Earth.'

Todd Hart hears their voices and comes over and sits beside them. He has been working with his editor. All the reports he filed at the hotel in Tirana were siphoned into the simulacrum of the news agency's offices in the Library of Dreams, and he has had to make them all over again. The first segment has just gone out, a small snippet about the sudden end of the Children's Crusade added to most of the world's cycling news channels. Larger segments, about Glass's and Antoinette's apotheoses, and the defence of Leskoviku, are still to be edited for the specialty newsgroups.

'The conspiracy theorists will have a fine old time,' Alex tells Todd, thinking of Max.

Todd takes a hit from Mrs Powell's joint. 'The UN are waiting for the Crusaders at the border of the neutral zone. I saw this one officer when I was kidnapped, and now I get to thinking that maybe they were in on it too. There are levels and levels to something like this, in a place like this. You never get to the bottom of it. Was it all down to Antoinette? I seriously doubt it.'

'Well, I wouldn't be surprised. I think she worked most of it out a long time ago. We're just loose ends she needn't be bothered with. Luckily for the feys, or she would have destroyed them. She was manipulating the Web cowboys and the mercenaries through the Twins. I'm sure of that.'

'I have contacts in the Web administration,' Todd says, 'but they haven't noticed any disturbance. Maybe she just went and died after all.'

'You'd like to think it didn't happen, because you don't like to feel that you've been manipulated. I can understand that, who better? But I don't think she's gone away. That's the odd thing. She's simply distributed herself into the world.'

Todd takes another hit off the joint and passes it back to Mrs Powell. He blows out a huge volume of smoke and says, 'Would you do it? If you could?'

Alex thinks of the white room. He shakes his head.

'Most definitely not,' Mrs Powell says.

'Come on, even if you were dying? I think most people would.'

'I think most people of my generation are already halfway there,' Mrs Powell says, 'but that isn't a good reason to join them.'

Todd says, 'I thought the Children's Crusade was something, but this . . . You should let me interview you, Alex. Really. The world should know.'

Alex says, 'I'm beginning to wish I hadn't told you.'

Todd says, 'It's a big story. You owe it to the world to tell it. I can negotiate a really good fee for you, or you can get an agent, get him to talk with me. You're coming out of this with nothing, right?'

'I'm very tired.'

'We'll talk in the morning,' Todd Hart says. 'We do need to talk.'

Alex turns over, and after a while the journalist goes away.

Mrs Powell says, 'Goodnight, Mr Sharkey. Sweet dreams.'

Ray watches the humans sleep. Big animals tossing and turning. Muttering and snorting. Eyeballs jerking under lids. His dreams are simple. Dreams of things, of places. Static, unpopulated, untroubled. He wakes and understands those things a little better. Humans always want to make connections. They spin webs of thought, and they are trapped in those fragile webs. But Ray can undo the knots of his memory. If something troubles him that's what he does. He starts over.

Many of the feys want to do just that. Some of them want to kill the humans, and so Ray stands watch over the humans. He has an attachment to Alex, and more especially to Katrina. He likes Katrina. He would never say so, but he does. He will never undo her knot. He fingers it as he watches her sleep, her lined face buried in the crook of her elbow.

Ray whispers to her as she sleeps. He walks through her dreams, sharing with her the voices in his blood.

And later, when it's day and they're about to leave, Ray runs up to Katrina and says with an urgency he knows she can't refuse, 'Give me your hands, to show we're friends.'

She grips him, fierce and strong, makes as if to pull him off his feet. Alarmed, Ray turns this into a dance, there in the stony field, amongst the smudged, cold ashes of the campfires.

The Crusade has already left for the UN relief teams that wait just over the border – no longer the Crusade, just men and women walking back into their lives, dazed as if they've slept for years. As, in a way, they have.

'All will be mended,' Ray says to Katrina, and then he swarms up her and kisses her and runs off.

'Silly little fucker,' Katrina says to Alex Sharkey, who watched this with an amused knowing smile. But she is smiling, too.

Fairies run ahead and on either side of them, silent and swift, their blue bodies half-glimpsed amongst the trees that crowd the edges of the old road. It's easy to believe there's nothing there but shadows. Soon, no one bothers to look for them, not even Mrs Powell.

All will be mended. In the night, the assemblers in Ray's blood edited the code extracted from Crusade fembots. A new meme plague will spread through the humans, and they will forget. The fairies will become no more than legends and stories, classified in the caches of the Web along with Bigfoot and other apparitions. They will become an unsolved mystery, glimpsed sidelong in dreams, never in life.

It is Ray's gift. It's all he has to give to his friends. As for himself, he brought a doll here, all the way from Paris. He took it from a fast-food outlet in the early hours of the morning after the fall of the Magic Kingdom.

Ray has learnt more from the humans than they can know. He doesn't need control chips or cocktails of hormones to make over a doll. No more chimeras constructed from slaves, forever indebted to human interference. As the humans retreat into their dreams, brave new creatures will claim the world.

Ray has the doll stashed in a ruined, roofless farmhouse the forest claimed long ago, and as he scampers through the trees he hopes it hasn't wandered off, or been taken by a warewolf. But he told it to hide, and it's dumb enough to be good at hiding. He'll call out, and let it taste his own wise blood. A myriad microscopic workers will spin a neural net through its cortex, construct hormone-secreting islands in its liver, and quicken its loins.

It will be the first of his children.

ABOUT THE AUTHOR

A biologist by training, PAUL McAULEY is now a full-time writer of stunning hard SF and alternate reality novels. His first novel, *400 Billion Stars*, won the Philip K. Dick Award, while *Fairyland* won both the Arthur C. Clarke Award and the John W. Campbell Memorial Award for Best SF Novel. *Pasquale's Angel* won the Sidewise Award for Alternate History.

He lives and works in London. Visit his blog at http://unlikelyworlds.blogspot.com